The Little Dragon That Could

A ribbon of fire sliced Jaxom's cheek, his right shoulder through the wherhide tunic, his forearm, his thigh. He felt, rather than heard, Ruth's bellow of pain.

They came out of *between* above the little mountain lake, Ruth whimpering with the pain in his foot and leg. All he wanted was to cool that Threadfire. Jaxom leaped from Ruth's neck and splashed water on his hide.

That was better.

"*We'll be much better at it next time,*" Ruth assured Jaxom. "*I'm faster than any of the big dragons. I can turn on my tail and go between in a single length from the ground.*"

Jaxom told Ruth fervently that he was without doubt the best, fastest, cleverest beast in all Pern. Ruth's green eyes whirled with pleasure. He was ready for any danger that might come.

"At last we have the long-awaited tale of Jaxom, a ruler who became a dragon-friend by chance, and Ruth, the white dragon, alone of his kind. If only one could hunt up a spaceport and invest in a ticket to Pern! At least *The White Dragon* gives us the illusion of such a joy." —Andre Norton

"*The White Dragon* is a triumph!"
                                —Marion Zimmer Bradley

Also by Anne McCaffrey
Published by Ballantine Books:

DECISION AT DOONA

DINOSAUR PLANET

DRAGONFLIGHT

DRAGONQUEST

GET OFF THE UNICORN

RESTOREE

THE SHIP WHO SANG

TO RIDE PEGASUS

THE
WHITE
DRAGON

Volume III of
"The Dragonriders of Pern"

Anne McCaffrey

A Del Rey Book

BALLANTINE BOOKS • NEW YORK

This book is irreverently dedicated
to my brothers
Hugh and Kevin
for sibling rivalries, and
the mature affections and loyalties that
develop from early brawling!

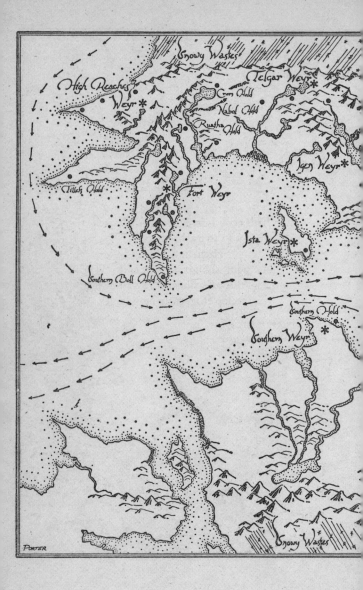

Lemos Hold

Bitra Hold

Benden Weyr

N
W · E
S

Keroon Hold

Nerat Hold

←Southern ← Current

Igen Hold

Cove Hold

Pern

Contents

PROLOGUE

RUKBAT, in the Sagittarian Sector, was a golden G-type star. It had five planets, two asteroid belts and a stray planet that it had attracted and held in recent millennia. When men first settled on Rukbat's third world and called it Pern, they had taken little notice of the strange planet swinging around its adopted primary in a wildly erratic elliptical orbit. For two generations, the colonists gave the bright Red Star little thought—until the path of the wanderer brought it close to its stepsister at perihelion. When such aspects were harmonious and not distorted by conjunctions with other planets in the system, the indigenous life form of the wandering planet sought to bridge the space gap between its home and the more temperate and hospitable planet. At these times, silver Threads dropped through Pern's skies, destroying anything they touched. The initial losses the colonists suffered were staggering. As a result, during the subsequent struggle to survive and combat this menace, Pern's tenuous contact with the mother planet was broken.

To control the incursions of the dreadful Threads—for the Pernese had cannibalized their transport ships early on and abandoned such technological sophistication as was irrelevant to this pastoral planet—the more resourceful men embarked on a long-term plan. The first phase involved breeding a highly specialized variety of a life form indigenous to their new world. Men and women with high empathy ratings and some innate telepathic ability were trained to use and preserve these unusual animals. These dragons—named for the mythical Terran beast they resembled—had two valuable characteristics: they could get from one place to another instantaneously and, after chewing a phosphine-bearing rock, they would emit a flaming gas. Because the dragons could fly, they were able to char Thread in midair, and then escape from its ravages.

It took generations to develop to the fullest the potential of these dragons. The second phase of the proposed defense against the deadly incursions would take even longer. For Thread, a space-traveling mycorrhizoid spore, with mindless voracity devoured all organic matter and, once grounded, burrowed and proliferated with terrifying speed. So a symbiote of the same strain was developed to counter this parasite, and the resulting grub was introduced into the soil of the southern continent. The original plan was that the dragons would be a visible protection, charring Thread while it was still skyborne and protecting the dwellings and the livestock of the colonists. The grub-symbiote would protect vegetation by devouring any Thread that managed to evade the dragons' fire.

The originators of the two-stage defense did not allow for change or for hard geological fact. The southern continent, overtly more attractive than the harsher northern land, proved unstable and the entire colony was eventually forced to move north to seek refuge from the Threads in the natural caves on the continental shield rock of the north.

The original Fort, constructed in the eastern face of the Great West Mountain Range, soon grew too small to hold the colonists. Another settlement was started slightly to the north, alongside a great lake conveniently formed near a cave-filled cliff. But Ruatha Hold, as the settlement was called, became overcrowded within a few generations.

Since the Red Star rose in the east, the people of Pern decided to establish a holding in the eastern mountains, provided a suitable cavesite could be found. Only solid rock and metal, both of which were in distressingly short supply on Pern, were impervious to the burning score of Thread.

The winged, tailed, fire-breathing dragons had by then been bred to a size that required more spacious accommodations than the cliffside holds could provide. But ancient cave-pocked cones of extinct volcanoes, one high above the first Fort, the other in the Benden mountains, proved to be adequate and required only a few improvements to be made habitable. However, such projects took the last of the fuel for the great stone-cutters, which had been programed only for regular mining operations, not for wholesale cliff excavations. Subsequent holds and weyrs had to be hand-hewn.

The dragons and their riders in their high places and the people in their cave holds went about their separate tasks, and each developed habits that became custom, which solidified into tradition as incontrovertible as law.

Then came an interval of two hundred Turns of the planet Pern around its primary—when the Red Star was at the other end of its erratic orbit, a frozen, lonely captive. No Thread fell on Pern. The inhabitants erased the depredations of Thread and grew crops, planted orchards from precious seed brought with them, thought of reforestry for the slopes denuded by Thread. They even managed to forget that they had once been in grave danger of extinction. Then the Threads fell again when the wandering planet returned for another orbit around Pern, bringing fifty years of attack from the skies. The Pernese once again thanked their ancestors, now many generations removed, for providing the dragons who seared the dropping Thread midair with their fiery breath.

Dragonkind, too, had prospered during that interval and had settled in four other locations, following the master plan of interim defense.

The significance of the southern hemisphere—and of the grub—had been lost in the immediate struggle to establish new settlements. Recollections of Earth receded further from Pernese history with each successive generation until memory of their origins degenerated into legend or myth and passed into oblivion.

By the Third Pass of the Red Star, a complicated socio-political-economic structure had been developed to deal with this recurrent evil. The six Weyrs, as the old volcanic habitations of the dragonfolk were called, pledged themselves to protect Pern, each Weyr having a geographical section of the northern continent literally under its wing. The rest of the population agreed to tithe to support the Weyrs since these fighters, these dragonmen, did not have arable land in their volcanic homes. They could not afford to take time away from nurturing their dragons to learn other trades during peacetime, nor could they take time away from protecting the planet during Passes.

Settlements, called Holds, developed wherever natural caves were found—some, of course, more extensive or strategically placed than others. It took a strong man to hold frantic, terrified people in control during Thread attacks; it took wise administration to conserve victuals when nothing could be safely grown, and it took extraordinary measures to control population and keep it productive and healthy until such time as the menace passed.

Men with special skills in metalworking, weaving, animal husbandry, farming, fishing, mining formed Crafthalls in each large Hold and looked to one Mastercrafthall where the precepts of their craft were taught and craft skills were preserved and guarded from one generation to another. One Lord Holder could not deny the products of the Crafthall situated in his Hold to others, since the Crafts were deemed independent of a Hold affiliation. Each Craftmaster of a hall owed allegiance to the Master of that particular craft—an elected office based on proficiency in that craft and administrative ability. The Mastercraftsman was responsible for the output of his halls and the distribution, fair and unprejudiced, of all craft products on a planetary rather than parochial basis.

Certain rights and privileges accrued to different leaders of Holds and Masters of Crafts and, naturally, to the dragonriders whom all Pern looked to for protection during the Threadfalls.

On occasion, the conjunction of Rukbat's five natural planets would prevent the Red Star from passing close enough to Pern to drop its fearful spores. To the Pernese these were Long Intervals. During one such Interval, the grateful people prospered and multiplied, spreading out across the land, carving more holds out of solid rock, just in case Thread returned. But they became so busy with their daily pursuits that they preferred to think that the Red Star had indeed passed beyond any danger to them.

No one realized that only a few dragons remained to take to the skies and that only one Weyr of dragonriders was left on Pern. Since the Red Star wasn't due to return for a long, long while, if ever, why worry? Within five generations, the descendants of the heroic dragonmen fell into disfavor; the legends of past braveries and the very reason for their existence fell into disrepute.

Volume One of THE DRAGONRIDERS OF PERN: DRAGONFLIGHT begins when the Red Star, obeying natural forces, began to spin closer to Pern, winking with a baleful red eye on its ancient victim. One man, F'lar, rider of the bronze dragon Mnementh, believed that the ancient tales had truth in them. His half-brother, F'nor, rider of brown Canth, listened to his arguments and believed in them. When the last golden egg of a dying queen dragon lay hardening on the Benden Weyr Hatching Ground, F'lar and F'nor saw an opportunity to gain control of the Weyr. Searching for a strong-minded woman to ride the soon-to-be-hatched queen, F'lar and F'nor discovered Lessa, the only surviving member of the proud Bloodline of Ruatha Hold. She Impressed young Ramoth, the new queen, and became Weyrwoman of Benden. Then F'lar's bronze Mnementh flew the young queen in her first mating, and F'lar became Weyrleader of Pern's remaining dragonriders.

The three—Lessa, F'lar and F'nor—then forced the Lord Holders and Craftsmen to recognize their imminent danger and to prepare their almost defenseless planet against Thread. Obviously the scant two hundred dragons of Benden Weyr would not be able to defend the sprawling settlements. Six full Weyrs had been needed in the olden days when the settled land had been more limited in area than it now was. An abortive attempt was even made to develop the by-now almost forgotten southern continent. But that didn't work.

However, in learning to direct her queen dragon

between one place and another, Lessa discovered that dragons could also move *between* one time and another. Risking her life as well as Pern's only queen dragon, Lessa and Ramoth went back in time, four hundred Turns, before the mysterious disappearance of the other five Weyrs, and just after the last Pass of the Red Star had been completed. The five Weyrs of that ancient time, seeing only the decline of their prestige and bored with inactivity after a lifetime of exciting combat, agreed to help Lessa's Weyr. These people from the past came forward to her time and saved Pern.

Volume Two of THE DRAGONRIDERS OF PERN: DRAGONQUEST picks up the story seven Turns later, when the initial gratitude and relief of Holds and Crafts had faded and soured. The Oldtimers themselves did not like the Pern of the future in which they were now living. Four hundred Turns had brought too many subtle changes. The Oldtimers, used to a more subservient and grateful population, found themselves at odds with the Lord Holders and the Crafthalls—and especially with Benden Weyr and its liberal leaders.

Tensions between the two factions came to a head in a petty quarrel involving F'nor and an Oldtimer Fort dragonrider. F'nor was sent off to the newly resettled southern continent to recover from his wound. Meanwhile F'lar confronted the Oldtimer, T'ron of Fort Weyr, in a meeting of all but two Weyrleaders. Little was decided at the meeting but it became apparent that the Oldtimers were not taking as much responsibility for their duties as they should. F'lar's arguments caused D'ram, Ista's Weyrleader, and G'narish of Igen Weyr, both Oldtimers, to take a good look at their contemporaries. Thread had begun to fall at unexpected times and the charts, carefully prepared by F'lar from the old Records, had somehow lost their validity. At that point Robinton, the Master Harper of Pern, and the Mastersmith, Fandarel, joined forces with the Benden leaders to try to cope with the new emergency. To help matters Fandarel developed a device that he hoped would provide communication among the Holds and Halls.

Meanwhile in the Southern Weyr, F'nor was being nursed by a young queenrider, Brekke, when he accidentally discovered that fire-lizards, previously dismissed as mere legends or fantasies, actually existed and could also be Impressed at Hatching in the same way their genetic cousins, the dragons, were. Kylara, a passionate and disgruntled Weyrwoman of Southern, found a clutch of fire-lizard eggs which she took to Lord Meron of Nabol, one of the most troublesome of the Lord Holders.

Summoned by F'nor's message about the fire-lizards, F'lar headed for Southern Weyr where he observed that T'bor, the young Leader, was having trouble with his Weyrwoman, the sensuous Kylara. When Threadfall came to Southern, F'lar joined in the fight. Observing a very curious phenomenon in the dense vegetation, he discovered a curious and very active insect in the soil and brought samples back to the Masterherdsman, Sograny, an opinionated man to whom the grubs were anathema. F'lar, remembering what he had observed, took issue with the man and pursued his investigation of the grubs with the aid of F'nor, now returned to the Weyr, and N'ton, craftbred young rider of bronze Lioth.

Soon Lord Lytol, guardian of the young Jaxom, the youth to whom Lessa had ceded her Bloodright to Ruatha Hold, visited Benden Weyr to discuss the tense situation with F'lar, Lessa, Robinton and Fandarel. He brought Jaxom with him as his ward was friendly with F'lessan, only son of F'lar and Lessa. While the adults were talking, the two boys sneaked into the unused passageways of Benden Weyr for a peek at Ramoth's latest clutch of eggs in the Hatching Ground. The boys became frightened by the unexpected return of the queen and quickly lost their way in the dark corridors, inadvertently discovering some long-forgotten rooms. A search party found the boys unconscious and discovered musty rooms in which they found a variety of curious objects, including an instrument which enlarged small things that quickly became the Mastersmith's special treasure. F'lar suggested that a discreet search be made of the older Holds and Weyrs to see if anything interesting should turn up to fill in the gaps of lost knowledge.

Shortly thereafter Kylara and Lord Meron appeared

7.

at the wedding of Lord Asgenar and Telgar's sister at
Telgar Hold with fire-lizards on their arms, causing considerable commotion. Suddenly a dragonrider appeared,
disrupting the wedding feast with the news that Thread
was unaccountably falling at Igen. F'lar requested the
help from the other Weyrleaders and T'ron found this
an excuse to challenge the Benden Weyrleader to a duel
from which F'lar, though wounded, emerged the victor
and banished T'ron and any other Oldtimer who
would not acknowledge that he was to be the overall
Weyrleader. Lord Holders and Craftmasters alike supported F'lar. Oldtimer Weyrleaders, D'ram of Ista,
G'narish of Igen and R'mart of Telgar, likewise stood
by him. T'kul of High Reaches joined T'ron in exile
with seventy other Oldtimers and Dragonfolk. F'lar,
despite his wound, insisted on flying Thread at Igen,
by going *between* time to the start of Threadfall.

The former Southern dragonriders, ousted by T'ron,
settled in the High Reaches Weyr which had been left
in a shocking state. Brekke, unaware that her queen
Wirenth was about to rise for her first mating, began to
restore order to the Weyr while Kylara enjoyed herself with Lord Meron. Unfortunately Kylara's queen,
Prideth, was also close to mating and when Wirenth
rose, so did Prideth. A battle ensued between the two
queens in which the other queens tried to separate the
combatants. Canth desperately attempted to save
Wirenth. But both queens were mortally wounded and
went *between*, leaving Kylara a mindless idiot and
Brekke hanging on the edge of sanity. Only F'nor's love
and Canth's devotion, and the constant companionship
of the little fire-lizards kept her alive.

Meanwhile, guided by the principles of the Benden
device, Fandarel and Wansor constructed a powerful
distance-viewer that made it possible to see both the
cloud-swirled surface of the Red Star and something of
the other planets in the system. Lessa, Robinton and
the dissident Lord Meron among others, arrived at Fort
Weyr, intent on testing the new far-viewer. But Meron
insisted that now that the face of the Red Star could
be seen, dragonmen somehow ought to be able to get
there. So he attempted to send his little fire-lizard on
the journey. The little creature not only disappeared in

fright, but managed to frighten the other fire-lizards as well.

When Ramoth's clutch was finally ready to Hatch, among the many guests were Lord Lytol and young Jaxom. An attempt to rouse Brekke from her stupor by presenting her as a candidate to the new queen failed but her bronze fire-lizard, Berd, succeeded in scolding her out of her grieving trance. When Jaxom noticed that the smallest egg—the very one he had been drawn to during his fateful peek at the clutch—was rocking but not cracking, he went to the assistance of the creature and made an Impression on the small white dragon he rescued. Jaxom, who had to remain Lord Holder of Ruatha, nonetheless became a weyrling. So it was decided to permit him to take Ruth to his Hold as it was possible that the tiny dragon might not survive his first Turn. F'lar, recovered from his wounds, used the opportunity of the Hatching to prove to various Craftmasters and Holders that grubs do attack and devour Thread. They also seem to restore and protect vegetation Thread damages. Then Masterfarmer Andemon remembered an ancient warning: *Watch the grubs*, and he realized that this saying had been misinterpreted and grubs had been systematically burned from the land when they should have been encouraged to proliferate.

So, after centuries, the secondary phase of protection initiated by the colonists was finally recognized as such. That being the case, F'lar began two campaigns with the help of F'nor and N'ton: the first to seed the Northern Continent with the grubs; the second, the dissemination of special knowledge to insure that no more important information would become lost or distorted.

But Lord Holders, prodded by Meron, continued to agitate for the dragonriders to go to the Red Star and remove the menace of Thread at its source. To forestall such dangerous attempts by F'lar, F'nor directed Canth to a cloud formation on the Red Star's surface. They took the massive leap *between* and nearly died in the Red Star's turbulent atmosphere, but were somehow called back from certain death by Brekke's need of them. F'nor's attempt made it obvious to every dragonrider and to everyone possessing a fire-lizard that the

Red Star could not be attacked directly. It was just too dangerous.

Having come to grips with the reality of the situation, F'lar directed his energies to spreading grubs and keeping a discreet watch on the South which, for the time being, would have to remain the province of the dissident Oldtimers whose situation, with no queens young enough to mate, was rapidly becoming critical. Other pressures, too, were being felt, pressures which Robinton believed were equally critical.

And now we begin THE WHITE DRAGON—the Third Volume of THE DRAGONRIDERS OF PERN . . .

CHAPTER I

At Ruatha Hold, Present Pass, 12th Turn

"IF HE ISN'T clean enough now," Jaxom told N'ton as he gave Ruth's neck ridge a final swipe with the oiled cloth, "I don't know what clean is!" He wiped his sweaty forehead on his tunic sleeve. "What do you think, N'ton?" he asked politely, suddenly aware that he had spoken without due regard for his companion's rank as Weyrleader of Fort.

N'ton grinned and gestured toward the grassy bank of the lake. They squelched through the mud created by rinsing soapsand from the little dragon and, as one, turned for a full view of Ruth gleaming wetly in the morning sun.

"I've never seen him cleaner," N'ton remarked after due consideration, adding hastily, "not to imply that you haven't always kept him immaculate, Jaxom. However, if you don't ask him to move out of that mud, he won't stay clean long."

Jaxom passed on the request hastily. "And keep your tail up, Ruth, till you are on the grass."

From the corner of his eye, Jaxom noticed that Dorse and his cronies were creeping away, just in case N'ton had any further hard work for them. Jaxom had somehow managed to keep the smugness he felt under control all during Ruth's bath. Dorse and the others hadn't dared disobey the dragonrider when N'ton had

blithely pressed them into service. To see them sweat-
ing over the "runt," the "oversized fire-lizard," unable
to tease and taunt Jaxom as they'd planned to do this
morning, had raised Jaxom's spirits considerably. He
entertained no hopes that the situation would last long.
But, if today the Benden Weyrleaders decided Ruth
was strong enough to bear his weight in flight, then
Jaxom would be free to fly away from the taunts he'd
had to endure from his milk-brother and his cronies.

"You know," N'ton began, frowning slightly as he
folded his arms across his damp-spattered tunic, "Ruth
isn't really white."

Jaxom stared incredulously at his dragon. "He's
not?"

"No. See how his hide has shadows of brown and
gold, and ripples of blue or green on the near flank."

"You're right!" Jaxom blinked, surprised at discovering something totally new about his friend. "I guess
those colors are much more noticeable because he's so
clean and the sun's so bright today!" It was such a
pleasure to be able to discuss his favorite topic with an
understanding audience.

"He's . . . more . . . all dragon shades than the lack
of any," N'ton continued. He slanted one hand against
the angle of Ruth's heavily muscled shoulder, then
cocked his head as he stared at the powerful hindquarters. "Beautifully proportioned, too. He may be
small, Jaxom, but he's a fine-looking fellow!"

Jaxom sighed again, unconsciously straightening his
shoulders and pushing out his chest with pride.

"Not too much flesh, not too little, eh, Jaxom?"
N'ton shot an elbow to catch Jaxom on the top of his
shoulder, a sly grin on his face for all the times Jaxom
had had to call on the Weyrleader to help him cope
with Ruth's indigestion. Jaxom had erroneously con-
cluded that if he could stuff the proper amount of
food down Ruth's gullet, the little dragon would grow
to match the size of his clutch-mates. The results had
not been good.

"Do you think he's strong enough to fly me?"

N'ton awarded Jaxom a thoughtful gaze. "Let's see,

12

The White Dragon

you Impressed him a Turn last spring, and we're into cool weather now. Most dragons achieve their full growth in their first Turn. I don't think Ruth's grown a half-hand in the last six months so we have to conclude that he has reached his full growth. Hey, now," N'ton reacted to Jaxom's sad sigh, "he's bigger than any runner beast by half a head, isn't he? They can be ridden for hours without tiring, right? And you're not exactly a heavyweight like Dorse there."

"Flying's a different sort of effort, isn't it?"

"True, but Ruth's wings are proportionately large enough to his body to support him in flight . . ."

"So he *is* a proper dragon, isn't he?"

N'ton stared at Jaxom. Then he put both hands on the boy's shoulders. "Yes, Jaxom, Ruth is a proper dragon, for all he's half the size of his fellows! And he'll prove it today when he flies you! So let's get you and him back to the Hold. You've got to get yourself fancied up to match his beauty!"

"C'mon, Ruth!"

I would rather sit here in the sun, Ruth replied, moving to Jaxom's left, his stride graceful as he kept pace with his friend and with the Fort Weyrleader.

"There's sun in our court, Ruth," Jaxom assured him, resting a light hand on Ruth's headknob, aware of the happy blue tone of Ruth's lightly whirling, jewel-faceted eyes.

As they walked on in silence, Jaxom raised his eyes to the imposing cliff face which was Ruatha Hold, the second oldest human habitation on Pern. It would be his to Hold when he came of age or when his guardian, Lord Lytol, former weaver-journeyman, former dragonrider, decided that he was wise enough—that is, if the other Lord Holders finally overcame their objections to his inadvertent Impression of the half-sized dragon, Ruth. Jaxom sighed, resigned to the fact that he would never be allowed to forget that moment.

Not that he wanted to, but Impressing Ruth had caused all kinds of problems for the Benden Weyrleaders, F'lar and Lessa, for the Lord Holders, and for himself since he was not allowed to be a real

dragonrider and live in a Weyr. He had to remain
Lord Holder of Ruatha or every younger Holdless son
of every major Lord would fight to the death to fill
that vacancy. The worst problem he had caused was
to the man he desperately wanted most to please, his
guardian, Lord Lytol. Had Jaxom only paused a moment to think before he jumped onto the hot sands of
Benden's Hatching Ground to help break the tough
shell for the little white dragon, he'd have realized
what anguish he would bring to Lord Lytol by a constant reminder of what the man had lost at the death
of his brown Larth. Never mind if Larth had died
Turns before Jaxom's birth at Ruatha Hold, that tragedy was vividly, cruelly fresh in Lytol's mind, or so
everyone told Jaxom repeatedly. If this was so, Jaxom
often wondered, why then hadn't Lytol protested when
the Weyrleaders and Lord Holders agreed that Jaxom
must try to raise the little dragon at Ruatha?

Looking up to the fire-heights, Jaxom noticed that
N'ton's bronze Lioth was nose to nose with Wilth, the
elderly brown watch dragon. He wondered what the
two dragons were talking about. His Ruth? The trial
of the day? He noticed fire-lizards, tiny cousins to the
big dragons, executing lazy spirals above the two dragons. Men were driving wherries and runner beasts
from the main stables out to the pastures, north of the
Hold. Smoke issued from the line of smaller cotholds
that bordered the ramp into the Great Court and
along the edge of the main road east. To the left of
the ramp, new cots were being built since the inner
recesses of Ruatha Hold were considered unsafe.

"How many fosterlings does Lytol have at Ruatha
Hold, Jaxom?" N'ton suddenly asked.

"Fosterlings? None, sir." Jaxom frowned. Surely
N'ton knew that.

"Why not? You've got to get to know the others of
your rank."

"Oh, I accompany Lord Lytol quite often to the
other Holds."

"I wasn't thinking of socializing so much as having
companions here of your own age."

"There's my milk-brother, Dorse, and his friends from the cothold."

"Yes, that's true."

Something in the Weyrleader's tone made Jaxom glance at him but the man's expression told him nothing.

"See much of F'lessan these days? I remember that you two used to get into a lot of mischief at Benden Weyr."

Jaxom could not control the flush that rose to his hairline. Was it possible that N'ton had somehow found out that he and F'lessan had squeezed through a hole onto Benden's Hatching Ground for a close look at Ramoth's eggs? He didn't think F'lessan would have told that! Not to anyone! But Jaxom had often wondered if touching that little egg had somehow destined its occupant to be his!

"I don't see much of F'lessan these days. I don't have much time, taking care of Ruth and all."

"No, of course not," N'ton said. He seemed about to say more and then changed his mind.

As they walked on in silence, Jaxom wondered if he'd said something wrong. But he couldn't think about it for long. Just then N'ton's fire-lizard, brown Tris, whirled in for a landing on the padded shoulder of the Weyrleader, chirping excitedly.

"What's wrong?" asked Jaxom.

"He's too excited to make sense," N'ton replied with a laugh, and he stroked the little creature's neck, uttering a series of soothing noises until Tris, with a final chirp in Ruth's direction, folded his wings to his back.

He likes me, Ruth observed.

"All fire-lizards like you," Jaxom replied.

"Yes, I've noticed that too, and not just today when they were helping us wash him," N'ton said.

"Why do they?" Jaxom had always wanted to ask N'ton that, but he had never had the courage. He didn't like to take up the Weyrleader's valuable time with silly questions. But, today, it didn't seem like such a silly question.

N'ton turned his head to his fire-lizard and, in a

moment, Tris gave a quick chirp and then busily cleaned his forepaw. N'ton chuckled. "He likes Ruth. That's all the answer I get from him. I'd hazard the notion that it's because Ruth is nearer their size. They can see him without having to back up several dragon-lengths to do so."

"I suppose so." Jaxom still had reservations. "What-ever it is, fire-lizards come from all over to visit him. They tell him the most outrageous stories but that makes him happy, especially when I can't be right there with him."

They had reached the roadway and were heading for the ramp into the Great Court.

"Don't be long dressing, will you, Jaxom? Lessa and F'lar ought to arrive soon," N'ton said as he kept going straight on through the great gates toward the massive metal Hold door. "Finder'll be in his quarters at this hour?"

"He should be."

Then, as Jaxom and Ruth turned toward the kitchen and the old stables, the youth began to worry about the trial set for today. N'ton surely would not have raised his hopes about getting permission to fly Ruth if he wasn't pretty sure the Benden Weyrlead-ers would be agreeable.

To fly Ruth would be so marvelous. Besides it would prove once and for all that Ruth was a real dragon and not just an overgrown fire-lizard as Dorse so often teased him. And, too, he'd finally be able to get away from Dorse. Today was the first time in Turns he hadn't had to endure Dorse's teasing as he washed Ruth. Not that the boy was just jealous of Jaxom's having Ruth. Dorse had always taunted Jaxom, ever since he could remember. Before Ruth had come, Jaxom had managed to make himself scarce in the dark recesses of Ruatha's many levels. Dorse didn't like the dark, stuffy corridors and stayed away. But with Ruth's arrival, Jaxom no longer was able to disappear and avoid Dorse's attentions. He of-ten wished that he didn't owe Dorse so much. But he was Lord of Ruatha and Dorse was his milk-brother so he owed him his life. For if Deelan hadn't given birth to Dorse two days before Jaxom's unexpected arrival, Jaxom would have died in his first hours. Therefore, Jaxom had been taught by Lytol and the Hold harper, he must share everything with his milk-brother. As far as Jaxom could see, Dorse benefited far more than he did. The boy, a full hand taller than Jaxom and heavier set, certainly hadn't suffered for sharing his mother's milk. And Dorse made sure he got the best part of anything else Jaxom had.

Jaxom waved cheerily to the cooks, busy preparing a fine midday meal to celebrate, he fervently hoped, the occasion of his first flight on Ruth. He and the white dragon continued past the gates to the old stables which had been refitted as their quarters. Small though Ruth had been when he first arrived at Ruatha a Turn and a half ago, it had been obvious that he would quickly grow too large to enter the traditional apartment of the Lord Holder within the Hold proper.

So Lytol had decided that the old stables, with the vaulted ceiling, could be refurbished suitably for sleeping quarters and a work room for Jaxom and a fine spacious Weyr for the little dragon. New doors had been specially designed by Mastersmith Fandarel and hung with such ingenuity that a slightly built lad and an awkward hatchling could manage them.

I will sit here in the sun, Ruth told Jaxom, poking his head past the entrance to their quarters. *My bed hasn't been swept.*

"Everyone's been so busy cleaning for Lessa's visit," Jaxom said, giggling as he remembered the terror in Deelan's face when Lytol had told her that the Weyr-woman was coming. In his milk-mother's eyes, Lessa was still the only full-blooded Ruathan left alive after Fax's treacherous attack on the Hold over twenty Turns ago.

Jaxom stripped off his damp tunic as he entered his own room. The water in the jar by his sink was tepid and he grimaced. He really ought to be as clean as his dragon but he didn't think he'd have time to get to the Hold's hot baths before the Weyrleaders came. It wouldn't do for him to be absent when they arrived. He washed with soapsand and the tepid water.

They come, Ruth announced the words in Jaxom's mind just before old Wilth and Lioth heralded the visitors with appropriate trumpetings.

Jaxom rushed to the window and peered out, catching a glimpse of huge wings as the newcomers settled into the great courtyard. He didn't wait long enough to see the Benden dragons remove themselves to the fire-heights, accompanied by excited fairs of fire-lizards. Drying himself hurriedly, he wriggled out of his wet trousers. It didn't take him long to don his good new clothes and stamp into the boots made especially for this occasion and lined with downy wherry-hide for warmth in flight. Recent practice made it easy for him to rig the riding straps on the eager little dragon.

As Jaxom and Ruth emerged from their quarters, Jaxom was again assailed by apprehension. What if N'ton had been wrong? What if Lessa and F'lar decided to wait just a few more months to see if Ruth would grow? What if Ruth, being such a small dragon, didn't have enough strength to fly him? Supposing he hurt Ruth?

Ruth crooned encouragingly. *You couldn't hurt me. You are my friend.* And he butted Jaxom affectionately, whiffling against his face with warm sweet breath.

Jaxom inhaled deeply, hoping to settle his agitated belly. He then became aware of the gathering on the steps of the Hold. Why did there have to be so many people here today?

There are not many, Ruth told him, his tone surprised as he lifted his head to observe the gathering. *And many fire-lizards to see me, too. I know everyone here today. So do you.*

Jaxom realized that he did. Taking courage from his dragon's acceptance of such a large audience, he straightened his shoulders and strode forward.

F'lar and Lessa, as the chief dragonriders, were the most important guests. F'nor, brown Canth's rider and mate of the sad Brekke, was also present but he was a good friend to Jaxom. N'ton, of course, was there since he was Fort's Weyrleader and Ruatha was beholden to Fort Weyr. Master Robinton as Harper of Pern was here and, beside him, Jaxom was glad to see Menolly, the Harper girl who had often been his champion. Jaxom reluctantly admitted the right of Lord Sangel of South Boll and Lord Groghe of Fort to be present as representatives of the Holders.

At first Jaxom couldn't see Lord Lytol. Then Finder moved to say something to Menolly and Jaxom spotted his guardian. He hoped Lytol would *really* look at Ruth this once, if never again.

They had crossed the courtyard now and stood before the steps, Jaxom resting his right hand on Ruth's strong, gracefully curved neck, and squarely faced the judges.

Extending one hand in greeting towards Ruth, Lessa smiled at Jaxom as she stepped down to welcome him. "Ruth has filled out a great deal since last spring, Jaxom," she said, her manner reassuring as well as appreciative. "But you ought to eat more. Lytol, does Deelan never feed the child? He's nothing but bones."

Jaxom was shocked when he realized that he now was taller than Lessa, and she was cocking her head to look up at him. He'd always thought of Lessa as big. To be looking down on the Weyrwoman of Benden was somehow embarrassing.

"I'd say you've the advantage of F'lessan still, and he's getting longer every time I look," she added.

Jaxom began to stammer an apology.

"Nonsense, Jaxom, stand up to your inches," F'lar said, coming up beside his weyrmate. His attention was centered on Ruth, and the white dragon raised his head slightly to be at eye level with the tall Weyrleader. "You've made more hands of height, Ruth, than I'd have given you at your Hatching! You've done well by your friend, Lord Jaxom." The Benden Weyrleader put a slight emphasis on the title as he turned his gaze from dragon to rider.

Jaxom winced, disliking the reminder of his equivocal position.

"However, I can't see that you'll ever reach the

stature of our good Mastersmith, so I don't think you'll overburden Ruth in flight." F'lar glanced at the others on the steps. "Ruth's a full head higher in the shoulder than runner beasts. Sturdier, too."

"What's his wingspan now?" Lessa asked, her brows drawn in a thoughtful frown. "Jaxom, please ask him to extend?"

Lessa could easily have asked Ruth directly since she was able to speak to any dragon. Jaxom was considerably heartened to be accorded such a courtesy and he passed the request on to Ruth. Eyes whirling with excitement, the white dragon raised himself to his haunches and spread his wings, the muscles rippling through chest and shoulder with the clouded shades of all dragon colors.

"He's completely in proportion to himself," F'lar said, dipping under the wing to inspect the upper side of the broad, transparent membrane. "Oh, thank you, Ruth," he added as the white dragon obligingly tilted his wing. "I take it he's as eager to fly you as you are!"

"Yes, sir, because, sir, he *is* a dragon, and dragons all fly!"

The look F'lar shot him caused Jaxom to hold his breath, wondering if his quick answer had been too bold. When he heard Lessa laugh, he looked over at her. But she wasn't laughing at him, or at Ruth. Her eyes rested on her weyrmate. F'lar's right eyebrow arched as he grinned back at her. Jaxom felt they weren't aware of him or Ruth at all.

"Yes, dragons do fly, don't they, Lessa?" the Weyrleader said softly, and Jaxom realized they were sharing some private joke.

Then F'lar raised his head to the fire-heights where golden Ramoth, bronze Mnementh, and the two browns, Canth and Wilth, maintained keen interest in the scene in the courtyard below.

"What does Ramoth say, Lessa?"

Lessa grimaced. "You know she's always said Ruth would do well."

F'lar glanced first at N'ton, who grinned, and then at F'nor, who shrugged acquiescence. "It's unanimous,

Jaxom. Mnementh doesn't understand why we're all making such a fuss. Mount then, lad." F'lar stepped forward as if to give Jaxom a leg up to the neck of the white dragon.

Jaxom was torn between pleasure at having the Weyrleader of all Pern to assist him and indignation that F'lar thought him incapable of mounting unaided.

Ruth intervened by swinging his wings out of the way and bending his left knee. Jaxom stepped lightly on the proffered limb and swung to the proper position between the last two neck ridges. Those protuberances in a full dragon were sufficient to keep a man steady in ordinary flight, but Lytol had insisted that Jaxom use riding straps as a safety measure. As Jaxom secured the strap buckles to his belt's metal loops, he cast surreptitious glances at the crowd. But no one showed a trace of surprise or contempt for this precaution. When he was ready, that awful coldness of doubt rose once more in his belly. Supposing that Ruth couldn't . . .

He caught the confident grin on N'ton's face and saw Master Robinton and Menolly hold up their hands in salute. Then F'lar lifted his fist above his head in the traditional signal to rise.

Jaxom took a deep breath. "Let's fly, Ruth!"

He felt the bunching of muscle as Ruth assumed a semi-crouch, felt the tension through the back, the shift of musculature under his calves as the huge wings lifted for the all-important first downsweep. Ruth deepened his crouch slightly just as he kicked away from the ground with his powerful hind legs. Jaxom's head snapped on his neck. Instinctively he grabbed for the security of the straps, then hung on tightly as the little white dragon's powerful wing strokes lifted them upward, past the first rank of windows and the startled faces of the holders, up so quickly to the fire-heights that Jaxom saw the other tiers of windows in a blur. Then the great dragons extended their wings, bugling encouragement to Ruth. Fire-lizards swirled about them, adding their silvery voices. Jaxom just hoped they wouldn't startle Ruth or get in his way.

They are pleased to see us in the air together. Ramoth and Mnementh are very happy to see you on my back at last. I am very happy. Are you happier now?

The almost plaintive question caused a lump to lodge in Jaxom's throat. He opened his mouth to respond, only to have sound torn from his lips by the press of wind against his face.

"Of course, I'm happy. I'm always happy with you," he said joyfully. "I'm flying with you, just like I wanted to. This'll show everyone that you're a right dragon!"

You're shouting!

"I'm happy. Why shouldn't I shout?"

I'm the only one to hear you and I hear you very well indeed.

"You ought to. You're the one I'm happiest for."

They began a glide turn now and Jaxom leaned back away from the curve, holding his breath. Not that he hadn't flown on a dragon innumerable times before. But then he had been a passenger, usually crammed between two adult bodies. The intimacy of this flight was another sensation entirely, exhilarating, pleasantly scary and utterly marvelous.

Ramoth says you must grip more tightly with your legs as you do on runners.

"I didn't want to interfere with your breathing." Jaxom pressed his legs tightly into the warmth of the silken neck, heartened by the security the grip gave him.

That's better. You can't hurt my neck. You can't hurt me. You're my rider. Ramoth says we must land. Ruth sounded rebellious.

"Land? We just got airborne!"

Ramoth says I must not strain. Flying you is no strain. It is what I want to do. She says we may fly a little farther every day. I like that idea.

Ruth corrected his descending plane so that they approached the court from the southeast. People on the roadway stopped to stare and then to wave. Jaxom thought he heard cheers but the wind rushed past, making it difficult to be sure. Those in the court turned to follow his path. Every window on the second and first tier of the Hold had its observers.

"They'll all have to admit you're a proper flying dragon now, Ruth!"

The only thing Jaxom regretted was that this flight was so brief. A little longer every day, huh? Not Fall, fire or fog would keep him from flying every single day, longer and farther away from Ruatha.

Abruptly he was thrown forward, bruising his chest on a neck ridge as Ruth backwinged to settle neatly on the spot he had so recently vacated.

Sorry about that, Ruth said contritely. *I see that there are things I must learn now.*

Savoring the triumph of the airborne experience, Jaxom sat for a moment, rubbing his chest and reassuring Ruth. Then he was aware of F'lar, F'nor and N'ton coming towards him with expressions of approval. But why was the Harper looking so thoughtful? And why was Lord Sangel frowning?

The dragonriders say we can fly. They are the ones who matter, Ruth told him.

Jaxom could discern no expression at all on the face of Lord Lytol. That dulled Jaxom's pride in their achievement. How he had hoped that today of all days he might receive some flicker of approval, some kindly response from his guardian.

He never forgets Larth, Ruth said in his softest tone.

"See, Jaxom? I told you," N'ton cried as the three dragonriders ranged themselves by Ruth's shoulder. "Nothing to it."

"Very good first flight, Jaxom," F'lar said, running his eyes over Ruth for any signs of stress. "No bother to him at all."

"This fellow'll turn on a wing tip. Make sure you keep the straps on till you're used to each other," F'nor added, reaching up to grab Jaxom's forearm. It was the greeting gesture of equals, and Jaxom was enormously gratified.

"You've been mistaken then, Lord Sangel," Lessa's voice rang clearly to Jaxom. "There's never been any doubt that the white dragon could fly. We merely postponed the event until we were sure Ruth had reached his full growth."

F'nor winked at Jaxom and N'ton grimaced, while F'lar raised his eyes upward, indicating the need for patience. That intimacy made Jaxom realize that he, Jaxom of Ruatha, had indeed been admitted to a kinship with the three most powerful dragonriders of Pern.

"You're a dragonrider now, lad," N'ton said.

"Yes." F'lar frowned as he lengthened the word. "Yes, but you may not fly all over the world tomorrow, nor may you try going *between*. Not yet. You do realize that, I trust. Fine! You're to exercise Ruth in flight every day. Do you have a slate on those drills, N'ton?" F'lar passed N'ton's slate over to Jaxom. "Those wing muscles have got to be strengthened slowly, carefully, or you will place too great a strain on them. That's the danger. The time might come when you'd need speed or maneuverability and those unfit muscles wouldn't respond! You heard about that tragedy at High Reaches?" F'lar's expression was stern.

"Yes, sir. Finder told me." Jaxom didn't bother to mention that Dorse and his friends, once they'd heard of the incident, never let Jaxom forget the weyrling who had been dashed to death on the mountain slopes because he'd overflown his young dragon.

"You've a double responsibility at all times, Jaxom, to Ruth and to your Hold."

"Oh, yes sir; I know it, sir."

N'ton laughed and clapped Jaxom on the knee. "I'll wager you do, young Lord Jaxom, right up to the teeth!"

F'lar turned to the Fort Weyrleader, surprised at the tone of the rejoinder. Jaxom held his breath. Did Weyrleaders speak without thinking? Lord Lytol was always after Jaxom to think before he opened his mouth.

"I'll oversee Jaxom's initial training, F'lar, no need to worry about his sense of responsibility on that score. It's well ingrained," N'ton went on. "And, with your permission, I'll instruct him on flying *between* when I feel he's ready. I think," he gestured toward the two

Lord Holders arguing with Lessa, "the less publicity for that phase of training, the better."

Jaxom could feel the slight tension in the air as N'ton and F'lar regarded each other. Suddenly Mnementh and then Ramoth bugled from the heights.

"They agree," N'ton said in a soft voice.

F'lar shook his head slightly and brushed away the lock of hair that fell into his eyes.

"It's obvious, F'lar, that Jaxom deserves to be a dragonrider," F'nor said in the same persuasive tone. "It's a question of Weyr responsibility in the final analysis. But it's not for those Lord Holders to decide. Besides Ruth *is* a Benden dragon."

"Responsibility is the overriding factor," F'lar said, frowning at the two riders. He glanced up at Jaxom, who wasn't certain exactly what they were talking about except that he knew he and Ruth were under discussion. "Oh, very well. He's to be trained to fly *between*. Otherwise, I suppose you'd try it on your own anyhow, wouldn't you, young Jaxom, being of Ruathan Blood?"

"Sir?" Jaxom really didn't quite believe his good fortune.

"No, F'lar, Jaxom wouldn't try such a thing on his own," N'ton replied in a curious tone. "That's the trouble. I think Lytol has done his job too well."

"Explain," F'lar said curtly.

F'nor held up his hand. "Here's Lytol himself," he said in quick warning.

"Lord Jaxom, if you would settle your friend in his quarters, and then join us all in the Hall?" The Lord Warder bowed politely to everyone. A muscle in his face started to twitch as he quickly turned and walked back to the steps.

He could have said something then . . . if he'd wanted to, Jaxom thought, staring sadly at his guardian's broad back.

N'ton gave him another clout on his knee and, when Jaxom looked at the Fort Weyrleader, he winked. "You're a good lad, Jaxom, and a good rider." Then he sauntered after the other dragonriders.

"You wouldn't by any chance be serving a Benden wine on this auspicious occasion, would you, Lytol?" the Masterharper's voice rang across the court.

"What else would anyone dare serve you, Robinton?" Lessa asked, laughing.

Jaxom watched them filing up the steps and through the Hall doors. With a concert of shrieks, the fire-lizards abandoned their aerial display and dove toward the entrance, narrowly missing the Harper's tall figure as they swarmed to get into the Hold.

The incident lifted Jaxom's spirits and he directed Ruth to their quarters. As his glance swept the windows, he saw people pulling back. He sincerely hoped that Dorse and all his pals had witnessed every moment, had noticed the handgrasp of F'nor and seen how he'd been talking to the three most important dragonriders on all Pern. Dorse would have to be more careful now that Jaxom was also going to be allowed to take his Ruth *between*. Dorse had never figured on that, had he? Nor, thought Jaxom, had he. Wasn't it just capital of N'ton to suggest it? And when Dorse heard, he'd just have to chew it raw and swallow!

Ruth answered his thoughts with a smug croon as the dragon paced into the old stable courtyard and dropped his left shoulder for Jaxom to dismount.

"We can fly now, and get away from here, Ruth. And we'll be able to go *between*, too, and go anywhere we want on Pern. You flew just beautifully, and I'm sorry I was such a poor rider, walloping you like that on your ridges. I'll learn. You'll see!"

Ruth's eyes wheeled affectionately in a brilliant blue as he followed Jaxom into the weyr. Then Jaxom kept telling Ruth how marvelous he was, turning on a wing tip and all, as he brushed away the worst of the ridge dust and hide fuzz that had accumulated on Ruth's bed overnight. Ruth settled himself, angling his head at Jaxom in a subtle bid for caresses. Jaxom obliged, somehow reluctant to join festivities at which the real guest of honor must be absent.

26

Warned by the shrieks of the fire-lizards, Robinton moved quickly to flatten himself against the right-hand leaf of the great metal doors, then put his hands across his face as a shield. He'd been caught too of-ten in frantic fire-lizard fairs not to take precautions. Generally speaking, however, the fire-lizards at the Harper Hall, thanks to Menolly's teachings, were well behaved. He smiled as he heard Lessa's exclamation of surprise and dismay. After he had felt the wind of their passing, he remained where he was and, sure enough, the fair swept back through the doorway. He heard Lord Groghe call his little queen, Merga, to order. Then his own Zair found him and, scolding as if Robinton had deliberately tried to hide from him, the little bronze fire-lizard settled on his padded left shoulder.

"There! There's a lad!" Robinton said, stroking the agitated bronze with his finger and receiving a head-sweeping caress on his cheek in return. "I wouldn't leave you, you ought to know that. Were you flying with Jaxom, too?"

Zair stopped scolding and gave a happy cheep. Then he craned his neck to peer down the court. Cu-rious, Robinton leaned forward to see what had at-tracted Zair and saw Ruth pacing toward the old stables. Robinton sighed. He almost wished Jaxom had not been allowed to fly Ruth. As he'd antici-pated, Lord Sangel was still vehemently against the youngster enjoying dragonrider prerogatives. Nor would Sangel be the only one of the older generation of Lord Holders who would dispute that liberty. Robinton felt that he'd done a fair job of influencing Groghe toward the boy, but then Groghe was smarter than Sangel. Besides, he owned a fire-lizard and that made him more charitably inclined toward Jaxom and Ruth. Robinton couldn't remember whether Sangel didn't want or had been unable to Impress a fire-lizard. He must ask Menolly. Her queen, Beauty, ought to be clutching soon. Useful that his journeywoman had a queen fire-lizard so that he could dispose of the eggs where he deemed it would do everyone the most good.

He watched a moment longer, rather touched by the sight. Between Jaxom and Ruth there was an aura of innocence and vulnerability, of dependence and protection of each for the other.

Jaxom had entered the world at a decided disadvantage, torn from his dead mother's body, with his father fatally wounded in a duel a half-hour later. Bearing in mind what N'ton and Finder had disclosed to him just before Jaxom's flight, Robinton was annoyed with himself for not keeping a closer check on the boy. Lytol was not so stiff that he wouldn't take a hint, especially if it were for Jaxom's sake. But Robinton had so many claims on his time and his thinking, even with Menolly and Sebell in his confidence and as his devoted aides. Zair cheeped and brushed his head against the Harper's chin.

Robinton chuckled and stroked Zair. They weren't more than the length of a man's arm, these fire-lizards. They weren't as intelligent as dragons, but they were utterly satisfying as companions—and occasionally useful.

Now, he'd better join the others and see how he could insinuate his suggestion to Lytol. Young Jaxom would be a perfect addition to his scheme.

"Robinton!" F'lar called him from the doorway of the Hold's smaller reception room. "Hurry up here. Your reputation is at risk."

"My what? I'm coming . . ." The Harper's long legs brought him quickly into the room by the end of the sentence. From the smiles of those standing by the flasks of decanted wine, the Harper had no trouble guessing what was afoot.

"Ah! You think to catch me out!" he cried, dramatically gesturing at the wine. "Well, I'm sure I can manage to maintain my reputation here! Just as long as you've marked the flasks correctly, Lytol."

Lessa laughed and picked one up, exhibiting her choice to the assembled. She poured a glass of the deep red wine and held it out to Robinton. Aware that all eyes were on him, Robinton made his approach to the table, affecting a slow swaggering step.

His eyes caught Menolly's and she gave him the barest wink, completely at her ease now in such prestigious company. Like the little white dragon, she was ready to fly on her own. She had certainly come a long Turn from the unsure, unappreciated girl of an isolated SeaHold. He really must get her out of the Harper Hall now and on her own.

Robinton made a proper show of wine-tasting, since this was obviously expected of him. He examined the color of the wine in the sunlight that streamed into the room, sniffed deeply of its aroma, then sipped ever so delicately and made a huge business of swishing the wine in his mouth.

"Hmmm, yes, well. There's no trouble in recognizing this vintage," he said, a shade haughtily.

"Well?" Lord Groghe demanded, his thick fingers twitching a bit on the broad belt in which he had hooked his thumbs. He rocked on his booted feet with impatience.

"One never hastens a wine!"

"Either you know or you don't," Sangel said with a skeptical sniff.

"Of course I know it. It's the Benden pressing of eleven Turns back, isn't it, Lytol?"

Robinton, aware of the silence in the room, was surprised by the look on Lytol's face. Surely the man couldn't still be upset about Jaxom flying the little dragon, could he? No, the muscle twitch had gone from his cheek.

"I'm right," Robinton said, drawling as he pointed an accusing finger at the Lord Warder. "And you know it, Lytol. To be precise, this is the later pressing as the wine is nicely fruity. Furthermore, this is from the first Benden shipment you managed to wheedle out of old Lord Raid, on the strength of Lessa's Ruathan Blood." He altered his voice to imitate Lytol's heavy baritone. "'The Weyrwoman of Pern must have Benden wine when she visits her former Hold.' Am I not right, Lytol?"

"Oh, you're right on all counts," Lytol admitted with what sounded suspiciously like a chuckle.

"About wines, Master Harper, you're infallible."

"What a relief!" F'lar said, clapping the Harper on the shoulder. "I could never have borne your loss of reputation, Robinton."

"It is a proper wine to celebrate this occasion. I give you all Jaxom, young Lord of Ruatha Hold and proud rider of Ruth." Robinton knew he'd put a dragon among wherries with his words, but there was no point hiding from the fact that, though Jaxom was Lord-elect of Ruatha Hold, he was also and undeniably a dragonrider. Lord Sangel cleared his throat abruptly before taking the required sip. Lessa's scowl suggested she'd rather he made any other toast just then.

Then, after clearing his throat a second time, Sangel jumped in as Robinton had hoped he would. "Yes, about that, there must be some understanding as to how much of a dragonrider young Jaxom is to be. I was given to understand at his Hatching," Sangel waved his hand in the vague direction of the stables, "that the little creature was not likely to survive. Only reason I didn't protest at the time."

"We didn't deliberately mislead you, Lord Sangel," Lessa began in a testy voice.

"There will be no problem, Sangel," said F'lar diplomatically. "We've no shortage of large dragons in the Weyr. So he isn't needed to fight."

"We've no shortage of trained, Blooded men to take Hold here, either," Sangel said, shooting his jaw out belligerently. Trust old Sangel to come to the point, thought Robinton gratefully.

"Not with Ruathan Blood," Lessa said, her gray eyes flashing. "The whole point of my relinquishing my blood right to this Hold when I became Weyrwoman was to cede it to the one remaining male with any Ruathan Blood in his veins—Jaxom! As long as I live, I will not permit Ruatha, of all the Holds on Pern, to be the prize for continent-wide blood duels among younger sons. Jaxom remains as Lord Holder-elect of Ruatha; he will never be a fighting dragonrider."

"Just like to set matters straight," Sangel said, stepping aside to avoid the icy stare Lessa gave him. "But you've got to admit, Weyrwoman, that riding dragons, no matter in how limited a fashion, can be dangerous. Heard about that weyrling at High Reaches . . ."

"Jaxom's riding will be controlled at all times," F'lar promised. He threw a warning glance at N'ton. "He will never fly to fight the Thread. The danger would be too great."

"Jaxom is naturally a cautious lad," Lytol joined the debate, "and I've made him properly aware of his responsibilities."

Robinton saw N'ton's grimace.

"Too cautious, N'ton?" asked F'lar, who had also noticed the Fort Weyrleader's expression.

"Perhaps," N'ton replied tactfully, with an apologetic nod to Lytol. "Or perhaps, inhibited is a better description. No offense meant, Lytol, but I noticed today that the lad finds himself . . . isolated from others. Having his own dragon accounts for part of it, I'm sure. Since no lads his age have been allowed a chance to Impress fire-lizards, the hold boys have no appreciation of his problems."

"Dorse been nagging him again?" Lytol asked, pulling at his lower lip as he regarded N'ton.

"Then you're not unaware of the situation?" N'ton appeared relieved.

"Certainly not. It's one reason I myself have pressed you, F'lar, to permit the boy to fly. He would then be able to visit the Holds which have boys his age and rank."

"But surely you've fosterlings?" Lessa cried, looking about the room as if she had somehow overlooked the presence of Holder younglings.

"I was about to arrange a half-Turn fostering for Jaxom when he Impressed." Lytol spread one hand to indicate an end to that plan.

"I can't support the notion of Jaxom leaving Ruatha for fostering," Lessa said with a frown. "Not when he's the last of the Bloodline . . ."

31

"Nor do I," Lytol said, "but it is necessary to reciprocate in fostering—"

" 'Tis not," Lord Groghe said, clapping Lytol on the shoulder. "In fact, it's a blessing not to. I've a lad Jaxom's age to be fostered. Be a relief not to have to take another boy back. When I see what you've done to put Ruatha back on its feet and so prosperous, Lytol, the lad would learn from you how to Hold properly. That is, if there should be anything for him to Hold when he gets his majority."

"That's another matter I'd like to broach," Lord Sangel said, stepping up to F'lar with a glance at Groghe for support. "What are we Holders to do?"

"To do?" asked F'lar, momentarily perplexed.

"With the younger sons," Robinton said smoothly, "for whom there are no more holds to manage in South Boll, Fort, Ista, and Igen—to name the Lords with the largest families of hopeful sons."

"The Southern Continent, F'lar, when can we start opening the Southern Continent?" Groghe asked. "That Toric, who stayed behind in the Southern Hold, maybe he could use a strong, active, energetic, ambitious lad or two, or three?"

"The Oldtimers are in the Southern Continent," Lessa said sternly. "They can do no one harm there, since the land is protected by grubs."

"I hadn't forgotten where the Oldtimers are, Weyrwoman," Groghe remarked, raising his eyebrows. "Best place for 'em, they don't bother us, they do what they want, without making honest folk suffer." There was a commendable lack of acrimony in Groghe's tone, Robinton noticed, considering how badly Fort Hold had suffered from T'ron's irresponsible conduct of Fort Weyr. "Point is, Southern's a fair size, grubbed, too, so it doesn't matter if the Oldtimers fly Thread or not, no real damage can be done."

"Have you ever remained outside your Hold during Threadfall?" F'lar asked Lord Groghe.

"Me? No! What d'you think I am, crazy? Not but what that gaggle of young men, fighting at the drop of a glove . . . Mind you, it's fists they fight with and I keep all weapons blunted, but their noise is enough to drive me *between* or outside. . . . Oh, I take your point, Weyrleader," Groghe added gloomily and his fingers did a rapid dance on his broad belt. "Yes, makes it difficult, doesn't it? We're not geared to live holdless, are we? Toric's not looking to increase his Holding at all? Something's got to be done about the youngbloods. Not just in my Hold, either, eh, Sangel?"

"If I may make a suggestion," Robinton broke in quickly when he saw F'lar hesitating. Considering the alacrity with which F'lar gestured him to proceed, he appeared grateful for the Harper's interruption. "Well, half a Turn ago, Lord Groghe's fifth son Benelek had an idea to improve a harvesting implement. The Fort Smithcraftmaster suggested that Fandarel ought to be interested. Indeed the good Mastersmith was. Young Benelek went to Telgar for special instruction and also talked one of the High Reaches' sons into joining him, that lad also having a mechanical bent. To shorten the tale, there are now eight Holder sons at the Smithcraft Hall, and three Crafthold boys who show an equal talent for the Smith's craft."

"What are you suggesting, Robinton?"

"Mischief needs idle hands. I'd like to see a special group of young people, recruited from all Crafts and Holds, exchanging ideas instead of insults."

Groghe grunted. "They want land to hold, not ideas. What about Southern?"

"That solution can surely be investigated," Robinton said, treating Groghe's insistence as offhandedly as he dared. "The Oldtimers won't live forever."

"In truth, Lord Groghe, we're by no means against expanding holds in the Southern," F'lar said. "It's just that . . ."

"The time must be chosen," Lessa finished when he faltered. There was a curious gleam in her eyes that suggested to the Harper she had other reservations as well.

"We'll not have to wait until the end of this Pass, I hope," Sangel said peevishly.

"No, just until we are in no danger of dishonoring our word," F'lar said. "If you'll think back, the Weyrs have agreed to explore the Southern Continent . . ."

"The Weyrs agreed to get rid of Thread and the Red Star, too," Sangel said, irritated now.

"F'nor here and Canth still bear the scars of that Star," Lessa reminded him, indignant at having the Weyrs criticized.

"Meaning no offense, Weyrwoman, F'lar, F'nor," Sangel said, mumbling and not very subtly masking his annoyance.

"Another reason why it might be salutary to have young minds trained to discover new ways of doing things," Robinton said, smoothly diverting Lord Sangel.

Robinton was no end pleased at Sangel's attitude. He'd reminded F'lar and Lessa recently that the older Lord Holders persisted in believing that the dragon-riders could, if they would put their minds to it, char Thread at its source on the Red Star and end forever the menace that kept people hold-fast. Mention, however, he deemed sufficient and quickly changed the subject.

"My archivist, Master Arnor, is going blind from trying to decipher eroding Record hides. He does well, but sometimes I think he doesn't at all understand what it is he is saving and thus unwittingly miscopies blurred words. Fandarel has commented on this problem, too. He's of the firm opinion that some of the mysteries from those old Records stem from miscopying. Now, if we had copyists who knew the discipline—"

"I'd like Jaxom to have some training that way," Lytol said.

"I was hoping you'd suggest him."

"Don't go back on your offer to take my son, Lytol," Groghe said.

"Well, if Jaxom's . . ."

"I see no reason why both solutions cannot be used," Robinton said. "We'd have boys his own age and rank fostering here where Jaxom must learn to

Hold, but Jaxom would also learn skills with others of different rank and background."

"After the famine, a feast?" N'ton said in so low a voice that only Robinton and Menolly heard him. "And speaking of feasts, here's our honored guest!"

Jaxom stood, hesitating, on the threshold, remembering his manners sufficiently to swing a bow to the assembled.

"Ruth's settled, has he, Jaxom?" Lessa asked in a kind voice, gesturing the boy to come to her side.

"Yes, Lessa."

"Some other settlings been done, too, kinsman," she went on, smiling when she saw his apprehensive look.

"You know my son, Horon, don't you? Your age?" Groghe asked.

Jaxom nodded, startled.

"Well, he's going to foster here as company for you."

"And possibly some other lads," said Lessa. "Would you like that?"

Robinton noticed the incredulous widening of Jaxom's eyes as he glanced from Lessa to Groghe and back to Lytol where his glance remained until Lytol had nodded solemnly.

"And, when Ruth is flying well, how about coming to my Hall to see what I can teach you about Pern that Lytol doesn't know?" Robinton asked.

"Oh, sir," and Jaxom looked again to his guardian, "may I really do all this?" There was unadulterated relief and joy in Jaxom's voice.

CHAPTER II

Benden Weyr, Present Pass, 13th Turn

DUSK WAS SETTLING in Benden Weyr as Robinton climbed the stairs to the queen's weyr, something he had done so many times in the past thirteen Turns. He paused as much to catch his breath as to speak to the man just behind him.

"We've timed it well, Toric. I don't think anyone noticed our arrival. And they'll certainly not question N'ton," he said gesturing to the Fort Weyrleader dimly seen crossing the Bowl to the lighted kitchen caverns.

Toric wasn't looking at him. He was staring up at the ledge where bronze Mnementh was seated on his haunches, regarding the new arrivals, his jewel-faceted eyes gleaming in the dim light. Robinton's Zair reacted by digging his claws sharply into the Harper's ear and twining his tail more tightly about his neck.

"He won't hurt you, Zair," Robinton said, but he hoped the message would also satisfy the Southern Holder whose face and bearing were taut with surprise.

"He's almost twice as big as any of the Oldtimers' beasts," Toric said in a respectfully hushed voice. "And I thought N'ton's Lioth was big!"

"I believe that Mnementh's the largest bronze,"

Robinton said, continuing up the last few steps. He was concerned by that twinge in his chest. He'd have thought that all his recent and unexpected rest would have eased that condition. He must remember to speak to Master Oldive about it. "Good evening, Mnementh," he said as he reached the top step, inclining his body toward the great bronze. "It strikes me as disrespectful to barge by without acknowledging him," he said in an aside to Toric. "And this is my friend, Toric, whom Lessa and F'lar are expecting."

I know. I have told them you are come.

Robinton cleared his throat. He never expected an answer to his pleasantries but was always extremely flattered on those occasions when Mnementh responded. However, he did not share the dragon's comment with Toric. The man seemed unnerved enough as it was.

Toric moved quickly toward the short corridor, keeping Robinton between himself and bronze Mnementh.

"I'd better warn you," Robinton said, keeping amusement out of his voice, "that Ramoth's even larger!"

Toric's response was a grunt which dissolved into a gasp as the corridor opened up into the large rocky chamber which served as the home of Benden's queen. She was asleep on her stone couch, her wedge-shaped head pointing in their direction, gleaming golden in the glows that illuminated the weyr.

"Robinton, you are indeed safely back," Lessa cried, running toward him, a wide smile lighting her unusual face. "And so tanned!"

To the Harper's delighted surprise, she threw her arms about him in a brief and totally unexpected embrace.

"I should get storm-lost more often," he managed to say in a light tone, grinning as raffishly as he could with his heart pounding in his chest. Her body had been so vibrant, so light against him.

"Don't you dare!" She flashed him a look compounded of anger, relief and outrage, then her mobile face assumed a more dignified smile for the other guest. "Toric, you are very welcome here, and thank you for rescuing our good Masterharper."

"I did nothing," Toric said, surprised. "He'd a dollop of pure unadulterated good luck. He ought to have drowned in that gale."

"Menolly's not a Seaholder's daughter for naught," the Harper said, clearing his throat as he remembered those grim hours. "She kept us afloat. Though at one point, I wasn't at all sure I wanted to stay alive!"

"You're not a good seaman, then, Robinton?" F'lar asked with a laugh. He gripped the Southerner's arm in greeting and with his left hand gave the Harper an affectionate crack on the arm.

Robinton suddenly realized that his adventure had had disturbing repercussions in this Weyr. He was both gratified and chagrined. True, at the time of the gale, he'd been far too occupied with his rebellious stomach to think beyond surviving the next wave that crashed over their little boat. Menolly's skill had kept him from realizing the acute danger they were in. Afterward he had come to appreciate their position and wondered if Menolly had suppressed her own fear lest she lose honor in his eyes. She'd gone about her seamanship, managing to save most of the wind-torn sail, rigging a sea anchor, lashing him to the mast as he'd been made weak by nausea and retching.

"No, F'lar, I'm no seaman," Robinton said now, with a shudder. "I'll leave that to those born to the craft."

"And follow their advice," Toric warned, somewhat tartly. He turned to the Weyrleaders. "He's got no weather sense either. And, of course, Menolly didn't realize the strength of the Western Stream at this time of the year." He raised his shoulders to indicate his helplessness against such stupidity.

"Is that why you were dragged so far from Southern?" F'lar asked, gesturing at the newcomers to seat themselves at the round table set in the corner of the big room.

"So I'm informed," said Robinton, grimacing over the long lectures he'd received on current, tide, drift and wind. He knew more than he'd take care ever to need about those aspects of the seaman's craft.

Lessa laughed at his droll tone and poured wine.

"Do you realize," he asked, twirling the glass in his fingers, "that there wasn't a drop of wine on board?"

"Oh, no!" Lessa cried in comic dismay. F'lar's laughter joined hers. "What deprivation!"

Robinton then got down to the purpose of this visit. "It was, however, a felicitous accident. There is, my dear Weyrleaders, considerably more of the Southern Continent than we'd ever thought." He glanced at Toric, who produced the map he'd hastily copied from the larger one in his Hold. F'lar and Lessa obligingly held the corners to flatten the stiff hide. The Northern Continent was detailed as was the known portion of the Southern Continent. Robinton pointed to the thumb of the Southern peninsula which contained the Southern Weyr and Toric's Hold, then gestured to the right and left of that landmark where the coastline and a good part of the interior, marked off by two rivers, had been topographically detailed. "Toric has not been idle. You can see how much he has extended knowledge of the terrain beyond what F'nor was able to do during his journey south."

"I asked permission of T'ron to continue the exploration," the Southerner's expression mirrored contempt and dislike, "but he barely heard me out and said I could do as I liked just as long as the Weyr was properly supplied with game and fresh fruit."

"Supplied?" exclaimed F'lar. "They'd only to walk a few dragon lengths from the weyrs and pick what they needed."

"Sometimes they do. Mostly I find it easier to have my holders supply their demands. They don't bother us then."

"Bother you?" Lessa's voice was indignant.

The White Dragon

"That's what I said, Weyrleader," Toric replied, a steely note in his voice; he turned back to the map. "My holders have been able to penetrate this far into the interior. Very difficult going. Tough jungle growth that dulls the keenest chopping blade in an hour. Never seen such vegetation! We know there are hills here and a mountain range farther back," he tapped the relevant area on the map, "but I'd not fancy carving my way there length by length. So we scouted along the shoreline, found these two rivers and proceeded up them as far as we could. The western river ends in a flat marshy lake, the southeastern one at a falls, six-seven dragon lengths high." Toric straightened, regarding the small portion of explored land with mild disgust. "I'd hazard the guess that even if the land went no farther south than that range, it's twice the size of South Boll or Tillek!"

"And the Oldtimers are not interested in examining what they have?" F'lar found that attitude unpalatable, Robinton realized.

"No, Weyrleader, they are not! And frankly, without some easier way to penetrate that vegetation," Toric tapped the hide, "I don't have the men, much less the energy, to bother. I've all the land I can hold right now and still be sure my people are safe from Thread." He paused. Although Robinton had a fair idea what he was hesitating about, the Harper wanted the Weyrleaders to know firsthand what this energetic Southerner thought. "Most of the time the dragonmen don't bother on that score, either."

"What?" Lessa exploded, but F'lar touched her shoulder.

"I'd wondered about that, Toric."

"How dare they?" Lessa continued, her gray eyes flashing. Ramoth stirred on her couch.

"They dare, all right," Toric said, looking nervously at the queen.

However, Robinton could see that Lessa's appalled reaction to the Oldtimers' delinquency gratified the man.

40

"But . . . but . . ." Lessa spluttered with indignation.

"Are you able to manage, Toric?" F'lar asked, calming his weyrmate with a firm hand.

"I've learned," he said. "We've plenty of flame-throwers, F'nor made sure they were left in my care. We maintain our holds grass-free and keep the beasts in the stone stables during Fall." He gave a diffident shrug, then grinned slightly at the indignant expression of the Weyrwoman. "They don't do us any harm, Lessa, even if they don't do us any good. Don't worry. We can handle them."

"That isn't the point," Lessa said angrily. "They are dragonmen, sworn to protect—"

"You sent them south because they weren't," Toric reminded her. "So they couldn't injure people here."

"That still doesn't give them any right to—"

"I told you, Lessa, they're not harming us. We manage fine without them!"

A sort of challenge in Toric's tone made Robinton hold his breath. Lessa had a quick temper.

"Is there anything you need from the North?" asked F'lar, in oblique apology.

"I was hoping you'd ask," the Southerner said, grinning. "I know you can't break your honor by interfering with the Oldtimers in the South. Not that I mind . . ." he added quickly as he saw Lessa about to protest again. "But we are running out of some things, like properly forged metal for my Craftsmith, and parts for the flamethrowers that he says only Fandarel can make."

"I'll see that you get them."

"And I'd like a young sister of mine, Sharra, to study with that healer the Harper was telling me about, a Master Oldive. We've some odd sorts of fevers and curious infections."

"Naturally she's welcome," Lessa said quickly. "And our Manora is adept in herb-brews."

"And . . ." Toric hesitated a moment, glancing at Robinton, who quickly reassured him with a smile and an encouraging gesture, "if there were some adventurous men and women who'd be willing to make do at my Hold, I think I could absorb them without the Oldtimers' knowing. Just a few, mind, because though we've all the space in the world, some people become unsettled when there aren't dragons in the sky during Threadfall!"

"Why, yes," F'lar said with a nonchalance that caused Robinton to stifle a laugh, "I believe there are a few hardy souls who would be interested in joining you."

"Good. If I've enough to Hold properly, then I can see my way clear to extending beyond the rivers next cool season." Toric's relief was visible.

"I thought you said it was impossible . . ." F'lar began.

"Not impossible. Just difficult," Toric replied, adding with a smile, "I've some men keen to continue despite the odds, and I'd like to know what's out there."

"So would we," Lessa said. "The Oldtimers won't last forever."

"That fact often consoles me," Toric replied. "One thing, though . . ." He paused, looking through narrowed eyes at the two Benden Weyrleaders.

So far, Toric's audacity had delighted Robinton. The Harper was very pleased at how he'd managed to prime the man into requesting the very thing that the North needed the most—a place to send the independent and capable men who had no chance of attaining holds in the North. The big Southerner's manner was quite a change for the Benden Weyrleaders: neither subservient and apologetic nor aggressive and demanding. Toric had become independent as a result of having no one, dragonmen, Craftmasters or Lord Holders, to fall back on. Because he had survived, he was self-confident and he knew what he wanted, and how to get it. Therefore he was addressing Lessa and F'lar as equals.

"One small matter," he continued, "which I'd like clarified?"

"Yes?" F'lar prompted him.

"What happens to Southern, to my holders, to me, when the last of those Oldtimers is gone?"

"I'd say that you will have more than earned the right to Hold," F'lar said slowly, with an unmistakable accent on the final word, "what you have managed to carve out of that jungle for yourself!"

"Good!" Toric gave a decisive nod of his head, his eyes never leaving F'lar's. Then, suddenly, his tanned face dissolved into a smile. "I'd forgotten what you Northerners can be like. Send me some more—"

"Will they hold what they have carved?" Robinton asked quickly.

"What they hold, they have," Toric replied in a grave manner. "But don't flood me with people. I've got to sneak them in when the Oldtimers aren't looking."

"How many can you sneak in . . . comfortably?" asked F'lar.

"Oh, six, eight, the first time. Then when we've got holds, the same again." He grinned. "The first ones build for themselves before the new ones come. But there's lots of room in the South."

"That's comforting because I've plans for the South myself," said F'lar. "That reminds me, Robinton, how far to the east did you and Menolly go?"

"I wish I could answer you. I know where we got to, when the storm finally blew out. The most beautiful place I've ever seen, a perfect semicircle of a white sanded beach, with this huge cone-shaped mountain far, far in the distance, right in the center of the cove . . ."

"But you came back along the shore, didn't you?" F'lar was impatient. "What was it like?"

"It was there," Robinton said uninformatively. "That's all I can say. . . ." He glared at Toric, who was chuckling at his discomfiture. "We had a choice of sailing very close to land which Menolly said was impossible as we didn't know the bottom, or with sufficient searoom to keep beyond the Western Current which would evidently have brought us right back to the cove. It is, as I've said, a very beautiful spot, but I was glad to leave it for a while. Consequently, while land was there, it was not close enough for any inspection by me."

"That's too bad." F'lar looked very unhappy.

"Yes and no," replied Robinton. "It took us nine days to sail back along that coast. That's a lot of land for Toric to explore."

"I'm willing, and I'll be ready if I get the supplies I need . . ."

"How do we get shipments to you, Toric?" F'lar asked. "Don't dare send them on dragonback, though that would be easiest and best from my point of view."

Robinton chuckled and gave a broad wink to the others. "As to that, if another ship should by chance be blown off course, south from Ista Hold . . . I had a word or two with Master Idarolan recently and he mentioned how bad the storms have been this Turn."

"Is that how you chanced to be South in the first place?" asked Lessa.

"How else?" Robinton said, assuming a very innocent expression. "Menolly was attempting to teach me to sail, a storm came up unexpectedly and blew us straight into Toric's harbor. Didn't it, Toric?"

"If you say so, Harper!"

CHAPTER III

Morning at Ruatha Hold, and Smithcrafthall at Telgar Hold, Present Pass, 15.5.9

WITH A FORCE that set all the cups and plates
bouncing, Jaxom brought down both fists on the
heavy wooden table.

"That is enough," he said into the stunned silence.
He was on his feet, jerking his broad, bony shoulders
back because his arms had been jarred by the blows.
"That is quite enough!"

He didn't shout, he was oddly pleased to recall
later, but his voice was deepened by this explosion of
long suppressed anger and carried clearly to the edge
of the Hall. The drudge who was bringing in another
pitcher of hot klah paused in confusion.

"I am the Lord of this Hold," Jaxom went on, staring first at Dorse, his milk-brother. "I am Ruth's rider.
He is unmistakably a dragon." Jaxom now bent his
gaze on Brand, the head steward whose jaw had
dropped in surprise. "He is, as usual," and Jaxom's
glance flickered across Lytol's blankly puzzled face,
"in the very good health he has enjoyed since his
Hatching." Jaxom passed over the four fosterlings who
were all too new at Ruatha Hold to have started jibing
at him. "And yes," he said directly to Deelan, his
milk-mother whose lower lip was quivering at her

nursling's startling behavior, "this is the day when I go to the Smithcrafthall where, as you all well know, I shall be served with the food and courtesy adequate to my needs and station. Therefore," and his glance swept the faces around the table, " the subjects of this morning's conversation do not need to be aired again in my presence. Have I made myself clear?"

He didn't wait for an answer but strode purposefully from the Hall, elated at having finally said something and half-guilty because he had lost control of his temper. He heard Lytol call his name but for once that summons did not exact obedience.

This time it would not be Jaxom, however young a Lord of Ruatha Hold he still was, who apologized for his behavior. The enormous backlog of similar incidents, manfully swallowed or overlooked for any number of logical reasons, swept aside every consideration except to put as much distance between himself and his invidious position, his too reasonable and conscientious guardian and the obnoxious group of people who mistook daily intimacy for license.

Ruth, picking up his rider's distress, came charging out of the old stable which made his weyr at Ruatha Hold. The white dragon's fragile-seeming wings were half-spread as he rushed to give whatever aid his mate needed.

With a breath that was half a sob, Jaxom vaulted to Ruth's back and urged him up out of the courtyard just as Lytol appeared at the massive Hold doors. Jaxom averted his face so that later he'd be able to say truthfully that he hadn't seen Lytol waving.

Ruth beat strongly upward, his lighter mass launched more readily than that of the regular-sized dragons.

"You're twice the dragon the others are. Twice! You're better at everything! Everything!" Jaxom's thought was so turbulent that Ruth trumpeted defiance.

The startled brown watchdragon queried them from the fire-heights and the entire Hold population of fire-lizards materialized around Ruth, dipping and swooping, chirping in echoed agitation.

Ruth cleared the fire-heights and then winked into *between,* unerringly going to the high mountain lake above the Hold which had become their special retreat.

The penetrating cold of *between,* brief passage though it was, reduced Jaxom's temper. He began shivering, since he wore only his sleeveless tunic, as Ruth glided down effortlessly to the water's edge.

"It's completely and utterly unfair!" he said, slamming his right fist into his thigh so hard that Ruth grunted with the impact.

What is troubling you today? the dragon asked as he landed daintily on the lake verge.

"Everything! Nothing!"

Which? Ruth reasonably wanted to know and turned his head to gaze at his rider.

Jaxom slid from the soft-skinned white back and encircled the dragon's neck with his arms, pulling the wedge-shaped head against him, for comforting.

Why do you let them *upset you?* Ruth asked, his eyes whirling with love and affection for his weyrmate.

"A very good question," Jaxom replied after a full moment's consideration. "But they know exactly how." Then he laughed. "This is where all that objectivity Robinton talks about ought to operate . . . and doesn't."

The Masterharper is honored for his wisdom. Ruth sounded uncertain, and his tone made Jaxom smile.

He was always being told that dragons had no ability to understand abstract concepts or complex relationships. Too often Ruth surprised him by remarks that cast doubt on the theory. Dragons, particularly Ruth in Jaxom's biased opinion, obviously perceived far more than others credited to them. Even Weyrleaders like F'lar or Lessa and even N'ton. Thinking about the Fort Weyrleader reminded Jaxom that he now had a particular reason for going to the Mastersmithhall this morning. N'ton, who would be there to hear Wansor, was the only rider Jaxom felt would be likely to help him.

"Shells!" Jaxom kicked rebelliously at a stone, watching the ripples it caused when it skittered across the surface of the lake and finally sank.

Robinton had often used the ripple effect to demonstrate how a tiny action produced multiple reactions. Jaxom let out a snort, wondering how many ripples he'd caused this morning by storming out of the Hall. And just why had this morning bothered him so much? It had begun like other mornings, with Dorse's trite comments about oversized fire-lizards, with Lytol's habitual query about Ruth's health—as if the dragon were likely to deteriorate overnight—and with Deelan snidely repeating that sickeningly old hoot about visitors starving at the Smithcrafthall. To be sure, Deelan's mothering had lately begun to irritate Jaxom, especially when the dear soul invariably fondled him in front of her seething natural son, Dorse. All the time-honored, worn-out nonsense that started a day, every day, at Ruatha Hold. Why, today, should it jerk him to his feet in a fury and drive him from the Hall he was Lord of, fleeing from people over whom, in theory, he had all control and right?

And there was nothing wrong with Ruth. Nothing.

No. I am fine, Ruth said, then added in a plaintive tone, *except that I didn't have time for my swim.*

Jaxom stroked the soft eye ridges, smiling indulgently. "Sorry to spoil your morning, too."

You haven't. I'll swim in the lake. Quieter here, Ruth said and nuzzled Jaxom. *It's better here for you, too.*

"I hope so." Anger was foreign to Jaxom and he resented the violence of his inner feelings and those who had driven him to such a point of fury. "Better swim. We've got to go on to the Smithcrafthall, you know."

Ruth had no sooner spread his wings than a clutch of fire-lizards appeared in the air above him, wildly chittering and loudly broadcasting thoughts of smug satisfaction at their cleverness in finding him. One winked out immediately and Jaxom felt another stab of resentment. Keeping track of him, huh? That'd be one more order from him when he got back to the Hold. Who did they think he was, an unbreeched child or an Oldtimer?

He sighed, repentant. Of course, they'd be worried about him when he'd stormed out of the Hold like that. Not that he was likely to go anywhere but to the lake. Not that he could possibly come to harm with Ruth, and not that he and Ruth could go anywhere on Pern where fire-lizards couldn't find them.

His resentment flared anew, this time against the silly fire-lizards. Why, of all dragons, did every fire-lizard have an insatiable curiosity about Ruth? Wherever they went on Pern, every fire-lizard in the neighborhood came popping in to gawk at the white dragon. This activity used to amuse Jaxom because the fire-lizards would give Ruth the most incredible images of things they remembered, and Ruth would pass the more interesting ones to him. But today, as with everything else, amusement had soured to irritation.

"Analyze," Lytol was fond of directing him. "Think objectively. You can't govern others until you can control yourself and see the broader, forward-looking view."

Jaxom took a couple of deep breaths, the kind Lytol recommended he take before speaking, to organize what he was going to say.

Ruth had winged over the deep-blue waters of the little lake now, fire-lizards outlining his graceful figure. He suddenly folded his wings and dove. Jaxom shuddered, wondering how Ruth could enjoy the biting cold waters fed by the snowcapped peaks of the High Ranges. In the muggy midsummer heat, Jaxom often found it refreshing, but now, with winter barely past? He shuddered again. Well, if dragons didn't feel the three-times-more-intense cold of *between,* a plunge in an icy lake would not be bothersome.

Ruth surfaced, waves lapping against the bank at Jaxom's feet. Jaxom idly stripped a branch of its thick needles and launched them one after another into the incoming ripples. Well, one wave of reaction to this morning's outburst was the dispatch of fire-lizards to find him.

Another, the look of stunned amazement on Dorse's face. That had been the first time Jaxom had ever rounded on his milk-brother, though, Shells, it was only the thought of Lytol's displeasure at his loss of control that had kept Jaxom's temper in check so long. Dorse loved nothing better than to taunt Jaxom about Ruth's lack of stature, masking his malicious jibes in mock-brotherly quarrels, knowing all too well that Jaxom could not retaliate without a rebuke from Lytol for conduct unbecoming his rank and station. Jaxom had long outgrown the need for Deelan's fussing but innate kindness and gratitude to her for the milk which had nourished him after his premature birth had long prevented Jaxom from asking Lytol to retire her.

So why, today, had all this suddenly come to a boil?

Ruth's head emerged from the waters again, the many-faceted eyes reflecting the bright morning sun in greens and brilliant clear blues. The fire-lizards attacked his back with rough tongues and talons, scrubbing off infinitesimal motes of dirt, splashing water over him with their wings, their own hides darkened by the wetting.

The green turned to batter her nose at one of the two blues and swatted the brown with her wing to make him work to her satisfaction. Despite himself, Jaxom laughed to see her scolding. She was Deelan's green and so much in manner like his milkmother that he was reminded of the weyr axiom that a dragon was no better than his rider.

In that way, Lytol had done Jaxom no disservice. Ruth was the best dragon in all Pern. If—and now Jaxom recognized the underlying cause of his rebellion—Ruth was ever *allowed* to be. Immediately all the frustrated anger of the morning returned, disrupting what little objectivity he had gained at the peaceful lakeside. Neither he, Jaxom, Lord of Ruatha, nor

Ruth, the white runt of Ramoth's clutch, were allowed to be what they really were.

Jaxom was Lord Holder in name only, because Lytol administered the Hold, made all its decisions, spoke in Council for Ruatha. Jaxom had yet to be confirmed by the other Lord Holders as Lord of Ruatha. True, a matter of form only since there was no other male on Pern with Ruathan Blood. Besides, Lessa, the only living full-blooded Ruathan, had relinquished her blood right to Jaxom at the moment of his birth.

Jaxom knew he could never be a dragonrider because he had to be Lord Holder of Ruatha. Only he was not really a Lord Holder because he couldn't go up to Lytol and just say: "I'm old enough to take over now! Thanks and good-bye!" Lytol had worked too hard and long to make Ruatha prosper to take second place to the bumblings of an untried youth. Lytol only lived for Ruatha. He'd lost so much else: first his own dragon, then his small family to Fax's greed. All his life now centered about Ruathan fields and wheat, and runners, and how many wherry bucks . . .

No, in all fairness, he would simply have to wait until Lytol, who enjoyed vigorous health, died a natural death before he started Holding at Ruatha.

But, Jaxom continued his thoughts logically, if Lytol is active so that Ruatha Hold is not in dispute, why couldn't he and Ruth occupy their time learning to be proper dragon and rider. Every fighting dragon was needed now, what with Thread falling from the Red Star at unexpected intervals. Why should he have to trudge about the countryside, lugging a clumsy flamethrower when he could more effectively fight Thread if Ruth were only allowed to chew firestone? Just because Ruth was half the size of the other dragons didn't mean he wasn't a proper dragon in all other respects.

Of course I am, Ruth said from the lake.

Jaxom grimaced. He'd been trying to think quietly.

I heard your feelings, not your thoughts, Ruth said calmly. *You are confused and unhappy.* He arched out of the water to shake his wings dry. He half-paddled, half-flew to the shore. *I am a dragon. You are my rider. No man can change that. Be what you are. I am.*

"But not really. They won't let us be what we are," Jaxom cried. "They're forcing me to be everything but a dragonrider."

You are a dragonrider. You are also, and Ruth said this slowly as if trying to understand it all himself, *a Lord Holder. You are a student with the Mastersmith and the Masterharper. You are a friend of Menolly, Mirrim, F'lessan and N'ton. Ramoth knows your name. So does Mnementh. And they know me. You have to be a lot of people. That is hard.*

Jaxom stared at Ruth, who gave his wings a final flick and then folded them fastidiously across his back.

I am clean. I feel well, the dragon said as if this announcement should resolve all of Jaxom's internal doubts.

"Ruth, whatever would I do without you?"

I don't know. N'ton comes to see you. He went to Ruatha. The little brown who followed looks to N'ton.

Jaxom sucked in his breath nervously. Trust Ruth to know which was whose fire-lizard. He had assumed the brown looked to someone at Ruatha Hold.

"Why didn't you tell me sooner?" Hurriedly Jaxom made to mount Ruth. He did most urgently want to see N'ton, and he wanted with equal intensity to keep in N'ton's good favor. The Fort Weyrleader didn't have that much free time to chat.

I wanted my swim, Ruth replied. *We will be in time.* Ruth rose from the ground when Jaxom had barely settled on his back. *We will not keep N'ton waiting.* Before Jaxom could remind Ruth that they weren't supposed to go *between* time, they had.

"Ruth, what if N'ton finds out we've been timing it," Jaxom said through chattering teeth as they broke out of *between* into the hot midmorning sun of Telgar over the Mastersmithcrafthall.

He will not ask.

Jaxom wished that Ruth wouldn't sound so complacent. But then, the white dragon wouldn't have to take N'ton's tongue-lashing. Timing was bloody dangerous!

I always know when I'm going, Ruth replied, not at all perturbed. *That's something few other dragons can say.*

They were barely in a landing circle above the Smithcrafthall complex before N'ton's great bronze Lioth burst into the air above them.

"And how you know how to time it that close, I'll never know," Jaxom said.

Oh, Ruth said easily, *I heard when the brown returned to N'ton and just came to that* when.

Jaxom knew that dragons were not supposed to laugh but the feeling from Ruth was so close to laughter as to make no difference.

Lioth winged close enough to Jaxom and Ruth for the young Lord to see the bronze rider's expression—a pleased grin. Jaxom thought Ruth had said N'ton had been at Ruatha first. Then Jaxom noticed that N'ton raised his hand and was holding what could only be Jaxom's wherhide riding jacket.

As they circled downward, Jaxom saw that they were by no means the first arrivals. He counted five dragons, including F'lessan's bronze Golanth and Mirrim's green Path who warbled a greeting. Ruth landed lightly on the meadow before the Smithcrafthall with Lioth touching down the next moment. As N'ton slid down the bronze shoulder, his brown firelizard, Tris, appeared and settled impertinently on Ruth's upper crest, chirping smugly.

"Deelan said you'd gone off without this," N'ton said and tossed the jacket at Jaxom. "Well, I suppose you don't feel the cold the way my old bones do. Or are you practicing survival tactics?"

"Ah, N'ton, not you, too!"

"Me, too, what, young fella?"

"You know . . ."

"No, I don't know." N'ton gave Jaxom a closer look. "Or did Deelan's babbling this morning have real significance?"

"You didn't see Lytol?"

"No. I just asked the first person in the Hold where you were. Deelan was weeping because you'd gone off without your jacket." N'ton drolly pulled down his lower lip in a trembling imitation of Deelan. "Can't stand weeping women—at least women that age—so I grabbed the jacket, promised on the shell of my dragon to force it about your frail body, sent Tris to see where Ruth was and here we are. Tell me, did something momentous happen this morning? Ruth looks fine."

Embarrassed, Jaxom looked away from the quizzical regard of the Fort Weyrleader and gave himself a bit more time by shrugging into his jacket.

"I told the entire Hold off this morning."

"I told Lytol it wouldn't be long now."

"What?"

"What tipped the scales? Deelan's blubbering?"

"Ruth is a dragon!"

"Of course he is," N'ton replied with such emphasis that Lioth turned his head to regard them. "Who says he's not?"

"They do. At Ruatha. Everywhere! They say he's nothing but an overgrown fire-lizard. And you know that's been said."

Lioth hissed. Tris took wing in surprise, but Ruth warbled complacently and the others settled.

"I know it's been said," N'ton replied, taking hold of Jaxom's shoulders. "But there isn't a dragonrider I know who hasn't corrected the speaker—somewhat forcefully on occasion."

"If *you* consider him a dragon, why can't he act like one?"

"He does!" N'ton gave Ruth a long look as if the creature had somehow changed in the last moment.

"I mean like other full fighting dragons."

"Oh." N'ton grimaced. "So that's it. Look, lad . . ."

"It's Lytol, isn't it? He's told you not to let me fight Thread on Ruth. That's why you'll never let me teach Ruth how to chew firestone."

"It's not that, Jaxom . . ."

"Then what is it? There isn't a place on Pern we

can't get to, first time, right on. Ruth's small but he's faster, turns quicker midair, less mass to move—"

"It's not a question of ability, Jaxom," N'ton said, raising his voice slightly to make Jaxom hear what he had to say, "it's a matter of what is advisable."

"More evasions."

"No!" N'ton's firm negative cut through Jaxom's resentment. "Flying with a fighting wing during Threadfall is bloody dangerous, lad. I'm not impugning your courage, but bluntly, however keen you are, however quick and clever Ruth is, you'd be a liability to a fighting wing. You haven't the training, the discipline . . ."

"If it's only training—"

N'ton grabbed Jaxom by the shoulders to stop his contentiousness.

"It isn't." N'ton drew a deep breath. "I said it's not a question of Ruth's abilities or yours; it is solely a question of advisability. Pern can't afford to lose either you, young Lord of Ruatha, or Ruth, who is unique."

"But I'm not Lord of Ruatha either. Not yet! Lytol is. He makes all the decisions . . . I just listen, and nod my head like a sunstruck wherry." Jaxom faltered, aware he was implying criticism of Lytol. "I mean, I know Lytol has to manage until the Lord Holders confirm me . . . and I don't really want Lytol to leave Ruatha Hold. But if I could be a dragonrider, it wouldn't come to that. You see?"

As Jaxom caught the expression in N'ton's eyes, his shoulders slumped in defeat. "You see, but the answer's still no! It would just make different ripples, probably bigger ones, wouldn't it? So I've got to muck on as something in between everything. Not a real Lord Holder, not a real dragonrider . . . not a real anything except a problem. A real problem to everybody!"

Not to me, Ruth said clearly and reassuringly touched his rider with his muzzle.

"You're not a problem, Jaxom, but I do see that you have one," N'ton said with quiet sympathy. "If it were up to me, I'd say it would do you a world of good

to join a wing and teach Ruth to chew firestone. For
the firsthand knowledge no other Lord Holder could
contest."

For one hopeful moment, Jaxom thought N'ton was
offering him the chance he so wanted.

"*If* it were my decision, Jaxom, which it isn't and
can't be. But," and N'ton paused, his eyes searching
Jaxom's face, "this is a matter that had better be discussed. You're old enough to be confirmed as Lord
Holder *or* to do something else constructive. I'll speak
to Lytol and F'lar on your behalf."

"Lytol will say that I am Lord Holder, and F'lar
will say Ruth isn't big enough for a fighting wing—"

"And I won't say anything if you act like a sulky
boy."

A bellow overhead interrupted them. Two more
dragons were circling, indicating that they wanted to
land. N'ton waved acknowledgment, and then he and
Jaxom jogged out of the way toward the Smithcrafthall. Just short of the door, N'ton held him back.

"I won't forget, Jaxom, only . . ." and N'ton grinned,
"for the sake of the First Shell, don't let anyone *catch*
you giving Ruth firestone. And be bloody careful when
you go!"

In a state of mild shock, Jaxom stared at N'ton as
the Weyrleader hailed a friend inside the building.
N'ton had understood. Jaxom's depression lifted instantly.

As he crossed the threshold of the Smithcrafthall,
he hesitated, adjusting his sight to the interior after
the bright spring sun. Intent on his own problems, he'd
also forgotten how important a session this was to be.
Masterharper Robinton was seated at the long work
table, cleared for this occasion of its usual clutter, and
F'lar, Benden's Weyrleader, was beside him. Jaxom recognized three other Weyrleaders and the new Masterherdsman Briaret. There were a good half a wing of
bronze riders and Lord Holders, the leading smiths
and more harpers than any other craft to judge by the
color of tunics on men he didn't recognize immediately.

Someone was calling his name in an urgent hoarse whisper. Looking to his left, Jaxom saw that F'lessan and the other regular students had gathered humbly by the far window, the girls perched on stools.

"Half Pern's here," F'lessan remarked, pleased, as he made room against the back wall for Jaxom.

Jaxom nodded to the others who appeared far more interested in watching the new arrivals. "Didn't think there'd be so many people interested in Wansor's stars and maths," Jaxom said in a low voice to F'lessan.

"What? And miss a chance to ride dragonback?" F'lessan asked with good-natured candor. "I brought four in myself."

"A lot of people have assisted Wansor in collating the material," Benelek said in his usual didactic manner. "Naturally they want to hear what use has been made of their time and effort."

"They sure didn't come for the food," F'lessan said with a snicker.

Now why, wondered Jaxom, doesn't F'lessan's remark annoy me?

"Nonsense, F'lessan," Benelek replied, too literal-minded to understand when someone was being facetious. "Food's very good here. You eat enough of it."

"I'm like Fandarel," F'lessan said. "I make efficient use of anything edible. *Sush!* Here he is himself. Shells!" The young bronze rider grimaced with disgust. "Couldn't someone have made him change his clothes?"

"As if clothes mattered for a man with a mind like Wansor's." Benelek dropped his voice but he was nearly sputtering with contempt for F'lessan.

"Today of all days, Wansor should look tidy," Jaxom said. "That's what F'lessan meant."

Benelek grunted but did not pursue the subject. Then F'lessan nudged Jaxom in the ribs with a wink for Benelek's reaction.

Halfway inside the door, Wansor suddenly realized that the hall was filled. He stopped, peered around him, at first timidly. Then, when he recognized a face, he bobbed his head and smiled hesitantly. From all sides he met with encouraging grins and murmured greetings and gestures for him to continue to the front of the hall.

"Well, my, my . . . All for my stars? My stars, my, my!" His reaction sent a ripple of amusement through the hall. "This is most gratifying. I'd no idea . . . Most gratifying. And Robinton, you're *here* . . ."

"Where else?" The Masterharper's long face was suitably serious but Jaxom thought he saw the man's lips twitch in an effort not to smile. Robinton then half-guided, half-pushed Wansor toward the platform at the far end of the hall.

"Come on, Wansor," Fandarel said in his rolling tones.

"Oh yes, so sorry. Didn't mean to keep you waiting. Ah, and there's Lord Asgenar. How very good of you to come. I say, is N'ton here, too?" Wansor executed a full circle. Being nearsighted, he peered closely at faces, trying to spot N'ton. "He really should be—"

"Here I am, Wansor," N'ton raised his arm.

"Ah." The worried frown vanished from the round face of the Starsmith as Menolly had impudently, if accurately, labeled him. "My dear N'ton, you must come up front. You've done so much work, watching and looking at the most dreadful hours of the night. Come, you must—"

"Wansor!" Fandarel half-rose to project his commanding bellow. "You can't put everyone up front and they've all watched. That's why they're here. To see what their watching was all for. Now get up here and get on with it. You're wasting time. Sheer inefficiency."

Wansor muttered protestations and apologies as he bounced up the short distance to the platform. He did indeed look, Jaxom noticed, as if he'd been sleeping in those clothes. He probably hadn't changed since the last Threadfall to judge by the sharpness of the creases in the back of his tunic.

But there was nothing sloppy about the charts of star positions which Wansor now tacked up on the wall. Where did Wansor get that lurid red color for the Red Star—the color almost pulsed on the paper. Nothing dithering about his spoken presentation. Out of deference and respect for Wansor, Jaxom tried to pay close attention but he had heard it all before and his mind returned inexorably to N'ton's parting shot. "Don't let anyone catch you giving Ruth firestone!"

As if he would be that foolish. Here Jaxom hesitated. Although he knew in theory the whys and hows of teaching a dragon to chew firestone, he had also learned in his classes that between theory and practice anything could happen. Maybe he could enlist F'lessan's help?

He glanced at the friend of his boyhood, who had Impressed a bronze two Turns ago. Candidly, Jaxom did not consider F'lessan more than a boy and certainly not serious enough about his responsibilities as a bronze rider. He was grateful that F'lessan had never told anyone that Jaxom had actually touched Ruth's egg when the dragon was still in its shell on the Hatching Ground. Of course, that would have been a serious offense against the Weyr. F'lessan would scarcely regard teaching a dragon to chew firestone as anything at all remarkable.

Mirrim? Jaxom glanced toward the girl. The morning sun slanted through her browny hair, catching golden glints which he'd never noticed before. She was oblivious to anything but Wansor's words. She'd probably give Jaxom an argument about not precipitating the Weyr into more problems and then set one of those fire-lizards of hers on him to be sure he didn't set himself ablaze.

Jaxom was privately convinced that T'ran, the other young bronze rider from Ista Weyr, thought Ruth was essentially an overgrown fire-lizard. He'd be even less help than F'lessan.

Benelek was out, too. He ignored dragons and fire-lizards as completely as they ignored him. But give Benelek a diagram or a machine, even the assorted parts of a machine found in the old holds and weyrs, and he'd spend days trying to figure out what it was supposed to be or do. Generally he could make a full machine work, even if he had to dismantle the whole thing to find out why it wasn't operating. Benelek and Fandarel understood each other perfectly.

Menolly? Menolly was just the person, if he did need someone, in spite of her predilection for putting anything she heard into a tune—a trick that was occasionally a real nuisance. But that talent made her an excellent Harper, in fact she was the first girl to be one in living memory. He stole a long look at her. Her lips were vibrating slightly and he wondered if she were already putting Wansor's stars to music.

"The stars mark time for us in every Turn and help us distinguish one Turn from another," Wansor was saying and Jaxom brought his attention guiltily back to the speaker. "The stars guided Lessa on her courageous trip back through time to bring the Oldtimers forward." Wansor cleared his throat at his somewhat unfortunate mention of the two dragonrider factions. "And the stars will be our constant guides in future Turns. Lands, seas, people and places may change but the stars are ordered in their courses and remain secure."

Jaxom remembered hearing some talk of trying to alter the course of the Red Star, deflecting it away from Pern. Had Wansor just proved that that couldn't be done?

Wansor went on to emphasize that once you understood the basic orbit and speed of any star, you could compute its position in the heavens as long as you also calculated the effect of its nearest neighbors at conjunction, at any given time.

"So, there is no doubt in our minds that we can now accurately predict Threadfall, according to the position of the Red Star when in conjunction with our other near neighbors in the skies."

Jaxom was amused that, whenever Wansor made a sweeping statement, he said *we* but when he announced a discovery, he said *I*.

"We believe that as soon as this blue star is released from the influence of the yellow star of our spring horizon and swings to the high east, Threadfall will resume the pattern which F'lar originally observed.

"With this equation," Wansor rapidly jotted the figures down on the board, and Jaxom again noticed that for a sloppy looking person, his notations were conversely precise, "we can compute further conjunctions which will affect Threadfall during this Pass. Indeed, we can now point to where the various stars have been at any time in the past and will be at any time in the future."

He was writing equations at a furious pace and explaining which stars were affected by which equations. He turned then, his round face settling into a very serious expression. "We can even predict, on the basis of this knowledge, the exact moment when the next Pass will begin. Of course, that's so many Turns in the future that none of us need worry about it. But I think it's comforting to know nonetheless."

Scattered chuckles caused Wansor to blink and then hesitantly grin, as if he belatedly realized that he'd said something humorous.

"And we must make sure that no one forgets in the long Interval this time," Mastersmith Fandarel said, his bass voice startling everyone after Wansor's light tenor. "That's what this union is all about, you know," Fandarel added, gesturing to the audience.

Several Turns before, when Ruth's life expectancy had been short, Jaxom had held a private if egocentric theory about the sessions at the Smithcrafthall. He had convinced himself that they had been initiated to give him an alternative interest in living in case Ruth died. Today's meeting let the substance out of that notion, and Jaxom snorted at his self-centered whimsy. The more people—in every Hold, in the Weyrs—who knew what was being done in each of the Crafthalls, by the individual Craftmasters and by their chief technicians, the less chance there was that the ambitious plans to preserve all Pern from the ravages of Thread would be lost again.

Jaxom, F'lessan, Benelek, Mirrim, Menolly, T'ran, Piemur, various other likely successors to Lord Holders

61

and advanced junior craftsmen formed the nucleus of the regular school at the Smith and Harper crafthalls. Each student learned to appreciate the other crafts.

Communication is essential. That was one of Robinton's tenets. Wasn't he always saying, "Exchange information, learn to talk sensibly about any subject, learn to express your thoughts, accept new ones, examine them, analyze. Think objectively. Think toward the future."

Jaxom let his eyes drift about the room at the gathering, wondering how many of them could accept all of Wansor's explanations. True, with this lot he had the advantage that most of them had watched the stars form and reform their patterns, night after night, season after season until those stately patterns could be reduced to Wansor's clever diagrams and numbers. The trouble was that everyone was here in this room because he was willing to listen to new ideas and accept new thoughts. The ones who needed to be influenced were those who hadn't listened—such as the Oldtimers now exiled to the Southern Continent.

Jaxom surmised that some sort of a discreet watch was kept on happenings there. N'ton had once made an oblique reference to the Southern Hold. The students had a very detailed map of the land about the Hold and of some of the neighboring areas which indicated that the Southern Continent extended far deeper into the Southern seas than anyone had guessed even five Turns ago. During one of his talks with Lytol, Robinton had once let slip something that led Jaxom to believe the Masterharper had been in the Southern lands recently. It amused Jaxom to wonder how much the Oldtimers knew of what occurred on the mainland. There were some obvious changes which even those with the most closed minds would have to admit seeing. What of the ever-increasing spreads of forestland about which the Oldtimers had protested—expanses now protected by the burrowing grubs that farmers had once tried to exterminate, erroneously considering them a bane instead of a carefully contrived blessing and safeguard.

Jaxom's attention was reclaimed by the stamping of feet and the clapping of hands. He hastily added his own applause, wondering if he'd missed anything vital during his ruminations. He'd check with Menolly later. She remembered everything.

The ovation continued long enough to make Wansor blush with pleased embarrassment, until Fandarel rose and spread his tree-limb arms for silence. But Fandarel no more got his mouth open to speak when one of the Ista Hold watchers jumped to his feet to ask Wansor to clarify an anomaly concerning the fixed position of the trio of Stars known as the Day Sisters. Before Wansor could answer him, someone else informed the man that no anomaly existed and a spirited argument began.

"I wonder if we could use Wansor's equations to go ahead in time safely," F'lessan mused.

"You deadglow! You can't go to a time that hasn't happened!" Mirrim answered him tartly before the others could. "How would you know what's happening there? You'd end up in a cliff or a crowd, or surrounded by Thread! It's dangerous enough to go back in time when at least you can check on what happened or on who was there. Even then you could, and *you* would, muddle things. Forget it, F'lessan!"

"Going ahead could serve no logical purpose at this time," Benelek remarked in his sententious way.

"It'd be fun," F'lessan said, undeterred. "Like knowing what the Oldtimers are planning. F'lar's sure they're going to try something. They've been far too quiet down there."

"Close your jaw, F'lessan. That's Weyr business," Mirrim said sharply, glancing anxiously around her for fear some of the adults might have overheard his indiscreet remark.

"Communicate! Share your thoughts!" F'lessan spouted back some of Robinton's taglines.

"There's a difference between communication and gossip," Jaxom said.

F'lessan gave his boyhood friend a long measuring look. "You know, I used to think this school idea was a good one. Now I think it's turned the whole lot of us into do-nothing talkers. And thinkers!" He rolled his eyes upward in disgust. "We talk, we think everything to death. We never do anything. At least I have to do first and think later when we fight Thread!" He turned on his heel and then, brightening, announced, "Hey, there's food!" He began to weave through the crowd to the doors where heavily laden trays were being passed through to the central table.

Jaxom knew F'lessan's remarks had been general, but the young Lord keenly felt the jibe about fighting Thread.

"That F'lessan!" Menolly said at his ear. "He wants to keep glory in the bloodline. A bit of derring-do . . ." and her sea-blue eyes danced with laughter as she added, "for me to tune about!" Then she sighed. "And he's not the type at all. *He* doesn't think beyond himself. But he's got a good heart. C'mon! We'd better lend a hand with the food."

"Let us *do!*" Jaxom's quip was rewarded by Menolly's smile of appreciation.

There was merit in both viewpoints, Jaxom decided as he relieved an overburdened woman of a tray of steaming meatrolls, but he'd *think* about it later.

The Mastersmith's kitchen had prepared for the large gathering, and besides succulent meatrolls there were hot fish balls, bread slabbed with the firm cheeses of the High Range, two huge kettles of klah.

As he passed food around, Jaxom became conscious of something else that annoyed him. The other Lords Holder and Craftmasters were all cordial, inquiring courteously after Ruth and Lytol. They all seemed quite willing to exchange pleasantries with him but would not discuss Wansor's theories. Perhaps, Jaxom thought cynically, they hadn't understood what Wansor had said and were ashamed to show their ignorance before the younger man. Jaxom sighed. Would he ever be old enough to be considered on equal terms?

"Hey, Jaxom, dump that," F'lessan grabbed his sleeve. "Got something to show you."

Believing he had done his duty, Jaxom pushed his tray onto the table and followed his young friend out the door. F'lessan kept going, grinning like a dimwit, and then swung round to point at the roof of the Smithcrafthall.

The Hall was a large building with steep gables. The roof appeared to be in colorful motion, rippling with sound. A veritable fair of fire-lizards were perched on the gray slates, chirping and humming to one another in earnest conversation—a perfect parody of the intent discussions going on inside the building. Jaxom began to laugh.

"There can't be that many fire-lizards looking to those inside," he said to Menolly, who had just joined them. "Or have you acquired a couple more clutches?"

Brushing the laugh-tears from her eyes, she denied guilt. "I've only the ten and they go off on their own, sometimes for days. I don't think I could account for more than two besides Beauty, my queen. She sticks by me constantly. You know," she turned a serious face to him, "they're going to be a problem. Not mine, because I make mine behave, but this sort of thing." She gestured toward the covered roof. "They're such dreadful gossips. I'll wager most of those don't look to the people within. They've been attracted by the dragons and by your Ruth in particular."

"A fair gathers like that wherever Ruth and I go," Jaxom said a bit sourly.

Menolly looked across the valley to where Ruth was lying on the sunny riverbank with three other dragons and the usual wing or two of ministering fire-lizards.

"Does Ruth mind?"

"No," Jaxom grinned tolerantly, "I think he rather enjoys it. They keep him company when I have to be elsewhere on Hold business. He says they have all sorts of fascinating and unlikely images in their minds. He likes looking . . . most times. Sometimes he gets annoyed—says they get carried away."

"How can they?" Menolly was bluntly dubious.

The White Dragon

"They don't have much imagination, not really. They only tell what they see."

"Or think they see, maybe?"

Menolly considered that. "What they see is usually pretty reliable. I know . . ." Then she stopped, looked dismayed.

"Never mind," Jaxom said. "I'd be as thick as a hold door if I didn't realize you Harpers keep busy down South." Jaxom then turned around to say something to F'lessan, who was nowhere to be seen.

"I'll tell you something, Jaxom," Menolly dropped her voice, "F'lessan was right. Something is going on down South. Some of my lot have been very agitated. I get an image of a single egg but it's not in an enclosed weyr. I thought maybe my Beauty had hidden another clutch. She sometimes does that. Then I got the impression that what she was seeing happened long ago. And Beauty's no older than Ruth, so how could she remember any more than five Turns back?"

"Fire-lizards with delusions of locating the First Shell?" Jaxom laughed heartily.

"I can't quite seriously laugh at their memories. They do know the oddest sorts of things. Remember F'nor's Grall not wanting to go to the Red Star? For that matter *all* the fire-lizards are terrified of the Red Star."

"Aren't we all?"

"They *knew,* Jaxom, knew before the rest of Pern had any knowledge."

Instinctively they both turned eastward, toward the malevolent Red Star.

"So?" Menolly asked cryptically.

"So? So what?"

"So fire-lizards have memories."

"Ah, leave off, Menolly. You can't ask me to believe that fire-lizards could remember things Man can't?"

"Got another explanation?" Menolly asked belligerently.

"No, but that doesn't mean there isn't one," and Jaxom grinned at her. His smile turned to alarm. "Say,

66

what if some of those fellows up there are from the Southern Hold?"

"I'm not worried. The fire-lizards are outside, for one thing. For another, they can only visualize what they've understood." Menolly chuckled, a habit of hers which Jaxom found a pleasant change from the giggling of Holder girls. "Can you imagine what nonsense someone like T'kul would make of Wansor's equations? Seen through lizard eyes?"

Jaxom's personal recollections of the High Reaches Oldtimer Weyrleader were sparse, but he'd heard enough from Lytol and N'ton to realize that man's mind was closed to anything new. Though nearly six Turns of fending on his own down in the Southern Continent might have broadened his outlook.

"Look, it isn't me alone who's worried," Menolly went on. "Mirrim is, too. And if anyone today understands fire-lizards, it's Mirrim."

"You don't do badly yourself—for a mere Harper."

"Well, thank you, my Lord Holder." She gave him a facetious salute. "Look, will you find out what the fire-lizards are telling Ruth?"

"Don't they talk to Mirrim's green dragon?" Jaxom was reluctant to have more to do with fire-lizards at the moment than was absolutely necessary.

"Dragons don't remember things. You know that. But Ruth's different, I've noticed . . ."

"Very different . . ."

Menolly caught the sour note in his voice. "What's got your back up today? Or has Lord Groghe been to see Lytol?"

"Lord Groghe? What for?"

Menolly's eyes glinted with devilment and she beckoned him closer, as if anyone were near enough to hear what they'd been saying. "I think Lord Groghe fancies you for that beast-bosomed third daughter of his."

Jaxom groaned in horror.

"Don't worry, Jaxom. Robinton squashed the idea. He wouldn't do you a disservice there. Of course," Menolly glanced at him from the corners of her laughing eyes, "if you have anyone else in mind, now's the time to say so."

Jaxom was furious, not with Menolly but with her news, and it was hard to dissociate tidings and bearer.

"The one thing I don't want just now is a wife."

"Oh? Got yourself taken care of?"

"Menolly!"

"Don't look so shocked. We Harpers understand the frailties of human flesh. And you're tall, and nice-looking, Jaxom. Lytol's supposed to be giving you instruction in all the arts . . ."

"Menolly!"

"Jaxom!" She mimicked his tone perfectly. "Doesn't Lytol ever let you off to have some fun on your own? Or do you just *think* about it? Honestly, Jaxom," her tone became acerbic and her expression registered impatience with him, "between Robinton, though I love the man, and Lytol, F'lar, Lessa and Fandarel, I think they've turned you into a pale echo of themselves. Where is Jaxom?"

Before he could sort out a suitable answer for her impertinence, she gave him a piercing look through slightly narrowed eyes. "They do say the dragon is the man. Maybe that's why Ruth is so different!"

On that cryptic remark she rose and made her way back to the others.

Jaxom had half a mind to call Ruth and leave if all he was going to get were insults and slights.

"Like a sulky boy!" N'ton's words came back to him. Sighing, he settled back to the grass. No, he would not depart hastily from an awkward scene for the second time that morning. He would not act in an immature fashion. He would not give Menolly the satisfaction of knowing that her provocative comments bothered him at all.

He stared down the river where his dear companion played, and wondered. Why *is* Ruth different? Is the dragon the man? To be sure, if Ruth were different, he shared it. His birth had been as bizarre as Ruth's Hatching—he from a dead mother's body, Ruth from an eggshell too hard for the half-sized beak to break.

Ruth was a dragon, but not weyrbred. He was Lord Holder, but not confirmed so.

Well then, to prove one would be to prove the other and hail the difference!

Don't let anyone catch you giving Ruth firestone! N'ton had said.

Wellaway, that would be his first goal!

CHAPTER IV

Ruatha Hold, Fidello's Hold, and Various
Points *Between,* 15.5.10–15.5.16

OVER THE NEXT few days, Jaxom realized that it
was one thing to form the resolution to teach Ruth to
chew firestone, and quite another to find the time to do
so. It was impossible to contrive a free hour. Jaxom
entertained the unworthy thought that perhaps N'ton
had tipped his plan to Lytol so that the Warder had
consciously found activities to fill his days. As quickly,
Jaxom discarded the notion. N'ton was not a treacherous or sly man. On sober examination, Jaxom had
to admit that his days had always been full: with
Ruth's care first, then lessons, Hold duties and, in past
Turns, meetings at other Holders which Lytol felt he
must attend—as a silent observer—to extend his knowledge of Hold management.

Jaxom simply hadn't realized the extent of his in-
volvement until now, when he desperately wanted time
to himself which did not have to be explained or
arranged in advance.

The other problem which he hadn't seriously considered was that no matter where he and Ruth went,
a fire-lizard was sure to appear. Menolly was correct in
calling them gossips and he had no wish for them to
oversee his unauthorized instruction. He experimented
by popping Ruth up to a mountain ledge in the High
Reaches which had been a practice ground when he was

teaching Ruth to fly *between*. The area was deserted, barren, without so much as mountain weed peeping up from under the late hard snow. He'd given Ruth directions while they were airborne and, at that particular moment, unaccompanied by fire-lizards. He'd counted no more than twenty-two breaths before Deelan's green and the Hold steward's blue arrived over Ruth's head. They squeaked in astonishment and then began to complain about the location.

Jaxom then tried two more equally unfrequented locations, one in the plains of Keroon and another on a deserted island off the coast of Tillek. He was followed to both places.

At first he seethed over such surveillance and envisioned himself tackling Lytol on the matter. Common sense urged that Lytol would scarcely have asked either the steward or Deelan to set their creatures on Jaxom. Misplaced zeal! If he tried to tell Deelan straight out, she'd weep and wail, wring her hands and run straight to Lytol. But Brand, the steward, was a different matter. He had come from Telgar Hold two Turns back when the old steward had proved unable to control the lustiness of the fosterlings. Jaxom paused. Now then, Brand *would* understand the problems of a young man.

So, when Jaxom returned to Ruatha Hold, he found Brand in his office, giving out discipline to some drudges for the depredations of tunnel-snakes in the storage rooms. To Jaxom's astonishment, the drudges were instantly dismissed with the injunction that if they didn't present him with two dead tunnel-snake carcasses apiece, they'd do without food for a few days.

Not that Brand had ever been lacking in courtesy to Jaxom, but such prompt attention surprised him, and he required a breath or two before he spoke. Brand waited with all the deference he would show to Lytol or a ranking visitor. With some embarrassment Jaxom remembered his outburst of a few mornings before and wondered. No, Brand wasn't the obsequious type. He had the steady eye, the steady hand, firm mouth and stance that Lytol had often told Jaxom to look for in the trustworthy man.

"Brand, I can't seem to go anywhere without fire-lizards from this Hold appearing. Deelan's green, and if you don't mind my saying so, your blue. Is all that really necessary anymore?"

Brand's surprise was honest.

"Occasionally," Jaxom hurried on, "a fellow likes to get off by himself, completely by himself. And, as *you* know, fire-lizards are the world's greatest gossips. They might get the wrong impression . . . if you know what I mean?"

Brand did but, if he was amused or surprised, he dissembled well.

"I do apologize, Lord Jaxom. An oversight, I assure you. You know how anxious Deelan used to be when you and Ruth first started flying *between* and the fire-lizards followed as a safeguard. I should have long ago altered that arrangement."

"Since when am I Lord Jaxom to you, Brand?"

The steward's lips actually twitched. "Since the other morning . . . Lord Jaxom."

"I didn't mean it like that, Brand."

Brand inclined his head slightly, forestalling further apology. "As Lord Lytol remarked, you are well old enough to be confirmed in your rank, Lord Jaxom, and we—" Brand grinned with uninhibited ease "—should act accordingly."

"Ah, well, yes. Thank you." Jaxom managed to leave Brand's office without further loss of poise and strode rapidly to the first bend of the corridor.

There he stopped, mulling over the implications of that interview. "Old enough to be confirmed in your rank . . ." And Lord Groghe thinking to marry him to his daughter. Surely the canny Fort Holder wouldn't do that if there was any doubt of Jaxom's being confirmed in rank. The prospect now alarmed and annoyed Jaxom whereas the day before it would have pleased him enormously. Once he officially became Lord of Ruatha, any chance he might have had of flying with the fighting wings would be gone. He didn't want to be

Lord of Ruatha—at least not yet. And he certainly
didn't want to be saddled with a female not of his own
choosing.

He should have told Menolly that he had no trouble
with any of the Holder girls . . . when he was of the
mind. Not that he had followed some of the bawdier
fosterlings' examples. He wasn't going to have the reputation of a lecher like Meron or that young fool of
Lord Laudey's, whom Lytol had sent back to his home
Hold with some cover excuse that no one really believed. It was all right for the Lord Holder to beget
a few halfbloods, quite another to dilute Holder Blood
with other lines. Nonetheless, he would have to find
a pleasant girl to give him the alibi he needed, and
then take the time for more important things.

Jaxom pushed himself off the wall, unconsciously
straightening his shoulders. Brand's deference had been
rather bracing. Now that he thought about it, he remembered other evidences of a change of attitude toward him, something his preoccupation with firestone
had blinded him to until now. He suddenly realized
that Deelan had not pestered him at the breakfast table
to eat more than he wanted, that Dorse had been inex-
plicably absent the past few days. Nor had Lytol's
morning remarks been prefaced with inquiries after
Ruth's health but, rather, had concerned the day's up-
coming business.

The night he had returned from the Mastersmithhall,
Lytol and Finder had been eager to learn about
Wansor's stars and that recital had taken up the whole
evening. If the fosterlings and others had been unusually silent, Jaxom had only attributed that state of
affairs to their interest in the discussion. Lytol, Finder
and Brand had not had trouble finding their tongues.

The next morning there had been no time for more
than a cup of klah and a meatroll as Thread was due
to fall across the spring-planted fields in the southwest
and they had a long ride ahead.

I should have spoken out months ago, Jaxom
thought as he entered his own quarters.

It had been established that Jaxom was not to be

disturbed when he was caring for Ruth; a privacy
that he was only now beginning to appreciate. Generally, Jaxom attended his dragon, oiling his skin and
grooming him in the early morning or late evening.
He hunted with Ruth every fourth day since the white
dragon required more frequent meals than the larger
ones. The Hold's fire-lizards usually accompanied
Ruth, feasting with him. Most people fed their pets
daily by hand, but the urge for hot, fresh-killed or
self-caught food could never be trained out of the
fire-lizards and it had been decided not to interfere
with that instinct. Fire-lizards were quixotic creatures
and although there was no doubt that they became
genuinely attached at Hatching, they were subject to
sudden fits and frights and would disappear, often for
long periods of time. When they returned, they acted
as if they'd never been gone, except for transmitting
some rather outrageous images.

Ruth would be ready to hunt today, Jaxom knew.
He heard his weyrmate's impatience to be off. Laughing, Jaxom shrugged on the heavy riding jacket and
stamped into his boots as he politely inquired what
sort of eating Ruth fancied.

*Wherry, a juicy plain wherry, none of those stringy
mountain ones.* Ruth emphasized his distaste for the
latter with a snort.

"You even sound hungry," Jaxom said, entering the
dragon's weyr and approaching him.

Ruth laid his nose lightly on Jaxom's chest, his
breath cool even through the heavy riding jacket. His
eyes were wheeling with the red overtone of active
appetite. He made his way to the huge metal doors
that opened onto the stable courtyard and pushed them
open with his forelegs.

Alerted by Ruth's hungry thoughts, the Hold's fire-
lizards swirled about in eager anticipation. Jaxom
mounted and directed Ruth aloft. The old brown
watchdragon called good hunting from the fire-
heights, and his rider waved.

From Hold tithings, the six Weyrs of Pern maintained their own herds and flocks on which the Weyr

dragons fed. No Lord Holder ever objected to an occasional rider feeding his dragon off his land. As Jaxom was Lord Holder and technically had the right to anything within Ruatha's borders, Ruth's hunting was primarily a matter of courtesy. Lytol had not needed to instruct Jaxom to spread his beast's appetite so that no holder was overburdened.

On this particular morning Jaxom gave Ruth coordinates of a rich grass holding where Lytol had mentioned buck-wherries were being fattened for spring slaughtering. The holder was out on his runner when Jaxom and Ruth appeared, and he greeted the young Lord politely enough and replied to Jaxom's courteous inquiries for his health, the progress of the flock and the laying weight of the hens.

"A thing I'd like you to mention to Lord Lytol," the man began, and Jaxom detected resentment in his manner. "I've asked for a fire-lizard egg time and again. It's my due as a holder and I've the need. I can't hatch wherry eggs proper if vermin burrow under and crack shells. There are four or five from each clutch gone, lost to snakes and the like. Fire-lizard would keep 'em off. They do for your man down at Bald Lake Hold and others I've spoken to. Fire-lizards are mighty handy creatures, Lord Jaxom, and being a holder now these past twelve Turns, it's only my due. Bald Lake Palon, now he's got a fire-lizard and he's only held for ten Turns."

"I can't imagine why you've been slighted, Tegger. I'll see that something is done about it. We haven't a clutch at the moment but I'll do what I can when we have."

Tegger gave surly thanks and then suggested that Jaxom hunt the buck flock to be found browsing at the far end of the plain meadow. He wanted to take the nearer flock for slaughter and a hunting dragon ran a sevenday's weight off bucks.

Jaxom thanked the man and Ruth warbled his gratitude, startling Tegger's runner into bucking. Tegger grimly yanked the beast's head about, preventing a bolt.

Tegger was unlikely to Impress a fire-lizard, Jaxom thought as he leaped to Ruth's shoulder.

Ruth agreed. *That man had an egg once. The little one went* between *and never returned to its hatching place.*

"How did you remember that?"

The fire-lizards told me.

"When?"

When it happened. I have just remembered it. Ruth sounded very pleased with himself. *They tell me many things that are interesting when you're not with me.*

Jaxom only then became aware that the usual fire-lizard escorts weren't about, even though Ruth was hunting. He hadn't meant that Brand should curtail all fire-lizards excursions with them.

Ruth plaintively asked if they couldn't get on with the hunting since he was hungry. So they proceeded to the suggested area and Ruth let Jaxom down on a grassy rise with a good view of the hunt where he made himself comfortable. No sooner had Ruth become airborne than a flight of fire-lizards appeared, courteously landing to await the dragon's summons to join him after his kill.

Some dragons took their time selecting their meal, swooping on flock or herd to scatter it and isolate the fattest. Either Ruth made up his mind quickly or else he was influenced by Jaxom's knowledge that Tegger would not appreciate overrun wherries. Whatever, the white dragon dispatched the first buck in one deft swoop, cracking the creature's long neck as he brought it down.

Ruth left the delighted fire-lizards picking the bones and killed a second time, eating as daintily as ever. The flock had barely settled at the far end of the meadow when he launched himself unexpectedly for the third.

I told you I was hungry, Ruth said so apologetically that Jaxom laughed and told him to stuff himself with all he wanted.

I am not stuffing myself, Ruth replied with a mild rebuke that Jaxom would think such a thing of him. *I am very hungry.*

Jaxom regarded the feasting fire-lizards thoughtfully. He wondered if any were from Ruatha. Ruth replied immediately that they had come from the surrounding area.

So, mused Jaxom, I've only solved the problem of keeping Ruathan fire-lizards from following. But what one fire-lizard knew, they all seemed to know so he would still have to keep his activities from their sight.

Jaxom knew a dragon needed time to chew and digest firestone for the best effect. Dragonriders would begin to feed their beasts stone several hours before Thread was due to fall. How fast could Ruth work up a full enough gullet of stone to produce the fire breath? He wondered. He'd have to go carefully. Since dragons differed in capacity and readiness, each rider had to find out for himself what his beast's peculiarities were. If only he could have trained Ruth in a Weyr and have the benefit of a weyrlingmaster's experience . . .

Well, firestone was no problem. The old watchdragon had to be supplied so there was a goodly pile on the fire-heights. And Ruth wouldn't need as much as a big dragon.

When still remained the problem. Jaxom had his morning free because Ruth was to hunt and it wasn't sound practice to take a full dragon *between*—all that rich warm food would sour a dragon belly in cold *between*. So Jaxom would have to take the time to fly Ruth straight to Ruatha Hold. This afternoon would be taken up with overseeing spring planting, and if Lytol were really going to arrange for him to be confirmed as Lord Holder, he couldn't get out of making an appearance.

Idly Jaxom wondered if the Lord Holders ever worried whether he might try to imitate his tyrannical father's taking ways or not. They would run on about Bloodlines, and blood telling, but weren't they the least bit nervous about his Fax blood telling? Or were they counting on the influence of his mother's blood. Everyone was right willing to discuss his Lady Mother Gemma with him, but did they ever fumble and fight to find another subject if he mentioned his unlamented father. Were they afraid to have him get ideas from his father's aggressive ways? Or was it merely courtesy not to talk about the dead unkindly? They certainly had no bar about discussing the living in destructive terms.

Jaxom toyed with the idea of conquest. How would *he* set about reducing Nabol or—since Fort Hold was too big a bite—Tillek? Or Crom, perhaps, though he liked Lord Nessel's oldest son, Kern, far too much to do him out of what was rightfully his. Shells, he was a fine one to talk of conquest, when he couldn't even control the destiny of himself and his dragon!

Ruth, waddling with a full, bulging belly, belched happily as he made his way to his rider. He settled himself in the sun-warmed sweet grasses and began to lick his talons. He was always neat.

"Can you fly when you're stuffed?" Jaxom asked when Ruth had finished tidying up.

Ruth turned his head, his eyes whirling in reproach. *I can always fly.* The dragon exhaled, his breath rather meaty and sweet. *You are worried again.*

"I want us to be proper dragon and rider, and fight Thread, me on your back, you flaming."

Then we will do it, Ruth said with unshakable faith. *I am a dragon, you are my rider. Why does this become a problem?*

"Well, wherever we go the fire-lizards come."

You told the thick man with the blue—Ruth's identification of Brand—*they were not to follow. They did not come here.*

"Others did, and you know how fire-lizards chatter." Then Jaxom recalled Menolly's comments. "What are that lot thinking of now?"

Their full bellies. The wherries were juicy and tender. Very good eating. They do not remember better in many Turns.

"Would they go away if you told them to?"

Ruth snorted, his eyes whirling a bit, more with amusement than irritation. *They would wonder why and come to see. I will tell them if you want me to. Maybe they would stay away long enough.*

"Just like them: they've more curiosity than sense. Well, as Robinton is always saying, there's a way to solve every problem. We'll just have to find a way."

On their return to Ruatha Hold, Ruth's digestion was working noisily. He wanted nothing more than to curl up on a sun-warmed rock and sleep, and since the brown watchdragon was away from his usual post, Ruth settled there. Jaxom waited in the Great Courtyard until he saw Ruth safely ensconced, and then he sought Lytol.

If Brand had commented on Jaxom's request to Lytol, the Lord Warder gave no sign, greeting Jaxom with his usual reserve and enjoining him to eat quickly as they had rather a long ride to make. Tordril and one of the other older fosterlings living under Lytol's supervision would accompany them. Master-farmer Andemon had sent a new seed he had developed for a high-yield, fast-growing wheat. Southern fields, grub-infested and planted with this wheat seed, had produced phenomenally healthy, blight-resistant crops, that were able to survive long dry spells. Andemon wondered how the wheat would fare in a rainier, Northern climate.

Many of the older small holders were stubborn about trying something new. "As hidebound as Old-timers," Lytol would mutter, but somehow or other he managed to prevail. For instance, Fidello, who owned the hold they were seeding, was only two Turns in the holding, the previous man having died of a fall while tracking wild wherries.

So, after a quick meal, the travelers set off on some of the specially bred runners that could pace a long summer's day without tiring. Though Jaxom used to find it tedious to take hours to cross country he could fly *between* on Ruth in a few breaths, he did enjoy an occasional runner ride. Today, with spring in the air and secure in the knowledge that he was still in Lytol's good graces, he enjoyed the trip.

Fidello's holding was in northeast Ruatha, on a

plateau with the snow-capped mountains of Crom in the background. When they reached the plateau, the blue fire-lizard that rode on Tordril's arm shrilled a greeting and took off to make an aerial circle of introduction to a brown that was probably looking to Fidello and set to watch for the visitors. Immediately the two fire-lizards winked *between*. Tordril and Jaxom exchanged glances, knowing that a welcoming cup of klah and sweetbreads would be waiting at the holding. Their ride had given them an appetite.

Fidello himself rode out to escort them on the last part of the road. He was mounted on a sturdy work-beast whose summer coat gleamed with health through the rough and patchy winter fur. His hold, to which he welcomed them in an earnest but restrained manner, was small and well kept. His dependents, including those of the last holder, had assembled to serve the visitors.

"He's got a good cook," Tordril said in an aside to Jaxom as the three younger men made conspicuous inroads on the food laid out on the long Hall table. "And a deuced pretty sister," he added as the girl approached them bearing a steaming pitcher of klah.

She was pretty, Jaxom agreed, looking at her closely for the first time. Trust Tordril to spot the prettiest girl. Brand would have to keep his eye on this one when he ventured out of the Hold to the workers' cots below the bridge. This pretty girl, however, had a timid smile for Jaxom, not Tordril, and even though the prospective Lord of Ista tried to engage her in conversation, she gave him short answers, keeping her smiles for Jaxom. She left his side only when her brother joined them to say that perhaps they'd better seed the fields or it would be a long, dark ride back to the Hold.

"I wonder would you have got her so quick if I'd been Lord of Ruatha?" Tordril asked Jaxom as they checked their saddle girths before mounting.

"Got her?" Jaxom stared blankly at Tordril. "We only chatted."

"Well, you could have her next time you . . . ah,

have a chance to chat. Or does Lytol mind a few halfbloods around? Father says it keeps the full ones on
their toes! Ought to be easy for you with Lytol weyrbred, and not as stuffy about such things."

Lytol and Fidello joined them at that point but
Tordril's envious comment set Jaxom's thoughts on a
very fruitful tack. What was her name? Corana? Well,
Corana could be very useful. There was only the one
fire-lizard about the Plateau Hold—and, if Ruth could
just dissuade that creature from following them . . .

When they returned to the Hold late that night,
Jaxom quietly climbed to the fire-heights and took a
good sackful of firestone from the brown's supply while
the old watchdragon and his rider were having a brief
evening flight to stretch wings.

The next morning he casually asked Lytol if he
thought they had brought enough seed for Fidello.
Theirs did seem to be a very large field. Lytol regarded his ward from under half-closed lids for a moment and then agreed that perhaps another half-sack
might be to the wise. Tordril's expression mirrored
surprise, envy and, Jaxom felt, some respect for plausi-
bility. Lytol duly ordered a half-sack of Andemon's
seed from Brand's locked stores, and Jaxom sauntered
off with it to don his riding gear.

Ruth, full of himself after a good feed, wanted to
know if there was a nice lake near the hold. Jaxom
thought that the river was wide enough for a respectable dragon's bath, but they weren't going there for
water sports. They managed to take off without anyone seeing the second sack slung on Ruth—or the
fighting straps. Although the fire-lizards engaged in
their usual dizzy pattern around them while Ruth was
becoming airborne, none emerged with them at the
Plateau Hold.

Fidello himself took receipt of the additional
seed with such profuse thanks that Jaxom was a bit
abashed at his duplicity.

"Didn't like to mention it in front of the Lord
Warder, Lord Jaxom, but that's a fair big field I've
ready for this seed and I'd want to see a good return

to justify Lord Lytol's opinion of me. Would you care for refreshment? My wife . . ."

Only his wife? "It would be welcome. The morning's nippy." He patted Ruth affectionately and dismounted, following Fidello into the hold. He was pleased to notice that the main Hall was as tidy as it had been for their expected visit. Corana was not in evidence, but Fidello's very pregnant wife was in no way misled by his casual return.

"Everyone else has gone to the river, to the place where it forms an island, to gather withies, Lord Jaxom," she said, glancing at him coquettishly, as she served him hot klah. "On your beautiful dragon, that's no more than a moment's trip for you, my Lord."

"Now why would Lord Jaxom want to see withies gathered?" Fidello asked, but received no direct answer.

The social amenities discharged, Jaxom directed Ruth aloft, circled while waving down at Fidello, and then took them *between* to the mountain well beyond the keenest eye of any hold. The brown fire-lizard followed.

"Shells! Ruth, tell him to get lost."

Immediately the brown winked out.

"Good, now I can teach you to chew firestone."

I know.

"You think you know. I've been around dragonriders long enough to know that doing so is not quite as simple as that."

Ruth gave a sort of sniff as Jaxom dug a lump of firestone the size of his own generous fist out of the sack.

"Now *think* of your other stomách!"

Ruth lidded his eyes completely as he accepted the firestone. The noise as he chewed the lump startled him. His eyes came wide open, making Jaxom exclaim: "Should you make that much noise?"

It is *rock.*

He threw one lid over his eyes as he suddenly swallowed. *I am thinking of my other stomach,* he told Jaxom before he could be reminded. Later Jaxom

swore that he could all but hear the chewed fragments
rolling down the dragon's gullet. The two sat and regarded each other, waiting for the next step.

"You're supposed to belch."

I know. I know how to belch. But I can't.

Jaxom politely offered him another largish piece of
firestone. This time the chewing did not resound so
noticeably. Ruth swallowed, then seemed to settle
more on his haunches.

OH!

On the heels of the mental exclamation, a rumble
started that made Ruth look quickly at his white belly.
His mouth opened. With a startled shout, Jaxom
launched himself to one side just as a tiny trickle of
flame appeared at the white dragon's muzzle. Ruth
jerked backward, only saved from falling over by the
set of his tail.

*I think I need more firestone to make a respectable
flame.*

Jaxom offered several smallish lumps. Ruth made
quick work of the chewing. And quicker work of the
eruption of gas.

That was much more the thing, Ruth said with satisfaction.

"Wouldn't do much against Thread."

Ruth just opened his mouth for more firestone. What
Jaxom had brought was all too quickly consumed. But
with it, Ruth managed to sear a fair swath among the
rock weeds.

"I don't think we've got the hang of it."

We also haven't burned any Thread midair.

"We aren't exactly ready to do that yet. But we
have proved that you *can* chew firestone."

I never doubted it.

"I never did either, Ruth, but," Jaxom sighed
heavily, "we're going to need a lot of firestone at hand,
until you learn the way of sustaining a continuous
eruption."

Ruth looked so disconsolate that Jaxom hastily reassured him, stroking his eye ridges and caressing his
headbone.

"We should have been allowed to train you properly with the other weyrlings. It's just not fair. I've always said so. You can't help your difficulties today. But, by the First Shell, we'll eventually succeed together."

Ruth allowed himself to be reassured, then brightened. *We will work harder, that's all. But it would be easier with more firestone. Brown Wilth never uses much anymore. He's really too old to chew at all.*

"That's why he's a watchdragon."

Jaxom emptied the sack of any firestone rubble, tied it up by the neck thong and looped it around his belt. He hadn't needed the rope for fighting straps, after all. He was about to tell Ruth to transfer directly to Ruatha when he remembered that he had better consolidate his alibi for future use. He had no trouble finding the withie gatherers by the river island, and Corana eagerly came to meet him. She was very pretty, he realized, with a delicate flush to her skin and round greenish eyes. Her dark hair had escaped the braids about her face and now clung to her cheeks in damp waves.

"Has there been Thread?" she asked, her green eyes becoming round with alarm.

"No. Why?"

"I can smell firestone."

"Oh, these riding clothes. I always use them during Fall. Smell must cling to them. I just didn't notice." That was one hazard he hadn't considered and he'd have to do something about it. "I flew up with more seed for your brother . . ."

She thanked him sweetly for taking so much trouble for such a small hold as theirs. Then she became shy. Jaxom rather liked drawing her out and sent her into another spin by insisting on helping with the withie gathering.

"This Lord Holder wants to know how to do everything he requires of his holders," he said, to silence her protests.

Actually, he enjoyed himself. When they had amassed a huge bundle, he offered to fly it home on Ruth if she'd ride with him. Corana was honestly frightened but he assured her they'd only fly straight since she wasn't dressed for cold *between*. Jaxom got in a couple of kisses before Ruth circled to land his passengers at the hold. He decided that one way or another, Corana would no longer be just an excuse.

When he had deposited her and the withies, he directed Ruth *between* to their mountain lake. Though he was in no mood for a cold bath, Jaxom knew they'd better scrub off the firestone stink before going back to Ruatha. It took time to sandscrub the smell from Ruth's fair hide. Then Jaxom had to dry his impregnated shirt and pants, spreading them in full sun on the bushes. By that time the sun was well past zenith and he had spent far more time than dallying with Corana would cover. So he took a risk and returned to Ruatha *between* time to when the sun was still on the morning side of the sky. But one detail he forgot to take into his calculations nearly gave away their endeavor.

He was at dinner when his dragon let out a call for him, an urgent call. "Ruth!" he explained as he sprang from his chair at the table and raced across the Hall to the corridor to his quarters.

My stomach burns, Ruth began telling him in great distress.

"Shells, it's the stones," Jaxom replied as he ran down the deserted hallway. "Go outside, to the fireheights. Where Wilth leaves his."

Ruth wasn't sure he could fly in his condition.

"Nonsense. You can always fly." Ruth had to disgorge his second stomach outside the weyr. Lytol might just follow to see what ailed the beast for him to interrupt Jaxom at dinner.

I can't move. I'm weighed down in the middle.

"You're just going to regurgitate the firestone ash. Dragons don't keep that in their stomachs: they can't pass it. The stuff has got to come back up."

I feel as if it will.

"Not in the weyr, Ruth. Please!"

Scarcely a second later, Ruth eyed him apologetically. In the middle of the weyr floor, a small pile of what looked like brownish gray wet sand exuded steam.

I feel much better now, Ruth said in a very small voice.

"Can you hear Lytol coming?" Jaxom asked Ruth, because his heart was pounding so from running that that was all he could hear. He dashed out the metal doors and into the kitchen yard to fetch a bucket and shovel. "If I can just get this outside before it smells up the place . . ." He worked as fast as he could and fortunately the mess just filled the one bucket. It wasn't as if Ruth had chewed enough firestone for a full four-hour Threadfall.

Jaxom pushed the bucket out and sprinkled sweet sand on the spot.

"No Lytol?" he asked, somewhat surprised.

No.

Jaxom exhaled heavily with relief, patted Ruth reassuringly. He wouldn't forget to have Ruth regurgitate in a safe spot next time.

When he resumed his place at the table, Jaxom offered no explanation and none was asked—one more example of the new respect from his familiars.

The next night he and Ruth filched as much firestone as the dragon could carry from the most logical place—the firestone mines in Crom. Half a dozen fire-lizards appeared during their raid, and Ruth merely sent each one on its way as soon as it appeared.

"Don't let them follow us."

They were only being courteous. They like me.

"There's such a thing as being too popular."

Ruth sighed.

"Is this too much firestone?" Jaxom asked, not wanting to overburden the beast.

Of course not. I'm very strong.

Jaxom directed Ruth *between* to the Keroon desert destination. There was the sea to bathe in afterward and plenty of sweetsand to scrub off firestone stench, and sun hot enough to dry his clothing in next to no time.

CHAPTER V

Morning in Harpercraft Hall, Fort Hold,
Afternoon in Benden Weyr, Late
Afternoon in Harpercraft Hall, 15.5.26

ANOTHER THREADFALL PASSED before Jaxom could get off to the Plateau hold again. He seemed to have more success with Corana than in getting Ruth to sustain flame properly. The white dragon's throat was nearly burned from keeping in belches when fire-lizards would suddenly appear at the most inopportune times. Jaxom was certain that every single one in Keroon Hold had had a look-in. Even Ruth's patience was tried and they had to time it by a six-hour span so that their absence from Ruatha would not be considered exceptional. Timing it tired him, Jaxom realized, as he fell into bed that night, exhausted and frustrated.

To make matters worse he would have to go to the Masterharperhall the next day with Finder because the Ruathan Harper was scheduled to learn how to use Wansor's star equations. Every Harper was expected to master that so at least one other person besides the Holder could make an accurate check on Threadfall.

The Masterharperhall was part of the sprawling complex of dwellings inside and outside the Fort Hold cliffs. When Jaxom and Finder, on Ruth, burst into the air above the Harpercrafthall, they met chaos. Fire-lizards were swooping and diving, screaming in an ecstasy of agitation. The watchdragon on Fort Hold's fire-heights was up on his hind legs, front ones pawing the air, wings fanning at the stretch, bellowing in fury.

Angry! They are angry! was Ruth's startled comment. *Ruth! I am Ruth! Ruth!* he called in his inimitable tenor bugle.

"What's happened?" Finder demanded in Jaxom's ear.

"Ruth says they're angry."

"Angry? I've never seen a dragon that angry before!"

Filled with apprehension, Jaxom directed Ruth to the courtyard of the Harpercrafthall. So many people were dashing around, with fire-lizards zipping wildly about, that he had trouble finding a clear spot. No sooner had he landed than a wing of fire-lizards danced about him, projecting anxious, agitated thoughts that Ruth told Jaxom made no sense to him —and even less to Jaxom when he received them secondhand. He did perceive that these were Menolly's beasts, sent to find out where he was.

"There you are! You got my message?" Menolly came racing out of the Hall up to them, dragging on her flying gear as she ran. "We've got to go to Benden Weyr. They've stolen the queen egg."

She was scrambling up behind Finder on Ruth's back, apologizing for crowding him and urging Jaxom to get a move on. "Are three too many for Ruth?" Menolly asked with belated concern as the white dragon seemed to hesitate before launching himself.

Never.

"Who stole Ramoth's egg? How? When?" Finder asked.

"This half-hour past. They're calling in all the bronzes and the other queens. They're going to Southern in force and make them give the egg back."

"How do they know it was Southern?" asked Jaxom.

"Who else would need to steal a queen egg?"

Then all conversation was suspended as Ruth took

them smartly *between.* They erupted into the air over
Benden, and suddenly three bronzes were arrowing
out of the sun right at them, flaming. Ruth let out a
squeal and went *between,* emerging over the lake and
chattering at his would-be attackers at the top of his
voice.

I'm Ruth. I'm Ruth. I'm Ruth!

"That was close!" Finder said, gulping. His hands
were pinching Jaxom's arms nerveless.

*You just missed my wing tip. I'm Ruth! They apol-
ogized,* the white dragon added in a calmer tone to his
rider. But he turned his wing tip for a close look.

Menolly groaned. "I forgot to tell you we were to
come in yelling who we were. You'd think Ruth at
least would be passed without challenge."

As she spoke, more dragons appeared, trumpeting
to the three bronzes guarding from the heights. The
new arrivals circled tightly to land their riders by a
crowd gathered around the entrance to the Hatching
Ground. Jaxom, Finder and Menolly started across the
Bowl to join them.

"Jaxom, have you ever seen so many dragons?"
Menolly looked around at the crowded Weyr rim, at
the dragons on weyr ledges, all with wings spread,
ready for instant flight. "Oh, Jaxom, what if it comes
to dragon fighting dragon?"

The terror in her voice echoed his own feelings
perfectly.

"Those fool Oldtimers must be desperate," Finder
said grimly.

"How could they get away with such bare-faced
thievery?" Jaxom wanted to know. "Ramoth never
leaves a clutch." Not since the time F'lessan and I
disturbed her eggs, he added guiltily to himself.

"F'nor brought us the news," Menolly said. "He
said she'd gone to feed. Half the Benden fire-lizards
were in the Ground. They always are—"

"With an odd one or two visiting from the Southern
Weyr, no doubt," Finder added.

Menolly nodded. "That's what F'nor said. So the
Oldtimers would have known when she wasn't there.

F'nor said she'd just killed when three bronzes appeared, passed the watchdragon. . . . I mean, why would the watchdragon question bronze dragons? They ducked in the upper tunnel to the Hatching Ground, Ramoth gave an almighty shriek and went *between*. The next thing three bronzes came flying out of the upper entrance, they had heard Ramoth scream. She came charging out of the Hatching Ground but they had gone *between* before she'd got a winglength off the ground."

"Didn't they send dragons after them?"

"Ramoth went after! With Mnementh but a breath behind her. Not that it did any good."

"Why not?"

"The bronzes went *between* time."

"And not even Ramoth would know *when*."

"Exactly. Mnementh checked the Southern Weyr and Hold and half the hot beaches."

"Not even the Oldtimers could be stupid enough to take a queen egg straight back to Southern."

"But surely the Oldtimers would not know," Finder added wearily, "that we know they took the egg."

By that time they had reached the outskirts of the crowd, where dragonriders from other Weyrs as well as Lords Holder and Craftmasters had gathered. Lessa stood on the ledge of her weyr, F'lar beside her along with Fandarel and Robinton, who both looked extremely grim and anxious. N'ton stopped halfway down the steps, talking earnestly and with angry gestures to two other bronze riders. Slightly to one side were the three other Benden weyrwomen, and several other women who must be queenriders from the other Weyrs. The atmosphere of outrage and frustration was oppressive. Dominating the entire scene was Ramoth, who paced up and down in front of the Hatching Ground, pausing now and again to peer in at the eggs remaining on the hot sands. Her tail started lashing and she let out angry buglings that obscured the discussions going on above her on the ledge.

"It's dangerous to take an egg *between*," someone in front of Jaxom and Menolly said.

"I suppose it could go a ways, so long as the egg was good and warm to start and took no hurt."

"We ought to just mount up and go down and sear those Oldtimers out of the Weyr."

"And have dragon fight dragon? You're as bad as the Oldtimers."

"But we can't have dragons stealing our queen eggs! This is the worst insult Benden's ever taken from the Oldtimers. And I say, make them pay for it."

"The Southern Weyr is desperate," Menolly said in an undertone to Jaxom. "None of their queens has risen to mate. The bronzes are dying, and they don't even have any young greens."

Just then Ramoth gave a piteous cry, throwing her head up toward Lessa. Every dragon in the Weyr answered her call, deafening the humans. Jaxom could see Lessa leaning over the ledge, one hand outstretched toward the despairing queen. Then, because he was a good head above most of the crowd and looking that way, Jaxom saw something dark fluttering in the Hatching Ground. He heard a muffled cry of pain.

"Look! What's that? In the Hatching Ground!"

Only those around him heard his exclamation or noticed him pointing. All Jaxom could think of was that if the Southern bronzes were indeed dying, the Oldtimers might use this confusion to try and steal a bronze egg as well.

He took to his heels, followed by Menolly and Finder, but he was overcome by such a wave of weakness that he was forced to stop. Something seemed to be sapping his strength, but Jaxom had no idea what it could be.

"What's the matter, Jaxom?"

"Nothing." Jaxom pulled Menolly's hands from his arm and all but pushed her toward the Ground. "The eggs. The eggs!"

His injunction was drowned in Ramoth's bellow of surprise and exultation.

"The egg. The queen egg!"

By the time Jaxom had recovered from his inexplicable vertigo and reached the Hatching Ground, everyone was staring with relief at the sight of the queen egg, now safely positioned once again between Ramoth's forelegs.

A fire-lizard, reckless with curiosity, got a scant winglength into the Ground before Ramoth's bellow of fury sent it streaking away.

In relief, people began to chatter, as they moved back out of the Hatching Ground to where the sand was not so uncomfortable underfoot. Someone suggested that perhaps the egg had merely rolled away and Ramoth only thought it had been taken. But too many had seen the empty place, where the queen egg had too obviously been missing. And what about the three strange bronzes streaking out of the high entrance to the Ground. More acceptable was the notion that the Oldtimers had had second thoughts about the theft, that they, too, were reluctant to pit dragon against dragon.

Lessa had remained in the Ground, trying to persuade Ramoth to let her see if the egg had come to any harm. Soon she came hurrying out of the Ground to F'lar and Robinton.

"That's the same egg but it's older and harder, ready to Hatch anytime now. The girls must be brought."

For the third time that morning, Benden Weyr was in a state of high excitement—happier fortunately, but still generating as much chaos. Jaxom and Menolly managed to keep out of the way but remained close enough to hear what was going on.

"Whoever took that egg kept it at least ten days or more," they heard Lessa saying angrily. "That demands action."

"The egg is back safely," Robinton said, trying to calm her.

"Are we cowards to ignore such an insult?" she asked the other dragonmen, turning away from Robinton's calmer words.

"If to be brave," Robinton's voice laid scorn on the quality, "means to pit dragon against dragon, I'd rather be a coward."

Lessa's white-hot outrage noticeably cooled.

Dragon against dragon. The words echoed through the crowd. The thought turned sickeningly in Jaxom's mind and he could feel Menolly beside him shutting off the implications of such a contest.

"The egg was somewhen for long enough to be brought close to hatching hardness," Lessa went on, her face set with her anger. "It's probably been handled by their candidate. It could have been influenced enough so that the fledgling won't Impress here."

"No one has ever proved how much an egg is influenced by pre-Hatching contact," Robinton was saying in his most persuasive voice. "Or so you've had me understand any number of times. Short of dumping their candidate on top of the egg when it hatches, I can't think their conniving can do them any good or the egg any more harm."

The assembled dragonfolk were still very tense but the initial impetus to rise in wings and destroy the Southern Weyr had cooled considerably with the return of the egg, however mysterious that return was.

"Obviously, we can no longer be complacent," said F'lar, glancing up at the watchdragons, "or secure in the delusion of the inviolability of the Hatching Ground. Any Hatching Ground." Nervously he pushed the hair back from his forehead. "By the First Shell, they've a lot of gall, trying to steal one of Ramoth's eggs."

"The first way to secure this Weyr is to ban those dratted fire-lizards," Lessa said heatedly. "They're little tattlers, worse than useless . . ."

"Not all of them, Lessa," Brekke said, stepping up beside the Weyrwoman. "Some of them come on legitimate errands and give *us* a lot of assistance."

"Two were playing that game," Robinton said without humor.

Menolly dug Jaxom in the ribs, reminding him that

the Harperhall's fire-lizards, hers included, did a lot of assisting.

"I don't care," Lessa told Brekke and glared around at the assembled, looking for fire-lizards. "I don't want to see them about here. Ramoth's not to be pestered by those plaguey things. Something's to be done to keep them where they belong."

"Mark 'em with their colors!" was Brekke's quick reply. "Mark 'em and teach them to speak their name and origin the way dragons do. They're quite capable of learning courtesy. At least the ones who come to Benden by order."

"Have them report to you, Brekke, or Mirrim," Robinton suggested.

"Just keep them away from Ramoth and me!" Lessa peered in at Ramoth and then whipped around. "And someone bring up that wherry that Ramoth didn't eat. She'll be the better for something in her belly right now. We'll discuss this violation of our Weyr later. In detail."

F'lar ordered several dragonmen to get the wherry and then courteously thanked the rest of the assembled for their prompt reply to his summons. He gestured to several of the Weyrleaders and Robinton to join him in the weyr above.

"There's not a fire-lizard in sight," Menolly said to Jaxom. "I told Beauty to stay away. She's answered me scared to her bones."

"So's Ruth," Jaxom said as they crossed the Bowl to him. "He's turned almost gray."

Ruth was more than scared, he was trembling with anxiety.

Something is wrong. Something is not right, he told his rider, his eyes whirling erratically with gray tones.

"Your wing was injured?"

No. Not my wing. Something is wrong in my head. I don't feel right. Ruth shifted from all four legs to his hindquarters, and then back again to all four, rustling his wings.

"Is it because all the fire-lizards have gone? Or the excitement about Ramoth's egg?"

94

Ruth said it was both and neither. The fire-lizards were all frightened; they remembered something which frightened them.

"Remembered? Huh!" Jaxom felt exasperated with fire-lizards and their associative memories, and their ridiculous images which were making his sensible Ruth miserable.

"Jaxom?" Menolly had detoured to the Lower Caverns and shared with him the handful of meat-rolls, she'd cadged from the cooks. "Finder says Robinton wants me to go back to the Harpercrafthall and let them and Fort Hold know what's been happening. I'm also to start marking my fire-lizards. Look!" She pointed to the Weyr rim and the Star Stones. "The watch dragon is chewing firestone. Oh, Jaxom!"

"Dragon against dragon." He shuddered violently.

"Jaxom, it can't come to that," she said in a choked voice.

Neither of them could finish their meatrolls. Silently they mounted Ruth, who took them aloft.

As Robinton climbed the steps to the queen's weyr, he was thinking faster than he had ever done. Too much was going to depend on what happened now—the whole future course of the planet, if he read reactions correctly. He knew more than he ought about conditions in the Southern Weyr but his knowledge had done him no service today. He berated himself for being so naive, as unseeingly obtuse as any dragonrider for assuming that the Weyrs were inviolable and a Hatching Ground untouchable. He had had warnings from Piemur; but he simply hadn't correlated the information properly. Yet, in light of today's occurrence, he ought to have arrived at the logical conclusion that the desperate Southerners would make this prodigious attempt to revive their failing Weyr with the blood of a new and viable queen. Even if he had reached the proper conclusion, Robinton thought ruefully, how ever would he have been able to persuade Lessa and F'lar that that was what the Southerners planned today. The Weyrleaders would have been properly scornful of such a ridiculous notion.

No one was laughing today. No one at all.

Strange that so many people had assumed that the Oldtimers would meekly accept their exile and remain docilely on their continent. They had not been cramped in their accommodation, merely in their hope of a future. T'kul must have been the motivating force—T'ron had lost all his vigor and initiative after that duel with F'lar. Robinton was reasonably certain that the two Weyrwomen, Merika and Mardra, had had no part in the plan; they wouldn't wish to be deposed by a young queen and her rider. Had one of them returned the egg?

No, thought Robinton, it had to be someone with an intimate knowledge of the Benden Weyr Hatching Ground . . . or someone possessed of the blindest good luck and skill to go *between* into and out of the cavern.

Robinton relived briefly the compound terror he had experienced during the egg's absence. He winced thinking of Lessa's fury. She was still likely to arouse the Northern dragonriders. She was quite capable of sustaining the unthinking frenzy that had all but dominated the events of the morning. If she continued in her demand for vengeance against the guilty Southerners, it could be as much a disaster for Pern as the first Threadfall had been.

The egg had been returned. Robinton clung to the comforting fact that it was apparently unharmed despite its ageing in that elapsed subjective time. Lessa could choose to make its condition an issue. And, if the egg did not hatch an unimpaired queen, there was no doubt in Robinton's mind that Lessa would insist on retribution.

But the egg had been returned! He must drum in that fact, must emphasize that obviously not all Southerners had been party to this heinous action. Some Oldtimers still honored the old codes of conduct. No doubt one of them had been perceptive enough to guess what punitive action would be launched against the criminals and wished, as fervently as Robinton, to avoid such a confrontation.

"This is indeed a black moment," someone with a deep sad voice said. The Harper turned, grateful for the sane support of the Mastersmith. Fandarel's heavy features were etched with worry and, for the first time, Robinton noticed the puffiness of age blurring the man's features, yellowing his eyes. "Such perfidy must be punished—and yet it cannot be!"

The thought of dragon fighting dragon again seared Robinton's mind with terror. "Too much would be lost!" he said to Fandarel.

"*They* have already lost all they had, being sent into exile. I often wondered why they didn't rebel before."

"They have now. With a vengeance."

"To be met with more vengeance. My friend, we must keep our wits today as never before. I fear Lessa may be unreasonable and unthinking. Already she has let emotion dominate common sense." The Smith indicated the leather patch on Robinton's shoulder where his fire-lizard, Zair, customarily perched. "Where is your little friend now?"

"Brekke's weyr with Grall and Berd. I wanted him to return to the Harpercrafthall with Menolly, but he refused."

The Smith shook his great head again in sad slow sweeps as the two men entered the Council Chamber.

"I do not have a fire-lizard myself but I know only good of the little creatures. It never occurred to me that they constituted any threat for anyone."

"You will support me in this then, Fandarel?" asked Brekke, who had entered behind them with F'nor. "Lessa is not herself. I do really understand her anxiety but she cannot be allowed to damn all fire-lizards for the mischief of a few."

"Mischief?" F'nor was perturbed. "Don't let Lessa hear you call what happened mischief. Mischief? Stealing a queen egg?"

"The fire-lizard's part was only mischief . . . popping in to Ramoth's cave like how many others have been doing since the eggs were laid." Brekke spoke more sharply than she usually did, and the tightness about F'nor's eyes and mouth indicated to Robinton that this couple were not in accord. "Fire-lizards have no sense of wrong or right."

"They'll have to learn . . ." F'nor began with more heat than discretion.

"I fear that we, who have no dragons," said Robinton, quickly intervening—lest today's event fracture the bond between the two lovers—"have been making too much of our little friends, carting them about with us wherever we go, doting as parents of a late child, permitting too many liberties of conduct. *But* a more restrained attitude toward fire-lizards in our midst is a very minor consideration in today's affair."

F'nor had dampened his aggravation. He nodded now at the Harper. "Suppose that egg hadn't been returned, Robinton . . ." His shoulders jerked in a convulsive shake and he pushed at his forehead as if trying to eliminate all memory of that scene.

"If the egg hadn't been returned," Robinton said implacably, "dragon would have fought dragon!" He spaced out his words, putting as much force and distaste as he could in his tone.

F'nor quickly shook his head, denying that outcome. "No, it would not have come to that, Robinton. You were wise . . ."

"Wise?" Spat out by the infuriated Weyrwoman, the word cut like a knife. Lessa stood at the entrance to the Council Room, her slender frame taut with the emotions of the morning, her face livid with her anger. "Wise? To let them get away with such a crime? To let them plot even more base treacheries? Why did I ever think it necessary to bring them forward? When I remember that I pleaded with that excrescence T'ron to come and help us. Help us? He helps himself! To my queen's egg. If I could only undo my stupidity . . ."

"Your stupidity is in carrying on in this fashion," the Harper said coldly, knowing that what he had to say before the Weyrleaders and Craftmasters assembled in the Council Room might well alienate them all. "The egg has been returned—"

"Yes, and when I—"

"That was what you wanted half an hour, an hour ago, was it not?" Robinton demanded, raising his voice commandingly. "You wanted the egg returned. To achieve that end you were within your rights to send dragon against dragon, and no one to fault you. But the egg has been returned. To set dragon against dragon for revenge? Oh, no, Lessa. That you have no right to do. Not in revenge.

"And if you must have revenge to satisfy your queen and your angry self, just think: *They* failed! They don't have that egg. Their actions have put all the Weyrs on guard so they could never succeed a second time. They have lost their one chance, Lessa. Their one hope of reviving their dying bronzes has failed. They have been thwarted. And they face . . . nothing. No future, no hope.

"You can do nothing worse to them, Lessa. So with the return of that egg, you have no right in the eyes of the rest of Pern to do anything more."

"I have the right to revenge that insult to me, to my queen, and to my Weyr!"

"Insult?" Robinton gave a short bark of laughter. "My dear Lessa, that was no insult. That was a compliment of the highest order!"

His unexpected laughter as well as his startling interpretation stunned Lessa into silence.

"How many queen eggs have been laid this past Turn?" Robinton demanded of the other Weyrleaders. "And in Weyrs the Oldtimers would know more intimately than Benden. No, they wanted a queen of Ramoth's clutch! Nothing but the best that Pern could produce for the Oldtimers!" Adroitly Robinton left that argument. "Come, Lessa," he said with great sympathy and compassion, "we're all overwrought by this terrible event. None of us is thinking clearly . . ."

He passed his hand across his face, no sham gesture for he was perspiring with the effort to redirect the mood of so many. "Emotions are running far too high. And you've borne the brunt of it, Lessa." He took her by the arm and led the shocked but unresisting Weyrwoman to her chair, seating her with great concern and deference. "You must have been half-crazed by Ramoth's distress. She is calmer now, isn't she?"

Lessa's jaw dropped in amazement and she continued to stare at Robinton with wide-open eyes. Then she nodded, closing her mouth and moistening her lips.

"So you'll be more yourself then, too." Robinton poured a cup of wine and passed it to her. Still bemused by his startling attitude, she even sipped it. "And able to realize that the worst catastrophe that could happen to this world would be for dragon to fight dragon."

Lessa set the cup down then, spilling wine on the stone table. "You . . . with your clever words . . ." and she pointed at Robinton, rising from the chair like an uncoiling spring. "You . . ."

"He was right, Lessa," F'lar said from the entrance where he'd been watching the scene. He walked into the room, toward the table where Lessa sat. "We only had cause to invade Southern to search for our egg. Once it was returned, we would be damned by all Pern to pursue vengeance." He spoke to her but his eyes had gone to each Weyrleader and Craftmaster to judge their reactions. "Once dragon fights dragon, for whatever reason," his gesture wiped away any possible consideration, "we, the dragonriders of Pern, lose the rest of Pern!"

He gave Lessa a long hard look which she returned with frozen implacability. Squarely he faced the room. "I wish with all my heart that there'd been some other solution that day at Telgar for T'ron and T'kul. Sending them to the Southern Continent seemed to be the answer. There they could do the rest of Pern scant harm . . ."

"No, just us—just Benden!" Lessa spoke with palpable bitterness. "It's T'ron and Mardra, trying to get back at you and me!"

"Mardra would not favor a queen to depose her," said Brekke, who did not turn aside when Lessa whirled on her.

"Brekke's right, Lessa," F'lar said, putting his hand on Lessa's shoulder with apparent casualness. "Mardra wouldn't like competition."

Robinton could see the pressure of the Weyrleader's fingers whitening his knuckles, although Lessa gave no sign.

"Neither would Merika, T'kul's Weyrwoman," said D'ram, the Istan Weyrleader, "and I knew her well enough to speak with surety now."

More than any of the others in this room, Robinton thought that the Oldtimer felt this turn of events most keenly. D'ram was an honest, loyal, fair-minded man. He had felt compelled to support F'lar against those of his own Time. By such backing, he had influenced R'mart and G'narish, the other Oldtime Weyrleaders, to side with the Benden Weyr at Telgar Hold. So many undercurrents and subtle pressures abounded in this chamber, Robinton thought. Whoever had conceived of kidnapping the queen egg might not have succeeded in that stratagem, but they had effectively shattered the solidarity of the dragonriders.

"I can't tell you how badly I feel about this, Lessa," D'ram continued, shaking his head. "When I heard, I couldn't believe. I just don't understand what good such an action would do them. T'kul's older than I. His Salth couldn't hope to fly a Benden queen. For that matter, none of the dragons in the South could fly a Benden queen!"

D'ram's puzzled comment did as much as Robinton's pointed remarks to ease the multiple strains in the Council Room. Unconsciously D'ram had supported Robinton's contention that an oblique compliment had been paid Benden Weyr.

"Why, for that matter, by the time the new queen was old enough to fly to mate," D'ram added as if he'd just realized it, "their bronzes would likely be dead. Eight Southern dragons have died this past Turn. We all know that. So they tried to steal an egg for nothing . . . for nothing." His face was lined with tragic regret.

"Not for nothing," Fandarel said, his voice heavy with sadness. "For just look at what has happened to us who have been friends and allies for how many Turns? You dragonriders," his great forefinger stabbed at them, "were a fingernail away from setting your beasts against the old ones at Southern." Fandarel shook his head slowly from side to side. "This has been a terrible, terrible day! I am sorry for all of you." His gaze rested longest on Lessa. "But I think I am sorrier for myself and Pern if your anger doesn't cool and your good sense return. I will leave you now."

With great dignity he bowed to each of the Weyrleaders and their women, to Brekke and last to Lessa, trying to catch her eyes. Failing, he gave a little sigh and left the room.

Fandarel had clearly stated what Robinton wanted to be sure Lessa heard and understood—that the dragonriders stood in grave peril of losing control over Hold and Craft if they permitted their outrage and indignation to control them. Enough had been said, in the heat of the moment, in front of those Holders summoned to the Weyr during the crisis. If no further action was to be taken now that the egg had been returned, no Holder or Craftmaster could fault Benden.

But how was anyone to get through to that stubborn Lessa, sitting there wallowing in fury and determined on a disastrous course of revenge? For the first time in his long Turn as Masterharper of Pern, Robinton was at a loss for words. Enough that he had lost Lessa's goodwill already! How could he make her see reason?

"Fandarel has reminded me that dragonriders can have no private quarrels without far-reaching effect,"

F'lar said. "I permitted insult to overcome sanity once. Today is the result."

D'ram's bowed head came up and he stared fiercely at F'lar, then shook his head vigorously. There were murmured disclaimers from other dragonriders, that F'lar had acted in all honor at Telgar.

"Nonsense, F'lar," Lessa said, roused from her immobility. "That wasn't a *personal* fight. You had to fight T'ron that day to keep Pern together."

"And today I cannot fight T'ron, or the other Southerners, or I won't keep Pern together!"

Lessa stared back at F'lar for another long moment and then her shoulders sagged as she reluctantly accepted that distinction.

"But . . . if that egg does not hatch, or if the little queen is in any way damaged . . ."

"If that should happen, we will certainly review the situation," F'lar promised her, raising his right hand to honor the condition.

Fervently Robinton hoped that the little hatchling would prove healthy and vigorous, not a whit the worse for its adventuring. By the Hatching, he ought to have some information that might appease Lessa and save F'lar's now pledged honor.

"I must return to Ramoth," Lessa announced. *"She* needs me." She strode from the room, past dragonriders who deferentially moved aside.

Robinton looked at the cup of wine he had poured for her and, taking it up, downed the contents in one gulp. His hand was trembling as he lowered the cup and met F'lar's gaze.

"We could all use a cup," F'lar said, gesturing the others to gather about while Brekke, rising quickly to her feet, began to serve them.

"We will wait until the Hatching," the Benden Weyrleader went on. "I don't think I have to suggest that you all take precautions against a similar occurrence."

"None of us have any clutches hardening right now, F'lar," said R'mart of Telgar Weyr. "And none of us have Benden queens!" He had a sly twinkle in his eye as he glanced toward the Harper. "So, if eight of their beasts died this past Turn, I make it that there are now two hundred and forty-eight dragonriders left, and only five bronzes. Who brought the egg back?"

"The egg is back: that's all that matters," F'lar said then half-emptied his cup at the first swallow. "Though I am deeply grateful to that rider."

"We could find out," N'ton said quietly.

F'lar shook his head. "I'm not sure I want to know. I'm not sure we need to know—just as long as that egg hatches a live and kicking queen."

"Fandarel has his finger in the sore," Brekke said, moving gracefully to refill cups. "Just look what has happened to those of us who have been friends and allies for many Turns. I resent that more than anything else. And," she looked at everyone in turn, "I also resent the antagonism for all fire-lizards because some few, who were only being loyal to their friends, had a part in this hideous affair. I know I'm prejudiced," she smiled sadly, "but I have so much reason to be grateful to our little friends. I would like to see sense prevail as regards them, too."

"We'll have to go softly on that score, Brekke," F'lar said, "but I have taken your point. Much was said this morning in the heat and confusion that was not meant to stand!"

"I hope so. I sincerely hope so," said Brekke. "Berd keeps telling me that dragons have flamed fire-lizards!"

Robinton let out a startled exclamation. "I got that wild notion from Zair, too, before I sent him to stay in your weyr, Brekke. But no dragon flamed here . . ." He looked about at the other Weyrleaders, some of whom were agreeing with Brekke's remark, others expressing concern over such an unlikely occurrence.

"Not yet . . ." Brekke said, nodding significantly toward Ramoth's weyr.

"Then we must make sure that the queen is not further upset by any sight of fire-lizards," F'lar said, his glance sweeping around the room for agreement. "For the time being," he added, raising his hand to stop the half-formed protests. "It *is* the better part of wisdom for them not to be seen or heard right now. I know they've been useful, and some are proving to be very reliable messengers. I know many of you have them. But direct them to Brekke if it is absolutely necessary to send them here." He looked directly at Robinton.

"Fire-lizards do not go where they are not welcome," Brekke said. Then she added with a wry smile to take the sting out of her comment: "They're scared out of their hides right now anyway."

"So we do nothing until the egg has Hatched?" N'ton asked.

"Except to assemble the girls found on Search. Lessa will want them here as soon as possible, to accustom Ramoth to their presence. We'll all assemble again for the Hatching, Weyrleaders."

"A good Hatching," D'ram said with a fervor that was sincerely seconded by everyone.

Robinton half-hoped that F'lar might hold him back as the others dispersed. But F'lar was in conversation with D'ram, and Robinton sadly decided that his absence would be appreciated. It grieved Robinton to be at odds with the Benden Weyrleaders and he felt weary as he made his way back to the weyr entrance. Still, F'lar had supported Robinton's plea for deliberation. As he reached the last turning of the corridor, he saw Mnementh's bronze bulk on the ledge, and he hesitated, suddenly reluctant to approach Ramoth's mate.

"Don't fret so, Robinton," N'ton said, stepping to his side and touching his arm. "You were so right and wise to speak out as you did, and probably the only one who could stop Lessa's madness. F'lar knows it." N'ton grinned. "But he does still have to contend with Lessa."

"Master Robinton," F'nor's voice was low as if he didn't wish to be overheard, "please join Brekke and me in my weyr. N'ton, too, if you're not pressed to return to Fort Weyr."

"I can certainly spare any time you need today,"

the younger bronze rider replied with cheerful compliance.

"Brekke will be right along." Then the wing second led the way across the Bowl, unnaturally silent except for the moans and mutters that issued in muffled echoes from Ramoth in the Hatching Ground. On his ledge, Mnementh swung his great head constantly so that every portion of the rim was scrutinized.

No sooner had the men entered the weyr than they were assaulted by four hysterical fire-lizards that had to be petted and reassured that no dragon would flame them—a fear which seemed to be common and persistent.

"What is this large darkness that I get from Zair's images?" Robinton asked when he had caressed his little bronze into a semblance of order. Zair shivered frequently and, whenever the Harper's gentle strokes lapsed, the bronze pushed imperiously at the negligent hand.

Meanwhile Berd and Grall were perched on F'nor's shoulders, stroking his cheeks, their eyes bright yellow with anxiety and still whirling at a frantic rate. "When they're calmer, Brekke and I will try to sort the whole thing out. I get the impression that they are remembering something."

"Not something like the Red Star?" N'ton asked. At his unfortunate reference, Tris, who had been lying quietly on his forearm, began to bat his wings and the others squealed in fright. "I'm sorry. Calm down, Tris."

"No, not something like that," F'nor said. "Just something . . . something they remembered."

"We do know that they communicate instantly with one another and apparently broadcast anything seen that is strongly felt or experienced," Robinton said, picking his words as he vocalized his thoughts. "So this could be evidence of a mass reaction. But picked up from which fire-lizard or fire-lizards? However, Grall and Berd, and certainly that little creature of Meron's, could not have known through one of their own kind that the . . . you know what . . . was dangerous to them. So how did they know to the point of hysterics? How could it be something they remembered?"

"Runner beasts seem to know when to avoid treacherous ground . . ." N'ton offered.

"Instinct." Robinton pondered. "Could be instinct." Then he shook his head. "No, avoiding treacherous ground is not the same use of an instinctive fear: that's a generality. The . . . R-E-D-S-T-A-R," he spelled letter by letter, "is a specific. Ah, well!"

"Fire-lizards are basically gifted with the same skills as dragons. Dragons, however, have no memories to speak of."

"Which, let us fervently hope," F'nor said, raising his eyes toward the ceiling, "wipes out what happened today in record time."

"Lessa does not suffer that gift," Robinton said with a heavy sigh.

"She's not stupid either, Masterharper," N'ton said, adroitly reaffirming his respect for the man by the use of his title. "Nor is F'lar. Just worried. They'll both come 'round and appreciate your intervention today." Then N'ton cleared his throat and looked the Masterharper squarely in the eyes. "Do you know who took the egg?"

"I had *heard* that something was being planned. I knew, which would have been obvious to anyone counting Turns, that the Southern men and dragons are slowing with age, and desperate. I've had only the experience of Zair wanting to mate . . ." Robinton paused, remembering that astounding revival of desires he had thought himself well past, shrugged and met the understanding twinkle in N'ton's eyes. "So I can appreciate the pressures that randy brown and bronze dragons can exert on their riders. Even a willing green, young enough to be flown, would help . . ." He looked questioningly at the two dragonriders.

"Not after today," F'nor said emphatically. "If they'd approached one of the Weyrs . . . D'ram for instance," he glanced at N'ton for corroboration, "perhaps a green would have gone, if only to prevent something disastrous. But to attempt to solve their problems by kidnapping a queen egg?" F'nor frowned. "How much do you know, Robinton, about what goes on down in the Southern Weyr? I know I gave you all the maps I'd made when I was timing it in the South."

"Frankly, I know more about happenings in the Hold. I did get a message from Piemur recently that the dragonriders had been more private than is their custom. They don't mix much with holders, following the pattern of their own Time, but a certain amount of coming and going into the Weyr was permitted. That ceased abruptly and then no holders were allowed near the Weyr. Not for any reason. Nor was there much flying done. Piemur says the dragons would be seen midair and then they'd pop *between*. No circling, no cruising. Just going *between*."

"Timing it," F'nor said thoughtfully.

Zair squeaked piteously and Robinton soothed him. Again the fire-lizard inserted in his mind the image of dragons flaming fire-lizards: the black nothingness, and a glimpse of an egg.

"Did you both get that picture, too, from your friends?" he asked though their startled expression made the question unnecessary.

Robinton pressed Zair for a clearer image, a view of where the egg was, and received nothing but the impression of flame and fear.

"I wish they'd a bit more sense," Robinton said, forcing down his irritation. Tantalizing to be so close, thwarted by the limited scope of fire-lizard vision.

"They're still upset," F'nor said. "I'll try with Grall and Berd later on. I wonder if Menolly's getting the same reaction from hers. You might ask her when you've got back to the Harpercrafthall, Master Robinton. With ten, she might get that much more clarity."

Robinton agreed as he rose, but thought of one last thing. "N'ton, weren't you among the bronzes who went to Southern Weyr, to see if the egg had been taken there?"

"I was. The Weyr was deserted. Not even an old dragon left behind. Completely deserted."

"Yes, that would follow, wouldn't it?"

When Jaxom and Menolly, on Ruth, entered the air above Fort Hold, Ruth called his name to the watch dragon and was almost smothered by fire-lizards. They so impeded his progress that he dropped a few lengths before he could get them to give him wing room. The moment he landed, the fire-lizards swarmed over him and his riders, keening with anxiety.

Menolly called out reassurances as fire-lizards clung to her clothing, got tangled in her hair. Jaxom found two trying to sit on his head, several had tails wrapped around his neck and three were beating their wings frantically to remain at eye level with him.

"What's got into them?"

"They're terrified! Dragons breathing fire at them," Menolly cried. "But no one's doing that to you, you silly clunches. You only have to stay away from the Weyrs for a bit."

Other harpers, attracted by the commotion, came to their rescue, either taking the fire-lizards bodily from Jaxom and Menolly, or sternly recalling the ones that looked to them personally. When Jaxom started to shoo them away from Ruth, the dragon told him not to bother—he, Ruth, would calm them down himself shortly. They were frightened because they remembered being chased by dragon fire. Since the harpers were all now clamoring for news from Benden, Jaxom decided to let Ruth handle the fire-lizards.

The Harpers had received some pretty distorted images from the fire-lizards returning, terrified, to the Harpercrafthall: Benden full of immense bronze dragons, breathing fire, ready to fight; Ramoth acting like a blood-maddened watchwher, and curious images of the queen egg solitary in the sand. But what made the Harpers extremely apprehensive was the vision of dragons flaming at fire-lizards.

"Benden dragons did not flame any fire-lizards," Jaxom and Menolly both said.

"But all the fire-lizards must stay away from Benden unless they're sent to either Brekke or Mirrim," Menolly added firmly. "And we're to mark all those that look to harpers with harper colors."

Jaxom and Menolly were ushered into the Harperhall and given wine and hot soup. Neither of them got to eat it hot because no sooner were they served than some of the Hold people arrived, soliciting the news. Menolly recounted the major portion of the happening, being the trained Harper. Jaxom's respect for the girl increased greatly as he listened to her flowing voice evoke the emotions appropriate to each part of her narrative, without distorting what he knew to have happened. One of the senior Harpers, soothing the blue fire-lizard in the crook of his arm, kept nodding his head as if approving her use of Harper tricks.

When Menolly stopped speaking, a respectful murmur of thanks was heard throughout the room. Then the listeners became the speakers, dissecting the news, wondering who had returned the egg and how—and why, which was still the biggest question. How were the Weyrs going to protect themselves? Were the main Holds in any danger? Who knew to what lengths the Oldtimers might go if they'd steal a Benden egg. Now, there'd been some mysterious occurrences—insignificant in themselves but in total highly suspicious—which the Harpers felt ought to be reported to Benden Weyr. Those mysterious shortages at the iron mines, for instance. And what about those young girls who were carried off and no one could trace where? Could the Oldtimers be looking for more than dragon eggs?

Menolly eased her way out of the center of the audience and beckoned Jaxom to follow her. "I'm talked dry," she said with a heavy sigh and led him down the corridor to the huge copyroom where moldy Records were transcribed before their messages were lost forever. Her lizards suddenly appeared and she signaled them to land on one of the tables. "You lot are about to wear the very latest design for fire-lizards!" She rummaged in the cabinet under the table. "Help me find white and yellow, Jaxom. This can is dried up." She chucked it into a bin in the corner.

"And what is your design for fire-lizards?"

"Hmmmm. Here's white. Harper blue with journeyman light blue, separated by white and framed by Fort Hold lattice yellow. That ought to label them accurately, don't you think?"

Jaxom agreed and found himself required to hold fire-lizard necks still. This assignment was rendered all the more difficult because the fire-lizards seemed to want to look him straight in the eye.

"If they're trying to tell me something, I'm not getting the message," Jaxom told Menolly as he patiently endured the fifth soulful scrutiny.

"I suspect," Menolly said, speaking in disjointed phrases as she carefully applied her root colors, "what you've got—hold him still, Jaxom—is the only . . . dragon on Pern . . . that . . . they're not—hold him— scared silly of right now. Ruth doesn't . . . after all . . . chew firestone."

Jaxom sighed because he could see that Ruth's sudden popularity was going to ruin his private plans. Much as he was loath to do so, he was going to have to time it because if the fire-lizards didn't know *when* they went they couldn't follow him! That reminded him of his original errand to the Harpercrafthall.

"I started out this morning to get Wansor's equations from you. . . ."

"Hmmm, yes." Menolly grinned at him over a squirming blue fire-lizard. "That seems like Turns ago. Well, we'll just patch the white on Uncle, and I'll give 'em to you. I've also got some winter-summer season charts you might as well have, seeing as you've been so cooperative. Piemur hasn't written out many yet."

A blue fire-lizard came zipping into the paint room, chirping with relief when it saw Jaxom.

It is the thick man's blue, Ruth said from outside.

"I've only the one blue fire-lizard and we just did him, didn't we?" Menolly asked in surprise, glancing about the room at the others.

"It's Brand's. I'd better get back to Ruatha Hold. I should've gone back hours ago."

"Well, don't be a fool and meet yourself coming," she said with a laugh. "You've been on legitimate business this time."

Managing a light laugh, Jaxom caught the roll of charts she threw in his direction. She couldn't know what he had in mind. He was entirely too sensitive to her random remarks. Sign of a guilty conscience.

"Then you'll alibi me to Lytol?"

"Anytime, Jaxom!"

Back at Ruatha Hold, he had the whole tale to tell again with an audience as rapt, astonished, angered and relieved as the harpers and the Fort Holders. He found himself unconsciously using Menolly's turns of phrase and he wondered how long before she'd make a Ballad of the event.

He finished by directing everyone owning a fire-lizard to band the creature with Ruatha colors: brown with red squares, banded by white and black. He got that task organized when he noticed that Lytol was still seated in his heavy chair, one hand playing with the corner of his lower lip, his eyes fixed on some indistinct point on the flagstones.

"Lytol?"

The Lord Warder recalled himself to the present with an effort and frowned at Jaxom. Then he sighed. "I've always feared that the conflict might come to dragon against dragon."

"It's not come to that, Lytol," Jaxom said quietly and as persuasively as he could.

The man looked intently into Jaxom's eyes. "It could, lad. It so easily could. And I, and you, owe so much to Benden. Should I go there now?"

"Finder remained."

Lytol nodded and Jaxom wondered if the Lord Warder felt he'd been slighted. "Better for Finder to travel on dragonback." He passed his hand over his eyes and shook his head.

"You're not well, Lytol. A cup of wine?"

"No, I'll be all right, lad." Lytol pushed himself

vigorously to his feet. "I don't suppose in all the fuss that you remembered what you went to the Harper-crafthall for?"

Much relieved to hear Lytol sound like himself, Jaxom lightly announced that he had not only Wansor's equations but some charts to work with. From then until the evening meal, Jaxom wished he'd not been so thoughtful because Lytol had him instructing Brand and himself in accurately timing Thread-fall.

Teaching someone else a method is a very good way to make it easier to do yourself, as Jaxom found later that night when he worked some private equations of his own, poring over the rough map he had of the Southern Continent. There was too much activity all over Pern for him to go to an alternate "when" with any safety. And since he was going to time it, he might just as well go back at least twelve Turns, before anyone had started using the Southern Continent at all. He knew just where firestone could be mined so there'd be no problem supplying Ruth. The night stars were halfway to morning before he felt he could find his way to the then he wanted to find.

Just before daybreak, he was awakened by the sound of Ruth's whimpering. He struggled from his furs and stumbled barefoot on the cold stones, blinking sleep from his eyes. Ruth's forelegs were churning and his wing elbows twitched with whatever dream disturbed him. Fire-lizards burrowed about him; most of them did not wear Ruathan colors. He shooed the creatures away and Ruth, sighing, dropped into a deeper, quiet sleep.

CHAPTER VI

Ruatha Hold and Southern Hold,
15.5.27–15.6.2

THE HOLD DAY began by sending out fire-lizards with messages to all the smaller holds and craftcottages, ordering that every fire-lizard be appropriately marked and individually warned about approaching any Weyr. Some of the nearby holders had ridden in during the morning for reassurances about the garbled accounts the fire-lizards had given. So Lytol, Jaxom and Brand were kept busy all day. The next day, Thread was due to fall, and it fell at precisely the moment Lytol had calculated. This gave him great pleasure and reassured the more nervous holders.

Jaxom good-naturedly took his place with the flamethrower crew, not that any Thread escaped the Fort Weyr dragons. It amused Jaxom to think that at the next Threadfall, he too might be above ground on a fire-breathing Ruth.

The third day after the egg was stolen, Ruth was famished and wanted to hunt. But the fire-lizards came in such droves to accompany him that he killed only once and ate the beast up, bones and hide.

I will not kill for them, Ruth told Jaxom so fiercely that he wondered if Ruth might eventually flame the fire-lizards.

"What's the matter? I thought you liked them!"

Jaxom met his dragon on the grassy slope and caressed him soothingly.

They remember me doing something I do not remember doing. I did not do it. Ruth's eyes whirled with red sparks.

"What do they remember you doing?"

I haven't done it. And there was a tinge of fearful uncertainty to Ruth's mental tone. *I know I haven't done it. I couldn't do such a thing. I am a dragon. I am Ruth. I am of Benden!* His last words sounded in a despairing tone.

"What do they remember you doing, Ruth? You've got to tell me."

Ruth ducked his head, as if he wished he could hide, but he turned back to Jaxom, his eyes wheeling piteously. *I wouldn't take Ramoth's egg. I know I didn't take Ramoth's egg. I was there by the lake all the time with you. I remember that. You remember that. They know where I was. But somehow they remember that I took Ramoth's egg too.*

Jaxom clung to Ruth's neck to keep from falling. Then he took several very deep breaths.

"Show me the images they've been giving you, Ruth!"

And Ruth did, the projections growing more clear and vivid as Ruth calmed in response to his rider's encouragement.

That's what they remember, he said finally with a deep sigh of relief.

Jaxom told himself to think logically so he said out loud, "Fire-lizards can only tell what they've seen. You say they remember. Do you know *when* they remember seeing you take Ramoth's egg?"

I could take you to that when.

"Are you sure?"

There are two queens—they've bothered me most because they remember best.

"They wouldn't just happen to remember it at night, when the stars are out, would they?"

Ruth shook his head. *Fire-lizards are not big enough to see enough stars. And that's when they got*

flamed. The bronzes who guard the egg chew firestone.
They don't want any fire-lizards near.

"That's smart of them."

None of the dragons like fire-lizards anymore. And
if they knew what the fire-lizards remember about
me, they won't like me, either.

"Then it's just as well that you're the only dragon
who'll listen to fire-lizards, isn't it?" That observation
wasn't much comfort to either Ruth or Jaxom. "But
why, if the egg is already back in Benden Weyr, are
the fire-lizards bothering you about it?"

Because they don't remember me going yet.

Jaxom felt he'd better sit down. This last statement
would take a lot of thinking. No, he contradicted
himself. F'lessan had been right. We think and talk
things to death. He wondered briefly if Lessa and
F'nor had been seized by this same sort of irrational
compulsion at the moment of their decisions. He decided he'd better not think about that either.

"You're sure you know *when* we have to go?" he
asked Ruth once more.

Two queens flitted up, crooning lovingly: one even
bold enough to light on Jaxom's arm, her eyes wheeling with joy.

They know. I know.

"Well, I'm glad they're willing to take us. I sure
wish they'd seen stars!"

Jaxom permitted himself one more deep breath and
then he swung to Ruth's neck and told him to take
them home.

Once he'd made his decision to act, it was amazing
how easy it was to go ahead, just as long as he didn't
think about it. He assembled his flying gear, the rope,
a fur robe to cover the egg. He gobbled down some
meatrolls, casually winked at Brand as he sauntered
out of the Hall, overwhelmingly glad that he had a
handy excuse in his suspected affair with Corana.

It took longer to persuade Ruth to roll in the black
tidal mud of the Telgar River delta, but Jaxom managed to persuade his weyrmate that a white hide was
remarkably visible against the black tropical night or

in full daylight inside the Hatching Ground where he planned for them to stay in the shadows.

From the images given Ruth by the two queens, Jaxom felt he could safely assume that the Oldtimers had taken the egg back in time but lodged it in the most logical and fitting spot for an egg, in the warm sands of the old volcano that would eventually become Southern Weyr in the appropriate time. He had already memorized the positions of Southern night stars so he'd probably be able to tell *when* he was, within a Turn or two. He'd have to count heavily on Ruth's boast that he always knew *when* he was.

The fire-lizards arrived in full fair at the delta and enthusiastically helped him sully Ruth's white coat with the clinging black mud. Jaxom dabbed it on his hands and face, and the shiny parts of his accoutrements. The fur robe was already dark enough.

Somehow Jaxom wasn't quite sure that all this was happening to him, that he could be mixed up in such a wild venture. But he had to be. He was moving in inexorable steps toward a predestined event and nothing could stop him now. So he mounted Ruth calmly, trusting as he had never done before in his dragon's abilities. Jaxom took two deep breaths.

"You know *when,* Ruth. We'd better get there!"

It was without doubt the longest, coldest jump he had ever made. He had one advantage over Lessa, he expected it. But that didn't keep the jump from being frighteningly dark, or relieve a silence that was a noisy pressure in his ears, or keep the cold from striking his bones. He couldn't come straight back with the egg; he'd have to take several steps to warm it.

Then they were above a darkened moist warm world that smelled of lush greenery and slightly decaying fruit. For a moment Jaxom had the hideous feeling that this was all a sun-dream of the fire-lizards. But something in the eerie way that Ruth glided as noiselessly as possible, a part of the gentle night breeze, made it real and immediate. Then he saw the egg below, a luminescent spot slightly to the right of Ruth's searching head.

Jaxom let him glide a little farther to catch a glimpse of the Weyr's eastern edge, the point from which he wanted to enter at all possible speed, at early dawn. Then he told Ruth to change and there seemed to be no time spent *between*. All at once the rising sun was warm on their backs. Ruth arrowed in, winging low and fast, over the backs of the drowsy bronzes and their napping riders. A quick deft swoop, Ruth grabbing the egg in his sturdy forearms, a lunge up and, before the startled bronzes could rise to their feet, the little white dragon had enough free air to go *between* again.

Ruth was still only a winglength above the Weyr when they came out of *between,* a Turn in time ahead of Ruth's sunrise plunge.

Ruth had just enough strength left in his forearms and wings to let the egg down carefully into the warm sands. Jaxom dropped from the dragon's neck to check the egg for any cracks, but it looked all right. Certainly it was hard enough and still warm. With his gloved hands, he shoveled sun-hot sand over the egg and then, like Ruth, collapsed to catch his breath.

"We can't stay long. They might just try it day by day. They'd know we can't take the egg far at once."

Ruth nodded, his breath still coming in ragged gasps. Then he stopped, taut until Jaxom started with alarm. Two fire-lizards, a gold and a bronze, were watching them from the edge of the Weyr. In the brief glimpse Jaxom had of them before they winked out, he saw no colored bands about their necks.

"Do we know them?"

No.

"Where're those two queens?"

They showed me when. *That's all you wanted.*

Jaxom felt bereft of their fragile guidance and stupid because he hadn't insisted they stay.

There's firestone, Ruth said. *And flame scar. The bronzes did flame at the fire-lizards here! A long time ago. The scar is growing weed.*

"Dragon against dragon!" Apprehension nagged at Jaxom. He didn't feel safe here. He wouldn't feel safe until they actually had that egg back in Benden where it belonged.

"We've got to make another jump, Ruth. We don't dare wait here."

Resolutely he unlooped the rope from about his waist and started making a rough sling with the fur rug. There'd be less strain on Ruth if the egg were strapped between his forelegs. Jaxom had completed the corners when he heard a loud crunching.

"Ruth! You're not going to flame dragons!"

No, of course I'm not. But will they dare approach me if I am flaming?

Jaxom was unsettled enough not to protest. When Ruth had a gulletful, he called him over and got the sling around the egg. He looped the rope comfortably over Ruth's shoulders to take the weight. He started to check the knots again and then, some inner caution prompting him, he just mounted.

"We'll go five Turns more into Keroon, to our place there. Do you know when?"

Ruth thought a moment and then said he knew when.

In *between* Jaxom had time to worry if he was making the jumps too long to keep the egg warm. It hadn't actually Hatched before he'd left. Maybe he should have waited, to find out if the egg had Hatched properly: then they'd've known how to judge the forward jumps. Maybe he'd even killed the little queen trying to save her. No, his mind reeled with *between* and paradoxes; the most important act, returning the queen egg, was in process. And dragon had not fought dragon—not yet.

The shimmering heat of Keroon desert warmed his failing spirit as well as his body. Ruth looked a ghastly shade under the caking black mud. Jaxom released the rope and lowered the egg to the sand. Ruth helped him cover it. It was midmorning, and not far from the hour when the egg must be back but at least six Turns in time-distance.

Ruth asked if he couldn't wash off the mud in the sea but Jaxom told him they'd have to wait until they'd got the egg safely back. No one had known who'd done it then: no one should know, and the safest way was not to have a white hide showing.

The fire-lizards?

That had worried Jaxom but he thought he had the answer. "They didn't know who brought the egg back that day. There weren't any in the Hatching Ground, so they don't know what they haven't seen." Jaxom decided not to think further on that subject.

He was very tired as he leaned back against Ruth's warm flank. They'd rest a little while and let the egg warm up well in the midmorning sun before they'd make that last and trickiest jump. They had to position themselves to land just inside the Hatching Ground, where the arch of the entrance sloped abruptly down and obscured the view of anyone looking from the Bowl into the Ground. In fact, directly opposite the peephole and slit that F'lessan and Jaxom had used so many Turns ago. It was just luck that Ruth was small enough to risk going *between* inside the Ground but it'd been his own Hatching place so his feeling was innate. Thus far he'd lived up to his boast that he always knew when he was going. . . .

Even in the hot desert plains of Keroon there was some noise: infinitesimal rustlings of insect life, hot breezes riffling through dead grasses, snakes burrowing in the sand, the distant rush of water on the beach. The cessation of such sounds can be as remarkable as a thunderclap, and so it was the utter stillness and a minute change of air pressure that roused Jaxom and Ruth from somnolence to alarm.

Jaxom glanced up, expecting bronze dragons to appear and reclaim their prize. The sky above was clear and hot. Jaxom glanced around and saw the danger, the silver mist of descending Thread raining down across the desert. He slithered and scrambled to the egg, Ruth right beside him, both digging it free, pushing it into the sling, frantically trying to judge the leading edge of Fall, wondering and worrying that the skies weren't full of fighting dragons.

As fast as they worked to secure the precious burden to Ruth for flight, they were not quite quick enough. The leading edge of Threadfall fell hissing to the sand around them as Jaxom got to Ruth's neck and directed him upward. Ruth, giving a belch of flame, vaulted skyward, trying to sear a path far enough above the ground to go *between*.

A ribbon of fire sliced Jaxom's cheek, his right shoulder through the wherhide tunic, his forearm, his thigh. He felt, rather than heard, Ruth's bellow of pain, lost in the black of *between*.

Somehow Jaxom kept his mind on where and when they should be. They were finally in the Hatching Ground, Ramoth bellowing outside. Ruth could not quite suppress his cry as the hot sand rubbed the raw Threadscore on his hind foot. Jaxom bit his lips against his pain as he struggled with the rope. There was so little time and it seemed to take ages to release the sling. Ruth lowered the egg to the sand but it rolled down the slight incline from their shadowy corner of the Ground. They couldn't wait. Ruth sprang up toward the high ceiling and went *between*.

Dragon would not now fight dragon!

It was no surprise to Jaxom that Ruth came out of *between* above the little mountain lake. In what relative when, Jaxom was too concerned for his dragon to care at that moment. Ruth was whimpering with the pain in his foot and leg; all he wanted was to cool that Threadfire. Jaxom leaped from his neck to the shallows and splashed water on the sweaty gray hide, cursing himself that the nearest numbweed was at Ruatha Hold. He was so clever, he was, that he never thought one of them might get hurt.

The cool lake water was taking the sting from the Threadscores but Jaxom worried now about the mud causing an infection. Surely he could have used something less dangerous for camouflage than river mud. He didn't dare scour the wounds with sand: it would be too painful for Ruth and might just rub the cursed mud deeper into the wounds. For the first time in many days, Jaxom regretted the total absence of fire-lizards who could have helped him scrub his very dirty dragon. Once again he briefly wondered when, besides high noon of the day, they were.

It is the day after the evening we left, Ruth announced. *I always know when I am,* he added with justifiable pride in his ability. *Along the left dorsal, a terrible itch. You've left some mud.*

Jaxom could and did use sand on the rest of Ruth's hide and managed to ignore the way it smarted in his own scores. He was dead weary and aching by the time Ruth allowed that he was clean enough for a last plunge in the deeper part of the lake.

The ripples lapping around his soaked ankles brought Jaxom's memory back to that not so distant day of his rebellion.

"Well," he said with a self-deprecatory chuckle, "among other things, we did get to fight Thread." And what a dismal showing they'd made of it with proof patent on their hides.

We weren't exactly giving our complete attention to Thread, Ruth reminded him with a note of reproach. *I know how now. We'll be much better at it next time. I'm faster than any of the big dragons. I can turn on my tail and go between in a single length from the ground.*

Jaxom told Ruth fervently and gratefully that he was without doubt the best, fastest, cleverest beast in all Pern, North and South. Ruth's eyes whirled greenly with pleasure and he paddled to the shore, wings extended to dry.

You are cold and hungry and sore. My leg hurts. Let's go home.

Jaxom knew that was the wisest course; he had to get numbweed on Ruth's leg and on his own injuries. But scores they were and undeniably caused by Thread. How in the name of the First Shell was he ever going to explain all of this to Lytol?

Why explain anything? Ruth asked logically. *We only did what we had to do.*

"Think logically, huh?" Jaxom replied with a laugh, and patted Ruth's neck before he wearily pulled himself up. With understandable reluctance and apprehension, he told Ruth to take them home.

The watchdragon caroled a greeting and a mere half-dozen fire-lizards, all banded in Hold colors, swarmed up to escort Ruth down to his weyr courtyard.

One of the drudges came hurrying out of the kitchen entrance, eyes wide with excitement.

"Lord Jaxom, there's been a Hatching. The queen egg Hatched, it did. You were sent to come but no one could find you."

"I had other business. Fetch me some numbweed!"

"Numbweed?" The drudge's eyes widened further with concern.

"Numbweed! I'm sunburned."

Rather pleased with his resourcefulness considering he was shivering in wet clothes, Jaxom saw Ruth comfortably situated in his weyr, his injured leg propped up.

It hurt Jaxom to get the tunic over his shoulder because Thread had scored right down the muscle, caught him at the wrist and continued to cut a long furrow down his thigh.

A timid scratching on the door to the main Hold announced the incredibly speedy return of the drudge. Jaxom opened the door wide enough to get the jug of numbweed, and still keep his Threadscores from the curious eyes.

"Thanks, and I'll want something hot to eat, too. Soup, klah, whatever's on the fire."

Jaxom closed the door, scooped up a bathing sheet which he knotted about his middle as he made his way to Ruth. He slathered a fistful of the numbweed on his dragon's leg and grinned at the sigh of intense relief that Ruth gave as the salve took immediate effect.

Jaxom gratefully echoed the sentiments as he smeared his own wounds. Blessed, blessed numbweed. Never again would he begrudge his labor in gathering the plaquey, thorny greenery from which this incredible balm was stewed. He peered into his looking glass as he daubed his face cut. It'd leave a finger-long scar.

No getting around that. Now if he could get around Lytol's wrath . . .

"Jaxom!"

Lytol strode into the room after the most perfunctory knock at the door. "You've missed the Hatching at Benden Weyr and—" At the sight of Jaxom, Lytol stopped so quickly in midstride that he rocked back on his heels. Clad only in a bathing sheet, the marks on Jaxom's shoulder and face were quite visible.

"The egg Hatched all right then? Good," Jaxom responded, picking up his tunic with a nonchalance he wasn't feeling. "I . . ." then he stopped, as much because his voice would be muffled in the fabric of his tunic as because he had been about to explain with his customary candor his bizarre night's work. He balked at the task. Ruth perhaps was right—they had only done what they had to. It was sort of his and Ruth's private affair. You might even say his actions reflected his unconscious wish to atone for violating Ramoth's Hatching Ground as a boy. He pulled the shirt over his head, wincing as it caught the numbweed on his cheek. "I heard at Benden," he said then, "that they were worried whether it would Hatch after all the coming and going *between*."

Lytol approached Jaxom slowly, his eyes on the young man's face, begging the question.

Jaxom settled his tunic, belted it, then smoothed the numbweed into the cut again. He didn't know what to say.

"Oh, Lytol, would you mind taking a look at Ruth's leg? See if I doctored it right?" Jaxom waited then, facing Lytol calmly. He noticed, with a sadness for the inevitability of this moment of reserve, that Lytol's eyes were dark with emotion. He owed the man so much, never more than at this moment. He wondered that he had ever considered Lytol cold or hard and unfeeling.

"There's a trick of ducking Thread," Lytol said quietly, "that you'd better teach Ruth, Lord Jaxom."

"If you'd be kind enough to tell me how, Lord Lytol . . ."

CHAPTER VII

Morning at Ruatha Hold, 15.6.2

"I CAME TO TELL you that we have guests, Lord Jaxom; Master Robinton, N'ton and Menolly are above, just back from the Hatching. First, let's see to Ruth."

"Didn't you go to Benden for the Hatching?" Jaxom asked.

Lytol shook his head as he walked toward Ruth's weyr. The white dragon was settling in for a well-deserved nap. Lytol bowed courteously to him before peering closely at the thickly smeared scorings.

"You washed first in the lake, I presume." Lytol's glance took in Jaxom's damp hair. "That water's pure enough, and the numbweed's been applied in good time. We'll check again in a few hours. But I think he's all right." Lytol's gaze went then to Jaxom's all-too-obvious scoring.

"I had no reason to excuse you to our guests." He sighed. "Be grateful it's N'ton above and not F'lar. I suppose Menolly knew what you were about?"

"I told no one what I intended, Lord Lytol," Jaxom said with some formality.

"At least you've learned discretion." The Lord Warder hesitated, his eyes sweeping the figure of his ward. "Ah, well, I'd best ask N'ton to take you for weyrling practice—safer that way and you'd be with others. Robinton will guess what you've been about, but he'd learn in due course no matter how we evaded. Come then, they'll not give you too hard a time for your clumsiness. Not that you don't deserve more than a ribbing, taking such a chance with yourself and Ruth. And right now, when order is all in pieces anyhow . . ."

"I apologize for distressing you, Lord Lytol . . ."

The man subjected his charge to another shrewd scrutiny.

"No distress, Lord Jaxom. Any apologies are on my head. I ought to have realized your need to prove Ruth's abilities. I *wish* that you were a few Turns older and that matters were in such order that I could let you take Hold—"

"I don't want to take Hold from you, Lord Lytol—"

"I don't think I'd be permitted to step down right now anyway, Jaxom. As you'll hear for yourself. Come, we've kept our guests waiting long enough as it is."

N'ton was facing the door of the smaller hall used at Ruatha when guests required privacy for their discussions. The bronze rider took one look at Jaxom's face and groaned. At his reaction, Master Robinton slewed round in his chair, his tired eyes registering surprise and, Jaxom hoped, a certain measure of approval.

"You're Threadscored, Jaxom," Menolly cried, and her expression was one of shocked dismay. "How could you take such a risk right now?" She, who had taunted him about thinking, not doing, was now furious with him.

"I should have known you'd try it, young Jaxom," N'ton said with a weary sigh, a rueful smile on his face. "You were bound to break out soon, but your timing is atrocious."

Jaxom would have liked to say that, in point of fact, his timing had been faultless, but N'ton went on: "Ruth wasn't hurt, was he?"

"A single score on thigh and foot," Lytol replied. "Well doctored."

"I do sympathize with your ambition, Jaxom," Robinton said, unusually solemn, "to fly Ruth with other dragons but I must counsel you to patience."

"I'd rather he learned how to fly properly now, Robinton. With my other weyrlings," N'ton interrupted unexpectedly, winning Jaxom's gratitude. "Particularly if he's mad enough, brave enough, to try it on his own without any guidance."

"I doubt we could get Benden to approve," Robinton said, shaking his head.

"*I* approve," Lytol said in a firm voice, his face set. "I am Lord Jaxom's guardian, not F'lar or Lessa. Let her manage her own concerns. Lord Jaxom is my charge. He can come to little harm with the Fort Weyrlings." Lytol stared fiercely at Jaxom. "And he will agree not to put his teaching to the test without consulting us. Will you abide by that, Lord Jaxom?"

Jaxom was relieved enough to know that the Benden Weyrleaders would not be queried so that he agreed to more stringent conditions than he might have. He nodded and was immediately beset by conflicting emotions—amusement because everyone had assumed the obvious and annoyance because, having achieved so much more that day, he was now reduced to apprentice level. Yet, his experience at Keroon had demonstrated too sharply how much he still had to learn about fighting Thread if he wished to keep whole his and his dragon's hides.

N'ton had been peering intently at Jaxom and his frown deepened so that, for one moment, Jaxom wondered if N'ton had somehow guessed what he and Ruth had actually been doing when they were Threadscored. If they ever found out, Jaxom would be twice bound with added restrictions.

"I think I'll require a further promise from you, Jaxom," the bronze rider said. "No more timing it. You've been doing far too much of that lately. I can tell from your eyes."

Startled, Lytol examined his ward's face more closely.

"I'm in no danger on Ruth, N'ton," Jaxom said,

relieved at being accused of a lesser transgression. "He always knows *when* he is."

N'ton dismissed that talent impatiently. "Possibly, but the danger lies in the rider's mind—an inadvertent time clue that could set both in jeopardy. Coming too close to yourself in subjective time is dangerous. Besides it's draining for both dragon and rider. You don't need to time it, young Jaxom. You'll have time enough for all you need to do."

N'ton's words caused Jaxom to recall the inexplicable weakness that had overcome him in the Hatching Ground. Was it possible that at that very moment—

"I don't think you can have realized, Jaxom," Robinton began, interrupting Jaxom's thoughts, "just how critical matters are in Pern right now. And you should know."

"If you mean about the egg-stealing, Master Robinton, and how close it came to dragon attacking dragon, I was in Benden Weyr that morning . . ."

"Were you?" Robinton was mildly surprised and shook his head as if he ought not to have forgotten. "Then you can guess at Lessa's temper today. If that egg hadn't hatched properly . . ."

"But the egg *was* returned, Master Robinton." Jaxom was confused. Why would Lessa still be upset?

"Yes," the Harper replied, "apparently not everyone in Southern was blind to the consequences of the theft. But Lessa is not appeased."

"An insult was given Benden Weyr, and Ramoth and Lessa," N'ton said.

"Dragons can't fight dragons!" Jaxom was appalled. "That's why the egg was returned." If his risk and Ruth's injury had been futile . . .

"Our Lessa is a woman of strong emotions, Jaxom —revenge being one of those most highly developed in her. Remember how you came to be Lord here?" Robinton's expression indicated regret for reminding Jaxom of his origin. "I do not belittle the Benden Weyrwoman when I say that. Such perseverance in the face of incredible odds is laudable. But her tenacity over the insult could have a disastrous effect on all Pern. So far, reason has prevailed but currently that balance is shaky indeed."

Jaxom nodded, perceiving that he could never admit to his part, relieved that he had not blurted out his adventure to Lytol. No one must ever know that he, Jaxom, had returned the egg. Particularly Lessa. He sent a silent command to Ruth, who drowsily replied that he was too tired to talk to anyone about anything and couldn't he please sleep?

"Yes," Jaxom said in reply to Robinton, "I quite understand the need for discretion."

"There is another event," Robinton's mobile face drew into a sorrowful grimace as he sought the proper word, "an event which will shortly compound our problems." He glanced at N'ton. "D'ram."

"I think you're right, Robinton," the bronze rider said. "He's unlikely to remain Weyrleader if Fanna dies."

"If? I'm afraid we must say when. And, according to what Master Oldive told me, the sooner it happens, the kinder it will be."

"I didn't know that Fanna was ill," Jaxom said, and his thoughts leaped ahead to the sorrowful knowledge that Fanna's queen, Mirath, would suicide when her Weyrwoman died. A queen's death would upset every dragon—and Lessa and Ramoth!

Lytol's expression was bleak, as it always was whenever he was reminded of his own dragon's death. Jaxom swallowed the remainder of his pride and dismay about apprenticing as a weyrling; he would never risk injuring Ruth again.

"Fanna's been declining gradually," Robinton was saying, "a wasting sickness that nothing seems to halt. Master Oldive is at Ista with her now."

"Yes, his fire-lizard will summon me when he's ready to leave. I want to be available to D'ram," N'ton said.

"Fire-lizards, yes, hmmm," said Robinton. "Another sore subject at Benden Weyr." He glanced at his bronze, perched contentedly on his shoulder. "I felt naked without Zair at that Hatching. Upon my word!" He stared at his somnolent bronze, then over to N'ton's Tris, drowsy-eyed on the rider's arm. "They've calmed down!"

"Ruth's here," N'ton said, stroking Tris. "They feel safe with him."

"No, that isn't it," Menolly said, her eyes resting on Jaxom's face. "They were worried even with Ruth. But that wild restlessness is gone. No more visions of the egg!" She peered sideways at her little queen. "I suppose that makes sense. It's Hatched and healthy. Whatever was plaguing them hasn't happened. Or," she stared at Jaxom suddenly, "or has it?"

Jaxom affected surprise and confusion.

"They were worried about the egg hatching, Menolly?" Robinton asked. "Too bad we can't tell Lessa how concerned they've all been. It might help restore them to her good graces."

"I think it's high time something was done about fire-lizards," Menolly said severely.

"My dear girl . . ." Robinton was surprised.

"I don't mean ours, Master Robinton. They've proved to be extremely useful. Too many people take them for granted and make no effort to train them." She gave a peculiar laugh. "As Jaxom can vouch. They congregate wherever Ruth goes till he's driven *between* by their attentions. Isn't that right, Jaxom?" There was a strange quality about her gaze that puzzled him.

"I wouldn't say he objects . . . most of the time, Menolly," he replied coolly, casually stretching his long legs under the table. "But a fellow likes a little time to himself, you know."

Lytol gave a knowing snort which told Jaxom that Brand had had a word with the Warder about Corana.

"Why? To chew firestone?" N'ton asked, grinning.

"Was that what you were doing with your . . . time, Jaxom?" Menolly asked him, her eyes wide, affecting innocent inquiry.

"You might say so."

"Do the fire-lizards really present you with problems?" Robinton asked, "in their preference for Ruth's company?"

"Well, sir," Jaxom replied, "no matter where we go, every fire-lizard in the vicinity pops in to see Ruth. Generally it's no bother because they keep Ruth amused if I'm busy with Hold matters."

"They wouldn't by any chance have told Ruth why they've been troubled? Or did you know about those images?" Robinton leaned forward, eager to have Jaxom's answer.

"You mean fire-lizards being flamed? The dark nothingness and the egg? Oh yes, they've been driving Ruth frantic with that nonsense," said Jaxom. He scowled as if annoyed for his friend, and was careful not to look in Menolly's direction. "But that seems to have passed. Perhaps the disturbance was connected with the stolen egg. But it's hatched now and look, they're not the least bit as agitated as they've been, and they're letting Ruth sleep by himself again."

"Where were you when the egg was being Hatched?" Menolly pounced on Jaxom so swiftly with her question that Robinton and N'ton regarded her with surprise.

"Why," and Jaxom laughed as he touched his scored cheek, "trying to sear Thread!"

His ready answer threw Menolly into quiet confusion while Robinton, Lytol and N'ton all had another go at him for his foolhardiness. He endured the scolding in good part because it kept Menolly from plaguing him. She'd been suspicious after all. He wished that he could tell her the truth. Of all the people on Pern, she was the only one he could trust now that he knew how infinitely wiser it was to let everyone else believe a Southern dragonrider had returned the egg. He was discontented, though, because it would be a relief, a pleasure, to be able to tell *someone* what he'd done.

Food was served them and they kept the discussions to the problem of the fire-lizards—whether they were more nuisance than valuable—until Jaxom pointed out that everyone about the table was converted. What they needed was a way to pacify Lessa and Ramoth.

"Ramoth will forget her aggravation soon enough," N'ton said.

"Lessa won't, although I doubt there'll be that much reason for me to send Zair to Benden Weyr."

As N'ton and Lytol vigorously reassured the Harper, Jaxom realized there was a curious restraint about the man, an odd note in his voice when he mentioned Benden or the Weyrwoman. Robinton wasn't worried simply that Lessa had prohibited fire-lizards at Benden.

"There's another aspect of this affair that is nagging at the back of my overactive imagination," Robinton said. "The matter has brought Southern to everyone's attention."

"Why is that a problem?" Lytol asked.

Robinton took a sip of his wine, delaying his answer as he savored the taste. "Just this: these recent events have made everyone realize that that huge continent is occupied by a mere handful of people."

"So?"

"I know some restless Lord Holders whose halls are crowded, whose cots are jammed. And the Weyrs, instead of protecting the inviolability of the Southern Continent, were half-set to force their way in. What's to prevent the Lord Holders from taking the initiative and claiming whole portions of it?"

"There wouldn't be dragons enough to protect that much area, that's what," Lytol said. "The Oldtimers surely wouldn't."

"They don't really need dragonriders in the South," Robinton said slowly.

Lytol stared at him, aghast at such a statement.

"It's true," he said. "The land is thoroughly sowed by grubs. Traders have told me that they more or less ignore Falls; Holder Toric just makes certain everyone's safe and all stock is under cover."

"There will come a time when no dragonriders will be needed in the North either," N'ton said, slowly, compounding Lytol's shock.

"Dragonriders will always be needed on Pern while

there is Thread!" Lytol emphasized his conviction by banging the table with his fist.

"At least in our lifetimes," Robinton said soothingly. "But I could have wished less interest in Southern. Think it over, Lytol."

"More of your thinking ahead, Robinton?" Lytol asked, a sour note in his voice and a jaundiced expression on his face.

"Looking ahead is far more constructive than looking behind," said Robinton. He held his clenched fist up. "I'd all the facts in my grasp and I couldn't see the water for the waves."

"You've been down to the Southern Continent often, Masterharper?"

Robinton gave Lytol a long considering look. "I have. Discreetly, I assure you. There are some things that must be seen to be believed."

"Such as?"

Robinton idly stroked Zair as he gazed out, over Lytol's head, at some distant view.

"Mind you, there are times when looking back can be helpful," he said and then turned back to the Lord Warder. "Are you aware that we originally, all of us, came from the Southern Continent?"

Lytol's first surprise at such a sudden turn of the conversation melded into a thoughtful frown. "Yes, that was implicit in the oldest Records."

"I've often wondered if there aren't older Records, moldering somewhere in the South."

Lytol snorted at the notion. "Moldering is right. There'd be nothing left after so many thousands of Turns."

"They had ways of tempering metal, those ancestors of ours, ways that made it impervious to rust and wear. Those plates found at Fort Weyr, the instruments, like the long-distance viewer that fascinates Wansor and Fandarel. I don't believe that time can have erased all traces of such clever people."

Jaxom glanced at Menolly, recalling hints that she'd let slip. Her eyes were sparkling with suppressed excitement. She knew something that the Harper wasn't saying. Jaxom looked then at the Fort Weyrleader and realized that N'ton knew all about this.

"The Southern Continent was ceded to the dissident Oldtimers," Lytol said heavily.

"And they have already broken their side of the agreement," N'ton said.

"Is that any reason for us to break ours?" Lytol asked, drawing his shoulders back and scowling at both Weyrleader and Harper.

"They occupy only a small tongue of land, jutting out into the Southern Sea," said Robinton in his smooth way. "They have been unaware of any activity elsewhere."

"You've already been exploring in the South?"

"Judiciously. Judiciously."

"And you'd not have your . . . judicious intrusions discovered?"

"No," answered Robinton slowly. "I shall make the knowledge public soon enough. I don't want every disgruntled apprentice and evicted small holder running about indiscriminately, destroying what should be preserved because they haven't the wit to understand it."

"What have you discovered so far?"

"Old mine workings, shored up with lightweight but so durable a material that it is as unscratched today as when it was put in place in the shaft. Tools, powered by who can guess—bits and pieces that not even young Benelek can assemble."

There was a long silence which Lytol broke with a snort. "Harpers! Harpers are supposed to instruct the young."

"*And* first and foremost, to preserve our heritage!"

CHAPTER VIII

Ruatha Hold, Fort Weyr, Fidello's Hold, 15.6.3–15.6.17

JAXOM WAS DISAPPOINTED that all Lytol's coaxing could not draw more facts from the Harper about his explorations in the South. At the point where Jaxom's fatigue made it difficult for him to keep his eyes open, it occurred to him that Robinton had indeed succeeded in rousing Lytol to support his and N'ton's desire to keep interest in the South to a minimum.

Jaxom's last waking thought was one of admiration for the Harper's devious methods. No wonder he had not objected to Jaxom training with N'ton when he saw Lytol was in favor of it. The Harper needed the older man as the Lord Holder at Ruatha. Training Ruth to chew firestone kept the young Lord from wanting to take Hold in Lytol's place.

The next morning Jaxom was positive that he couldn't have moved during the night. He was bindingly stiff, his face and shoulder stung with the Threadscore and that reminded him of Ruth's injury. With no regard for his own discomfort, he whipped aside the furs and, grabbing the numbweed pot as he went, burst into Ruth's weyr.

The faintest rumble told him that the white dragon was still sound asleep. He also seemed not to have moved for his leg was propped in the same position.

That made it easier for Jaxom to work and he smeared a new coating of numbweed along the line of the score. Only then did it occur to Jaxom that he and Ruth might have to wait until they'd healed before they could join the weyrlings at Fort Weyr.

Lytol did not share his thought. The reason Jaxom was going to Fort Weyr was to avoid scoring, to learn how to take care of his dragon and himself during Threadfall. If he got teased because he hadn't ducked fast enough, he deserved it. So, after breaking his fast, Jaxom flew Ruth to the Weyr.

Fortunately two of those in training were near his own age of eighteen Turns—not that being older would have bothered Jaxom as long as he could train Ruth properly. He did have to suppress the insidious urge to excuse Ruth's scoring with the real reason for the supposed clumsiness. He took refuge in knowing that he had achieved more than they'd ever guess—a small consolation.

His first problem in the weyrling class was to relieve Ruth of the embarrassment of the endless fire-lizards that settled on him. No sooner was one group dislodged and sent off than another appeared, to the disgust and exasperation of K'nebel, the weyrlingmaster.

"Does this go on all day wherever you are?" the man asked Jaxom irritably.

"More or less. They just . . . come. Especially since . . . what happened at Benden Weyr."

K'nebel snorted his aggravation even as he nodded his understanding. "I don't like to put truth to these notions that dragons flamed fire-lizards, but you'll never get Ruth going if the fire-lizards don't leave him alone. And if they don't leave him alone, one of 'em will get flamed!"

So Jaxom had Ruth shoo the fire-lizards away as quickly as they arrived. It took time before Ruth remained unencumbered for any appreciable period. Then, either all the fire-lizards in the vicinity had looked in, or Ruth had been sufficiently firm and the rest of the morning's class was undisrupted.

Despite all the interruptions, K'nebel kept the weyrlings working until the noonday meal was called. Jaxom was invited to stay and, as a mark of his rank, was shown to the large table reserved for senior dragonriders.

The conversation was dominated by continued speculation about the return of the egg and which one of the queen riders had returned it. The discussions served to reinforce Jaxom's decision to remain silent. He cautioned Ruth, needlessly it appeared, since the white dragon was more interested in chewing firestone and dodging Thread than in past events.

The fire-lizards about him had lost all their previous agitation. Their primary concern now was eating, the secondary one was their hides. With the advent of the warmer weather, they had begun shedding and were plagued by itching. The images they projected to Ruth no longer had alarming content.

Since he was engaged at Fort Weyr in the mornings, Jaxom had to forego the classes at the Harper and Smith crafthalls. That meant he wouldn't have to endure Menolly's tendency to ask searching questions, and he was well pleased. He was also heartily amused when he realized that Lyton was leaving him several uncommitted hours in the afternoons. Obligingly he and Ruth took off for the Plateau Hold to see how the new wheat was prospering—of course.

Corana was about the hold these days since her brother's wife was near her time. When she showed a pretty concern for his healing score, he did not abuse her notion that he'd acquired it in a legitimate Fall, protecting the Hold from Thread. She rewarded him for that protection in a fashion that embarrassed him even as it relieved him. He'd as soon save his favors for honest endeavor. But he couldn't be annoyed with her when, in the languor that followed their pleasure, she made several references to fire-lizards and asked if he'd ever had a chance to find a clutch when he was fighting Thread.

"Every beach in the North is well staked," he told her and, noting her intense disappointment, added,

"Of course, there are lots of empty beaches in the Southern Continent!"

"Could you fly in on your Ruth without those Old-timers knowing?" Clearly Corana knew little of the most recent events, another relief to Jaxom, who was beginning to be bored by the Weyr's preoccupation with that topic.

Fly in on Ruth made the whole thing seem simple enough; especially as Ruth would not upset strange fire-lizards since he had apparently made friends with them all.

"I suppose I could." His hesitation was due to the complications of planning an absence long enough to allow him to go South. Corana misconstrued what he said, and again, he was too tenderhearted and too gratified to correct her.

As he and Ruth winged homeward from the Plateau, it occurred to Jaxom that the ripples from his initial outburst just a short while ago were still spreading. He had finally achieved proper training for Ruth and, if he hadn't taken Hold, at least he was finally enjoying more of the prerogatives of a Lord Holder. He grinned, savoring Corana's sweetness. Judging by her sister's warm welcome, he assumed the Plateau Hold would not object to a half-blooded addition. Success in that area would do him no harm in the eyes of Lord Holders. He considered bringing Corana to the Hold, but decided against it. That would be unfair to the other fosterlings and cause trouble for Brand and Lytol. It wasn't as if he didn't have Ruth and couldn't come and go at his leisure and speedily. Furthermore, if he brought Corana to his quarters, she'd demand more of his attention at Ruth's expense than he was willing to give.

The third afternoon he went to the Plateau Hold, Fidello's wife was in labor and Corana too distracted to do more than beg his pardon for the fuss and excitement. He asked if they wished the Hold's healer, but Fidello said that one of his dependents was skillful in such matters and had said that his wife would have no trouble with the birth. Jaxom made all the appropriate remarks, then left, feeling slightly put off by this unanticipated obstacle to his expectations.

Why are you laughing? Ruth asked as they winged back to the Hold.

"Because I'm a fool, Ruth. I'm a fool."

I don't think you are. She makes you feel good, not a fool.

"That's why I'm a fool now, silly dragon. I went up there expecting . . . expecting to feel good and she's too busy. And only a few sevendays ago I wouldn't have dreamed I'd be as lucky with her. That's why I'm a fool now, Ruth."

I will always love you, was Ruth's reply because he felt that was the response Jaxom needed.

Jaxom reassuringly caressed his dragon's neck ridge, but he couldn't suppress his self-deprecatory mirth. He discovered a second obstacle when he returned to the Hold. Lytol informed him that the remainder of Ramoth's clutch would probably Hatch the next day, and that Jaxom would have to put in an appearance at Benden. The Lord Warder peered intently at Jaxom's healed score and nodded.

"Do try to keep out of the Weyrleaders' sight. They'd know at a glance what that was," Lytol said. "No sense advertising your folly."

Jaxom privately thought the scar gave him a more mature appearance but he promised Lytol he'd stay well away from Lessa and F'lar.

Jaxom rather enjoyed Hatchings, more so when Lytol was not present. He felt guilty about that but he knew that, at each Hatching, painful memories of Lytol's beloved Larth tortured the man.

News of the imminent Hatching came to Fort Weyr while Jaxom was flying wing tip in weyrling Fall practice. He finished the maneuver, begged the weyrlingmaster's pardon and took Ruth *between* to Ruatha so that he could change into proper clothing. Lytol along with Menolly's Rocky reached him at the same moment and requested that he collect Menolly, since Robinton was already at Ista Weyr with the Harperhall's dragon and rider.

Jaxom put a good face on the request since he could think of no excuse to refuse. Well, he'd hurry her out of the Hall and into the Weyr so quickly that she wouldn't have time to ask any questions.

When he and Ruth arrived at the Harpercrafthall, Ruth bellowing his name to the watchdragon on the fire-heights, Jaxom became furious. Why, there were enough Fort Weyr dragons on the meadow to take half the Hall. Why hadn't she asked one of them? He was determined that she wouldn't have a chance to nag at him and asked Ruth peremptorily to tell her fire-lizards that he was here and waiting in the meadow. He had barely formed the words in his mind when Menolly came dashing out of the archway toward him, Beauty, Rocky and Diver chittering in circles above her head. She began shrugging into her riding jacket, awkwardly juggling something from one hand to the other.

"Get down, Jaxom," she ordered imperiously. "I can't do it when your back's to me."

"Do what?"

"This!" She held up one hand to show him a small pot. "Get down."

"Why?"

"Don't be dense. You're wasting time. This is to cover that scar. You don't want Lessa and F'lar to see it, do you, and ask awkward questions? Come down! Or we'll be late. And you're not supposed to time it, are you?" She added the last comment as he still hesitated, not altogether reassured by her altruism.

"I've got my hair brushed over—"

"You'll forget and push it back," she said, gesturing him to do so now as she unscrewed the pot lid. "I got Oldive to make some without scent. There. Only takes a dab." She had applied it to his face and then brushed the residue on the skin of his wrist above his glove. "See? It blends in." She stared critically at him. "Yes, that does the trick. No one would ever know you've been scored." Then she chuckled. "What does Corana think of your scar?"

"Corana?"

"Don't glare at me. Get up on Ruth. We'll be late.

Very clever of you, Jaxom, to cultivate Corana.
You'd've made a good harper with your wits."

Jaxom mounted his dragon, furious with her but
determined not to rise to her lure. It was just like
her to find out such things, hoping to aggravate him.
Well, she wasn't going to succeed.

"Thanks for thinking of the salve, Menolly," he said
when he got his voice under control. "It certainly
wouldn't do to annoy Lessa right now, and I do have
to be at this Hatching."

"Indeed you do."

Her tone was loaded but he'd no time to figure out
what she meant as Ruth took them up and, with no
further direction, *between* to Benden Weyr. No, he
wouldn't let her rouse him. But she was bloody clever,
this Harper girl.

Ruth came out of *between* midsyllable. " . . . *uth.
I'm Ruth. I'm Ruth.*"

Which reminded Jaxom and he twisted his head
about to look at Menolly's left shoulder.

"Don't worry. They're safely in Brekke's weyr."

"All of them?"

"Shells, no, Jaxom. Only Beauty and the three
bronzes. She may be mating soon and the boys won't
leave her alone for a moment." Menolly chuckled
again.

"Are all that clutch spoken for?"

"What? Count the eggs before they're laid? Not at
all!" Menolly sounded repressive. "Why? You don't
want one, do you?"

"Not I."

Menolly burst out laughing at his telling rejoinder and he groaned. Well, let her have her laugh.

"What would I do with a fire-lizard?" he went on
to settle her. "I promised Corana I'd see if I could
get one for her. She's been very . . . kind to me, you
know." He was rewarded by the sound of Menolly's
gulp of surprise.

Then she smacked him across the shoulder blade
with her closed fist and he winced, then ducked away
from her.

"Leave off, Menolly! I've a score on that shoulder, too." He spoke with more irritation than he meant and then cursed himself for reminding her of what he avoided mentioning.

"I am sorry, Jaxom," she said with such contrition that Jaxom was mollified. "How much scoring did you get?"

"Face, shoulder and thigh."

She caught at his other shoulder. "Listen! They're thrumming wildly. And, look, there are candidates entering the Hatching Ground. Can we fly right in?"

Jaxom directed Ruth in through the upper entrance of the Hatching Ground. Bronzes were still bearing visitors to the Ground. As Ruth entered, Jaxom found his gaze going immediately to the spot by the arch where he and Ruth had transferred to return the egg. He felt a sudden surge of pride at his feat.

"I see Robinton, Jaxom. There on the fourth tier. Near the Istan colors. Would you sit with us, Jaxom?" There was an entreaty in her tone, and a slight emphasis that puzzled Jaxom. Who wouldn't want to sit with the Masterharper of Pern?

Ruth angled close to the tier, catching at the ledge with his claws and hovering long enough to permit Menolly and Jaxom to dismount.

As Jaxom settled his tunic before seating himself, he got a good long look at Master Robinton. He could understand Menolly's entreaty. The Harper seemed different. Oh, he had greeted Jaxom and Menolly brightly enough with a smile for his journeyman and a buffet on the shoulder for Jaxom but he had turned back to his own thoughts which, to judge by his expression, were sad. The Masterharper of Pern had a long face, generally mobile with quick expressions and reaction. Now, while the Harper apparently watched the progress of the young candidates as they moved across the warm sands of the Hatching Ground, his face was lined, his deep-set eyes shadowed with fatigue and worry, the skin of his cheeks and chin sagged. He looked old, tired, and bereft. Jaxom was appalled and looked quickly away, avoiding Menolly's gaze because his thoughts must have been all too apparent to the observant Harper girl.

Master Robinton old? Tired, worried, yes. But ageing? A cold emptiness assailed Jaxom's innards. Pern deprived of the humor and wisdom of the Master Harper? Even harder to contemplate was being without his vision and eager curiosity. Resentment replaced the sense of loss as Jaxom found himself, loyal to Robinton's precepts, trying to rationalize this wave of unpalatable reflection.

An urgent thrumming brought his attention back to the Hatching Ground. He'd been to enough Hatchings to realize that Ramoth's presence, when there was no queen egg, was unusual; her attitude was daunting. He wouldn't have wanted to brave her red whirling eyes, or the stabs of her head as she kept poking toward the oncoming candidates. Instead of fanning out so that they loosely circled the rocking eggs, the boys were in a tight group, as if that way they stood a better chance against her attentions.

"I don't envy them," Menolly said to Jaxom in an undertone.

"Will she let them Impress, sir?" Jaxom asked the Harper, momentarily forgetting his awareness of the man's mortality.

"You'd think she was inspecting each one to see if he smelled of the Southern Weyr, wouldn't you?" the Harper replied, his voice light with humor.

Jaxom glanced at him and wondered if there hadn't been some unflattering trick of lighting for the Harper grinned with mischief, very much his customary self.

"I'm not sure I'd care for such a scrutiny right now," he added, giving his left eyebrow a quirk upward.

Menolly coughed, her eyes dancing. Jaxom supposed they'd been South recently and wondered what they had learned.

Shells, he thought, in a sudden sweaty panic, the Southerners *knew* that none of them had returned the egg. Suppose Robinton had found that out?

An angry hiss from the Hatching Ground brought

such a reaction from the audience that Jaxom quickly transferred his attention. One of the eggs had split, but Ramoth had moved so protectively over it that none of the candidates dared approach. Mnementh bellowed from his ledge outside and the bronzes within thrummed. Ramoth's head went up, her wings, shimmering gold and green, extended and she warbled a defiant answer. The other bronzes answered her in conciliating tones but Mnementh's bugle was clearly an order.

Ramoth is very upset, Ruth said to Jaxom. The white dragon had discreetly retired to a sunny spot by the Bowl lake. His absence did not keep him from knowing what was happening within the Ground. *Mnementh tells her she is being silly. The eggs must Hatch; the Hatchlings must make Impression. Then she will not have to worry about them again. They will be safe with men.*

The croon of the bronzes deepened and Ramoth, still protesting an inevitable cycle of life, stepped slowly away from the eggs. Whereupon one of the older boys who had bravely led the first rank bowed formally to her and then stepped up to the split egg from which a young bronze was emerging, squealing as it tried to balance itself on wobbly legs.

"That boy has good presence of mind," Robinton said, nodding his approbation. He was intent on the scene below. "Just what Ramoth needed, that courtesy. Her eyes are slowing and she's retracting her wings. Good. Good!"

Following the example set, two more of the older candidates bowed to Ramoth and moved quickly toward eggs that had begun rocking violently with the efforts of the Hatchlings to pierce their shells. If subsequent obeisances were jerky or skimped, Ramoth had been mollified although she emitted curious little barks as each dragonet made its Impression.

"Look, he got the bronze! He deserved him!" Robinton said, applauding, as the newly linked pair moved toward the entrance of the Ground.

"Who's the lad?" Menolly asked.

"From Telgar Hold; he's got the build and coloring of the old Lord—and his wits."

"Young Kirnety from Fort Hold has another bronze," Menolly reported, delighted. "I told you he'd do it."

"I have been wrong before and will be again, my dear girl. Infallibility would be a bore," Master Robinton replied equably. "Are there any lads here from Ruatha, Jaxom?"

"Two, but I can't recognize them from this angle."

"It's a good-sized clutch," Robinton replied. "Plenty to choose from."

Jaxom was watching five boys who had circled one large egg covered with green splotches. He caught his breath as the dragonet's head emerged, turning to look at each of the boys as it shook shell fragments from its body. "And many boys disappointed," Jaxom said as the little brown dragon pushed past the five boys, out into the sands, crooning piteously, swinging its head from side to side. What if, Jaxom thought with a pang of cold in his guts, Ruth had not found me suitable? Almost all the candidates had left the Ground when he'd freed Ruth from the overhard shell.

The searching dragonet stumbled, its nose burying into the warm sand. It righted itself, sneezed and cried again. Ramoth called out in warning and the boys nearest her retreated hurriedly. One of them, a dark-haired, long-legged lad whose bony knees were scarred, almost stumbled over the little brown. He caught himself with a wild flailing of his arms, started to back away and then halted, staring at the brown dragon. Impression occurred!

I was there. You were there. We are now together, said Ruth, responding to Jaxom's emotion at that scene. Jaxom blinked away an excess of moisture that collected in his eyes at that reaffirmation of their bond.

"It's all over so soon," Menolly said, her voice

petulant with regret. "I wish it wouldn't all happen in such a rush!"

"I'd say we'd had quite an afternoon," Robinton stated, gesturing toward Ramoth. The queen was now glowering at the retreating pairs and shifting from foreleg to foreleg.

"D'you suppose now that they're all safely Hatched and Impressed, her temper will improve?" Menolly asked.

"And Lessa's as well?" Robinton's lips twitched to suppress his amusement. "No doubt once Ramoth can be persuaded to eat, both will feel more charitable."

"I hope so." Menolly's reply was low and fervent, not meant, Jaxom thought, to be heard by Robinton, for the Harper had turned to the back of the tiers, evidently looking for someone.

Robinton had heard, however, and gave his journeyman a warm grin. "Too bad we can't postpone this meeting until the happy restoration has occurred."

"Can't I come with you this once?"

"To protect me, Menolly?" The Harper gripped her by the shoulder, smiling affectionately. "No, it's not a general meeting and I cannot offend by including you."

"He can come . . ." Menolly jerked her thumb at Jaxom, glaring at him with resentment.

"I can what?"

"You hadn't learned from Lytol that a meeting's been called after the Impression?" the Harper asked. "Ruatha must attend."

"They couldn't exclude you as Masterharper," said Menolly in a tight voice.

"Why would they?" Jaxom asked, surprised by Menolly's uncharacteristic defensiveness.

"Because, you dim glow . . ."

"That's enough, Menolly. I appreciate your concern, but all things come to pass in the fullness of time. My head is neither bloodied or bowed. Once Ramoth has killed, I'll have no fear of being dragon bait, either." Robinton patted her shoulder, reassuringly.

The queen was making her way out of the Hatching Ground and, as they watched, she took wing.

"There, you see. She's gone to feed," the Harper said. "I have nothing to fear anymore."

Menolly gave him a long sardonic look. "I just wish I could be with you, that's all."

"I know. Ah, Fandarel," The Harper raised his voice and waved to catch the eye of the big Mastersmith. "Come, Lord Jaxom, we've business in the Council Chamber."

This must be what Lytol had meant by his being required to attend the Hatching. But oughtn't Lytol to have been there if the meeting was as important as Menolly intimated? Jaxom was flattered by his guardian's confidence.

The two Masters, having met on their way down the tiers, attached other Craftmasters who nodded greetings with more solemnity than a Hatching generally occasioned. Menolly's hint that this was to be an unusual meeting was reinforced. Again Jaxom wondered that Lytol was not here. He had, Jaxom knew, agreed to support Robinton.

"Thought Ramoth was going to prevent Impression for a moment there," Fandarel said, nodding at Jaxom. "Hear you've deserted me for your favorite pastime, huh, lad?"

"Training only, Master Fandarel. All dragons must learn to chew firestone."

"Upon my soul," Masterminer Nicat exclaimed. "Never thought he'd live long enough to do that."

Jaxom caught the Masterharper's warning expression as he was about to reply with some heat, and rephrased his answer. "Ruth is very good at it, thank you."

"One forgets the passage of time, Master Nicat," Robinton said, smoothly, "and that growth and maturity come to those we remember first as very young. Ah, Andemon, how are you today?" The Harper beckoned to the Masterfarmer to join them as they made their way across the hot sands.

Nicat fell in beside Jaxom, chuckling. "Teaching

the little white to chew firestone, huh? That wouldn't happen to be why some of our supplies appear short in the morning?"

"Master Nicat, I'm training at Fort Weyr and have all the firestone Ruth needs there."

"Training at Fort Weyr, are you?" Nicat's grin widened as his eyes flicked to Jaxom's cheek, stayed and moved on. "With dragonriders, huh, Lord Jaxom?" There was the barest stress of the title before Nicat looked ahead at the steps up to the queen's weyr and the ledge where Mnementh generally perched.

The bronze had gone off to watch his queen feed in the meadow below. Jaxom looked for the white hide of Ruth by the lake and felt his dragon's mental presence.

"Good Hatching, with a nice bit of suspense for starters, huh?" Nicat said conversationally.

"Did you have any lads on the Ground today?" Jaxom asked politely.

"Only one this time. Two lads had already gone to Telgar's last Hatching so no complaints. No complaints. Although, if you've a clutch of fire-lizard eggs going a-begging, I wouldn't say no to a couple."

Nicat's gaze was guileless, and it certainly would be no hair off his hide if Jaxom chose to teach Ruth to chew firestone and had appropriated sacks from the mines.

"We've none presently, but you never can tell when a clutch'll be found."

"I only mention it in passing. They're pure death for those pesky, ruinous tunnel snakes, not to mention being very clever about discovering gas pockets *we* don't smell. And gas pockets is about all we're mining at present."

The Masterminer sounded depressed and worried. Jaxom wondered what was in the air these days to produce such a general atmosphere of anxiety and sorrow. He'd always liked Master Nicat and, during their lessons in the mines, had come to respect the short heavyset craftmaster whose face was still black-pored from working as an apprentice below the ground. As they climbed the stone steps to the queen's weyr, Jaxom wished again that he wasn't bound by that promise to N'ton not to time it. He had too many demands on ordinary daytime to risk a hop *between* to the Southern beaches although Ruth might be lucky enough to locate a clutch quickly. He would like to oblige Master Nicat; he'd also like to find an egg for Corana. It also wouldn't hurt to indulge the disgruntled Tegger, who might have learned how to keep a fire-lizard now. But there was no way, short of timing it, that Jaxom could complete a trip south right now.

Just as they reached the entrance, a bronze dragon appeared above the Star Stones, bugling. The watch-dragon replied. Jaxom noticed that everyone had stopped stock still to hear the exchange. Shells and shards, but they were nervous here in Benden. He wondered who had arrived.

The Weyrleader from Ista, Ruth told him.

D'ram? It wasn't incumbent on other Weyrleaders to attend Hatchings, though generally, unless Thread-fall was imminent in their own area, they did come—especially to Benden. Jaxom had already spotted N'ton, R'mart of Telgar Weyr, G'narish of Igen, T'bor of the High Reaches among those gathered. Then he remembered the Master Harper's talk about D'ram's Weyrwoman, Fanna. Was she worse?

When they reached the Council Chamber, Nicat parted from him. Jaxom took one look at Lessa, seated in the Weyrwoman's huge stone chair, her face intense in its frown, and he quickly moved to the far corner of the room. Her keen eyes wouldn't be able to spot the score on his cheek at that distance.

This was not to be a large meeting, the Harper had said. Jaxom watched the Mastercraftsmen file in, the other Weyrleaders, the major Lord Holders, but there were no weyrwomen or wing-seconds except for Brekke and F'nor.

D'ram arrived in the company of F'lar and a younger man Jaxom didn't recognize though he wore wing-second colors. If Jaxom had been upset by the glimpse of the Masterharper's ageing, he was shocked by the change in D'ram's appearance. The man seemed to have shrunk in the past Turn to a husk, dried up and frail. The Istan Weyrleader's step was jerky and his shoulders rounded.

Lessa rose in one of her swift graceful gestures and went to meet the Istan, her hands outstretched, her expression unexpectedly compassionate. Jaxom had had the impression that she had been totally immersed in her brooding. Now, all her attention was centered on D'ram.

"We're all assembled as you asked, D'ram," Lessa said, pulling him to the chair beside her and pouring him a cup of wine.

D'ram thanked her for the wine and welcome, took a sip but, instead of seating himself, he turned to face the meeting. Jaxom could see that his face was marred by lines of fatigue as well as of age.

"Most of you already know my situation and Fanna's . . . illness," he said in a low hesitant voice. He cleared his throat, took a deep breath. "I wish to step down now as Istan Weyrleader. None of our queens is due to mate but I have no heart to continue longer. My Weyr has agreed. G'dened," and D'ram indicated the man who had accompanied him, "has led the past ten Falls on his Barnath. I should have stepped down sooner but . . ." he shook his head, smiling sadly, "we so hoped the illness would pass." He straightened his shoulders with an effort. "Caylith is oldest queen and Cosira a good Weyrwoman. Barnath has flown Caylith already and there's been a large strong clutch to prove them." Now he hesitated, glancing warily at Lessa. "It was the custom in the Oldtime, when a Weyr was leaderless, to throw open the first queen's flight in that Weyr to all young bronzes. In this fashion a new leader was fairly chosen. I would invoke that custom now." He said it almost belligerently and yet his manner toward Lessa was entreating.

"You must be very sure of G'dened's Barnath then,"

R'mart of Telgar Weyr said in a disgusted tone of voice that rose over the startled murmurs.

G'dened, grinning broadly, managed to avoid meeting anyone's glance.

"I want the best leadership for Ista," D'ram said, stiffly, resenting R'mart's implication of a token flight. "G'dened has proved his competence to my satisfaction. But he ought to prove it to everyone's."

"That's fairly put." F'lar rose to his feet, holding up his hands for silence. "I don't doubt G'dened has a good chance, R'mart, but D'ram's offer is exceedingly generous at this critical time. I'll inform all my bronze riders but I, for one, will permit only those whose dragons haven't yet had a chance to mate with a queen. I don't think it's fair to pile too many odds against Barnath, now is it?"

"Isn't Caylith a Benden queen?" Lord Corman of Keroon Hold asked.

"No, she's one of Mirath's laying. Pirith is the Benden Hatched queen."

"Caylith's an Oldtimer queen?"

"Caylith is an Istan queen," F'lar said firmly but quickly.

"And G'dened?"

"I was born in the old time," the man said in a quiet voice but the expression he turned to Lord Corman bore no trace of apology.

"He is also a son of D'ram," Lord Warbret of Ista Hold said, speaking directly to Lord Corman as if that qualification should ease the Holder's tacit objection.

"Good man. Good blood," Corman replied, not at all ruffled.

"His leadership is in question, not his bloodline," F'lar said. "The custom is a good one . . ."

Jaxom clearly heard someone remark that it was the only good Oldtime custom he'd ever heard about, and he hoped that the low whisper hadn't carried far.

"D'ram would be within his right to keep to the Weyr for leadership," F'lar continued, addressing the craftmasters and Lord Holders. "I, for one, deeply appreciate his offer and the willingness of the Weyr to open the mating flight."

"I only want the best leadership for my Weyr," D'ram repeated. "This is the only way to be certain Ista gets it. The only way, the only right way."

Jaxom suppressed the urge to cheer and glanced about the room, willing the reactions to be favorable. All the Weyrleaders seemed to agree. As they should, since one of their riders might gain from it. Jaxom hoped that G'dened's Barnath would fly Caylith anyhow. That would prove there was good metal in the younger Oldtimers. No one would be able to say anything against Ista leadership once it was proved by competition!

"I have stated Ista's intention," D'ram said, raising his tired voice over the murmur of individual conversations. "It is the will of my Weyr. I must go back now. My duty to you, Lords, Masters, Weyrleaders, all."

He gave a quick sweeping nod to everyone, bowed more formally to Lessa, who rose, touched his arm in sympathy and let him pass.

To Jaxom's surprise and elation, everyone rose as D'ram left, but the Istan Weyrleader's head remained down. Jaxom wondered if he'd been aware of that spontaneous show of respect and felt a lump rise in his throat.

"I will take my leave as well, in case I'm needed," G'dened said, bowing formally to Benden's leaders and the others.

"G'dened?" Lessa incorporated a wealth of question in his name.

The man shook his head slowly. "I will inform all the Weyrs when Caylith is ready to fly." He quickly followed D'ram.

As the sound of his footsteps diminished down the corridor, voices began to rise. The Lord Holders weren't certain they approved of such an innovation. The Craftmasters were apparently divided, though Jaxom rather thought Robinton had known of D'ram's decision and was neutral. The Weyrleaders expressed complete satisfaction.

"Hope Fanna doesn't expire today," Jaxom heard a Craftmaster murmur to his neighbor. "A death at a Hatching is a bad sign."

"Besides spoiling the feast. I wonder just how strong G'dened's bronze is. Now if a Benden bronze rider got into Ista . . ."

Speaking of the feast reminded Jaxom that his stomach was roiling for lack of food. He'd been up early for his training as usual, and had had no more than time to change into good clothing at his Hold so he began to sidle to the exit. He could always coax a meatroll or a sweetbread from one of the Lower Cavern women to stay his hunger.

"Is this all the meeting there is?" Lord Begamon of Nerat Hold asked, his rasping voice falling into a momentary silence. He sounded peevish. "Haven't the Weyrs yet found out who took the egg? Even who returned it? That's what I thought we'd hear today."

"The egg was returned, Lord Begamon," F'lar said, extending his hand to Lessa.

"I know the egg was returned. I was right here when it happened. Was at its Hatching, too."

F'lar continued to lead Lessa down the length of the room.

"This is another Hatching, Lord Begamon," F'lar said. "A happy occasion for all of us. There will be wine below." And the two Weyrleaders had left the room.

"I don't understand." Begamon turned in confusion to the man beside him. "I thought we'd learn something today."

"You did," F'nor said, guiding Brekke past him. "That D'ram is stepping down as Weyrleader at Ista."

"That doesn't concern me," Begamon was growing more, rather than less, annoyed with the replies he was getting.

"That concerns you more than any puzzle over the egg," F'nor said as he and Brekke left the room.

"I think that's all the answer you're going to get," Robinton said to Begamon, a wry smile on his face.

"But . . . but aren't they doing anything about it? They're not just letting the Oldtimers insult them like that and not doing something?"

"Unlike Lord Holders," N'ton said, coming forward, "dragonriders are not free to indulge their passions or honors at the expense of their primary duty, which is to protect all of Pern from Thread. *That* is the important occupation of dragonriders, Lord Begamon."

"C'mon, Begamon," Lord Groghe of Fort Hold said as he took the man by the arm. "It's Weyr business, not ours, you know. Can't interfere. Shouldn't. They know what they're doing. And the egg was returned. Too bad about D'ram's woman. Hate to see him go. Sensible fellow. F'lar didn't say but it must be Benden wine."

Jaxom saw Lord Groghe searching the faces about him.

"Ah, Harper, it ought to be Benden wine here?"

The Harper agreed and left the Council room in the company of the two Lords, Begamon still protesting the lack of information. Jaxom followed them out as the room was clearing. When he got to the base of the weyr steps, Menolly pounced on him.

"Well, what happened? Did they speak to him at all?"

"Did who speak to whom?"

"Did F'lar or Lessa address the Harper?"

"No reason why they would."

"Plenty of reason why they wouldn't. What happened?"

Jaxom sighed for patience with her as he rapidly reviewed what had occurred.

"D'ram came here to ask—no, to tell them that he's stepping down as Istan Weyrleader . . ." Menolly nodded encouragingly as if this were no news to her. "And he said he was invoking an Oldtime custom to throw the first queen's mating flight open to all bronzes."

Menolly's eyes widened and she made her mouth round with surprise. "That must have rocked 'em back on their heels. Any protests?"

"From the Lord Holders, yes." Jaxom grinned. "From the other Weyrleaders, no. Except that R'mart made a snide remark about G'dened being so strong there'd be no contest."

"I don't know G'dened, but he's a son of D'ram's."

"That doesn't always mean anything."

"True."

"D'ram kept saying that he wanted the best leadership for Ista Weyr and this was the way to achieve it."

"Poor D'ram . . ."

"Poor Fanna, you mean."

"No, poor D'ram. Poor us. He was very strong as a leader. Did Master Robinton speak at all?" she asked then, throwing off her reflections on D'ram for the more important consideration.

"He spoke to Begamon."

"Not to the Weyrleaders?"

"No reason to. Why?"

"They've been such close friends for so long . . . and they're so unfair about it. He had to speak up. Dragons can't fight dragons."

To which Jaxom stoutly agreed, his comment echoed by a rumble from his stomach so audible that Menolly glared at him. Jaxom was torn between embarrassment and amusement at such an internal betrayal. The laughter won and, even as he apologized to Menolly, he could see that the incident had triggered her sense of the ridiculous.

"Oh, come on. I won't get any sense out of you until you've eaten."

It was not the most memorable of Hatching feasts nor particularly merry. A restraint touched the dragonriders. Jaxom did not try to figure out how much was due to D'ram's resignation or how much to the theft of the egg. He preferred not to hear any more about that. He was uncomfortable in Menolly's company because he couldn't put aside his feeling that she knew he'd brought the egg back. The fact that

The White Dragon

she said nothing about her suspicions worried him more because he also felt that she was leaving him in suspense on purpose. He didn't particularly wish to share a table with F'lessan and Mirrim, who might notice the Threadscore. Benelek was not his choice of a companion at any time and he certainly wouldn't have been at ease taking the place at the main tables to which his rank entitled him. Menolly had been dragged away from him by Oharan, the Weyr's Harper, and he could hear them singing. Had there been new music he might have stayed by them, just to be part of some group. But the Lord Holders were asking for their favorite songs and so were the proud parents of boys who had Impressed.

Ruth was enjoying the emotional feast of the newly Hatched dragons but he did miss the ministrations of the fire-lizards.

They don't like being cooped up in Brekke's weyr, Ruth told his rider. *Why can't they come out? Ramoth's asleep with a very full belly. She wouldn't even know.*

"Don't be too sure of that," Jaxom said, glancing up at Mnementh, curled on the queen's ledge, his softly glowing eyes bright points on the other side of the darkening Weyr Bowl.

The outcome was that he and Ruth left the feast as soon after eating as courtesy permitted. While they were circling in to Ruatha Hold Jaxom began to worry about Lytol. His guardian would be extremely upset when Fanna died and her queen suicided. He wished he didn't have to bring the news of D'ram's resignation. He knew that Lytol respected the Oldtimer. He wondered what Lytol's reaction would be to the open mating flight.

Lytol merely grunted, gave a sharp nod of his head and asked Jaxom if any further development over the theft of the egg had been discussed. For Jaxom's recital of Lord Begamon's complaint, Lytol issued another sort of grunt, disgusted and contemptuous. Then he asked if there were any fire-lizard eggs available;

156

two more small holders had been pressing him for eggs. Jaxom said he'd ask N'ton in the morning.

"Considering the bad odor of fire-lizards, I wonder anyone wants them," the Fort Weyrleader remarked the next day when Jaxom told him his errand. "Or maybe that's why there's so many requests. Everyone is convinced no one else will want 'em, so they get in there now. No, I don't have any. But I wanted to speak with you. Fort Weyr flies with the High Reaches Weyr tomorrow during the northernly Fall. If it were over Ruatha, I'd ask you to join the weyrling wing. As it is, I'd better not. Can you understand?"

Jaxom allowed that he could, but did N'ton mean that he would be able to fight Ruth the next time Thread was over Ruatha.

"I discussed it with Lytol." N'ton grinned, his eyes twinkling. "Lytol's reasoning is that you'd be so far above ground no Ruathan would realize his Lord Holder was risking his life and word wouldn't get back to Benden."

"I risk my life and limbs far more surely on the ground with that flamethrower crew."

"Quite likely, but we still don't want someone blurting the truth out to Lessa and F'lar. I've had a good report of you from K'nebel. Ruth is all you told me he could be—fast, clever and unusually quick in the air." N'ton grinned again. "Between you and me, K'nebel says the little beast changes direction on his tail. His chief concern is that some of the others might get the notion that their dragons can do the same thing, and we'd have riders coming adrift."

So the following morning, while the Weyr dealt with falling Thread, Jaxom hunted Ruth and then directed him to the lake for a good scrub and swim. While the fire-lizards were grooming Ruth's neck ridges, Jaxom did a careful brushing of the scar on his leg.

Suddenly the white dragon whimpered. Apologetic, Jaxom looked around and noticed that the fire-lizards had suspended their labors. All the animals had their heads cocked, as if listening to something beyond Jaxom's hearing.

"What's the matter, Ruth?"

The woman dies.

"Take me back to the Hold, Ruth. Hurry."

Jaxom gritted his teeth as his wet clothing froze against his body in the cold of *between*. Teeth chattering, Jaxom glanced toward the watchdragon on the fire-heights. Strangely enough, the beast was indolent in the sun when he ought to be responding to the death.

Now *she is not yet dying,* Ruth said.

It took Jaxom a moment to realize that Ruth had acted on his own initiative and timed it to just before the fire-lizards' alarm at the lake.

"We promised not to time it, Ruth." Jaxom could appreciate the circumstances but he didn't like the notion of going back on his word for any reason.

You promised. I did not. Lytol will need you in time.

Ruth landed Jaxom in the courtyard and the young Lord pelted up the stairs to the main Hall. He startled the drudge who was sweeping the dining hall with a demand to know Lytol's whereabouts. The drudge thought Lord Lytol was with Master Brand. Jaxom knew that Brand kept wine in his office but he ducked into the serving hall, grabbed up a wineskin by its thong, swept two cups into his other hand and strode to the steps of the inner hall, which he took two at a time. Catching the heavy inner door with the point of his shoulder, he worked the latch with his right elbow and continued without much loss of forward speed down the corridor to Brand's quarters.

Just as he threw open the door, Brand's little blue fire-lizard struck the very listening pose that had alerted Jaxom at the lake.

"What's the matter, Lord Jaxom?" Brand cried, rising to his feet. Lytol's face showed his disapproval of such a mannerless entrance and he was about to speak when Jaxom pointed to the fire-lizard.

The blue suddenly sat back on his haunches, opened his wings and began the shrill high ululation that was the keening of the fire-lizards. As all color drained from Lytol's face, the men heard the deeper, equally piercing cries of the watchdragon and Ruth, each giving voice to the passing of a queen dragon.

Jaxom splashed wine in a cup and held it to Lytol.

"It doesn't stop the pain, I know," he said in a rough tone, "but you can get drunk enough not to hear or remember."

CHAPTER IX

Early Summer, Harpercraft and Ruatha Hold, 15.7.3

THE FIRST HINT Robinton had was from Zair, who woke abruptly from a sound morning's sleep in the sun on the window ledge and flew to Robinton's shoulder, wrapping his tail firmly about the Harper's neck. Robinton, not having the heart to rebuke his friend, tried to ease the tension of the tail so that he didn't have the sensation of choking to death. Zair rubbed his cheek against the Harper's, crooning.

"Whatever is the matter with you?"

Just then the watchdragon on the fire-heights rose to his haunches and bugled. A dragon appeared in midair, answered the summons smartly before beginning a circle to land.

A knock on the door was followed so closely by its opening that the courtesy was hardly observed. Robinton was forming a reprimand as he slewed round in his chair and saw Menolly, with Beauty clinging tightly to her shoulder, Rocky, Diver and Poll doing an aerial dance about her.

"It's F'lar and Mnementh," she cried.

"So I had just perceived, my dear. Why the panic?"

"Panic? I'm not in a panic. I'm excited. This is

the first time since the egg was taken that Benden has come to you."

"Then be a polite child and see if Silvina has any sweetbreads to eat with our klah. It is," he sighed wistfully, "a shade too early in the morning to offer wine."

"It's not too early in Benden's morning," Menolly said as she left the room.

Robinton sighed again, sadly, as he looked at the empty doorway. She had grieved over the estrangement of the Harper Hall and Benden Weyr. So, in his own way, had he. He brought his thoughts sharply away from that. There'd been no hint of distress in Mnementh's acknowledgement of the watchdragon's challenge. What had brought F'lar to Benden? And, more important, did the Weyrleader come with Lessa's knowledge? And consent?

Mnementh had landed now. F'lar would be striding across the meadow. Robinton began to twitch with more impatience for that final walk than he had felt during the four sevendays of coolness between Weyr and Hall.

Robinton rose and paced to the window just as F'lar entered the inner courtyard of the Crafthall. He was walking with long strides, but F'lar always did, so there did not seem to be any haste in his errand. Then why was he coming to the Hall?

F'lar spoke to a journeyman, who was packing a runner for a trip. Fire-lizards congregated on the roof. Robinton saw F'lar raise his head and notice them. The Harper briefly considered whether he ought to ask Zair to leave while F'lar was present. No sense firing resentment of any consequence right now.

F'lar had entered the Hall. Through the open window, Robinton could hear the Weyrleader's voice and the pause for an answer. Silvina? More likely his journeyman, he thought, smiling to himself, lying in wait for the Weyrleader. Yes, he was right. He could hear Menolly's voice and F'lar's as they came up the stairs. The sounds of the voices were unmarked by emotion. Good girl! Easy does it.

"Ah, Robinton, Menolly informs me that her firelizards refer to Mnementh as 'the biggest one,'" F'lar said with a slight smile on his face as he entered the room.

"They're chary of awarding accolades, F'lar," Robinton replied, taking the tray from Menolly, who withdrew, closing the door. Not that her absence precluded her knowing what would happen, not with Beauty attuned to Zair.

"There's no trouble at Benden, is there?" Robinton asked the Weyrleader as he handed him a cup of klah.

"No, no trouble." Robinton waited. "But there is a puzzle that I thought you might be able to answer for us."

"If I can, I will," the Harper said, gesturing to F'lar to seat himself.

"We can't find D'ram."

"D'ram?" Robinton almost laughed in surprise. "Why can't you find D'ram?"

"He's alive. We know that much. We don't know where."

"Surely Ramoth could touch Tiroth?"

F'lar shook his head. "Perhaps I should have said *when*."

"When? D'ram's timed it somewhere? I mean, somewhen?"

"That's the only explanation. And we can't see how he could possibly have gone *back* to his own Time. We don't believe that Tiroth has that much strength in him. Timing it, as you know, is very draining on both dragon and rider. But D'ram has gone."

"That's not unexpected surely," Robinton said slowly, his mind turning rapidly over the possibilities of *when*.

"No, not unexpected."

"He wouldn't have gone to the Southern Weyr?"

"No, because Ramoth would have no trouble locating him there. And G'dened went back quite a distance, before Threadfall, at Ista itself, thinking D'ram would stay where his memories are."

"Lord Warbret offered D'ram any one of those caves on the south side of Ista Island. He seemed agreeable." Then as F'lar's shrug negated that suggestion, the Harper added, "Yes, he was too agreeable."

F'lar rose, striding restlessly about, turning back to the Harper. "Have you any ideas where the man could have gone? You were with him a great deal. Can you remember anything?"

"He wasn't talking very much toward the end, just sat there holding Fanna's hand." Robinton found that he needed to swallow. As accustomed as he was to mortality, D'ram's devotion to his Weyrwoman and his silent grief at her death had the power to bring tears to the Harper's eyes. "I tendered offers of hospitality to him from Groghe and Sangel. In fact, I gather he could have gone anywhere on Pern and been welcome. Obviously he prefers the company of his memories. Might I ask if there is any reason to know where he is?"

"No reason other than our concern for him."

"Oldive said that he was completely in possession of his reason, F'lar, if that's your worry."

F'lar made a grimace and impatiently stroked back a forelock which invariably fell into his eyes when he was agitated. "Frankly, Robinton, it's Lessa. Ramoth can't find Tiroth. Lessa's certain he's gone far enough back in time to suicide without giving us distress. It's in D'ram's nature to do so."

"It is also his option," Robinton said gently.

"I know. I know. And no one would fault him but Lessa is very worried. D'ram may have stepped down, Robinton, but his knowledge, his opinions are valuable and valued. Right now more than ever. Bluntly we need him . . . need him available to us."

Robinton thought briefly about the possibility that D'ram had realized this and deliberately removed himself and Tiroth from easy access. But D'ram would serve Pern, and dragonfolk at any time.

"He perhaps needs time to recover from his grief, F'lar."

"He was worn out with tending Fanna. You know that. He could also be sick and who would be there to help? We're both worried."

"I hesitate to suggest this, but has Brekke tried with the fire-lizards? Hers as well as those at Ista Weyr."

A grin tugged at the worried line of F'lar's mouth. "Oh, yes. She insisted. No luck. The fire-lizards need a direction to go *between* time just like dragons."

"I didn't exactly mean sending them. I mean, asking them to *remember* a lone bronze dragon."

"Asking those creatures to *remember?*" F'lar laughed with incredulity.

"I'm serious, F'lar. They have good memories which can be triggered. For instance, how could the fire-lizards have known that the Red Star . . ." He was interrupted by a squeal of protest from Zair, who launched himself so quickly from Robinton's shoulder that he scratched the Harper's neck. "I will mention it in his presence!" Robinton said, ruefully patting the scratch. "My point is, F'lar, that the fire-lizards all knew that the Red Star was dangerous and could not be reached *before* F'nor and Canth tried to go there. If you can get a fire-lizard to make any sense when you mention the Red Star, they say they remember being afraid of it. They? Or their ancestors when our ancestors first attempted to go to it?"

F'lar gave the Masterharper a long searching stare.

"That isn't the first memory of theirs that has proved to be accurate," Robinton went on. "Master Andemon believes that it's entirely possible that these creatures can remember unusual events that one of their number has witnessed or felt. Instinct plays a part with all animals—why not in their memories, too?"

"I'm not sure I see how you intend to get this—

this fire-lizard memory to work in helping to find D'ram, whenever he's got to."

"Simple. Ask them to remember seeing a lone dragon. That would be unusual enough to be noted . . . and remembered."

F'lar was not convinced it would work.

"Oh, I think so if we ask Ruth to ask them."

"Ruth?"

"When every fire-lizard was scared to death of the other dragons, they beleaguered Ruth. Jaxom's told me that they talk with his white wherever they are. With so many, there's bound to be one that might remember what we want to know."

"If I could relieve Lessa's fears, I'd even forget my antipathy to those nuisances."

"I trust you'll remember that statement." Robinton grinned to soften the remark.

"Will you come with me to Ruatha Hold?"

In that moment, Robinton remembered Jaxom's Threadscoring. Of course, it would be long healed. But he couldn't remember if N'ton had ever discussed Jaxom's training with Benden Weyr.

"Shouldn't we find out if Jaxom's at the Hold?"

"Why wouldn't he be?" F'lar asked, frowning.

"Because he's often about the Hold, learning the land, or at Fandarel's with the other young people."

"A point." F'lar looked away from the Harper, out the window, his eyes unfocused. "No, Mnementh says Ruth's at the Hold. See, I have my own message sender," F'lar added with a grin.

Robinton hoped that Ruth would think to tell Jaxom that Mnementh had bespoken him. He wished that he'd had time to send Zair with a message to Ruatha but he had no excuse and certainly no wish to jeopardize this gesture of F'lar's.

"More reliable than mine and farther reaching than Fandarel's little wire." Robinton donned the thick wherhide jacket and helmet he used when flying. "Speaking of Fandarel, he's got his lines as far as Crom's mines, you know." He gestured F'lar to precede him out of the room.

"Yes, I know. That's another reason to locate D'ram."

"It is?"

F'lar laughed at the Harper's bland question, a laugh that held no constraint so that Robinton sincerely hoped that this visit mended their relationship.

"Hasn't Nicat been at you, too, Robinton? To go south to those mines?"

"The ones Toric's been trading from?"

"I thought you'd know."

"Yes, I know that Nicat's worried about mining. The ores are getting very poor. Fandarel's a good sight more worried than Nicat. He needs the better quality metals."

"Once we allow the Crafts into the South, the Lord Holders will press for entry . . ." F'lar instinctively lowered his voice though the courtyard they were crossing was empty.

"The Southern Continent is large enough to take all of Northern Pern and rattle it. Why, we've only touched the fringes of it, F'lar. Great Shells and Shards!" Robinton slapped his forehead. "Talk about fire-lizards and associative memories. That's it! That's where D'ram has gone."

"Where?"

"At least I think that's where he might have gone."

"Speak, man. Where?"

"The problem is still when, I fancy. And Ruth is still our key."

They had only several dragonlengths to go before they reached Mnementh in the meadow. Zair fluttered above Robinton's head, chittering anxiously well away from the bronze dragon. He refused to alight on Robinton's shoulder, though the Harper gestured for him to land.

"I'm going to Ruatha to the white dragon, to Ruth. Join us there, then, you silly creature, if you won't ride on my shoulder."

"Mnementh doesn't mind Zair," F'lar said.

"It's still the other way round, I'm afraid," Robinton said.

A hint of anger danced in the bronze rider's eyes. "No dragon flamed a fire-lizard."

"Not here, Weyrleader, not here. But all of them remember seeing it happen. And fire-lizards can only tell what they or one of them have actually seen."

"Then let's get to Ruatha and see if one of them has seen D'ram."

So the fire-lizards were still tender subjects, thought Robinton sadly as he climbed up Mnementh's shoulder to sit behind F'lar. He wished that Zair had not been so wary of Mnementh.

Jaxom and Lytol stood on the Hold steps as Mnementh bugled his name to the watchdragon and circled to land in the huge courtyard. As the two visitors were being greeted, Robinton scanned Jaxom's face to see if the Threadscore was obvious. He couldn't see a trace of it and wondered if he was examining the right cheek. He could only hope that Ruth had healed as well. Of course, F'lar was so involved with this business of D'ram he wouldn't be looking for scoring on Ruth or Jaxom.

"Ruth said Mnementh inquired for him, F'lar," Jaxom said. "I trust nothing is wrong?"

"Ruth may be able to help us find D'ram."

"Find D'ram? He hasn't . . ." Jaxom paused, looking anxiously at Lytol, who was frowning and shaking his head.

"No, but he has timed it somewhen," Robinton said. "I thought perhaps if Ruth asked the fire-lizards, they might tell him."

Jaxom stared at the Harper, who wondered why the lad looked so stunned and, curiously, scared. Robinton did not miss the quick flick of Jaxom's eyes toward F'lar nor the convulsive swallowing.

"I remembered hearing you comment that fire-lizards often tell Ruth things," Robinton went on in a casual manner, giving Jaxom time to recover his composure. Whatever was bothering the boy?

"Where? Possibly. But when, Master Robinton?"

"I've a hunch I know where D'ram went. Would that help?"

"I'm not sure I understand," Lytol said, looking from one to the other. "What's this all about?" Lytol had been guiding the visitors into the Hold and toward the small private room. Wine and cups had been set on the table, together with cheese, bread and fruits.

"Well," Robinton said, eyeing the wineskin, "I'll explain . . ."

"And you'll be dry, I'm sure," Jaxom said, as he strode to the table to pour. "It's Benden wine, Master Robinton. Only the best for our distinguished visitors."

"The lad's growing up, Lytol," F'lar said, taking the cup and raising it approvingly toward Lytol.

"The lad has grown up," Lytol said in a half-growl. "Now, about those fire-lizards . . ."

Zair appeared midair, squealed and swooped to Robinton's shoulder, wrapping his tail tightly about the Harper's neck and chittering in a nervous tone as he reassured himself that Robinton had taken no harm riding the biggest one.

"Pardon me," Robinton said, and soothed Zair to silence. Then he explained to Lytol his theory that fire-lizards shared a vast pool of common knowledge which would explain their fear of—he cleared his throat and pointed east to spare them all his bronze's antics. Fire-lizards were able to communicate strong emotions as evidenced by Brekke's call to Canth that fateful night. They had had this fright about the queen's egg and all had been in a high state of turmoil until the egg had Hatched properly. They seemed to remember seeing it near a black nothingness, and they seemed to remember being flamed. Jaxom had told him on several occasions that the fire-lizards regaled Ruth with incredible things they said they'd remembered seeing. If this curious talent of theirs was not the sun-dreams of silly creatures—he had to placate an outraged Zair—then here was a case in which it could be proved, with Ruth's cooperation. D'ram had apparently gone off on his own, to a time when

Ramoth could not reach the mind of his dragon. It was upsetting Ramoth and Lessa, who were worried that D'ram might be in physical distress. Despite his resignation as Weyrleader, Pern still had a need of and a place for D'ram and certainly did not wish to lose contact with him.

"Now," Robinton went on, "there have been occasions in recent Turns . . ." He cleared his throat, glanced toward F'lar for permission and received the nod. ". . . occasions when I have ventured South. On one such instance, Menolly and I were blown off course, far to the east where we came to rest in a beautiful cove, white-sanded, with red fruit trees abounding; the waters of the cove teemed with yellowtail and white fingerfish. The sun was warm and the waters of a stream just inland was sweet as wine." He looked into his cup wistfully. With a laugh, Jaxom refilled it. "I told D'ram of it, I've forgotten why now. I'm reasonably certain I described it well enough for a dragon of Tiroth's abilities to find his way there."

"D'ram would not wish to cause complications here," Lytol said slowly. "He'd have gone to a time when the Oldtimers were not in the South. A jump back of ten-twelve Turns wouldn't overtax Tiroth."

"A point, Robinton, that might complicate matters," F'lar said. "If these creatures can remember significant events that happened to their predecessors" —and F'lar was patently skeptical—"then none of the fire-lizards here could possibly have any recollections for our purpose. No ancestors from the area." He indicated Zair. "He's from that clutch Menolly brought up from below Half-Circle Sea Hold, isn't he?"

"Fire-lizards from all over converge on Ruth," Robinton said, looking to the young Lord for corroboration.

"F'lar has made a good point," Jaxom said.

"Not if you go to that cove, Jaxom. I'm sure the fatal fascination fire-lizards all have for Ruth will operate even there."

"You want me to go to the Southern Continent?"

169

Robinton noted the incredulity and sudden start of intense interest in Jaxom's eyes. So, the boy had discovered that flying a fire-breathing dragon was not enough to keep him content with his life.

"I don't *want* anyone to go South," F'lar replied, "since that . . . is a breach of our agreement, but I can't see any other way of locating D'ram."

"The cove is a long way from the Southern Weyr," Robinton said gently, "and we know the Oldtimers don't venture far from it."

"They ventured far enough from it a little while ago, didn't they?" F'lar asked with considerable heat in his voice and an angry shine in his amber eyes.

Wearily Robinton saw that the breach between Harper Hall and Benden Weyr was only thinly healed.

"Lord Lytol," the Benden Weyrleader continued, "I am remiss. May we have your permission to recruit Jaxom to this search?"

Lytol shook his head and gestured toward Jaxom. "It is entirely up to Lord Jaxom."

Robinton could see F'lar digesting the implications of that referral, and he gave Jaxom a long keen look. Then he smiled. "And your answer, Lord Jaxom?"

With commendable poise, Robinton thought, the young man inclined his head. "I'm flattered to be asked to assist, Weyrleader."

"You don't happen to have any maps of the Southern Continent in this Hold, do you?" asked F'lar.

"As a matter of fact, I do." Then Jaxom added a hasty explanation. "Fandarel gave us several sessions of chartmaking at his Hall."

The charts were, however, incomplete. F'lar recognized them as copies of F'nor's original explorations of the Southern Continent when the Benden wingsecond had taken Ramoth's first clutch back ten Turns to mature before Thread would fall again—an undertaking marked by partial success.

"I have more comprehensive maps of the coastline," Robinton said casually and scribbled a note to Menolly which he attached to the clasp on Zair's collar. He sent the little bronze back to the Harper Hold with an entreaty not to forget his errand.

"And he'll bring the charts back directly?" F'lar asked, skeptical and somewhat contemptuous. "Brekke and F'nor keep trying to convince me of their usefulness, too."

"I suspect with something as important as the charts, Menolly will wheedle the watchdragon into bringing her." Robinton sighed, wishing he'd thought to insist she return the charts by fire-lizard. No opportunity should be wasted.

"How much timing it have you done, Jaxom?" F'lar asked suddenly.

A flush suffused Jaxom's face. With a start, Robinton saw the thin line of scar white against the reddened cheek. Luckily that side of Jaxom's face was turned away from the Weyrleader.

"Well, sir . . ."

"Come, lad, I don't know any young dragonrider who hasn't used the trick to be on time. What I want to establish is how accurate Ruth's time sense is. Some dragons don't have any at all."

"Ruth always knows when he is," Jaxom replied with quick pride. "I'd say he has the best time memory on Pern."

F'lar considered that for a long moment. "Have you ever tried any long jumps?"

Jaxom nodded slowly, his eyes flicking to Lytol whose face remained impassive.

"No wavering of the leap? No unduly long stay *between?*"

"No, sir. It's easy to be accurate anyhow if you jump at night."

"I'm not sure I follow that reasoning."

"Those star equations that Wansor worked out. I think you were at that session in the Smithcrafthall . . ." The young man's voice trailed off uncertainly until F'lar caught his drift and looked his surprise. "If you work out the position of the dominant stars in the skies, you can position yourself most accurately."

"If you jump at night," the Masterharper added, never having thought to put that use to Wansor's equations.

"Never occurred to me to do that," F'lar said.

"There is a precedent," Robinton remarked, grinning, "in your own Weyr, F'lar."

"Lessa used the stars from the tapestry to go back for the Oldtimers, didn't she?" Jaxom had clearly forgotten that, and also, to judge by the sudden comic dismay on his face, forgotten that his reference to the Oldtimers was not adroit.

"We can't ignore them, can we?" the Weyrleader said with more tolerance than Robinton had anticipated. "Well, they exist and can't be ignored. To the present problem, Robinton. How long is it likely to take your fire-lizard?"

Just outside the Hold window a multivoiced squabbling arose, so obviously that of fire-lizards that they all hurried to the window.

"Menolly did it," Robinton said in an undertone to Jaxom. "They're here, F'lar."

"Who? Menolly with the watchdragon?"

"No, sir," Jaxom said, his voice triumphant, "Zair, and Menolly's queen and her three bronzes. They've all got charts strapped to their backs."

Zair flew in, chittering in a combination of anger, concern and confusion. Menolly's four followed. The little queen, Beauty, started scolding all of them as she circled about the room. Robinton easily lured Zair to his arm. But Beauty kept her bronzes in circulation, out of reach, while F'lar, grinning sardonically, and Lytol, expressionless, watched the attempts of Robinton and Jaxom to land the other four fire-lizards.

"Ruth, would you tell Beauty to behave and come to my arm?" Jaxom cried as his futile attempts to coax the little queen began to assume ludicrous proportions in front of someone he was trying to impress.

Beauty let out a startled squawk but immediately came to rest on the table. She scolded Jaxom furiously as he undid the chart. She kept up her monologue as the bronzes timidly landed, not quite furling their wings, to have their burdens removed. Once free of their encumbrances, the bronzes retreated out the window. Beauty gave everyone in the room one final raucous harangue and then, with a flick of her tail, disappeared from sight. Zair let out one sort of apologetic cheep and hid his face in Robinton's hair.

"Well," Robinton said as welcome silence settled on the room, "they did return promptly, didn't they?"

F'lar burst out laughing. "Return, yes. Delivery was another problem. I'd hate to have to argue for every message brought me."

"That was just because Menolly wasn't here," Jaxom said. "Beauty wasn't certain whom she could trust, you know. Meaning no offense, F'lar," he added hastily.

"Here's the one I need," Robinton said, unwinding it fully. He gestured for the others to unroll the segments they held. Shortly the maps were placed in sequence across the table, the curling ends weighted down with pieces of fruit and wine cups.

"It would appear," Lytol said mildly, "that you have been blown off course in every direction, Master Robinton."

"Oh, not me, sir," the Harper replied ingenuously. "SeaHolders have been very helpful here, here and here," and he pointed to the western portions where an intricate coastline was carefully delineated. "This is the work of Idarolan and the captains reporting to him." He paused, toying with the notion of mentioning just how much of Idarolan's explorations had been assisted by the various fire-lizards of the crews. "Toric and his holders, of course," he went on, deciding against gilding the matter now, "have a perfect right to discover their land. They've detailed this portion . . ." His hand swept across the peninsular thumb that was the Southern Hold and Weyr and substantial portions of the territory on either side.

"Where're those mines located that Toric's trading from?"

"Here." Robinton's finger dropped to the foothilled

shading, slightly to the west of the settlement and well inland.

F'lar considered the location, walking his fingers back across the well-stretched hide to the Weyr's location. "And where's this cove of yours?"

Robinton pointed to a spot which was as far distant from the Southern Weyr as Ruatha was from Benden. "In this area. There're quite a few small coves in the coastline. I couldn't say exactly which one it was, but in this general location."

F'lar mumbled about his recollection being all too general and how would a dragon take the specific direction he'd need to go *between*.

"Dead center in the cove is the cone of an old mountain, perfectly symmetrical." Robinton gestured appropriately. "Zair was with me and could give Ruth the proper image." Robinton turned his head slightly and gave Jaxom a private wink.

"Could Ruth take a direction from a fire-lizard?" F'lar asked Jaxom, frowning at the unreliability of the source.

"He has," Jaxom remarked, and Robinton caught the glint of amusement in the lad's eyes. He began to wonder where fire-lizards had already led the white dragon. Would Menolly know?

"What is this?" F'lar demanded suddenly. "A conspiracy to restore fire-lizards to good odor?"

"I thought we were forming a cooperative venture to locate D'ram," Robinton replied in mild rebuke.

F'lar snorted and bent to study the maps.

The cooperation, Robinton realized, would be all on Ruth's part. The outcome would finally depend on whether or not the Southern fire-lizards were attracted to the white dragon. Otherwise, Jaxom had agreed to try judicious time jumps backward in the cove . . . if, F'lar amended, Jaxom was able to find the proper one.

The subject of fire-lizard memory was discussed again; F'lar unwilling to concede that, unlike the dragons they otherwise resembled, the little creatures were capable of recall. Their tales might all be imaginary, the results of sun-dreams and insubstantial. To that Robinton replied that imagination relied on memory—without one, the other was impossible. The afternoon drew to a close, emphasized by the return of the fosterlings to the Hold after a day's field tour with Brand. F'lar noted that he'd been gone far longer than he had intended when he set out from Benden. He cautioned Jaxom to be careful timing it—advice which Robinton suspected F'lar had best take to heart himself—and to take no risks with himself or his dragon. If he didn't locate the cove, he was not to waste time and energy but return. If he did find D'ram, preferably he was to mark the time and place and return immediately to Benden with the coordinate for F'lar. F'lar did not want to intrude on D'ram's grief unnecessarily, and if Jaxom could avoid being seen, so much the better.

"I think you could trust Jaxom to handle the situation diplomatically," Robinton said, watching the young man through the side of his eyes. "He's already proved to be discreet." Now why would Jaxom react so to a simple compliment, Robinton wondered and smoothly made a fuss of rolling up the charts to divert attention from the discomposed young rider.

Robinton told Jaxom to get a good night's sleep, a good morning's breakfast, and to report to the Harpercrafthall immediately thereafter to acquire his guide. Then Robinton and F'lar left the Hold. As the Weyrleader and Mnementh brought the Harper back to his Hall, Robinton forebore to go beyond offering ordinary courtesies. The needs of Pern had brought the Benden Weyrleader back to the Hall. One step at a time!

As Robinton watched F'lar and bronze Mnementh climb above the fire-heights and wink out, Beauty appeared, scolding at Zair, who resumed his customary perch on the Harper's shoulder. Zair did not respond to her crackling, causing Robinton to grin. Menolly must be agitating for an account of the afternoon's doings. She wasn't presumptuous enough to nag at him, but that didn't keep Beauty from badgering his bronze.

A good child, Menolly, and worth her weight in marks. He hoped she'd approve of a trip with young Jaxom. He hadn't mentioned her participating in front of Lytol since F'lar had long ago enjoined him to the strictest secrecy about his Southern trips. Zair would not have been enough for Jaxom to find the right cove, but with Menolly, who had been with him on that stormy trip, and her fire-lizards to act as reinforcement, they'd have no trouble at all. But the fewer people who knew about it the better.

The next day when the Harper informed Jaxom of this added insurance for success, Jaxom looked relieved and surprised.

"Mind you, young Jaxom, it's not to be discussed that Menolly and I have been exploring so far south. In point of fact, we hadn't planned that trip . . ."

Menolly chuckled. "I told you there'd be a storm."

"Thank you. I've heeded your weather wisdom since, as you well know." He grimaced as he recalled three days of storm-sickness and a desperate Menolly clinging to the tiller of their light craft.

He saddled them with no further advice, urged them to take a supply of food from the kitchens and said he hoped they'd have a favorable report.

"Of D'ram's whereabouts?" Menolly asked, her eyes dancing at him, "or the performance of the fire-lizards?"

"Both, of course, saucy girl. Away with you."

He had decided not to query Jaxom about his strong reactions to timing it and discretion. When he had told Menolly of his intention to send her and her fire-lizards to accompany Jaxom, she, too, had reacted in an unexpected fashion. He had casually asked her what was so amusing and she had merely shaken her head, convulsed in laughter. He couldn't imagine what the two of them had been up to together. Now, as he watched Ruth circle into the skies above the Hold, he reviewed their interactions. Good-natured chaffing, certainly—a dollop of contention for leadership but nothing beyond the exchanges of old friends. Not, he hastily told himself, that Menolly would not make an excellent Lady Holder for Jaxom if the two were sincerely attached. It was just that . . . the Harper chided himself for interfering and turned to dull matters of Craft management which he had been delaying far too long.

CHAPTER X

From Harpercraft Hall to the Southern Continent, Evening at Benden Weyr, 15.7.4

As RUTH FLEW upward from the meadow, Jaxom experienced a tremendous sense of relief and excitement as well as the usual tension that gripped him when making a long jump *between*. Beauty and Diver were perched on Menolly's shoulders, tails twined about her neck. He had given shoulder room to Poll and Rocky since these four had accompanied the Harper and Menolly on that initial trip. Jaxom would have liked to ask what they'd been doing sailing in the Southern Continent. The boat made some sense since Menolly, being SeaHold-bred, was a good sailor. But there'd been a challenging gleam in Menolly's eyes that had kept him from asking. He was wondering, too, if she had told the Harper anything of her suspicions about his part in returning the egg.

They went *between* first to Nerat's tip, circling again while Menolly and her fire-lizards concentrated on imagining the cove far to the southeast. Jaxom had wanted to time it to the night before; he'd spent hours working out star positions in the Southern Hemisphere. Menolly and Robinton had overruled him unless Ruth couldn't get a vivid enough picture of the cove from the combination of Menolly and the fire-lizards.

Somewhat to Jaxom's disgruntlement, Ruth announced that he could clearly see where he was to go. *Menolly makes very sharp pictures,* he added.

Jaxom had no option but to ask him to change.

The quality of the air was Jaxom's first impression of the new location: softer, cleaner, less humid. Ruth was gliding toward the little cove, expressing pleasure in anticipation of a good swim. Their guiding mountain peak glistened in the sun, distant, serene and unusually symmetrical.

"I'd forgotten how lovely it was," Menolly said, breathing out a sigh in his ear.

The water had a clarity that made the sandy bottom of the cove quite visible, though Jaxom was sure that the water was by no means shallow. He noticed the brilliant reflection of yellowtails and the darting movements of whitefingers in the clear waters. Ahead of them was the perfect crescent of a white-sanded cove, trees of all sizes, some bearing yellow and red fruits, forming a shady border. As Ruth descended to the beach, Jaxom could see dense forest extending unbroken toward the low range of foothills that culminated in that magnificent mountain. Just beyond this cove, on both flanks, were other little bays, not perhaps as symmetrically shaped, but equally peaceful and untouched.

Ruth came to a back-winging halt on the sands, urging his passengers to disembark as he intended to have a proper bath.

"Go ahead, then," Jaxom said, patting Ruth's muzzle affectionately and laughing as the white dragon, too eager to dive, waddled ungracefully into the sea.

"These sands are as hot as at Hatching Grounds," Menolly explained, picking up her feet in fast order and heading toward the shaded area.

"They're not that hot," Jaxom said, following her.

"My feet are sensitive," she replied, casting herself down on the beach. She glanced up and down and then grimaced.

"No signs, huh?" Jaxom asked.

"Of D'ram?"

"No, fire-lizard."

She unslung the pack with their provisions.

"They're likely sleeping off their early-morning feed. You're still on your feet. See if there're some ripe redfruits in that tree there, would you, Jaxom? Meatroll makes dry eating."

Jaxom found sufficient ripe fruit to feed a Hold and brought as much as he could carry back to Menolly. He knew her fondness for them. Ruth was disporting himself in the water, diving and surfacing to tail length before crashing down with great splashings and wave-makings, the fire-lizards encouraging him with shrieks and buglings.

"Tide's full in," Menolly said as she bit into red-fruit peel, tearing off a large hunk and squeezing the pulp for the juice. "Oh, this is heavenly! Why does everything Southern taste so good?"

"Forbidden, I guess. Does the tide make a difference to the fire-lizards' appearing?"

"Not that I know of. Ruth will make the difference, I think."

"So we have to wait until they notice Ruth?"

"That's the easiest way."

"Do we actually know there *are* fire-lizards in this part of the South?"

"Oh, yes, didn't I mention?" Menolly pretended to be contrite. "We saw a queen mating, and I nearly lost Rocky and Diver to her. Beauty was furious."

"Anything else that hasn't been mentioned that I should know?"

Menolly grinned at him. "I need to have the old memory jogged by association. You'll know what is needed when the time comes."

Jaxom decided that two could play that word game and grinned back at her, before choosing a redfruit to eat. It was so warm that he set aside his riding jacket and helmet. Ruth continued to enjoy a leisurely and lengthy bath as Menolly's fire-lizards performed alongside him, their combined show affording their indulgent audience considerable amusement.

It got hotter, the white sands reflecting the sun's

rays and baking the cove even where they were in shade. The clear water and the fun the beasts were having was too much for Jaxom to watch any longer. He unlaced his boots, wriggled out of his trousers, whipped off his shirt and raced for the water. Menolly was soon splashing beside him before he was a dragonlength from the shore.

"We'd better not take too much sun," she told him. "I got a colossal burning the last time." She grimaced in recollection. "Peeled like a tunnel snake."

Ruth erupted beside them, blowing out water, all but swamping them with strokes from his wings, and then, solicitously extending a helping tail as the two choked and spluttered from the water they'd swallowed.

Menolly's body was trimmer than Corana's, Jaxom noticed as they waded out, happily exhausted by their swim with Ruth. She was longer in the leg and not nearly as rounded in the hip. A bit too flat in the breast, but she moved with a grace that fascinated Jaxom more than courtesy allowed. When he looked back, she had put on pants and overtunic, so that her slim bare arms were exposed to the sun as she dried her hair. He preferred long hair in a girl though, with all the dragonriding Menolly did, he could see why she'd keep it short enough to wear under a helmet.

They shared a yellow fruit which Jaxom had never eaten before. Its mild taste was well seasoned by the salt in his mouth.

Ruth emerged from the water, shaking water all over Jaxom and Menolly.

The sun is warm, he said when they complained of the shower. *Your clothes will dry quickly. They always do at Keroon.*

Jaxom shot a glance at Menolly but she evidently hadn't caught the significance of the remark. She was resettling herself, disgusted by the wet sand that now speckled her clothes and bare arms.

"It's not the wet that bothers," Jaxom told Ruth, as he brushed his face before lying down again, "it's the gritty sand."

Ruth worked himself into a good wallow of dry sand and the fire-lizards, giving little tired cheeps, nestled down against him.

Jaxom thought that one of them should stay awake to see if local fire-lizards responded to the lure of the white dragon, but the combination of exercise, food, sun and the limpid air of the cove were too much.

Ruth's soft call woke him. *Do not move. We have visitors.*

Jaxom was on his side, his head pillowed on his left hand. Opening his eyes slowly, he looked directly at Ruth's shade-dappled body. He counted three bronze fire-lizards, four greens, two golds and a blue. None of them wore neck paint or bands. As he watched, a brown came gliding in to land by one of the golds. The two exchanged nose touches and then cocked their heads at Ruth's head which was on the sand at their level. Ruth had the lids of one eye half-opened.

Beauty, who had been asleep on the other side of Ruth, minced carefully across the white dragon's shoulders and returned the courtesies of the strangers.

"Ask them if they remember seeing a bronze dragon?" Jaxom thought to Ruth.

I have. They're thinking about it. They like me. They've never seen anything like me before.

"Nor will again." But Jaxom was amused at the delight in his dragon's tone. Ruth did so like to be liked.

A long time ago there was a dragon, a bronze one, and a man who walked up and down the beach. They did not bother him. He didn't stay long, Ruth added, almost as an afterthought.

Now what did that mean? Jaxom wondered, apprehensive. Either we came and got him. Or he and Tiroth suicided.

"Ask them what else they remember about men," Jaxom said to Ruth. Maybe they saw F'lar with D'ram.

The new fire-lizards became so excited that Ruth's head came up out of the sand and his eyes flashed open and began to whirl with alarm. At his movement, Beauty lost her grip on his ridge and slid out of sight, reappearing with wings working furiously as she repositioned herself, squawking over her disarrangement.

They remember men. Why don't I remember such things?

"And dragons?" Jaxom suppressed a spurt of alarm, wondering how on earth the Oldtimers could know he and Menolly were here. Then his common sense asserted itself. They couldn't know.

He nearly jumped to his feet at the touch on his arm.

"Find out when, Jaxom," Menolly said in a soft whisper, "when was D'ram here?"

No dragons. But many many men, Ruth was saying and added that the fire-lizards were too excited now to remember anything about one man and a dragon. He didn't understand what they were remembering; each one seemed to have different memories. He was confused.

"Do they know we're here?"

They haven't seen you. They've only looked at me. But you aren't their men. Ruth's tone indicated he was as perplexed by this message as Jaxom.

"Can't you get them back to the subject of D'ram?"

No, Ruth said sadly and with some disappointment. *All they want to remember is men. Not my men, but their men.*

"Maybe if I stand up they will recognize me as a man." Slowly Jaxom got to his feet, gesturing cautiously to Menolly to rise as well. What the fire-lizards needed was the proper perspective.

You aren't the men they remember, Ruth said as the fire-lizards, startled by the two figures rising from the sands, took wing. They circled once, at a safe distance, and then disappeared.

"Call them back, Ruth. We've got to find out when D'ram is."

Ruth was silent for a moment, his eyes decreasing the speed of their whirl. Then he shook his head as he told his rider that they had gone away to remember their men.

"They couldn't mean Southerners," Menolly said, having received some images from her friends. "That mountain is in the background of their images." And she turned in that direction though she couldn't see the mountain for the trees. "And they wouldn't have meant Robinton and myself when we got storm-tossed here. Did they remember a boat, Ruth?" Menolly asked the white dragon, then looked at Jaxom for the answer.

No one told me to ask about a boat, Ruth said plaintively. *But they did say they saw a man and a dragon.*

"Would they react if . . . if Tiroth had gone *between,* Ruth?"

By himself? To the end? Yes, they didn't remember sadness. I remember sadness. I remember Mirath's going very well. The white dragon's tone was sad.

Jaxom hurried to comfort him.

"Did he?" Menolly asked anxiously, not hearing Ruth.

"Ruth doesn't think so. And besides, a dragon wouldn't let his rider harm himself. D'ram *can't* suicide with Tiroth alive. And Tiroth won't if D'ram is still alive."

"When?" Menolly sounded upset. "We still don't know when."

"No, we don't. But if D'ram was here, long enough for the fire-lizards to remember him, if he planned to stay here as he must have, he would have had to build some sort of shelter for himself. There are rains in this part of the world. And Thread . . ." Jaxom had started toward the verge of the forest to test his theory. He called, "Hey, Menolly, Thread's only been falling for the past fifteen Turns. That wouldn't be too long a jump for Tiroth. They came forward in time at twenty-five Turn intervals. I'll bet anything that's his when, before Thread. D'ram's had enough of Thread for several lifetimes." Jaxom scrambled across the sand back to his clothes and continued talking as he got dressed. That sense of rightness colored his speculation. "I'd say Dram's gone back about twenty or twenty-five

Turns. I'll try then first. If we see any sign of D'ram or Tiroth, we'll come right back, I promise." He vaulted to Ruth's back, fastening his helmet as he urged the white dragon to wing.

"Jaxom, wait! Don't be so quick . . ."

Menolly's words were lost in the noise of Ruth's wings. Jaxom grinned to himself as he saw her jumping up and down in the sands in her frustration. He concentrated on the moment in time to when he wished to jump: predawn, with the Red Star far east, a pale, malevolent pink, not yet ready to swoop down on an unsuspecting Pern. But Menolly had a final say. He felt a tail wrapping about his neck just as he told Ruth to transfer *between* time.

It seemed a long moment, suspended in that cold nothingness that was *between*. He could feel that chill inching its way through skin and bones warmed by a kind sun. He steeled himself for the ordeal. Then they were out in the cool dawn, the pink gleam of the Red Star low on the horizon.

"Can you sense Tiroth, Ruth?" Jaxom could see nothing in the crepuscular light of this new day so many Turns before his birth.

He sleeps, so does the man. They are here.

Elation brimming inside him, Jaxom told Ruth to get back to Menolly but not too soon. Jaxom pictured the sun well over the forests and that was what he saw as Ruth burst back into *now* over the cove.

For a moment he couldn't see Menolly on the beach. Then Beauty and the other two bronzes—it was Rocky who had accompanied him—exploded beside them, Beauty blistering the air with her angry comments, while Diver and Poll chittered anxiously. Then Menolly appeared from the forest, planted both hands on her hip bones and just watched. He didn't need to see her face to know she was furious. She continued to glare balefully at him while Ruth settled to the sand, careful not to flick it over the girl.

"Well?"

Menolly was very pretty, Jaxom thought, with her eyes flashing like that, but she was daunting, too.

"D'ram was *then*. Twenty-five Turns back. I used the Red Star as a guide."

"I'm glad you used something constant. Do you realize that you've been gone from this time for hours?"

"You knew I was all right. You sent Rocky with me."

"That didn't help! You went so far Beauty couldn't touch him. We had no idea where you were!" She flung her arms wide with her exasperation. "You could've met up with those men the other fire-lizards saw. You could've miscalculated and never come back!"

"I'm sorry, Menolly, really I am." Jaxom was genuinely contrite, if only to spare himself the sharp edge of her tongue. "But I couldn't remember what time it was when we left, so I made sure we didn't double up on ourselves coming back."

She calmed down a trifle. "You didn't need to be that cautious. I was about to send Beauty for F'lar."

"You were worried!"

"Bloody right." She swooped and gathered up the pack, shrugging into her jacket and slapping her helmet on. "Incidentally I found the remains of a lean-to, near a stream back there," she said as she slung him the pack. Vaulting neatly to Ruth's back, she looked around for her fire-lizards that had disappeared. "Off again." She gave a call, and Jaxom instinctively ducked from the rush of wings about his head.

Menolly settled them down, Beauty and Poll on her shoulders, Rocky and Diver on Jaxom's, and they were ready.

When they emerged above Benden Weyr, Ruth caroled his name. Menolly's fire-lizards cheeped uncertainly.

"I wish I dared take you into the queen's weyr, but that wouldn't be smart. Off you go to Brekke!"

As they disappeared, the watchdragon let out an outraged roar, wings extended, neck arching, eyes flashing with angry red. Startled, Menolly and Jaxom turned to see a fair of fire-lizards arrowing toward them.

"They followed us from the South, Jaxom. Oh, tell them to go back!"

The fair winked out abruptly.

They only wanted to see where we came from, Ruth said to Jaxom in an aggrieved tone.

"At Ruatha Hold, yes. Here, no!"

They won't come again, Ruth said sadly. *They got frightened.*

By that time the watchdragon's alarm had stirred up the Weyr. With sinking spirits, Jaxom and Menolly saw Mnementh raise himself on his ledge. They could hear Ramoth's bellow and before they had landed in the Bowl, half the dragons were bellowing, too. The unmistakable figures of Lessa and F'lar appeared on the ledge by Mnementh.

"We're in for it now," Jaxom said.

"Not as bearers of good tidings, we're not. Concentrate on that."

"I'm too bloody tired to concentrate on anything," Jaxom replied with more feeling than he'd intended. His skin itched, probably the sand. Or too much sun, but he was uncomfortable.

I am very hungry, Ruth said, looking wistfully toward the fenced killing ground of the Weyr.

Jaxom groaned. "I can't let you hunt here, Ruth." He gave his friend an encouraging pat and, noticing F'lar and Lessa waiting for them, he hitched up his trousers, settled his tunic and gestured to Menolly that they'd better go.

They'd taken no more than three steps, during which time Mnementh had turned his wedge-shaped head to F'lar, when the Weyrleader had spoken to Lessa and the two Benden leaders started down the steps, F'lar gesturing to Jaxom to move Ruth on to the killing ground.

Mnementh is a kind friend, Ruth said. *I may eat here. I am very very hungry.*

"Let Ruth go, Jaxom," F'lar was calling across the intervening distance. "He's gray!"

Ruth did indeed look gray, Jaxom realized, which was the shade he himself felt, now that the exhilaration of their quest was ebbing. Relieved, he signaled the white dragon to proceed to the ground.

As he and Menolly walked toward the Weyrleaders, he felt his knees weaken unaccountably and he lurched against Menolly. She had her hand under his arm instantly.

"What's the matter with him, Menolly? Is he ill?" F'lar strode to her assistance.

"He jumped back twenty-five Turns to find D'ram. He's exhausted!"

The next few moments were a blank to Jaxom. He re-established contact with the here and now when someone held a rank-smelling vial under his nose, the fumes of which cleared his head and made him back away from the stink. He realized that he was sitting on the steps to the queen's weyr, his body braced between F'lar and Menolly, with Manora and Lessa in front of him, everyone looking extremely anxious.

A high-pitched squeal told him that Ruth had killed and, curiously, he felt better immediately.

"Drink this slowly," Lessa ordered, curling his fingers about a warm cup. The soup was rich with meat juice, savory with herbs and just the right temperature for drinking. He took two long gulps and opened his mouth to speak when Lessa gestured him imperiously to keep drinking.

"Menolly's given us the salient points," the Weyrwoman said, pulling a disapproving grimace. "But you disappeared long enough to scare Menolly out of her harpered wits. How under the sun did you conclude he'd gone twenty-five Turns back? Don't answer that yet. Drink. You're transparent and I'd never hear the last of it from Lytol if you came to any harm over this numbwitted escapade." She glared at her weyrmate. "Yes, I've been worried over D'ram but not to the point where I would risk a fingertip of Ruth's hide to find him if he's trying that hard to be lost. Nor am I very pleased to find fire-lizards involved." She was tapping one foot now and her glare was divided equally between Menolly and Jaxom. "I still think they're pests. Barging in where they're not wanted. I suppose that unmarked fair that popped in followed you up from the South? I won't sanction that."

"Well, I can't keep them from following Ruth," Jaxom said, too weary to be prudent. "Don't think I haven't tried!"

"I'm sure you have, Jaxom," Lessa said in a milder tone.

A series of frightened wherry whistles was plainly heard from the killing ground. They saw Ruth swoop to dispatch a second fowl.

"He certainly is neat," Lessa remarked approvingly. "Doesn't run a flock to bone making a choice. Can you stand, Jaxom? I think you'd best plan on spending the night here. Send one of those dratted fire-lizards of yours to Ruatha Hold, Menolly, and tell Lytol. It'll take Ruth time to digest anyhow and I won't permit this lad to risk *between* tired out of his mind and on a tired and sated dragon."

Jaxom got to his feet.

"I'm all right now, thank you."

"Not when you're leaning at that angle," F'lar said with a snort as he slipped one arm around Jaxom. "Up to the weyr."

"I'll bring a proper meal," Manora promised and turned to go. "You can help me, Menolly. And send your message."

Menolly hesitated, obviously wanting to stay with Jaxom.

"I don't intend to eat him, girl," Lessa said, shooing Menolly off. "Much less scold him when he's reeling. I'll save that for later. Come up to the weyr when you've sent word to Ruatha."

Jaxom felt obliged to protest their assistance, but they were convinced he needed it and by the time they'd reached the top of the weyrsteps, he ruefully sagged against their support. Mnementh regarded him kindly as Lessa and F'lar guided him into the weyr.

This was not the first time Jaxom had been there, and, as they led him to the living corner, he wondered if he was always going to enter Ramoth's weyr consumed with guilt. Could Ramoth perceive his thoughts? Her jeweled eyes turned idly without a trace of agitation as he was solicitously settled in a chair, and a foot rest positioned. When Lessa was spreading a fur over him, muttering about watching for chills after exertion, she paused, staring at him. She put her hand under his chin and turned his head slightly, then traced the line of Threadscore with a light finger.

"Where did you acquire that, young Lord Jaxom?" she asked harshly, her eyes forcing him to look at her.

F'lar, alerted by the tone in her voice, returned to the table with the wine and cups he'd taken from the wall chest.

"Acquire what? Oh ho, the young man has trained his dragon to chew firestone but not to duck!"

"I thought it was decided that Jaxom was to remain in Holding at Ruatha."

"I thought you said you wouldn't scold him," F'lar replied as he winked at Jaxom.

"About timing it. But this . . ." she gestured angrily at Jaxom, "this is entirely different."

"Is it, Lessa?" F'lar asked in a tone that embarrassed Jaxom. They were momentarily unaware of him. "I seem to remember a girl wanting desperately to fly her queen."

"Flying was no danger. But Jaxom could be—"

"Jaxom has evidently learned a lesson. Haven't you? About ducking, that is."

"Yes, sir. N'ton's put me in with the weyrlings at Fort."

"Why wasn't I informed?" Lessa demanded.

"Jaxom's training is Lytol's responsibility and we've no complaints on that score. As far as Ruth is concerned, I'd say that he too falls under N'ton's jurisdiction. How long has this been going on, Jaxom?"

"Not that long, sir. I asked N'ton because . . . well . . ." Here Jaxom's conscience interfered with his glibness. Above all else, Lessa must not think he had any part in returning that blasted egg.

F'lar rescued him. "Because Ruth *is* a dragon, and

dragons ought to fight Thread with firestone? Right?"
He shrugged at Lessa. "What did you expect? He's
Ruathan-blooded, like yourself. Just keep your hide
and Ruth's intact."

"We haven't flown in a Threadfall yet," Jaxom
admitted realizing as he spoke how much resentment
showed in his voice.

F'lar gave him a friendly clout on the shoulder.

"He's a sound lad, Lessa, stop glowering. If he's
singed himself once, he's less likely to risk doing so
again. Was Ruth hurt?"

"Yes!" The anguish of that experience was plain in
Jaxom's admission.

F'lar gave a laugh and waggled a finger at Lessa,
who was still glaring at Jaxom. "There! That's the
best deterrent in the world. Ruth wasn't badly hurt, was
he? I can't say I've seen you that often recently . . ."
F'lar turned toward the killing ground as if conjuring
up the white dragon.

"No," Jaxom said quickly and F'lar grinned again
at the relief in his reply. "It's well healed. You can
barely see the scar. On his left thigh."

"I can't say that I like all this," Lessa said.

"We would have asked you, Weyrwoman," Jaxom
began, not entirely truthful, "but there was so much
trouble just then. . . ."

"Well . . ." she began.

"Well," echoed F'lar, "it really isn't up to you,
Lessa, but you do understand, Jaxom, how awkward it
would be for you to be seriously hurt right now. We
can't afford to have a major Hold in contention."

"I appreciate that, sir."

"Nor, I'm afraid, is it wise to press your confirmation
as Lord Holder—"

"I don't want Lytol to have to step down, sir. Not
ever."

"Your loyalty does you credit but I really can understand and appreciate your ambiguous position. It's
never easy to be patient, my friend, but patience can be
rewarding."

Again Jaxom was embarrassed by the look that Lessa and F'lar exchanged.

"And," the Weyrleader continued more briskly, as if he realized Jaxom's discomfiture, "you've already proved your resourcefulness today, though, believe me, had I known you to be so thorough, I'd have been more explicit in my instructions." F'lar's expression was severe but Jaxom found himself grinning in relief. "Twenty-five Turns timing it . . ." The Weyrleader was both appalled and impressed.

Lessa gave a snort.

"It was your jumps, Lessa, that first gave me the notion," Jaxom said, and when he saw her startled expression, explained: "Remember, you came forward in twenty-five Turn jumps when you brought the Old-timers forward. So I thought it likely that D'ram would go back that interval. It left him time enough before the Pass started so he wouldn't have to worry about Thread."

F'lar nodded approvingly, and Lessa appeared somewhat mollified.

Ramoth turned her head toward the entrance.

"Your meal is coming," Lessa said, smiling. "No more talk till you've eaten. Ruth's way ahead of you, just brought down his third wherry, Ramoth says."

"Don't worry about a bird or three or four," F'lar said, for Jaxom had winced at this report of Ruth's greed. "The Weyr can support the meal."

Menolly entered, breathing heavily from the climb and, to judge by the beads of perspiration on her brow, her haste. When Lessa exclaimed that she'd brought enough food to feed a fighting wing, Menolly replied that Manora said it was nearly dinnertime and they might as well all eat in the weyr.

If anyone had told Jaxom that morning that he'd enjoy a comfortable dinner with the Benden Weyr-leaders, he'd have told them to open their glow baskets. Despite the reassurances of Mnementh and Ramoth that they conveyed to him, he wouldn't sit still and eat until he'd checked on Ruth. So Lessa permitted him to walk to the ledge and see the white dragon grooming himself by the lake. When Jaxom resumed his place at the table, he found himself shaking, and he applied himself to the roast meats to restore his energy.

"Tell me again what those fire-lizards said about men," F'lar asked when they were relaxing around the table.

"You can't always get fire-lizards to explain," Menolly said, glancing first at Jaxom to see if he wished to answer. "They got so excited when Ruth asked them if they remembered men that their images made no sense. Actually," Menolly paused, drawing her brows together in concentration, "the images were so varied that you didn't see much."

"Why would their images be varied?" Lessa asked, interested in spite of her present antagonism to fire-lizards.

"Generally a group will come up with one specific image . . ."

Jaxom inhaled wearily: she couldn't be foolish enough to mention the egg pictures.

"They echoed Canth's fall from the Red Star. My friends will often come back with rather good images, I think each reinforcing the other, of places they've been."

"Men!" F'lar said thoughtfully. "They could mean men elsewhere in the South. It is a vast continent."

"F'lar!" Lessa's voice was sharp and warning. "You are not exploring the Southern Continent. And, might I suggest that if there were men there, somewhere, they would certainly have ventured far enough north to be seen at some stage or another by F'nor when he was south, or by Toric's groups. There would have been signs of them other than the unreliable recollections of some fire-lizards."

"You're quite likely correct, Lessa," F'lar said, looking so disappointed that Jaxom realized for the first time that being Benden's Weyrleader and First Dragonrider of Pern might not be as enviable a position as he'd previously assumed.

So often lately he'd come to realize that things were not as they seemed. There were hidden facets to everything. You'd think you had what you wanted in your grasp and, when you looked closely, it wasn't what it had seemed to be from a distance. Like teaching your dragon to chew firestone—and getting caught at it, in one sense, as he had. Now he had to train earnestly with N'ton's weyrlings, which was fine as far as it went but it didn't go far enough to please Jaxom—flying high in a Fort Weyr wing so his holders wouldn't even know he was there!

"The problem is, Jaxom, that we," F'lar indicated Lessa, himself and the entire Weyr, "have other plans for the South—before the Lord Holders start parceling it out to their younger sons." He brushed his hair back from his face. "We learned a lesson from the Oldtimers, a valuable one. And I know what happens to a Weyr in a long Interval." F'lar grinned broadly at Jaxom. "We've been mighty busy protecting land by seeding the grubs. By the next Pass of the Red Star, all the Northern Continent," and the Weyrleader's gesture was wide, "will be seeded. And safe at least from Thread burrowing. If the Holds thought dragonriders were superfluous before, they certainly will have more cause then."

"People always feel better *seeing* dragons flame Thread," Jaxom said hastily, from a sense of loyalty although, from the expression on F'lar's face, the Weyrleader didn't seem to be in need of any reassurance.

"True, but I'd prefer it if the Weyrs no longer needed the bounty of the Holds. If we had land enough of our own . . ."

"*You* want the South!"

"Not all of it."

"Just the best part of it," said Lessa firmly.

CHAPTER XI

*

Late Morning at Benden Weyr, Early Morning at Harpercraft Hall, Midday at Fidello's Hold, 15.7.5

JAXOM AND RUTH SPENT the night in an empty weyr, but Ruth felt sufficiently uneasy in a full-sized dragon bed that Jaxom bundled his furs and curled up against his mount. Jaxom was conscious of having to pull himself out of a soft, black enfolding pit from which he was loath to move.

"I know you must be flattened with fatigue, Jaxom, but you've got to wake up!" Menolly's voice penetrated the comfortable darkness. "Besides, you'll get a pain in your neck sleeping like that."

Menolly was upside down, Jaxom thought as he opened his eyes. Beauty was precariously perched, hind legs on the girl's shoulder, her forepaws well down Menolly's breast, peering anxiously at him. He felt Ruth stir.

"Jaxom, wake up! I've brought you all the klah you can drink." Mirrim moved into his line of vision. "But F'lar's eager to go and he wants Mnementh to talk to Ruth first."

Menolly winked solemnly at Jaxom, turning her shoulder to mask her action from Mirrim. Jaxom groaned because he was never going to keep straight in his mind who knew what was to be kept secret or who could be told. He groaned again because his neck was indeed stiff.

Ruth opened his inner lid just a crack, regarding his rider with displeasure. *I am tired. I need to sleep.*

"You can't sleep any longer now. Mnementh needs to speak to you."

Why didn't he speak to me last night?

"Because he probably wouldn't have remembered today."

Ruth's head came up and he turned one eye fully on Jaxom. *Mnementh would. He is the biggest dragon on all Pern.*

"Just because he let you gorge yourself on his killing ground, you like him. But he wants to speak to you so you'd better. Are you awake?"

If I am able to speak to you, I am not dreaming. I am awake.

"You are a bold fellow today," Jaxom said. In one massive heave, he pulled himself out of his impromptu bed. Dragging the furs about him, he half-fell toward the table where Menolly and Mirrim had politely withdrawn. The smell of klah was very welcome and he thanked the girls.

"What time is it?"

"Midmorning, Benden time," Menolly said, her face expressionless but her eyes dancing as she lightly stressed the last two words.

Jaxom grunted. They could all hear the creaks, groans and rumblings of Ruth as the dragon stretched himself in preparation for the day.

"When did you get Threadscored, Jaxom?" Mirrim asked with her usual forthrightness. She leaned over and traced the scar with a light touch, flattening her lips together in patent disapproval of the disfigurement.

"Teaching Ruth to chew firestone. At Fort Weyr," he added, after a malicious pause as he saw her gathering herself to scold him.

"Does Lessa know?" Mirrim asked, emphasizing the last word.

196

"Yes," Jaxom replied. Let Mirrim digest that truth. But Mirrim wouldn't let some matters alone.

"I don't think much of N'ton's weyrlingmaster then," she said, sniffing disapproval, "letting you get scored that way."

"Not his fault," Jaxom mumbled through half-chewed bread.

"Wasn't Lytol furious? You shouldn't be risking yourself."

Jaxom shook his head vigorously. He did wish Menolly hadn't brought Mirrim with her.

"And I just don't see what good it's going to do you. You can't expect to fight Ruth."

Jaxom choked. "I am too going to fight Ruth Mirrim."

"He already has," Menolly remarked, indicating the Threadscore. "Now shut your mouth and let the man eat."

"Man?" Mirrim's voice took a derisive swoop and she gave Jaxom a scathing glance.

Menolly made an exasperated sound. "If Path doesn't fly soon, Mirrim, you're not going to be on terms with anyone!"

Surprised, Jaxom looked at Mirrim, who was flushing deeply red.

"Oh ho, Path's ready to be flown! That'll sort out some of your high-headed notions." He couldn't resist crowing at her dismay. "Has Path shown a preference? Ha! Look at her blush! Never thought I'd see the day you'd lose the use of your tongue! And you'll be losing something more soon. I hope it's the wildest flight they've had at Benden since Mnementh first flew Ramoth!"

Mirrim exploded, her eyes narrowed with her anger, hands clenched into fists at her sides. "At least my Path will be flown! That's more than you'll ever do, with that white runt of yours!"

"Mirrim!" Menolly's sharp voice made the girl wince, but not soon enough to erase the angry retort that sank coldly into Jaxom's mind. He stared at Mirrim, trying to reject her taunt. "You take too much on

yourself, Mirrim," Menolly was saying. "I think you'd better leave."

"You just bet I'll leave. And I don't care if you have to climb down from this weyr, Menolly. Indeed I don't." Mirrim ran from the room.

"Shells and Shards, but it'll be a relief when that green of hers rises to mate. And it might even be today the way Mirrim's reacting." Menolly spoke in a casual tone, almost chuckling at her friend's behavior.

Jaxom swallowed against the dryness in his mouth. Rigidly he controlled his intense emotional reaction for Ruth's sake. A surreptitious glance at the white dragon showed that his friend was still stretching and extending wings and legs. Jaxom only hoped that the dragon had been too sleepy to attend to what they had been saying. He leaned toward Menolly.

"Do you know anything about . . ." he jerked his head at Ruth, "that I don't know?"

"About Path?" Menolly deliberately misconstrued his direction. "Well, if you've never seen a rider re-action to a proddy dragon, Mirrim's given you a classic example."

Path is a well-grown dragon, Ruth said thoughtfully. Jaxom groaned, covering his face with one hand; he should have known that Ruth missed little.

Menolly tapped his hand imperiously, her eyes demanding an explanation.

"Would you like to fly Path?" Jaxom asked Ruth, his eyes meeting Menolly's.

Why should I fly her? I have already outflown her in every race we flew at Telgar. She isn't as fast as I am in the air.

Jaxom repeated to Menolly exactly what Ruth had said, trying to keep his voice as close to Ruth's puzzled tone as possible.

Menolly burst out laughing. "Oh, I wish Ruth had said that in Mirrim's hearing. That would bring her down a peg or two."

Mnementh wishes to speak to me, Ruth said in a very respectful manner, raising his head and turning toward Mnementh's ledge.

"Do you know something I don't? About Ruth?" Jaxom asked in a fierce whisper as he caught hold of Menolly's hand to bring her closer to him.

"You heard him, Jaxom." Menolly's eyes were bright with amusement. "He's simply not interested in dragons, not that way yet."

Jaxom gave her hand a hard squeeze.

"Just think logically, Jaxom," she said, leaning over to him. "Ruth's small, he's maturing more slowly than other dragons."

"You mean, he may never mature enough to mate, don't you?"

Menolly regarded him steadily and he searched her eyes for pity or evasion; and found neither. "Jaxom, aren't you enjoying Corana?"

"Yes, I am."

"You're upset. I don't think you need be. I have never heard a word to suggest you should worry. Only that Ruth *is* unusual."

I have told Mnementh what he wishes to know. They go now, Ruth said. *Do you think I could take a bath in the lake?*

"Didn't you get enough bathing yesterday in the cove?" Jaxom was relieved to find himself answering his dragon calmly.

That was yesterday, Ruth replied equably. *I have eaten since then and slept on a dusty surface. You need a bath, too, I think.*

"All right, all right," Jaxom replied. "Go along with you then. But don't let Lessa see you with any fire-lizards."

How will I get my back properly cleaned? Ruth asked in mild reproach. He stepped down from the bedstone.

"What's his problem?" Menolly wondered aloud, grinning at Jaxom's expression.

"Wants his back scrubbed."

"I'll send my friends to you, Ruth, once you're at the lake. Lessa won't notice."

Ruth paused in his progress to the weyr entrance, cocking his head, patiently considering. Then he

199

arched his neck and moved forward confidently. *Yes, Mnementh has gone and Ramoth with him. They will not know that I will have a real bath with fire-lizards to scrub my ridges properly.*

Jaxom couldn't help but laugh at the smug satisfaction in Ruth's tone as he left the weyr.

"Sorry about inflicting Mirrim on you, Jaxom, but I couldn't get up to this level without Path. And her."

Jaxom took a long sip of klah. "I suppose, if Path's proddy, she has to be excused."

"Mirrim usually is, one way or another." Menolly's tone was acid.

"Huh?"

"Mirrim generally gets away with outrageous behavior—"

A sudden thought caused Jaxom to interrupt the harper girl abruptly. "You don't think Mirrim did sneak onto the Ground before that Hatching? I know she swears she didn't but I do know she wasn't supposed to Impress. . . ."

"Not any more than you were! Oh, for goodness sake, Jaxom, can't I tease you? No, I don't think she tried to influence Path in the shell. She had her fire-lizards and was always content with them. Who wouldn't be with three? Also, you surely know how furious Lessa was after she Impressed Path? Well, no one came forward then to say they'd ever seen Mirrim sneaking onto the Ground and they would have! Mirrim can be managing, tactless, difficult and exasperating, but she's not devious. Weren't you at the Hatching? Oh, well, I was. Path came staggering over to the spot where Mirrim was sitting, crying her heart out and refusing every single candidate on the Ground until F'lar was forced to decide that Path wanted someone sitting among the spectators."

Menolly shrugged. "Someone who turned out to be Mirrim. Oddly enough, her fire-lizards never uttered a chirp of objection. No, I think the partnering was as much . . . well, destined to be as you and Ruth. Not at all like my acquisition of Poll. As if I needed another fire-lizard." She grimaced ruefully. "But his shell cracked just as I was passing him to that addle-handed child of Lord Groghe's. *He's* never faulted me, and the child got a green. A bronze would have been wasted on that brat!"

Jaxom pointed a forefinger at Menolly. "You are blathering! What is it you're hiding? What is it that you know about Ruth that I don't?"

Menolly looked Jaxom straight in the eye. "I don't *know* anything, Jaxom. But, by your own account to me a few minutes gone by, Ruth greeted the news of Path's imminent mating with all the enthusiasm of a weyrling asked to change glow baskets."

"That doesn't mean—"

"Doesn't mean anything. So don't get defensive. Ruth is maturing late. That's all you need to think about it . . . especially with Corana on hand."

"Menolly!"

"Don't explode! You'll undo all the good rest you had last night. You were faded!" She put her hand on his arm, giving it a squeeze. "I'm not prying about Corana. I'm commenting, although you might not appreciate the distinction."

"It does occur to me that Ruatha Hold is not Harper business," he said, gritting his teeth against the words he'd like to use.

"You, Jaxom, rider of white Ruth, are the Harper's business—not young Jaxom, Lord of Ruatha."

"You're making distinctions again."

"Yes, I am, Jaxom," and although her voice was serious, her eyes twinkled. "When Jaxom influences what happens to Pern, then he becomes Harper business."

Jaxom stared at her, still baffled by her silence on the matter of the egg's return. Then he caught the odd warning expression in her eyes; for some reason beyond his comprehension, she did not want him to confirm that adventure.

"You're several people at once, Jaxom," she went on, earnestly. "The Lord of a Hold which cannot be in contention, the rider of an unusual dragon and a young man who's not quite sure who or what he should

be. You can, you know, *be* all and more, without being disloyal to anyone, or yourself."

Jaxom snorted. "Who's speaking? The Harper, or
Menolly the Meddler?"

Menolly shrugged, gave a rueful twist of her mouth,
neither smile nor denial. "Partly Harper, because I
can't look at most things without thinking Harper, but
Menolly mostly, right now, I think, because I don't
want you to be upset. Particularly not after that feat
you pulled off yesterday!" There was no doubt of the
warmth of her smile.

Her fair of fire-lizards came swooping into the weyr.
Jaxom suppressed his annoyance at the interruption
because he'd have preferred to keep Menolly talking
in this unusually expansive mood. But the fire-lizards
were clearly excited and, before Menolly could calm
them enough to find out, Ruth came into the weyr,
his eyes whirling with myriad colors.

*D'ram and Tiroth are here, and everyone is very
excited,* Ruth said, pushing his nose at Jaxom to be
caressed. Jaxom obliged, and went on to rub eye
ridges damp from Ruth's swimming. *Mnementh is very
pleased with himself.* There was a note of grievance in
that addition.

"Well, Mnementh couldn't have brought D'ram and
Tiroth back without your help, Ruth," Jaxom replied
staunchly. "Right, Menolly?"

*I could not have found D'ram and Tiroth without
the fire-lizards' help,* Ruth remarked graciously. *And
you thought of going back twenty-five Turns.*

Menolly sighed, unable to hear Ruth's last comment.

"Actually, we owe more to those Southern fire-
lizards."

"That's just what Ruth said . . ."

"Dragons are honest people!" Menolly exhaled
heavily and rose. "Come on, my friend. You and I
had better return to our own halls. We've done what
we were sent to do. Done it well. That's all the satisfaction we're likely to have." She shot him an amused
look. "Isn't that so?" She gathered up her pack.

"Which is the way some matters have to remain. Right?"

She slipped her arm through his, hauling him to his feet, grinning in a semi-conspiratorial fashion that oddly enough did dispel the resentment he was beginning to feel.

As they came out on the ledge, they could see the activity about the queen's weyr, as riders and women from the Lower Caverns came streaming across to greet D'ram and his bronze.

"I must admit, it's rather nice to leave Benden with everyone in a good frame of mind for a change," Menolly said as Ruth bore her and Jaxom upward.

Jaxom expected to deposit Menolly safely in the Harperhall and return home. No sooner had Ruth announced himself to the watchdragon on the fire-heights than Zair and a harper-banded little queen attached themselves with precarious talon holds to Ruth's neck.

"That's Sebell's Kimi. He's back!" There was an exultant ring to Menolly's voice that Jaxom had never heard before.

The watchdragon says that the Harper wants to see us. So does Zair, Ruth told Jaxom. *He means me, too,* Ruth added with a note of pleasant surprise.

"Why shouldn't the Harper want to see you, Ruth? He's sure to give you the credit you're due," Jaxom said, still nursing a bit of resentment as he slapped the arched neck affectionately. Ruth had turned his head to choose a landing space in the courtyard.

Master Robinton and a man with a master's knot on his shoulder came striding down the Hall's steps. Master Robinton's arms were outstretched so he could encircle both Menolly and Jaxom with an enthusiasm that almost embarrassed Jaxom. Then, to his complete surprise, the other Harper grabbed Menolly from Robinton's grasp and began to swing her around and around, all the time kissing her soundly. Instead of protesting this treatment of their friend, the fire-lizards went into spectacular aerial maneuvers of twined necks and overlapped wings. Jaxom knew that fire-lizard queens rarely indulged in tactile contact with

203

queens, but Beauty and the strange gold were as joyously indulging as Menolly and the man. Glancing to see what the Harper's reaction was to such excess, Jaxom was astonished to see Master Robinton grinning with smug pleasure, an expression quickly altered when he noticed Jaxom's regard.

"Come, Jaxom, Menolly and Sebell have several months' news to exchange and I want to hear *your* version of D'ram's discovery."

As Robinton guided Jaxom toward the Hall, Menolly cried out and pushed herself free of Sebell's arms, although Jaxom noticed that her fingers remained entwined in Sebell's as she took a hesitant step toward Robinton. "Master?"

"What?" Robinton affected dismay. "Cannot Sebell command a measure of your time after so long an absence?"

Jaxom was gratified to see Menolly caught by uncertainty and confusion. Sebell was grinning.

"Hear what *he* has to tell you first, girl," Robinton said, more kindly. "I'll make do admirably with Jaxom."

Glancing back at the pair as Robinton escorted him into the Hall, Jaxom saw their arms linked about each other's waists, heads inclined together. Their firelizards spiraled above, following them as they walked slowly toward the meadow beyond the Harper Hall.

"You brought D'ram and Tiroth back?" the Harper asked Jaxom.

"I found them. The Benden Weyrleaders returned them this morning, Benden time."

Robinton hesitated, his foot nearly missing the top step as he led Jaxom to his own quarters. "They were there, though, in that cove, all along? Just as I surmised."

"Twenty-five Turns back," and, with no further urging, Jaxom recounted the adventure from the beginning. His listener was more sympathetic and attentive than either Lessa or F'lar had been, so Jaxom began to enjoy his unaccustomed role.

"Men?" The Harper, who had been lounging in his

chair, one booted foot propped on the table, abruptly came off the end of his spine. His heel rang on the stone floor. "They'd seen men?"

Jaxom was momentarily startled. Whereas the Weryleaders had been alarmed and skeptical, the Master Harper acted almost as if he'd expected this news.

"I've always maintained that we came from the Southern Continent," the Harper said, more to himself than anyone else. Then he signaled Jaxom to continue.

Jaxom obeyed but was soon aware that only half the Harper's attention was on his narrative, though the man nodded and asked occasional questions. Jaxom told of his and Menolly's safe return to Benden Weyr, remembered to mention his gratitude to Mnementh for permitting Ruth to eat. He fell silent then, wondering how to ask a question of his own of the Harper, but Robinton was frowning at some private reflections.

"Tell me again what the fire-lizards said about these *men*," the Harper asked, leaning forward, elbows on the table, eyes fixed on Jaxom. On his shoulder, Zair echoed a querying note.

"They didn't *say* much, Master Robinton. That's the trouble! They got so excited, they made little sense at all. Menolly could probably tell you more because she had Beauty and the three bronzes with her. But—"

"What did Ruth say?"

Jaxom shrugged, unhappily aware that his half-answers were inadequate.

"He said the images were too confused, even if they were all about men, their men. And we, Menolly and I, weren't their sort of men."

Jaxom reached for the pitcher of klah, to slake the dryness of his mouth. He courteously filled a cup for the Harper who absently drained half of it while deep in thought.

"Men," Master Robinton said again, extending the last consonant and ending the sound with a click of his tongue. He got to his feet in such a fluid motion that Zair squawked, clawing for balance. "Men, and so long ago that the images the fire-lizards retain are vague. That is very interesting, very interesting indeed."

The Harper began to pace, stroking Zair, who chittered reprovingly.

Jaxom glanced out the window at Ruth, sunning himself in the courtyard, the local fire-lizards clustered about him. Jaxom listened idly to the chorus, wondering why they were stopped so often in the Ballad, for he couldn't detect discord in their harmonies. The breeze coming in the window was pleasant, soft with summer scents, and he was jerked back to his surroundings when Robinton's hand gripped his shoulder.

"You've done very well, lad, but you'd better get back to Ruatha now. You're half asleep. That time jump took more out of you than I think you realize."

As Master Robinton accompanied Jaxom to the courtyard, he had him rehearse the conversation with the fire-lizards just once more. This time the Harper nodded his head sharply at each point as if to insure accurate recall.

"That you found D'ram and Tiroth safe, Jaxom, is the least of this affair, I think. I knew I was right to involve you and Ruth. Don't be surprised if you hear more from me on this business, with Lytol's permission, of course."

With a final affectionate grip of his arm, Robinton stepped back to let Jaxom mount Ruth, the fire-lizards shrilling their disappointment at the end of their friend's visit. As Ruth obediently climbed higher, Jaxom waved a cheery farewell to the diminishing figure of the Master Harper. Then Jaxom looked down toward the river for Menolly and Sebell. He was annoyed with himself, at the same time, for wanting to know where they were—and further irritated, because, when he did spot them, the intimacy of their attitude proved that they enjoyed a relationship of which he had been totally unaware.

He did not go straight back to Ruatha Hold. Lytol would not be expecting him at any particular hour. As he also saw no fire-lizards abroad to betray his delinquency, he asked Ruth to take him to the Plateau Hold. In Ruth's cheerful compliance, he wondered if the white dragon knew his mind better than he did himself.

Now, it was close to midday in western Pern, and Jaxom wondered how he was going to attract Corana's attention without every dependent in the hold knowing of his visit. His need of her was great enough to make him irritable.

She comes, Ruth said, dipping his wing so that Jaxom could see the girl emerging from the hold, walking in the direction of the river, a basket balanced on one shoulder.

What could have been more fortuitous! He told Ruth to take them to the river edge where the women of her hold generally did their washing.

The stream is not very deep, Ruth said casually, *but there is a large rock in the sun where I can be comfortable and warm.* And before Jaxom could answer, he began to glide down to the river, past the rapid boiling waters flowing across treacherously strewn boulders, to the calm pool and the flat stone outcropping. Angling himself neatly so as not to foul his wings in the branches of the heavy shade trees that bordered the river, Ruth landed lightly on the biggest rock. *She comes,* he repeated, ducking his shoulder so that Jaxom could dismount.

Suddenly Jaxom was assailed by a conflict of desires and doubts. Mirrim's angry remarks resounded in his head. Ruth was indeed well beyond the usual age of mating and yet . . .

She comes and she is good for you. If she is good for you, it is good for me, Ruth said. *She makes you feel happy and relaxed and that is good. The sun here makes me warm and happy, too. Go.*

Startled by the strength of his weyrmate's tone, Jaxom stared up at Ruth's face. The eyes were whirling gently, with the blues and greens of a contentment at odds with the force of his voice.

Then Corana reached the last loop in the path to the river's edge and saw him. She dropped her basket, spilling the linen, and ran, embracing him so fiercely, kissing his face and neck with such uninhibited delight, that he was soon too involved to think.

Together they moved toward the soft moss that carpeted the ground beyond the stones, out of sight of the river bank, out of Ruth's actual vision. Corana was as willing and eager as he was to satisfy desires thwarted on his previous visit to the hold. As his hands touched her soft flesh and he felt her body press against his, he wondered briefly if she'd have been as willing a lover had he not been Ruatha's Lord. But he didn't care! He was her lover now! He gave himself to that pursuit with no further reservation. At the precise moment of his release, exquisite to the point of pain, he was aware of a gentle touch and knew, with a sense of relief that enhanced his own, that Ruth was joined to him then, as always.

CHAPTER XII

Ruatha Hold, Fidello's Hold, Threadfall, 15.7.6

KEEPING A SECRET from one's dragon was not easy. About the only safe time for Jaxom to think of anything he didn't wish Ruth to perceive was very late at night when his friend was sound asleep, or in the morning if Jaxom happened to wake before Ruth. He had seldom needed to shield his thought from Ruth, which further complicated and inhibited the process. Then, too, the pace of Jaxom's life—the now-boring training with the weyrling wing, helping Lytol and Brand to gear up the Hold to full summer activity, not to mention excursions to the Plateau Hold—caused Jaxom to fall asleep as soon as he pulled his bed furs about his shoulders. Mornings, he was often dragged out of his bed by Tordril or another fosterling just in time to keep appointments.

Nevertheless, the problem of Ruth's maturity cropped up in Jaxom's mind at inconvenient times during his waking hours and had to be rigidly suppressed before a hint of his anxiety reached his dragon.

Twice at Fort Weyr, to intensify the problem, a proddy green had taken off on a flight, pursued by such browns and blues as felt able to rise to her. The first time, Jaxom was in the middle of drill sequence and only happened to notice the flight above and beyond the weyrlings' wing. His attention was abruptly diverted from them as a most unconcerned Ruth continued in the wing's maneuver. Jaxom had to grab at the fighting straps to remain in place.

The second time, Jaxom and Ruth were aground when the mating shrieks of a green blooding her kill startled the Weyr. The other weyrlings were immature enough to be disinterested but the weyrlingmaster looked in Jaxom's direction for a long moment. All at once, Jaxom realized that K'nebel was apparently wondering if Jaxom and Ruth were going to join those waiting for the green to launch herself.

Jaxom was assailed by such a gamut of emotions —anxiety, shame, expectation, reluctance, and pure terror—that Ruth reared, wings wide, in alarm.

What has upset you? Ruth demanded, settling to the ground and curving his neck about to regard his rider, his eyes whirling in quick response to Jaxom's emotions.

"I'm all right. I'm all right," Jaxom said hastily, stroking Ruth's head, desperately wanting to ask if Ruth felt at all like flying the green and hoping in a muted whisper deep inside him that Ruth did not!

With a challenging snarl, the green dragon was airborne, the blues and browns after her while she repeated her taunting challenge. Quicker, lighter than any of her prospective mates, her facility strengthened by her sexual readiness, she achieved a conspicuous distance before the first male had become airborne. Then they were all after her. On the killing ground, their riders closed into a knot about the green's rider. All too quickly, challenger and pursuers dwindled to specks in the sky. The riders half-ran, half-stumbled to the Lower Caverns and the chamber reserved there.

Jaxom had never witnessed a mating flight of dragons. He swallowed, trying to moisten his dry throat. He felt heart and blood thudding and a tension that he usually experienced only as he held Corana's slender body against him. He suddenly wondered which dragon had flown Mirrim's Path, which rider had—

The touch on his shoulder made him jump and cry out.

"Well, if Ruth isn't ready to fly, you certainly are, Jaxom," K'nebel said. The weyrlingmaster glanced up at far-distant specks in the sky. "Even a green's mating can be unsettling." K'nebel's expression was understanding. He nodded at Ruth. "He wasn't interested? No, well, give him time! You'd better be off. Drill was all but over today, anyhow. I've just got to keep these younger ones occupied someplace else when that green gets caught."

Then Jaxom realized that the rest of the wing had dispersed. With a second encouraging clap on Jaxom's back, K'nebel walked off toward his bronze, agilely mounting and urging the beast up toward their weyr.

Jaxom thought of the skyborne beasts. Unwillingly he thought of their riders in the inner room, linked to their dragons in an emotional struggle that was resolved in a strengthening and fusing of the links between dragons and riders. Jaxom thought of Mirrim. And of Corana.

With a groan, he sprang on Ruth's neck, fleeing the emotional atmosphere of Fort Weyr, trying to flee from his sudden realization of what he had probably always known about riders but had only this very morning assimilated.

He had intended to go to the lake to immerse himself in the cold waters and let that icy shock cure his body and chill the torment in his mind. But Ruth took him instead to the Plateau Hold.

"Ruth! The lake. Take me to the lake!"

It is better for you to be here right now, was Ruth's astonishing reply. *The fire-lizard says the girl is in the upper field.* Once again Ruth seized the initiative, gliding toward the field where young grain waved, brilliantly green in the noonday sun, where Corana was diligently hoeing away the tenacious

211

creeper vine that grew from the borders of the field and threatened to strangle the crop.

Ruth achieved a landing on the narrow margin between grain and wall. Corana, recovering from surprise at his unexpected arrival, waved a welcome. Instead of rushing toward him as she usually did, she smoothed back her hair and blotted the perspiration beading her face.

"Jaxom," she began as he strode toward her, the urgency in his loins increasing at the sight of her, "I wish you wouldn't—"

He silenced her half-teasing scold with a kiss, felt something hard clout him along his side. Pinning her against him with his right arm, he found the offending hoe with his left hand. Wrenching it from her grasp, he spun it away from them. Corana wriggled to get free, as unprepared for this mood in him as he was. He held her closer, trying to temper the pressures rising within him until she could respond. She smelled of the earth and her own sweat. Her hair, covering his face as he kissed her throat and breast, also smelled of sun and sweat, and the odors excited him further. Somewhere in the back of his mind was a green dragon, shrieking her defiance. Somewhere, too, close to his need, was that vision of dragonriders in an inner room, waiting, with an excitement that matched his own, waiting until the green dragon had been captured by the fastest, the strongest or the smartest of her pursuers. But it was Corana he was holding in his arms, and Corana who was beginning to respond to his need. They were on the warm ground, the dampness of earth she had just hoed soft under his elbows and knees. The sun was warm on his buttocks as he tried to erase the memory of those riders half-stumbling toward the inner room, and the mocking taunt of a green dragon in flight. He did not resist or deny Ruth's familiar beloved touch as his orgasm released the turmoil of body and mind.

Jaxom could not bring himself to go to weyrling practice the next morning. Lytol and Brand were out early, riding to a distant holding with the fosterlings so no one questioned his presence. When he left the Hold in the afternoon, he firmly directed Ruth to the lake and scrubbed and scrubbed his dragon until Ruth meekly asked what was the matter.

"I love you, Ruth. You are mine. I love you," Jaxom said, wanting with all his heart to be able to add, with his former blithe confidence, that he would do anything in the world for his friend. "I love you!" he repeated through gritted teeth and dove from Ruth's back as deeply as he could into the ice-cold waters of the lake.

Perhaps I am hungry, Ruth said as Jaxom fought the pressure of water and airlessness in his lungs.

That could certainly provide a diversion, Jaxom thought as he erupted to the surface, gasping for breath. "There's a hold in South Ruatha where there're wherries fattening."

That would do very nicely.

Jaxom dried himself quickly, shrugged into his clothes and boots, absently coiling the damp bath sheet over his shoulders as he mounted Ruth and directed him up and *between* to the Southern Holding. He realized his foolishness the moment the deathly chill of *between* compounded the dampness about his neck. He'd surely contract a distressingly uncomfortable head cold from such stupidity.

Ruth hunted with his usual dispatch. Fire-lizards, local by their band colors, arrived, apparently invited by the white dragon to share the feast. Jaxom watched, freer to think while Ruth was totally involved with hunting and eating. Jaxom was not pleased with himself. He was thoroughly disgusted and revolted by the way he had used Corana. The fact that she seemed to have matched what he had to admit was a violent lust dismayed him. Their relationship, once innocent pleasure, had somehow been sullied. He wasn't at all certain that he cared to continue as her lover, an attitude that posed another unpleasant burden of guilt. One point in his favor, he had helped her finish the hoeing his importunity had interrupted. That way she'd not be in trouble with Fidello for shorting her task. The young grain was important. But he ought not to have taken Corana like that. Doing so was inexcusable.

She liked it very much. Ruth's thought touched him so unexpectedly that Jaxom jerked straight.

"How could you possibly know?"

When you are with Corana, her emotions are also very strong and just like yours. So I can feel her, too. Only at that time. Otherwise I do not hear her. Acceptance rather than regret colored Ruth's tone. Almost as if he were relieved that the contact was limited.

Ruth was padding up from the field as he spoke, having disposed of two fat wherries without leaving much for the fire-lizards to pick over. Jaxom regarded his friend, the whirl of the jeweled eyes slowing as the red of hunger paled into dark violet and then the blue of contentment.

"Do you like what you hear? Our lovemaking?" Jaxom asked, abruptly deciding to air his concern.

Yes. You enjoy it so much. It is good for you. I like it to be good for you.

Jaxom jumped to his feet, consumed by frustration and guilt. "But don't you want it for yourself? Why are you always worried about me? Why didn't you go fly that green?"

Why does that worry you? Why should I fly the green?

"Because you're a dragon."

I am a white dragon. Blues and browns, and occasionally a bronze, fly greens.

"You could have flown her. You could have flown her, Ruth!"

I did not wish to. You are upset again. I have upset you. Ruth extended his neck, his nose gently touching Jaxom's face in apology.

Jaxom threw his arms about Ruth's neck, burrowing his forehead against the smooth, spicy-smelling hide, concentrating on how very much he loved his

Ruth, his most unusual Ruth, the only white dragon on all Pern.

Yes, I am the only white dragon there has ever been on Pern, Ruth said encouragingly, moving his body so that he could gather Jaxom closer within the circle of his foreleg. *I am the white dragon. You are my rider. We are together.*

"Yes," Jaxom said, wearily admitting defeat, "we *are* together."

A chill shook Jaxom and he sneezed. Shells, if he was heard sneezing about the Hold, he'd be subjected to some of those noxious medicines Deelan foisted on everyone. He closed his jacket, folded the now dry bathing sheet about his neck and chest and, mounting Ruth, suggested that they get back to the Hold as fast as possible.

He escaped the dosing only because he kept out of Deelan's way by staying in his own quarters. He announced that he was occupied in a task for Robinton and did not care to interrupt it for the evening meal. He hoped that his sneezing would abate by evening. Lytol would be sure to visit him, which reminded Jaxom that if he didn't have something to show for his afternoon's occupation Lytol might be difficult. Actually, Jaxom had wanted to set down his observations about that beautiful cove, with the cone of the huge mountain center so neatly in its curve. Using the soft carbon stick that Master Bendarek had developed to use on his paper leaves, Jaxom became absorbed in the project. Much easier to work with these tools, he thought, than with sandtable. Errors, since his memory of the cove did not appear to be that precise, could be rubbed out with a blob of softwood tree sap as long as he was careful not to abrade the leaf's surface too much.

He had achieved a respectable map of D'ram's cove when a knock on the door broke his concentration. He sniffed mightily before calling permission to enter. His voice didn't seem too affected by the congestion in his head.

Lytol entered, greeted Jaxom and approached the

worktable, eyes courteously averted from the contents.

"Ruth did eat today?" he asked, "because N'ton sent to remind you that Thread falls north and you could fly with the wing. Ruth will have sufficient time to digest, won't he?"

"He'll be just fine," Jaxom replied, aware of both an excitement and a sense of inevitability at the prospect of fighting Thread from Ruth's back.

"Have you then completed your training with the weyrlings?"

So Lytol had noticed his morning's delinquency from the Weyr. Jaxom also heard the faint note of surprise in his guardian's voice.

"Well, you might say that I've learned about all I'd need to know since I'm not to fly regularly with a fighting wing. I've done this sketch of D'ram's cove. That's where we found him. Isn't it beautiful?" He offered the leaf to Lytol.

To Jaxom's satisfaction, Lytol's expression changed to one of surprised interest as he peered intently at the sketch and diagram.

"Your rendering of the mountain is accurate? It must surely be the largest volcano on Pern! You've got the perspective correct? How magnificent! And this area?" Lytol's hand washed across the space beyond the trees which Jaxom had carefully drawn in their variety and as accurately in position along the cove's edge as he could recall.

"Forest extends to low hills, but we stayed on the beach, of course—"

"Beautiful! One can appreciate why the Harper remembered the place so clearly."

With a noticeable reluctance, Lytol replaced the leaf on Jaxom's table.

"The drawing is a poor image of the real place," he said to his guardian, letting his voice end on an upward note. It wasn't the first time Jaxom regretted Lytol's aversion to riding on dragonback for any but the most vital excursions.

Lytol favored Jaxom with a brief smile, shaking his

head. "It is good enough to guide a dragon, I'm sure. But do remember to tell me when you've the notion to return there."

With that Lytol bade him good evening, leaving Jaxom a trifle unsettled. Was Lytol giving him oblique permission to go back to the cove? Why? Critically, Jaxom examined the sketch, wondering if he really had drawn the trees correctly. It would be nice to go back there again. Say, after Threadfall, if flying didn't overtire Ruth . . .

I would like to swim off firestone stench in the cove waters, Ruth said sleepily.

By tilting his chair back, Jaxom could see the white bulk of Ruth on his couch, head facing Jaxom's door, though both sets of the dragon's eyelids were closed.

I would like that very much indeed.

"And maybe we could find out more about those men from the fire-lizards." Yes, thought Jaxom, relieved to have a definite objective, it would be very good. Neither F'lar nor Lessa had forbidden him to return to the cove. It was certainly far enough away from the Southern Hold to put him in no danger of compromising the Weyrleaders. Now if he could learn more about the men, he'd be doing Robinton a favor. He might even be able to find a clutch somewhere along that coastline. Maybe that's what Lytol had had in mind by giving him that oblique permission. Of course! Why hadn't Jaxom realized that before?

Threadfall was calculated to arrive the next morning at just past the ninth hour. Although Jaxom was not to ride out in his usual place with the flamethrower crews, he was nevertheless awakened early by a drudge who brought him a tray of klah and sweetbread as well as a package of meatrolls for his lunch.

Jaxom was conscious of a stuffiness in his head, a tightness in his throat and a general sense of unfitness. Under his breath he cursed himself for that moment's thoughtlessness that was going to make his first Threadfall mighty uncomfortable. What under the sun had possessed him to dive into a chill-watered lake, go *between* half-soaked, then cavort in lustful exercise on damp, just-turned earth? He sneezed several times as he dressed. That cleared his nose, but left his head aching. He put on his warmest underfur, heaviest tunic, pants and extra liners in his boots. He was sweltering when he and Ruth left their quarters. Holders were bustling about the courtyard, mounting runners, securing flamethrowers and equipment. The watchdragon and the hold fire-lizards were chewing firestone on the heights. Catching Lytol's eye where the Lord Warder stood on the top step of the Hold entrance, Jaxom gestured skyward, saw Lytol salute in reply before he continued giving orders for the day's emergency. Jaxom sneezed once more, an exhalation that rocked him back on his heels.

Are you all right? Ruth's eyes whirled faster in concern.

"For a damn fool who's caught a cold, yes, I'm all right. Let's get going. I'm boiling inside these furs."

Ruth complied and Jaxom was more comfortable with wind cooling the sweat from his face. He had Ruth fly direct to the Weyr for they had plenty of time. He would never be foolish enough to go *between* again in a sweat. Maybe he'd better change to lighter flying gear once at the Fort. He'd be warm enough once they were fighting Thread. However, the Weyr was situated higher in the mountains than Ruatha Hold and he did not feel overheated once they landed.

Following instructions well drilled into him, Jaxom took Ruth to collect their firestone sack. Then he directed Ruth to take stones from the supply laid about the Bowl for that purpose. Ruth began to chew firestone, preparing his second stomach for flame. With a good start, he'd have a steady flame that could be easily replenished in flight by additional stone from the sack he carried. While Ruth was chewing, Jaxom got himself a large mug of steaming klah, hoping that would revive him. He felt miserable, his nose clogging repeatedly.

Fortunately the noise of so many dragons chewing stone masked his fits of sneezing. If this wasn't to be his very first time to fight Ruth, Jaxom might have hesitated about continuing. Then he convinced himself that since the weyrlings would undoubtedly be flying in the wake of the other wings on the after-edge of Threadfall, he could probably keep from having to go *between* frequently, if at all, and so he would run little risk of aggravating the congestion. He didn't fancy sneezing just as Ruth had to duck *between* to avoid Thread.

N'ton and Lioth appeared on the Star Stones, Lioth bugling for silence as the Weyrleader raised his arm. Fort's four queens flanked the big bronze, larger than he but, in Jaxom's eyes, only enhancing his magnificence with their brilliance. Dragons on all weyr ledges listened to Lioth's silent orders and then the wings formed. Jaxom needlessly tested the fighting straps that held him securely to his ridge seat on Ruth's neck.

We are to ride with the queens' wing, Ruth told his rider.

"All of the weyrlings?" Jaxom asked, since he'd heard nothing from K'nebel about a change of position.

No, just us. Ruth sounded pleased but Jaxom wasn't at all sure of the honor.

His hesitation was noticed by the weyrlingmaster, who gave him a curt signal to take his assigned position. So Jaxom directed Ruth upward to the Star Stones. As Ruth landed neatly on the left-hand side of Selianth, the youngest Fort queen, Jaxom wondered if he looked as silly as he felt, dwarfed by the golden dragon.

Lioth bugled again and the Weyrleaders took off from the Star Stones, dropping far enough for wing room before rising on strongly beating wings to the sky. Ruth needed no room at all for takeoff and hovered briefly before taking his position beside Selianth. Prilla, her rider, waved an encouraging fist and then Ruth told Jaxom that Lioth was giving him the command to go *between* to meet Threadfall.

When they emerged above the barren hills of

northern Ruatha, Jaxom found himself responding to an exhilaration he had never before experienced on Ruth. The wings of the fighting dragons spread above and all around his lower level position in the queens' wing. The sky appeared to be full of dragons, all facing east, the highest wing the first to contact the imminent Fall of Thread.

Jaxom snuffled back the mucus, irritated that his condition was dampening this personal triumph: Jaxom, Lord of Ruatha Hold, was actually going to fly his white dragon against Thread! Between his legs, he could feel Ruth's body rumbling with the stored gas and wondered if the feeling were in any way analogous to his own congested, heavy-headed state.

In a burst of speed, the uppermost wing moved forward and Jaxom had no further time for speculation as he, too, glimpsed the filming of the clear sky, that graying that heralded the advent of Thread.

Selianth wants me to stay above her at all times so her flamethrower won't singe me, Ruth said, his mental tone muffled as he retained fire-breath. He altered his position and now all the wings began to move.

The gray film visibly turned into the silver rain of Thread. Gouts of flame blossomed in the sky as the forward dragons seared their ancient mindless enemy into charred dust. Jaxom's excitement was tempered by the endless drills he had performed with the weyrlings, and by the cold logic of caution. He and Ruth would not return Threadscored today!

The queens' wing nosed slightly earthward, to fly under the first wave of dragons, set to destroy whatever shred might have eluded the first flames. They flew through patches of fine dust, the residue of crisped Thread. Wheeling sharply, the queens' wing turned back and now Jaxom did spy a silver strand. Urging an all too willing Ruth upward, Jaxom heard his white dragon warn others off as the novice team encountered and demolished Thread in proper style.

Proudly, Jaxom wondered if anyone else noted the economy of Ruth's deadly flame: just enough, no more than was necessary. He stroked his friend's neck and felt Ruth's delight in the praise. Then they were off on another tangent as the queens' wing headed for a heavier concentration of Thread, eluding an easterly flying wing.

From that moment onward, throughout the Fall, Jaxom had no time for further thought. He became aware of the rhythm to the queens' wing pattern. Margatta on her golden Luduth seemed to have an uncanny instinct for those heavier patches that could escape even the closest flying wing. Each time the queens would be under the silver rain, destroying it. It became apparent to Jaxom that his position in the queens' wing was neither sinecure nor protective. The golden dragons could cover more territory in the air, but they were not as maneuverable. Ruth was. Ever maintaining his upper position, the little white dragon could flit from one side of the queens' V formation to the other, assisting wherever he was needed.

Abruptly, the Thread stopped falling. The upper reaches of the sky were clear of the graying mist. The highest wing began to circle down leisurely, to begin the final phase of the defense, the low-level sweep which assisted ground crews in locating any trace of viable Thread.

The exhilaration of combat drained from Jaxom and his physical discomfort began to manifest itself. His head felt twice its proper size, his eyes were unaccountably filled with grit and ached hotly. His chest felt tighter, his throat raw. The illness had a good hold on him now. He'd been a fool to fight Thread. To compound his miseries, he didn't even have any sense of personal achievement after four hours of bloody hard work. He was thoroughly depressed. He earnestly wished that he and Ruth could retire now but he had made such an issue of flying with the fighting wings that he must complete the exercise. Dutifully he continued on above the queens.

The big queen says we must go, Ruth said suddenly, *before the ground crews see us.*

Jaxom glanced down at Margatta and saw her signal of dismissal. He could not suppress the sense of injury that gesture gave him. He hadn't expected a round of cheers but he did think that he and Ruth had acquitted themselves well enough to rate some indication of approval. Had they done something wrong? He could not think with his head hot and aching. But he obeyed, directing Ruth to change flight to the Hold when he saw Selianth rise toward him. Prilla gave her right fist the pumping motion that signaled well done and thanks.

Her recognition reduced his grievance.

We fought well and no Thread passed us, Ruth said in a hopeful tone. *I was quite comfortable sustaining my flame.*

"You were marvelous, Ruth. You were such a clever dodger, we didn't have to go *between* once." Jaxom slapped with affectionate force the flight-extended neck. "D'you have more gas to exhale?"

He felt Ruth cough and just the merest trickle flicked beyond his head.

No more flame but I shall be very glad to be rid of the fire-ash. This is the most firestone I have ever chewed!

Ruth sounded so proud of himself that despite his general discomfort, Jaxom laughed, his own spirits buoyed up by Ruth's ingenuous satisfaction.

It was also obscurely comforting to find the Hold occupied by a few drudges only. The other Thread fighters were hours away from the rewards he could now enjoy. While Ruth drank long and deep at the courtyard well, Jaxom asked a drudge to bring him any warm food available and a mug of wine.

As Jaxom entered his own quarters to change out of his stinking fighting gear, he passed his worktable and, seeing the cove sketch, remembered his promise of the previous evening. He thought longingly of the hot sun in that cove. It'd bake the cold out of his bones and dry the wetness in his head and chest.

I would like to swim in the water, Ruth said.

"You're not too tired, are you?"

I am tired but I would like to swim in the cove and then lie in the sand. It would be good for you, too.

"It'd suit me down to the shell," Jaxom said as he stripped off the fighting clothes. He was pulling on fresh riding furs when the drudge, tapping nervously on the half-open door, arrived with the food.

Jaxom gestured toward the worktable and then asked the man to take the discarded clothing to be cleaned and well aired. He was sipping the hot wine, blowing out against the sting of it in his mouth, when he realized that it would be hours before Lytol returned to the Hold and so he couldn't inform his guardian of his intention. But he needn't wait. He could be there and back before Lytol had returned to the Hold. Then he groaned. The cove was halfway on the other side of the world, and the sun which he had wanted to bake the illness out of his body would be well down now on the cove's horizon.

It will remain warm enough long enough, Ruth said. *I really want to go there.*

"We'll go, we'll go!" Jaxom gulped down the last of the hot wine, and reached for the toasted bread and cheese. He didn't feel hungry. In fact the smell of the food made his stomach queasy. He rolled up one of his sleeping furs, to keep the sand off his skin, slung the small pack over his shoulder and started out of his quarters. He'd leave word with the drudge. No, that wasn't sufficient. Jaxom whirled back to his table, the pack banging against his ribs. He wrote a quick note to Lytol and left it propped up between mug and plate where it was clearly visible.

When are we going? Ruth asked, plaintive now with his impatience to be clean and to wallow in the warm sands.

"I'm coming. I'm coming!" Jaxom detoured through the kitchens, scooping up some meatrolls and cheese. He might be hungry later.

The head cook was basting a roast and the smell of it, too, made him feel nauseated.

"Batunon, I've left a message for Lord Lytol in my room. But, if you see him first, tell him I've gone to the cove to wash Ruth."

"Thread is gone from the sky?" Batunon asked, ladle poised above the roast.

"Gone to dust, all of it. I'm away to wash the stink from both our hides."

The yellow tinge in Ruth's whirling eyes was reproachful but Jaxom paid that no heed as he scrambled to the dragon's neck, loosely fastening the fighting straps which would need to be soaked and sunned as well. They were airborne in such haste that Jaxom was glad he had the straps about him. Ruth achieved only the barest minimum of wing room before he transferred them *between*.

CHAPTER XIII

A Cove in the Southern Continent, 15.7.7–15.8.7

JAXOM ROUSED, felt something wet slip down from his forehead across his nose. He irritably brushed it aside.

You are feeling better? Ruth's voice held a volume of wistful hope that astonished his rider.

"Feel better?" Not quite awake, Jaxom attempted to lift himself up on one elbow but he couldn't move his head, which seemed to be wedged.

Brekke says to lie still.

"Lie still, Jaxom," Brekke ordered. He felt her hand on his chest preventing his movement.

He could hear water dripping somewhere nearby. Then another wet cloth, this one cool and aromatic with scent, was placed on his forehead. He could feel two large blocks, padded because they lay along his cheeks to his shoulder, on either side of his head, presumably to keep him from moving his head from side to side. He wondered what was wrong. Why was Brekke there?

You've been very sick, Ruth said, anxiety coloring his tone. *I was very worried. I called Brekke. She is a healer. She heard me. I couldn't leave you. She came with F'nor on Canth. Then F'nor went for the other one.*

"Have I been sick a long time?" Jaxom was dis-

mayed to think he'd needed two nurses. He hoped
that the "other one" wasn't Deelan.

"Several days," Brekke replied, but Ruth seemed to
think a longer period of time. "You'll be all right now.
The fever's finally broken."

"Lytol knows where I am?" Jaxom opened his eyes
then, found them covered by the compress and reached
to pull it away. But spots danced in front of his eyes,
even shielded by the fabric of the compress, and he
groaned and closed his lids.

"I told you to lie still. And don't open your eyes or
try to remove the bandage," Brekke said, giving his
hand a little slap. "Of course Lytol knows. F'nor
took word to him immediately. I sent word when your
fever had broken. Menolly's has too."

"Menolly? How could she catch my cold? She was
with Sebell."

Someone else was in the room because Brekke
couldn't speak and laugh at the same time. She began
quietly explaining that he hadn't had a cold. He'd had
an illness known as fire-head to Southerners; its initial
symptoms were similar to those of a cold.

"But I'm going to be all right, aren't I?"

"Are your eyes bothering you?"

"I don't really want to open them again."

"Spots? As if you were staring at the sun?"

"That's it."

Brekke patted his arm. "That's normal, isn't it,
Sharra? How long do they generally last?"

"As long as the headache. So keep your eyes covered,
Jaxom." Sharra spoke slowly, almost slurring her
words but her low voice had a rich lilt that made
him wonder if she looked as good as her voice sounded.
He doubted it. No one could. "Don't you dare look
about. You've still got that headache, haven't you?
Well, keep your eyes closed. We've got the place as
dark as we can but you could do permanent damage
to your eyes if you're not careful right now."

Jaxom felt Brekke adjust the compress. "Menolly
got sick, too?"

"Yes, but Master Oldive sent word that she's responding to the medicine very well." Brekke hesitated. "Of course, she hadn't flown Thread or gone *between,* which aggravated the illness for you."

Jaxom groaned. "I've gone *between* with a cold before and got no worse for it."

"With a cold, yes, not with fire-head," Sharra said. "Here, Brekke. This is ready for him now."

He felt a reed placed at his lips. Brekke told him to suck through it as he should not lift his head to drink.

"What is this?" he mumbled around the straw.

"Fruit juice," Sharra said so promptly that Jaxom sipped warily. "Just fruit juice, Jaxom. You need liquid in your body right now. The fever dried you out."

The juice was cool in his mouth and so mild in taste that he couldn't figure out from which fruit it came. But it was just what he wanted, not tart enough to irritate moisture-starved tissues in his mouth and throat, and not sweet enough to be nauseating to his empty stomach. He finished it and asked for more, but Brekke told him he'd had enough. He should try to sleep now.

"Ruth? Are you all right?"

Now that you are yourself again, I will eat. I will not go far. I don't need to.

"Ruth?" Alarmed by the thought that his dragon had neglected himself, Jaxom injudiciously tried to raise his head. The pain was incredible.

"Ruth is perfectly all right, Jaxom," Brekke said in a stern voice. Her hands had already pushed his shoulders flat to the bed. "Ruth's been covered with fire-lizards, and he's been bathed regularly morning and evening. He's never been more than two lengths from you. I've reassured him on every concern." Jaxom groaned, having completely forgotten that Brekke could speak to any dragon. "F'nor and Canth have hunted for him because he wouldn't leave you so he's by no means the skin and bones you are. He'll hunt now, none the worse for the waiting. You go to sleep."

He had no option and suspected as he drifted away from consciousness that there had been something besides fruit in that drink.

When he woke, feeling rested and restless, he remembered not to move his head. He began to cast back through distorted memories of being hot and cold. He distinctly remembered reaching the cove, staggering into the shade, collapsing at the base of a redfruit tree, struggling to reach the cluster of fruit, longing for the liquid to cool his parched mouth and throat. That must have been when Ruth realized he was ill.

Jaxom could vaguely recall fevered glimpses of Brekke and F'nor, could remember pleading with them to bring Ruth to him. He supposed they had erected some kind of temporary hold for shelter. Sharra had said something to that effect. He extended his left arm slowly, moved it up and down, without contacting more than the frame of the bed. He extended his right arm.

"Jaxom?" He heard Sharra's soft voice. "And Ruth too fast asleep himself to warn me. Are you thirsty?" She didn't sound contrite that she'd been asleep. She made a small sound of dismay as she touched the now dry compress. "Don't open your eyes."

She removed the bandage and he heard her dipping it in liquid, wringing it out and then he shivered at its touch on his skin. He reached up, holding the bandage against his forehead, lightly at first and then with more confident pressure.

"Hey, it doesn't hurt—"

"*Ssssh.* Brekke's asleep and she wakes so easily." Sharra's voice had been muted; now her fingers closed his lips.

"Why can't I move my head from side to side?" Jaxom tried not to sound as startled as he felt.

Sharra's low laugh reassured him. "We've got two blocks wedging your head so you can't move. Remember?" She guided his hands to them, then moved the restraints aside. "Turn your head, just a little now, from side to side. If your skin is no longer sensitive, you may be over the worst of the fire-head."

Gingerly he rotated his head, left and then right. He made a bolder motion. "It doesn't hurt. It actually doesn't hurt."

"Oh, no, you don't." Sharra grabbed his wrist as he reached for the compress. "I've a night light on. Wait till I shield it. The less light, the better."

He heard her fumbling with a glow-basket shield. "All right now?"

"I'm only permitting you to try," she stressed the last word as she covered his hand on the bandage with hers, "because it's a moonless hour of night and you couldn't do any harm. If you see even the tiniest patch of glare, cover your eyes instantly."

"It's that dangerous?"

"It can be."

Slowly she peeled the bandage back.

"I don't see anything!"

"Any glare or spots?"

"No? Nothing. Oh!" Something had been obscuring his vision for now he could see dim outlines.

"I had my hand in front of your nose, just in case," she said.

He could make out the dark blur of her body beside him. She must be on her knees. Slowly his sight improved as he blinked sandy incrustations from his lashes.

"My eyes are full of sand."

"Just a moment." Suddenly water was dribbled carefully into his eyes. He blinked furiously, complained loudly. "I told you to hush, you'll wake Brekke. She's worn out. Now, does that clear the sand?"

"Yes, it's much better. I didn't mean to be so much trouble."

"Oh? I thought you'd planned all this on purpose."

Jaxom caught one of her hands and brought it to his lips, holding it as fast as his weakened condition permitted because she gasped at the kiss and withdrew her hand.

"Thanks!"

"I'm putting your bandage back on," she said, the reproach in her voice unmistakable.

Jaxom chuckled, pleased to have disconcerted her. His only regret was the lack of light. He could see that she was slender. Her voice, despite her firmness, sounded young. Would her face be lovely enough to match that voice?

"Please drink all this juice," she said, and he felt the straw against his lips. "Another good sleep now and you're over the worst of it."

"You're a healer?" Jaxom was dismayed. Her voice had sounded so young. He'd assumed she was a fosterling of Brekke's.

"Certainly. You don't think they'd entrust the life of the Lord of Ruatha Hold to an apprentice? I've had a lot of experience getting people through fire-head."

The familiar floating sensation induced by fellis juice flooded him and he couldn't have answered her no matter how urgently he wanted to.

To his disappointment, when he awoke the next day, Brekke answered his call. It didn't seem courteous to inquire where Sharra was. Nor could he ask Ruth since Brekke could hear the exchange. But Sharra had evidently told Brekke of his middle-of-the-night awakening because her voice sounded lighter, almost gay as she greeted him. To celebrate his recovery, she permitted him a cup of weak klah and a bowl of moistened sweetbread.

Warning him to keep his eyes closed, she changed the bandage but the replacement was not as dense and when he opened his eyes, cautiously, he could distinguish light and dark areas about him.

Midday he was allowed to sit up and eat the light meal Brekke provided, but even that slight activity exhausted him. Nonetheless he complained petulantly to Brekke when she offered him more juice to drink.

"Fellis-laced? Am I expected to sleep my life away?"

"Oh, you'll be making up for this lost time, I assure you," she replied, a cryptic remark that puzzled him as he drifted off to sleep again.

The next day he chafed further at the restrictions imposed on him. He chafed but, when Sharra and Brekke assisted him to the bench so they could exchange rushbags on the bed, he was so weak after sitting up a few minutes that he was very grateful to be down again. He was all the more surprised then, that evening, to hear N'ton's voice in the other room.

"You look a lot better, Jaxom," N'ton said, walking quietly up to the bed. "Lytol will be immensely relieved. But if you ever," N'ton's harsh voice reflected his anxieties, "attempt to fight Thread again when you're ill, I'll . . . I'll . . . I'll throw you to Lessa's mercies."

"I didn't think I'd more than a stuffed head, N'ton," Jaxom replied, nervously poking at grassy bumps in his bedbag. "And it *was* my first Fall on Ruth . . ."

"I know, I know," N'ton said, his tone considerably less reproving. "You couldn't have known you were coming down with fire-head. You owe your life to Ruth, you know. F'nor says Ruth has more sense than most people. Half the dragons on Pern wouldn't have known what to do with their rider delirious; they would have been totally confused by the confusion in their riders' minds. No, you and Ruth are in very good odor at Benden. Very good! You just concentrate on getting your strength back. And when you're feeling stronger, D'ram said he'd be glad to bear you company and show you some of the interesting things he found while he was here."

"He didn't mind me and Ruth following him?"

"No." N'ton was genuinely surprised at Jaxom's question. "No, lad, I think he was surprised that he'd been missed and gratified that he's still needed as a dragonrider."

"N'ton!" Brekke's call was firm.

"I was told I couldn't stay long." Jaxom could hear N'ton's feet scraping on the ground as he rose. "I'll come again, I promise." Jaxom could hear Tris complaining and he visualized the little fire-lizard clutching N'ton's shoulder for balance.

"How's Menolly? Is she recovering? Tell Lytol that I'm very sorry to cause him worry!"

"He knows that, Jaxom. And Menolly's much better. I've seen her, too. She had a lighter touch of fire-head than you did. Sebell recognized the symptoms almost immediately and called in Oldive. Don't be in a rush to get up, though."

As glad as he'd been for N'ton's visit, Jaxom was relieved that it had been short. He felt limp and his head began to ache.

"Brekke?" Could he be having a relapse?

"She's with N'ton, Jaxom."

"Sharra! My head is aching." He couldn't help the waver in his voice.

Her cool hand touched his cheek. "No fever, Jaxom. You tire quickly, that's all. Sleep now."

The reasonable words, spoken in her gentle rich voice lulled him and, though he wanted to remain awake, his eyes closed. Her fingers massaged his forehead, descended to his neck, gently smoothing the tension, all the while her voice encouraged him to rest, to sleep. And he did.

The cool, moist sea breeze roused him at dawn, and he fumbled irritably to cover his exposed legs and back for he'd been sleeping on his stomach, tangled in the light blanket. Having rearranged himself with some difficulty, he couldn't drop back to sleep again though he had closed his eyes, expecting to do so. He opened them again, fretfully gazing beyond the raised curtains of the shelter. He exclaimed in surprise, tensing, just then aware that his eyes were no longer bandaged and his vision was unimpaired.

"Jaxom?"

Twisting around, he saw Sharra's tall figure swing from the hammock, noticed the length of dark hair streaming about her shoulders, obscuring her face.

"Sharra!"

"Your eyes, Jaxom?" she asked in a hushed worried tone and walked swiftly to his bed.

"My eyes are just fine, Sharra," he replied, catching her hand in his, keeping her where he could see her face clearly in the dim light. "Oh, no, you don't," he said with a low laugh as she tried to break his hold. "I've been waiting to see what you looked like."

With his free hand, he pushed aside the hair that covered her face.

"And?" She drawled the word in proud defiance, unconsciously straightening her shoulders and tossing her hair back.

Sharra was not pretty. He'd expected that. Her features were too irregular, in particular her nose was too long for her face, and though her chin was well shaped it was a shade too firm for beauty. But her mouth had a lovely double curve, the left side twitching as she contained the humor which her deep-set eyes echoed. She arched her left eyebrow slowly, amused by his scrutiny.

"And?" she repeated.

"I know you may not agree but *I* think you're beautiful!" He resisted her second attempt to free her hand and rise. "You must be aware that you have a beautiful speaking voice."

"I have tried to cultivate *that*," she said.

"You've succeeded." He exerted pressure on her hand, pulling her still closer. It was immensely important to him to determine her age.

She laughed softly, wriggling her fingers in his tight grasp. "Let me go now, Jaxom, be a good boy!"

"I am not good and I am not a boy." He had spoken with a low intensity which drove the good-natured amusement from her expression. She returned his gaze steadily and then gave him a small smile.

"No, you're neither good nor a boy. You've been a very sick man and it's my job," she stressed the word just slightly as he let her withdraw her hand from his, "to make you well again."

"The sooner, the better." Jaxom lay back, smiling up at her. She'd be nearly his height when he stood, he thought. That they would be able to look eye to eye appealed to him.

She gave him one long, slightly puzzled look and then, with a cryptic shrug, turned away from him, gathering her hair and twining it neatly about her head as she left the room.

Although neither of them mentioned that dawn confidence, afterward Jaxom found it easier to accept the restraints of his convalescence in good grace. He ate what he was given without complaint, took the medicines, and obeyed instructions to rest.

One worry fretted him until he finally blurted it out to Brekke.

"When I was fevered, Brekke, did I . . . I mean . . ."

Brekke smiled and patted his hand reassuringly. "We never pay any attention to such ramblings. Generally, they're so incoherent they make no sense whatever."

Some note in her voice bothered him, though. ". . . so incoherent, they make no sense?" He had babbled his head off, then. Not that he minded about Brekke if he had said something about that dratted queen egg. But if Sharra had heard? She was from the Southern Hold. Would she be as quick to discount his ramblings about that double-blasted shard-shelled egg? He couldn't relax. What wretched luck to fall ill when you had a secret that must be kept! He worried over that until he fell asleep, and picked right up on the same train of thought the next morning, though he forced himself to be cheerful as he listened to Ruth bathing with the fire-lizards.

He comes, Ruth said suddenly, sounding startled. *And D'ram brings him.*

"D'ram brings whom?" Jaxom asked.

"Sharra," Brekke called from the other room, "our guests have arrived. Would you escort them from the beach?" She came quickly into Jaxom's room, smoothing the light blanket and peering intently at his face. "Is your face clean? How are your hands?"

"Who's coming that has you in a flurry? Ruth?"

He's pleased to see me, too. Ruth's sound of surprise was colored with delight.

Jaxom was forewarned by that remark, but he could only stare, stunned, as Lytol came striding into the room. His face was tense and pale under the flying helmet, and he hadn't bothered to unfasten his jacket on the walk up from the beach, so perspiration beads formed on his forehead and upper lip. He stood in the doorway, just looking at his ward.

Abruptly, he turned toward the outside wall, harshly clearing his throat, stripping off helmet and gloves, unbelting his jacket, grunting in surprise when Brekke appeared at his elbow to relieve him of the gear. As she passed Jaxom's bed on her way out of the room, she gave him such an intense look that he couldn't fathom what she was trying to convey.

She says that he is crying, Ruth told him. *And that you are not to be surprised or embarrass him.* Ruth paused. *She is also thinking that Lytol is healed, too? Lytol hasn't been ill.*

Jaxom didn't have time to sort out that oblique reference because his guardian had already recovered his composure and turned.

"Hot here after Ruatha," Jaxom said, struggling to break the silence.

"You want a bit of sun, boy," Lytol said at the same moment.

"I'm not allowed out of bed, yet."

"The mountain is just as you sketched it."

They spoke again simultaneously, answering each other's comments.

It was too much for Jaxom, who burst out laughing, waving Lytol to sit beside him on the bed. Still laughing, Jaxom grabbed Lytol's forearm, holding it firmly, trying in that grasp to apologize for all the concern he'd caused. Abruptly he was engulfed in Lytol's rough embrace, his back soundly thumped when the man released him. Tears sprang to Jaxom's eyes, too, at the unexpected demonstration. Lytol had always been scrupulous in caring for his ward but the older Jaxom had grown, the more he had wondered if Lytol really liked him at all.

"I thought I had lost you."

"I'm harder to lose than you'd think, sir."

Jaxom couldn't stop grinning foolishly because Lytol actually had a smile on his face: the first one Jaxom recalled.

"You're nothing but bones and white skin," Lytol said in his customary gruff manner.

"That'll pass. I'm allowed to eat all I want," Jaxom replied. "Care for something?"

"I didn't come to eat. I came to see you. And I'll tell you this, young Lord Jaxom, I think you'd better go back to the Mastersmith for more drafting lessons: you did not accurately place the trees along the cove shore in that sketch of yours. Though the mountain is very well done."

"I knew I had the trees wrong, sir, one of the things I planned to check out. Only when I got back here, it went clean out of my head."

"So I understand," and Lytol gave a rusty laugh.

"Give me the news of the Hold." Jaxom was suddenly eager for those minor details that had once bored him.

They chatted away in a companionable fashion that astonished Jaxom. He'd been ill at ease with Lytol, he realized now, ever since he had inadvertently Impressed Ruth. But that strain had evaporated. If this illness of his did no other good, it had brought him and Lytol closer than Jaxom in his boyhood could ever have imagined.

Brekke entered, smiling apologetically. "I'm sorry, Lord Lytol, but Jaxom tires easily."

Lytol obediently rose, glancing anxiously at Jaxom.

"Brekke, after Lytol has come all this distance, on dragonback, he *must* be allowed to . . ."

"No, lad, I can return." Lytol's smile startled Brekke. "I'd rather not take a risk with him." He gave Brekke a second surprise then as he embraced Jaxom with awkward affection before striding from the room.

Brekke stared at Jaxom, who shrugged to indicate she could put her own interpretation on his guardian's behavior. She quickly left to escort the visitors back to the beach.

He was very glad to see you, Ruth said. *He is smiling.*

Jaxom lay back, wriggling his shoulders into the

rushes to get comfortable. He closed his eyes, chuckling to himself. He had got Lytol to see his beautiful mountain.

Lytol wasn't the only one to come to see the mountain, and Jaxom. Lord Groghe arrived the next afternoon, grunting and puffing from the heat, shouting at his little queen not to get lost with all those strangers, and not to get completely soaked because he didn't want a wet shoulder on the way back.

"Heard you'd got ill of that fire-head stuff like the harper girl," Lord Groghe said, swinging into Jaxom's room with a vigor that produced instant fatigue in the convalescent.

More unnerving was Lord Groghe's scrutiny. Jaxom was certain the man counted his ribs, he had looked at them so long. "Can't you feed him up better than this, Brekke? Thought you were a top-flight healer. Boy's a rake! Can't have that. Must say you picked a beautiful place to fall ill in. Must have a look about me since I'm down here. Not that it took all that long to come. Hmmm. Yes, must have a look about." Groghe stuck his chin out at Jaxom, frowning again. "Did you? Before that sickness got hold of you?"

Jaxom realized that Lord Groghe's totally unexpected visit might have several objectives: one, to assure the Lord Holders that the Lord of Ruatha was in the land of the living, all rumor to the contrary. The second purpose made Jaxom a little uneasy when he could so clearly recall Lessa's remark about wanting "the best part of it."

When Brekke tactfully reminded the blustering and genial Lord Holder that he mustn't tire her patient, Jaxom nearly cheered.

"Don't worry, lad. I'll be back again, never fear." Lord Groghe waved cheerfully to him from the doorway. "Beautiful spot. Envy you."

"Does everyone in the North know where I am?" Jaxom asked when Brekke returned.

"D'ram brought him," she said, sighing heavily and frowning.

"D'ram ought to have known better," Sharra said,

collapsing on the bench and plying a tree frond as a fan in exaggerated relief at the Lord's departure. "The man's enough to wear the healthy down, much less the convalescent."

"I would guess," Brekke continued, ignoring Sharra's remarks, "that the Lord Holders needed verification of Jaxom's recovery."

"He looked Jaxom over like a herdsman. Did you show him your teeth?"

"Don't let Lord Groghe's manner fool you, Sharra," Jaxom said. "He's got a mind as sharp as Master Robinton's. And if D'ram brought him, then F'lar and Lessa must have known he was coming. I don't think they'll like him returning—or scouting around here."

"If Lessa did permit Lord Groghe to come, she'll hear from me about it, you may be sure," Brekke replied, thinning her lips in disapproval. "He is not an easy visitor for a convalescent. You might as well know now, Jaxom, that you were ill of that fever for sixteen days . . ."

"What?" Jaxom sat upright in the bed, stunned. "But . . . but . . ."

"Fire-head is a dangerous disease for an adult," Sharra said. She glanced at Brekke, who nodded. "You nearly died."

"I did?" Appalled, Jaxom put his hand to his head.

Brekke nodded again. "So, if we seem to be restricting you to a very slow recovery, you will agree that we have cause."

"I nearly died?" Jaxom couldn't absorb that news.

"So we will go slowly to ensure your health. Now, I think it's time you had something to eat," Brekke said as she left the room.

"I nearly died?" Jaxom turned to Sharra.

"I'm afraid so." She sounded more amused by his reaction than concerned. "The important thing is that you didn't die." Involuntarily she glanced toward the beach and sighed, a quick exhalation of relief. She smiled, a brief one, but Jaxom noticed that her expressive eyes were dark with remembered sorrow.

"Who died of fire-head that saddens you, Sharra?"

"No one you know, Jaxom, and no one I knew very well. It's just . . . just that no healer likes to lose a patient."

He could tease no more from her on the subject and stopped trying to when he saw that she had felt that death so keenly.

The next morning, cursing with embarrassment at the unreliability of his legs, Jaxom was assisted to the beach by Brekke and Sharra. Ruth came charging up the sands, almost dangerous in his delight at seeing his friend. Brekke sternly ordered Ruth to stand still lest he knock Jaxom off his unsteady feet. Ruth's eyes rolled with concern and he crooned with apology as he extended his head very carefully toward Jaxom, almost afraid to muzzle him in greeting. Jaxom flung his arms about his dragon's neck, Ruth tightening his muscles to take the drag of his friend's body, almost thrumming with encouragement. Tears flowed down his cheeks which he quickly dried against his friend's soft hide. Dear Ruth. Marvelous Ruth. Unbidden came the thought to Jaxom's mind: "If I had died of fire-head . . ."

You did not, Ruth said. *You stayed. I told you to. And you are much stronger now. You will get stronger every day and we will swim and sun and it will be good.*

Ruth sounded so fierce that Jaxom had to soothe him with words and caresses until Brekke and Sharra insisted that he had better sit down before he fell. They had arranged a matting of woven streamer fronds against a landward-leaning trunk, well back from the shore, to avoid full exposure to the sun. To this couch they assisted him. Ruth stretched out so that his head rested by Jaxom's side, the jeweled eyes whirling with the lavenders of stress.

F'lar and Lessa arrived at midday, after Jaxom had had a short nap. He was surprised to find that Lessa, for all her abrasiveness on other occasions, made a soothing visitor, quiet and soft-voiced.

"We had to let Lord Groghe come in person, Jaxom, though I'm sure you didn't appreciate the visit. Rumor

had you dead and Ruth, too." Lessa shrugged expres-
sively. "Bad news needs no harper."

"Lord Groghe was more interested in where I was
than how I was, wasn't he?" Jaxom asked pointedly.

F'lar nodded and grinned at him. "That is why we
had D'ram bring him. The Fort Hold watchdragon is
too old to take a placement from Lord Groghe's mind."

"He also had his fire-lizard with him," Jaxom said.

"Those pesky creatures," Lessa said, her eyes
sparkling with annoyance.

"These same pesky creatures came in very handy
saving Jaxom's life, Lessa," Brekke said firmly.

"All right, they have uses but, as far as I'm concerned, their bad habits still outweigh the good ones."

"Lord Groghe's little queen may be intelligent,"
Brekke went on, "but not clever enough to get him
back here on his own."

"That isn't the real problem," F'lar grimaced. "He's
now seen that mountain. And the scope of the land."

"So, we put in our claim here first," Lessa replied
decisively. "I don't care how many sons Groghe wants
to settle, the dragonriders of Pern have first choice.
Jaxom can help—"

"Jaxom has some time to go before he can do very
much of anything," Brekke said, breaking in so
smoothly that Jaxom wondered if he'd misinterpreted
the surprise on Lessa's face.

"Don't worry, I'll think of some way to stall Lord
Groghe's ambitions," F'lar added.

"If one gets in, the others will follow," Brekke said
thoughtfully, "and I can hardly blame them. This part
of the Southern Continent is so much more beautiful
than our original settlement."

"I have a yearning to get closer to that mountain,"
F'lar said, turning his head to the south. "Jaxom, I
know you've not been very active yet, but how many
of those fire-lizards about Ruth are Southerners?"

"They're not from the Southern Weyr, if that's what
you're worried about," Sharra said.

"How can you tell?" Lessa asked.

Sharra shrugged. "They won't be handled. They go

between if anyone gets close to them. It's Ruth that fascinates them. Not us."

"We are not *their* men," Jaxom said. "Now that I can get to Ruth, I'll see what I can find out about them from him."

"I wish you would," Lessa said. "And if there are any from the Southern Weyr . . ." She let her sentence trail off.

"I think we ought to let Jaxom rest," Brekke said.

F'lar chuckled, gesturing for Lessa to precede him. "Fine guests we are. Come to see the man and never let him talk."

"I've done nothing lately to talk about," and Jaxom shot a fierce look at Brekke and Sharra. "When you come back, I will."

"If anything interesting occurs, have Ruth bespeak Mnementh or Ramoth."

Brekke and Sharra left with the Weyrleaders, and Jaxom was grateful for the respite. He could hear Ruth talking to the two Benden dragons and he chuckled when Ruth told Ramoth firmly that there were no fire-lizards from the Southern Weyr among his new friends. Jaxom wondered why it hadn't occurred to him sooner to ask Ruth's acquaintances about their men. He sighed. He hadn't been thinking about much lately except his extraordinary brush with death, and that occupied his mind too morbidly. Much better for him to explore a living puzzle.

He had several. The most worrisome was still what he might have said in his delirium. Brekke's rejoinder had been no real assurance. He tried to force his thought back to that time but all he remembered was heat and cold, vivid but vague nightmares.

He thought about his guardian's visit. So Lytol did like him! Shells! He'd forgotten to ask Lytol about Corana. He ought to have sent her some kind of word. She must have heard of his illness. Not but what this didn't make it easier for him to complete the break in their relationship. Now that he'd seen Sharra, he couldn't have continued with Corana. He must remember to ask Lytol.

What *had* he said when he was fevered? How did a fever patient talk? In bits and snatches? Whole phrases? Maybe he needn't worry. Not about what he could have said in fever.

He didn't like Lord Groghe just appearing like that, to check up on him. And, if he hadn't taken ill, Lord Groghe would never have known about this part of Southern. At least, until the dragonriders wanted him to know. And that mountain! Too unusual a feature to forget. Any dragon would be able to find it. Or would they? Unless the rider had a very clear picture, the dragon did not always see vividly enough to jump *between*. And a secondhand vision? D'ram and Tiroth had done so from Master Robinton's description. But D'ram and Tiroth were experienced.

Jaxom wanted to be well. He wanted to get closer to that mountain. He wanted to be first. How long would it take him to recover?

He was allowed to swim a bit the next day, an exercise which Brekke said would tone his muscles but which succeeded in proving he had none left. Exhausted, he was no sooner on his beachside couch than he fell deeply asleep.

Roused by Sharra's touch, he cried out and sat bolt upright, looking about him.

"What's the matter, Jaxom?"

"A dream! A nightmare!" He was sure something was wrong. Then he saw Ruth, stretched out, fast asleep, his muzzle only a handsbreadth from his feet, at least a dozen fire-lizards curled on and about him, twitching in their own dreams.

"Well, you're awake now. What's wrong?"

"That dream was so vivid . . . and yet it's all gone. I wanted so much to remember it."

Sharra placed a cool hand on his forehead. He pushed it away.

"I'm not fevered," he said, cranky.

"No, you're not. Any headache? Spots?"

Impatient and angry, he denied them, then sighed

and smiled an apology at her. "Bad-tempered, aren't I?"

"Rarely." She grinned, then eased to the sand beside him.

"If I swim a little longer and further every day, how long will it take me to recover fully?"

"What makes you so anxious?"

Jaxom grinned, jerking his head back in the direction of the mountain. "I want to get there before Lord Groghe does."

"Oh, I think you'll manage that quite easily." Sharra's expression was mischievous. "You will get stronger every day now. We just don't want you to push yourself too quickly. Better a few more days now, than suffer a relapse and go through all this again."

"A relapse? How would I know if I was having one?"

"Easy. Spots and headaches. Do please do it our way, Jaxom."

The appeal in her blue eyes was genuine, and Jaxom liked to think it was for him, Jaxom, not for him, the patient. Not taking his eyes from hers, he nodded slowly in acquiescence and was rewarded by her slow smile.

F'nor and D'ram arrived late that afternoon, in fighting gear, with full firestone sacks draped across their dragons.

"Thread tomorrow," Sharra told Jaxom as she caught his look of inquiry.

"Thread?"

"It falls on all Pern, and has fallen here in this cove three times since you took ill. In fact, the day after you took ill!" She grinned at his openmouthed consternation. "It's been a rare treat to watch dragons in the sky. We'd only to keep the shelter area free. Grub takes care of the rest." She chuckled. "Tiroth complains that he's not fighting full when he doesn't follow the Fall to its end. Just wait till you see Ruth in action. Oh, yes, nothing could keep him out of the sky. Brekke keeps her ear open for him and, of course, Tiroth and Canth are directing. He's so proud of himself, protecting you!"

Jaxom swallowed against a variety of emotions, chagrin being foremost as he heard Sharra's casual explanation.

"You were aware of Thread, by the way. Once a dragonrider, one evidently doesn't forget—even in fever. You kept moaning about Thread coming and not being able to get off the ground." Fortunately she was looking at the dragons as they glided to a landing on the beach because Jaxom was certain that his expression gave him away. "Master Oldive says that we humans have instincts, too, hidden deep in our minds, to which we respond automatically. As you reacted to Threadfall, sick as you were. Ruth is such a dote. I made much of him after each Fall, I assure you, and I made sure that the fire-lizards got all firestone stink out of his hide."

She waved a greeting to F'nor and D'ram as they strolled up the beach, loosening their fighting gear. Canth and Tiroth had already shrugged off the firestone sacks on the beach and, wings extended high, waddled with groans of pleasure into the soft warm water. Ruth came slithering through the water to join them. A great fair of fire-lizards chittered above the three dragons, overjoyed with such company.

"You've more color, Jaxom, you look better!" F'nor said, grasping Jaxom's arm in greeting.

D'ram nodded his head, agreeing with F'nor.

Aware of his indebtedness to both riders, Jaxom stammered out his gratitude.

"Tell you something, Jaxom," F'nor said, squatting on his haunches, "it's been a rare treat to watch your little fellow work in the air. He's a superb chop-and-change artist. Caught three times as much Thread as our big fellows could. You trained him well!"

"I don't suppose I'll be considered strong enough to fight Thread tomorrow?"

"No, nor for some time to come," F'nor replied firmly. "Know how you're feeling, Jaxom," he continued as he dropped beside him on the mats. "Felt the same way when I was wounded and not allowed to fly Thread. But now, your only responsibility to Hold and Weyr is to get fit. Fit enough to take a good look about this country! I envy you that chance, Jaxom. Indeed I do!" F'nor's grin was candidly envious. "Haven't had the time to fly far, even after Thread, down here. Forest extends a long way on either side." F'nor gestured broadly with one arm. "You'll see. Shall I bring you writing materials next trip down so you can make a Record? You may not fly Thread yet awhile, Jaxom, but you'll be working hard enough to make that a treat!"

"You're only saying that . . ." Jaxom broke off, surprised at the bitterness in his voice.

"Yes, because you need something to look forward to since you can't do what you want most," F'nor said. He reached out and gripped Jaxom's arm. "I understand, Jaxom. Ruth's been giving Canth a full report. Sorry. Awkward for you, but Ruth worries when you're upset, or didn't you know that?" He chuckled.

"I appreciate what you're trying to do, F'nor," Jaxom said.

Just then Brekke and Sharra emerged from the trees, Brekke walking quickly to her weyrmate. She did not, as Jaxom half-expected, embrace the brown rider. But the way she regarded him, the gentle, almost hesitant way she rested her hand on his arm, spoke more tellingly of the love between the two than any more demonstrative welcome. A bit embarrassed, Jaxom turned his head and saw Sharra watching Brekke and F'nor, a peculiar expression on her face which she erased the moment she realized that Jaxom was looking at her.

"Drinks all round," she said in a brisk tone, handing a mug to D'ram as Brekke served F'nor.

It was a pleasant evening and they ate on the beach, Jaxom managing to suppress his frustration in the face of the morning's Threadfall. The three dragons made nests in the still warm sands above the high-tide lines, their eyes glistening like jewels in the dark beyond the firelight.

Brekke and Sharra sang one of Menolly's tunes while D'ram added a rough bass line. When Brekke noticed Jaxom's head lolling to one side, he didn't resist her ordering him back to the shelter. He drifted to sleep, face turned toward the fireglow, lulled by the singing voices.

Ruth's excitement roused him and he blinked without comprehension as the dragon's voice penetrated his sleep. *Thread!* Ruth was going to fight Thread today with D'ram's Tiroth and F'nor's Canth. Jaxom threw aside the blanket, struggled into his trousers, and strode quickly from the shelter to the beach. Brekke and Sharra were helping the two dragonriders load their beasts with the firestone sacks. With the four fire-lizards on the ground at his feet, Ruth was industriously chewing away at the pile of stone on the beach. Dawn was just breaking in the east. Jaxom peered through the dim light, straining to see the filmy discoloration that meant Thread. The three Dawn Sisters winked with unexpected brilliance high above him, paling to insignificance the other morning stars in the west. Jaxom frowned at their display. He hadn't realized how bright they were, how close they seemed. In Ruatha, they were duller, barely visible points on the southeastern horizon at dawn. He reminded himself to ask if F'nor could have the use of a long-distance viewer, and if Lytol would send down his star equations and maps. Then Jaxom noticed the absence of the fairs of Southern fire-lizards which haunted Ruth day and night.

"Jaxom!" Brekke noticed him. The two riders waved a greeting and swung up on their beasts.

Jaxom checked Ruth to be sure he had enough stone in his gullet, caressing his friend and applauding his willingness to fly Thread though riderless.

I remember all the drills we were taught at Fort Weyr. I have F'nor and Canth, and D'ram and Tiroth to help. Brekke always watches me, too. I have never listened to a woman before. But Brekke is good! She

*is also sad but Canth says it is good for her to hear us.
She knows that she is never alone.*

They were all facing east where the Red Star pulsed, round and brightly orange-red. A film seemed to float across it and F'nor, raising his hand, called Ruth to take wing. Canth and Tiroth leapt strongly into the air, their wings beating in powerful strokes to assist their rising. Ruth was well aloft before them and straining ahead. Beside him four fire-lizards appeared, as dwarfed by him as he was by Canth and Tiroth.

"Don't meet Thread alone, Ruth!" Jaxom cried.

"He won't," Brekke said, her eyes twinkling. "He is young enough to want to be first. At that, he saves the older dragons a lot of effort. But we must go in."

As one, the three paused for a last look at their defenders and then moved quickly inside the shelter.

"You can't see much," Sharra told Jaxom, who had gone to stand by the open doorway.

"I'd see if Thread got into this greenery."

"It won't. We've clever riders."

Jaxom felt the skin on his back begin to crawl and he gave a massive shudder.

"Don't you dare catch a cold," Sharra said. She collected a shirt from his room which she threw at him.

"I'm not cold. I'm just thinking of Thread and this forest."

Sharra made a disparaging sound. "I forget. You're Northern Hold-bred! Thread can't do any more than tear or hole leaves which heal in Southern forests. It's all grubbed. And, in case you're interested, that's the first thing F'nor and D'ram did—check to be sure the land here is well-grubbed. It is!"

We have met Thread, Ruth told him, sounding elated. *I am flaming well. I am to do V-sweeps while Canth and Tiroth pass east and west. We are high. The fire-lizards flame well, too. Over there! Berd. You are closest! Meer, get it to your offside. Talla! Help him. I come, I come. Down. I come. I flame! I protect my friend!*

Brekke caught Jaxom's eyes, smiling at him. "He

delivers a running comment so we all know how well he fights!" Her eyes lost their focus on him and then she blinked. "Sometimes I see the Fall through three sets of dragon eyes. I don't know where I'm looking! It goes well!"

Later, Jaxom could not have said what he ate or drank. When Ruth's monologue resumed, Jaxom paid strict attention to what his dragon said, looking now and again at Brekke whose face reflected the intense concentration of listening to three dragons and four fire-lizards. Suddenly Ruth's commentary stopped and Jaxom gasped.

"It's all right. They don't pursue Thread through the Fall," Brekke said. "Just enough to insure our safety. Benden flies Thread tomorrow evening over Nerat. F'nor and Canth ought not overtire themselves today."

Jaxom rose so abruptly that his bench clattered to the floor. He mumbled an apology, righted it and then strode out the door in the direction of the beach. As he reached the sands, he kept peering westward and barely discerned the distant film of Thread. Another shudder gripped him and he had to smooth the hair down on the back of his neck. The cove before him, generally calm with leisurely waves, was roiled with the activity of fish diving, lifting their bodies above the surface and crashing awkwardly down again as if in the throes of pain.

"What's the matter with them?" he asked Sharra, who had joined him.

"The fish are having a good feed off Thread. They generally manage to clean up the cove in time for our dragons to bathe when they return. There! There they all are! Just popped back!"

It was a good Fall! Ruth was jubilant, then rebellious. *But we are not to follow it. Canth and Tiroth said that once across the big river there is nothing but stony waste and it is stupid to waste flame above what cannot be hurt by Thread. Ooooh!*

Sharra and Jaxom laughed as the little white dragon emitted a trail of flame, almost singeing his muzzle because he was at the wrong flight angle. He corrected instantly, continuing his downward glide on the correct plane.

Even as the big dragons landed, the waters had calmed. Ruth was full of boast that he'd not needed to replenish his fire once, that he now knew how much to take to last the Fall. Canth turned his head toward the little white in an attitude of amused tolerance.

Tiroth snorted and, relieved of his firesack, nodded once toward D'ram then waded into the water. Abruptly the air was full of fire-lizards, hovering eagerly above Tiroth. The old bronze threw his head skyward, snorted again and, with a loud sigh, rolled over in the water. The fire-lizards descended, dropping mouthsful of sand on him before attacking his hide with all four feet. Tiroth's eyes, lidded once against the water, gleamed just beneath the surface in an eerie submarine rainbow.

Canth bellowed and half the fair left Tiroth to minister to him as he splashed about. Ruth watched this pre-emption of his friends, blinked, gave himself a bit of a shake and meekly took to the water at some distance from the bronze and brown. Four fire-lizards, the banded ones, detached themselves from the big dragons and began to scrub the little white.

"Here, I'll help you, Jaxom," Sharra said.

Scrubbing a dragon's hide free of firestone stink is a tiring job under any circumstances and, although he only had to do one side of Ruth, Jaxom had to grit his teeth to finish.

"I told you not to overdo, Jaxom," Sharra said, her voice sharp as she straightened from scrubbing the fork of Ruth's tail and noticed Jaxom leaning against the dragon's rump. She gestured imperiously toward the beach. "Get out! I'll bring you some food. You're whiter than he is!"

"I'm never going to get myself fit if I don't try!"

"Stop muttering at me under your breath . . ."

"And don't tell me you're doing it for my own good . . ."

"No, for mine! I don't want to have to nurse you through a relapse!"

She glared at him so fiercely that he gathered himself erect and stalked out of the water. Though it wasn't far to his informal bed under the trees, his legs were leaden as he dragged them through the water. He lay down, heaving a sigh of relief, and closed his eyes.

When he opened them again someone was shaking him, and he discovered Brekke peering at him quizzically. "How do you feel now?"

"I was dreaming?"

"Hmmm. Bad ones again?"

"No, curious ones. Only nothing was in focus." Jaxom shook his head to clear the miasma of nightmare. He realized that it was midday. Ruth was asleep snoring, at his left. On the far right, he could see D'ram resting against Tiroth's front legs. There was no sign of F'nor or Canth.

"You're probably hungry," Brekke said, holding out the plate of food and the mug she'd brought.

"How long did I sleep?" Jaxom was disgusted with himself. He stretched his shoulders, feeling muscles stiff from the exercise of scrubbing a dragon.

"Several hours. Did you good."

"I dream an awful lot lately. Aftereffect of the fire-head?"

Brekke blinked, then frowned thoughtfully. "Come to think of it, I've been dreaming rather more than usual myself. Too much sun perhaps."

At that point, Tiroth woke, bellowed, struggled to his feet, sprinkled his rider with sand. Brekke gasped and rose quickly, her eyes on the old bronze as he shook his body free of sand and extended his wings.

"Brekke, I must go!" D'ram shouted. "Did you hear?"

"Yes, I heard. Do go quickly!" she called back, raising her hand in farewell.

Whatever had roused Tiroth excited the fire-lizards who began wheeling, diving, chittering raucously. Ruth raised his head, looked at them sleepily, then laid his head back on the sand, unmoved by the excitement. Brekke turned to regard the white dragon, with a curious frown.

"What's wrong, Brekke?"

"The bronzes at Ista Weyr are blooding their kills."

"Oh, Shards and Shells!" Jaxom's initial surprise melded into disappointed disgust with his weakness. He'd hoped to be allowed to attend that mating flight. He'd wanted to cheer G'dened and Barnath on.

"I'll know," Brekke said soothingly. "Canth will be there as well as Tiroth. They'll tell me all. Now, you eat!"

As Jaxom obeyed, still cursing his unfortunate condition, he noticed that Brekke was staring at Ruth again.

"What's the matter with Ruth?"

"Ruth? Nothing. Poor dear, he was so proud to fly Thread for you, and he's too tired to care about anything else right now."

She rose and as she left him Berd and Grall landed on her shoulders, murmuring softly as she disappeared into the shady forest.

CHAPTER XIV

Early Morning at Harpercraft Hall,
Midmorning at Ista Weyr, Midafternoon
at Jaxom's Cove, 15.8.28

IN THE DARK of the early morning Robinton was
awakened by Silvina.

"Master Robinton, word has come from Ista Weyr.
The bronzes are blooding their kill. Caylith will fly
soon. You're wanted there."

"Oh, yes, thank you, Silvina." He blinked against
the light from the glow baskets she was unshielding.
"You didn't by any chance bring me . . ." He saw
the steaming mug by his bed. "Oh, good woman! My
undying thanks!"

"That's what you always say," Silvina replied,
chuckling as she left him to proceed with his wake-up
routine.

He dressed quickly to avoid the predawn chill. Zair
took his accustomed shoulder perch, squeaking softly
as Robinton paced down the corridor.

With a glow torch to cast some light in the dark
lower hall, Silvina awaited him at the massive iron
doors. She whirled the release wheel and the great
bar lifted from ceiling and floor. He gave the yank
required to open the huge door and wondered at
the sudden stitch in his side. Then Silvina passed

him his gitar, stoutly encased against the bitter cold of *between.*

"I do hope Barnath flies Caylith," she said. "Look, here's Drenth now."

The Harper saw the brown dragon backwinging to land and he ran down the hall steps. Drenth was excited, his eyes gleaming orange and red in the night. Robinton greeted the dragon's rider, paused to sling his gitar across his back and then, reaching for D'fio's hand, climbed to the brown's back.

"How does the wagering stand?" he asked the rider.

"Ah, now Harper; Barnath is a fine beast. He'll fly Caylith. Although," a certain element of doubt tinged the man's voice, "the four bronzes N'ton is permitting to try are good strong young beasts, and mighty eager for the chance. It could be an upset. Put your mark where you will, it'll give you good value."

"I wish I could bet, but it's not the sort of thing I ought to do . . ."

"Now, if you were to pass me the marks, Master Robinton, I'd swear on the Shell of Drenth here that they were mine!"

"After the flight as well as before?" Robinton asked, amusement warring with his unprofessional desire to gamble.

"I'm a dragonrider, Master Robinton," D'fio said gruffly, "not one of those faithless Southerners."

"And I'm Master Harper of Pern," said Robinton. But he leaned into the man's back, pressing a two-mark piece into his hand. "Barnath, of course, and please let none be the wiser."

"As you wish, Master Robinton," D'fio sounded pleased.

They rose above the black shadow of the Fort Hold cliffs, the lighter darkness of night sky, moonless at this hour and season, just barely discernible. He felt the tension in D'fio's back, drew his own breath in sharply as they transferred *between,* and abruptly emerged with Drenth calling out his name to the Ista Weyr watchdragon.

Robinton shielded his eyes from the brilliance of the sun slanting off the water. As he glanced below, he saw the dramatic half-peak of Ista Weyr, the black stone like giant jagged fingers pointing to the bright blue skies. Ista was the smallest of the Weyrs, some of its complement of dragons making weyrs in the forest that surrounded the base. But the broad plateau beyond the cone was crowded with bronze beasts, their riders forming a cluster close to the golden queen who was crouched over her kill, sucking the blood from its body. At a farther and safe distance from this spectacle a large group of people looked on. Toward this area, Drenth glided.

Zair took wing from Robinton's shoulder, to join other fire-lizards in an aerial display of excitement. Robinton noticed that the little creatures kept a distance from the dragons. At least the fire-lizards were appearing at Weyrs again.

D'fio dismounted, too, and sent his brown for a swim in the warm waters of the bay below the Weyr plateau. Other dragons, uninvolved in this flight, were already taking advantage of the bathing at Ista Island.

Caylith vaulted from the ground toward the herd of beasts in the Weyr's corral. Cosira half-followed, keeping a firm control on her young queen so that she wouldn't gorge the meat and be too heavy for this all-important mating flight. Robinton counted twenty-six bronzes ringing the killing ground, gleaming in the harsh sunlight, their eyes wheeling red in rut agitation, their wings half-furled, their bodies at a crouch that would send them skyward the instant the queen ascended. They were all young, as F'lar had recommended, almost equal in size as they waited, never taking their glistening eyes from the object of their interest.

Caylith growled deep in her throat as she sucked the blood from the buck carcass. She raised her head to snarl contemptuously back at the bronze ring.

Suddenly the watch dragon roared a challenge and

even Caylith turned to look. Arrowing in from the south, over the sea, came two bronzes.

Just as Robinton realized that the beasts must have flown in at sea level to get this close to the Weyr undetected, he also realized that these were older beasts, muzzles graying, necks thickened. Southerners. Two of the Oldtimers' bronzes. That had to be T'kul with Salth, and probably B'zon with Ranilth. Robinton began to run toward the killing ground, toward the queen's prospective mates, for that was the obvious goal of the two bronzes sweeping in from the south.

Their timing had been perfect, Robinton thought then saw two others making for the landing bronzes —the stocky figure of D'ram and F'lar's lean body. T'kul and B'zon jumped off their beasts. The dragons took one final leap to range themselves with the other bronzes who hissed and growled at the newcomers. Robinton prayed under his breath that none of the bronze riders would act first, think later. Most of them were so young they'd not recognize T'kul or B'zon. But D'ram and F'lar certainly had.

Robinton felt his heart pounding in his chest and a totally unfamiliar ache that caused him to grimace and slow his trot momentarily. B'zon was facing him, a set smile on his face. The Oldtimer touched T'kul's arm and the former High Reaches Weyrleader spared the Harper a quick glance. T'kul considered him no threat and turned back toward the two Weyrleaders.

D'ram reached T'kul first. "You fool, this is for young beasts. You'll kill Salth."

"What option have you left us?" B'zon demanded just as F'lar and Robinton skidded to either side of the two Southerners. There was a hysterical note in the man's voice. "Our queens are too old to rise: there are no greens to give the males relief. We *must . . .*"

Caylith bugled as she left the blood-sucked corpse of the buck and half-flew, half-ran to scatter the herd, one sweeping forepaw impaling another victim on its flank and dragging it back to her.

"D'ram, you declared this flight open, didn't you?"

T'kul asked in a harsh voice, his features fine-drawn despite the tan of Southern suns. He looked from D'ram to F'lar.

"I did, but your bronzes are too old, T'kul." He gestured toward the eager young dragons. The difference between them and the two older ones was pathetically obvious.

"Salth's dying anyway. Let him go out flying. I made that choice, D'ram, when I brought him here." T'kul stared hard at F'lar, the bitterness and hatred so vivid that Robinton sucked in his breath. *"Why* did you take back the egg? How did you find it?" Desperation broke briefly through T'kul's cold pride and arrogance.

"Had you come to us, we would have helped you," F'lar said quietly.

"Or I," D'ram said, miserable before the plight of his one-time acquaintance.

Ignoring F'lar altogether, T'kul gave the Istan Weyrleader a long scornful glance then, straightening his shoulders, jerked his head at B'zon to move forward. F'lar was in his direct path to the other bronze riders. The Benden Weyrleader opened his mouth to speak, shook his head in regret and stepped to one side. The Southern riders moved the few paces forward just in time. Caylith, raising her bloody muzzle, seemed to pulse more golden than ever. Her eyes were whirling opalescence. With a fierce scream, she launched herself upward. Barnath was the first dragon off the ground after her, and, to Robinton's surprise, T'kul's Salth was not far behind the Istan bronze.

T'kul swung back to F'lar, the triumph on his face an insult. Then he strode to Cosira's side. The Weyrwoman was swaying with the effort of staying in mental contact with her queen. She didn't notice that it was G'dened and T'kul who were leading her back to her quarters to await the outcome of the flight.

"He'll kill Salth," D'ram was muttering, his face stricken.

That odd pressure against his chest kept Robinton from reassuring the worried man.

"And B'zon, too!" D'ram grabbed F'lar's arm. "Is there nothing we can do to stop it? Two dragons?"

"If they had come to us . . ." F'lar began, placing his hand consolingly on D'ram's. "But those Oldtimer riders always *took!* That was their error at the outset!" His face hardened.

"They're still taking," Robinton said, wanting to ease D'ram's distress. "They've taken what they wanted from the north all along. Here, there. What pleased them. Young girls, material, stone, iron, jewels. They looted with quiet system ever since they were exiled. I've had the reports. I've given them to F'lar."

"If only they had asked!" F'lar looked upward at the fast-dwindling specks of dragons in flight.

"What was that all about?" Lord Warbret of Ista Hold hurried up to them. "Those last two were old or I don't know dragons as well as I thought I did."

"The mating flight was open," F'lar replied, but Warbret was looking at D'ram's anxious face.

"To old dragons? I thought you stipulated young ones that hadn't had a chance at a queen before! I don't see the point myself, in having another older Weyrleader. No offense intended, D'ram. Change upsets holders." He gazed at the sky. "How'll they keep up with the younger ones? That's a gruelling pace."

"They have the right to try," F'lar said. "While we await the outcome, some wine, D'ram?"

"Yes, yes, wine. Lord Warbret . . ." D'ram recovered his composure sufficiently to gesture the Lord Holder to accompany him toward the living cavern. He beckoned to the other guests to follow, but his step was heavy and slow.

"Don't worry, D'ram. That other dragon might have been quick off the mark," Lord Warbret said as he thumped D'ram's shoulder encouragingly, "but I've all the faith in the world in G'dened and Barnath. Fine young man! Splendid dragon. Besides he's mated Caylith before, hasn't he? That always tells, doesn't it?"

While Robinton breathed with relief that the Lord

Holder was misinterpreting D'ram's concern, F'lar replied to the questions.

"Yes, Caylith had thirty-four eggs of her first clutch with Barnath. You don't want a young queen to overlay herself, but her hatchlings were healthy and strong. No queen egg, but that's often the case when a Weyr has enough queens. The bond of a previous mating can be a strong factor despite a queen's captiousness, but you never know."

Robinton noticed that the weyrfolk appeared to be somewhat tense as they served the visitors. He wondered how many had indeed identified the Southerners. He hoped no one blurted out their suspicions in front of the Lord Holder.

T'kul's Salth must have flown his queen dozens of times and won her. He'd be a canny old fellow, all right, but all his cleverness would be no good if he couldn't catch the queen in the first few minutes of flight. He simply wouldn't have the staying power of the younger dragons, and possibly not even the speed for the surge to catch her up. He flew against some fine beasts. Robinton knew how carefully N'ton had chosen the four bronze riders to present themselves from Fort. Each had been wing-seconds for Turns, men already proven in Falls as leaders with strong dragons. F'lar had also limited Benden's three contenders to men well able to lead a Weyr. Robinton could only assume that Telgar, Igen and High Reaches had honored D'ram's Weyr with good men. Ista was the smallest of the six Weyrs and needed a united folk.

He sipped at his wine, hoping his side would stop aching, wondering what had caused that unnerving pressure. Well, wine cured many ills. He waited until D'ram turned his head and then he refilled the man's cup, catching F'lar's approving gaze as he did.

Weyrfolk began to stop at the table now, greeting D'ram and Lord Warbret. Their obvious pleasure in seeing their former Weyrleader was a tonic for D'ram, and he responded with smiles and chatting. He looked tense but anyone would attribute that to understandable concern for the outcome of this flight.

Robinton had a puzzle to chew over: T'kul's bitter words about the egg. "Why did you take back the egg? How did you find it?" Didn't T'kul realize that someone from Southern had returned the egg? Then the Harper stiffened. No Southerner had returned that egg, for surely T'kul would have discovered the culprit by now.

Robinton began to hope fervently that neither of the two old dragons would die in their attempt to fly the young queen. Just like the Oldtimers to add a sour note to what ought to be a joyous occasion! Surely life in the Southern Weyr was not so unbearable that T'kul would cold-bloodedly allow his dragon to court death rather than continue there? Robinton knew the Weyr well; the setting in its own small valley was beautiful— a considerable improvement on T'kul's dour, barren High Reaches Weyr. There was a huge well-constructed hall in the center of a flagstone court where no Thread could find grass to burrow. Food for the picking, wild beasts in plenty to feed dragons, ideal weather, and their only obligation as dragonriders to the small Hold on the coast.

Then Robinton recalled the pulsing hatred for F'lar in T'kul's eyes. It was malice and spite that motivated the former High Reaches Weyrleader—and hatred for an exile not of his choosing.

The queens might be too old to rise, but that was only a recent occurrence, Robinton thought, and the bronzes could not be in that hard a case. They were ageing as well and the blood did not so easily quicken, so the old urgencies surely could be contained.

There was also the point that T'kul need not have gone South with Mardra, T'ron and the other obstinate and inflexible Oldtime weyrfolk. He could have accepted the leadership of Benden, acknowledged that Craft and Hold had earned rights for themselves in the four hundred Turns since the last Pass and conducted himself and his Weyr affairs accordingly.

Had any of the Southerners come forward, acting in honor, asking the assistance of the other Weyrs, he was certain such would have been forthcoming. He didn't doubt D'ram's sincerity, and he would have pressed for their requests himself, by the Shell he would have!

Looking at the worst possible conclusion to the day's events, what would happen to T'kul if Salth did overfly himself? The Harper sighed deeply, not liking to consider that possibility at all, but he'd better. The possibility meant that . . . Robinton glanced toward the Weyrwoman's quarters. T'kul had been wearing a belt knife. Everyone wore belt knives. Robinton felt his heart pounding. He knew it wasn't proper, but shouldn't he suggest to D'ram that someone be in the queen's weyr in case of trouble? Someone uninvolved in the mating flight. When a man's dragon died he could become insane, not know what he was doing. A vision of T'kul's hatred flashed vividly before the Harper's eyes. Robinton had many prerogatives but entering the chambers of a Weyrwoman whose dragon was mating was not one of them. Still . . .

Robinton blinked. F'lar was no longer seated at the table. The Harper glanced about the cavern, but caught no glimpse of the tall figure of the Benden Weyrleader. He rose, struggling to keep his progress casual, managed to nod pleasantly to D'ram and Warbret as he sauntered toward the entrance. The Istan Harper intersected his path.

"F'lar took two of our strongest riders with him, Master Robinton." The man nodded toward the Weyrwoman's quarters. "He's afraid of trouble."

Robinton nodded, blowing out with relief, then halted.

"How did he manage it? I saw no one using the steps."

Baldor grinned. "This Weyr is full of odd tunnels and entrances. It wouldn't do to compound the problem," he added, gesturing toward the guests in the cavern, "now would it?"

"Indeed not. Indeed not."

"We'll know what happens soon enough," Baldor said with a worried sigh. "Our fire-lizards'll tell us."

"True," and Zair on his shoulder cheeped at Baldor's brown.

Robinton was somewhat relieved by the precautions and made his way back to the table. He filled his cup again, and D'ram's. Not Benden wine, but it wasn't altogether unpalatable, if a trifle sweeter than he liked. Why was it that happy occasions seemed to fly past and one like today dragged interminably?

The watchdragon bugled, a fearful, unhappy sound. But not a keen! Not a death knell! Robinton felt the muscles in his chest relax. His relief was premature for there was a rustle of worried whispers sweeping through the living cavern. Several weyrfolk hurried out, looking up at the blue watchdragon, his wings extended. Zair crooned softly but Robinton sensed nothing definite from the creature. The little bronze merely repeated the dragon's muddled thoughts.

"One of the bronzes must have faltered," D'ram said, swallowing nervously, his face tinged gray under his tan. He looked hard at Robinton.

"One of those older ones, I'll wager," Warbret said, pleased at this justification of his opinion.

"You're likely right," Robinton said easily, "but the flight was declared open, so they had to be admitted."

"Aren't they taking a long time of it?" Warbret asked, frowning out at the sky just visible from their table.

"Oh, I don't think so," Robinton replied with what he hoped was a casual air, "though it sometimes seems that way. I expect that's because the outcome of this particular flight will have such consequences for the Weyr. Caylith is at least giving the bronzes a good run for her!"

"D'you think there'll be a queen egg this time?" Warbret asked eagerly.

"I would never make the error of counting eggs *this* soon, my Lord Warbret," the Harper said, trying to keep his countenance bland.

"Oh, yes, of course. I mean it would be quite an

accomplishment for Barnath, wouldn't it? Having his queen lay a golden egg this flight?"

"It would indeed. That is, if . . . Barnath succeeds in flying her."

"Really, Master Harper, of course he will. Where's your sense of justice?"

"Where it generally is, but I doubt that Caylith is attuned to justice right now."

The words were no sooner out of his mouth than Zair, his eyes the bright yellow of distress, gave a frightened, gibbering squeak at the Harper. Mnementh erupted into the air just above the ground of the Bowl, bugling in alarm.

Robinton was on his feet and running, glancing about him for Baldor. The Istan Harper was equally alert to the danger. He and four large riders began pelting toward the Weyr.

"What's the matter?" Warbret demanded.

"Stay there," Robinton shouted.

The air was suddenly full of dragons, bugling and keening, barely avoiding midair collisions as they swept about, riderless, disturbed. Robinton pumped his long legs as fast as he could, regardless of the fierce pain in his side that he eased somewhat by digging the heel of his hand into his flesh. The weight on his chest seemed worse; it kept breath which he needed for running.

Zair began squealing over Robinton's head, projecting an image of a falling dragon and fighting men. Unfortunately the little bronze could not project the information Robinton most wanted—which dragon, which men! F'lar must be involved or Mnementh would not be here.

The huge bronze was landing on the queen's weyr ledge, preventing Baldor's men from entering the weyr. They flattened themselves against the wall, trying to avoid the frantic sweeps of his wide wings.

"Mnementh! Listen to me! Let us pass! We're going to aid F'lar. Listen to me!"

Robinton charged right up the steps, past Baldor and his men, and grabbed one wing tip. He was all but hauled off his feet as Mnementh pulled it back, bending his head to hiss at the Harper. The great eyes whirled violently yellow.

"Listen to me, Mnementh!" the Harper roared. "Let us pass!"

Zair flew at the bronze dragon, screaming at the top of his lungs.

I listen. Salth is no more. Help F'lar!

The great bronze dragon folded his wings, lifted his head, and Robinton thankfully waved Baldor and his men to go ahead. He needed a moment to catch his breath.

As Robinton turned to enter the passage, hand pressed against his side, Zair zipped in front of him, his cries full of encouragement now. The Harper wondered fleetingly if the tiny creature thought that he, and he alone, had turned aside the great bronze. Robinton could only be grateful that the bronze dragon *would* listen to him.

As Robinton entered the weyr, he could hear the sounds of fighting in the Weyrwoman's sleeping chamber. The curtain across the entrance was suddenly ripped from its pole as two struggling bodies staggered out into the larger room. F'lar and T'kul! Baldor and two of his helpers were close behind, trying to separate the men. In the room beyond them, locked in the mating flight contact with their beasts, were the rest of the bronze riders and the Weyrwoman, oblivious to the combat. Someone had collapsed on the floor. B'zon, probably, he thought as the scene registered in his mind in one split second.

What caught Robinton's horrified attention was the fact that F'lar had no knife in either hand. His left was closed about T'kul's right wrist, straining to keep the man's long knife—no short-bladed belt but a skinning tool—away from his collarbone. His fingers began digging into the tendons of T'kul's wrist, trying to force the fingers open, or to deaden the nerves. His right hand held T'kul's left arm down and out from their sides. T'kul writhed savagely; the maniacal gleam in his reddened eyes told Robinton that the man was be-

yond himself. As he must have intended, thought
Robinton.

One of Baldor's men was trying to shove a knife in
F'lar's hand but F'lar had to keep T'kul's left hand
engaged.

"I'll kill you, F'lar," T'kul said through gritted teeth
as he struggled to force his right hand down, closer
and closer, the blade slanting toward the bronze rider's
neck. "I'll kill you. As you killed my Salth. As you
killed us! I'll kill you!" It sounded like a chant, the
beats emphasized by the spurts of strength T'kul called
up from the depths of his madness.

F'lar saved his breath, the strain of holding off that
knife showing in the cords that stood out in his neck,
in the drag on his face muscles, the tension in his legs
and thighs.

"I'll kill you. I'll kill you as T'ron ought! I'll kill
you, F'lar!"

T'kul's voice now came in ragged gasps as the point
of the knife inched toward its goal.

Abruptly, F'lar kicked out with his left leg and,
twining it about T'kul's left, yanked the foot out from
under the crazed, overbalanced Oldtimer. With a yell,
T'kul fell forward into F'lar, who neatly twisted him
over and down, breaking T'kul's left-hand hold but
keeping his own left hand firmly locked on T'kul's
right wrist. The Oldtimer kicked out, caught F'lar vi-
ciously in the stomach. Although the bronze rider did
not release the knife hand, he was doubled up, windless. A second kick from T'kul knocked his feet out
from under him. F'lar fell heaving as T'kul wrenched
his knife-hand free and scrambled to fall on the
younger Weyrleader. But F'lar continued the roll with
an agility that astonished the watchers, coming to his
feet again even as T'kul stood up and launched an immediate attack. But that interval had been time
enough for F'lar to grab the belt knife from Baldor.

The two antagonists faced each other. Robinton
knew by the grim determination on F'lar's face that
this time, with the man's beast already dead, the

Benden Weyrleader would finish off his opponent. If he could.

Robinton disliked having doubts about F'lar's skill as a fighter, but T'kul was no ordinary antagonist, driven as he was by the grief-madness of Salth's death. The man, older by some twenty Turns, had the reach of F'lar, and a longer, more deadly blade in his hand. F'lar would have to elude that slashing blade long enough to wear T'kul past the point of the mad energy that possessed the Oldtimer.

An exultant shout burst from the Weyrwoman's room and her piercing shriek followed. That was just enough to divert T'kul. F'lar was ready for that tiny break in concentration. He dove at T'kul, knife arm down and, before the man could parry and guard himself at the lower angle, F'lar's thrust went up and through the ribs to the heart. T'kul, eyes protruding, fell dead at his feet.

F'lar sagged, dropping to one knee, gasping with his exertions. Wearily he scrubbed at his forehead with the back of his left hand, every line of his body emphasizing the dejection he was experiencing.

"You could have done nothing else, F'lar," Robinton said softly, wishing he had the strength to move to F'lar's side.

From the Weyrwoman's chamber came the rejected suitors, dazed by their participation in the mating flight. They came out in a mass, and Robinton couldn't figure out who had remained with the Weyrwoman as her mate and was now the new Weyrleader of Ista.

His sudden inexplicable weakness confused the Harper. He couldn't catch his breath; he hadn't the energy to quiet Zair, who was chittering the wildest distress. The pain in his side had moved again to his chest, like a heavy rock sitting on him.

"Baldor!"

"Master Robinton!" The Istan Harper rushed to his side, his face expressing horror and consternation as he assisted Robinton to the nearest bench. "You're gray. Your lips. They're blue. What's wrong with you?"

"Gray is how I feel. My chest! Wine! I need wine!"

The room began pressing in on the Harper. He couldn't breathe. He was aware of shouts, sensed panic in the air and tried to bestir himself to take control of the situation. Hands pushed him down, then flat, making it totally impossible to breathe. He struggled to sit up.

"Let him. It will help his breathing."

Dimly Robinton identified the voice as Lessa's. How did she come to be here? Then he was propped against someone and could breathe more easily. If only he could rest, could sleep.

"Clear everyone from the weyr." Lessa was giving orders.

Harper, Harper, listen to us. Now listen to us. Harper, don't sleep. Stay with us. Harper, we need you. We love you. Listen to us.

The voices in his head were unfamiliar. He wished they would be silent so that he could think about the pain in his chest and the sleep he so desperately craved.

Harper, you cannot leave. You must stay. Harper, we love you.

The voices puzzled him. He didn't know them. It wasn't Lessa or F'lar speaking. The voices were deep, insistent, and he wasn't hearing them with his ears. The voices were in his mind where he couldn't ignore them. He wished they would leave him alone so that he could sleep. He was so very tired. T'kul had been too old to fly his dragon or win a fight. Yet he was older than T'kul, who now slept in death. If only the voices would let him sleep, too. He was so tired.

You cannot sleep yet, Harper. We are with you. Do not leave us. Harper, you must live! We love you.

Live? Of course, he would live. Silly voices. He was just tired. He wanted to sleep.

Harper, Harper, do not leave us. Harper, we love you. Do not go.

The voices were not loud, but they held on to him, in his mind. That was it. They were not letting his mind go.

Someone else, outside him, was holding something to his lips.

"Master Robinton, you must try to swallow the medicine. You must make the effort. It will ease the pain." That voice he recognized. Lessa. Distraught.

Of course, she would be, with F'lar having to kill a rider, and all the trouble with the theft of the egg, and Ramoth being so upset.

Harper, obey Lessa. You must obey Lessa, Harper. Open your mouth. You must try.

He could ignore Lessa, he could bat feebly at the cup at his lips and try to spit out the bitter-tasting pill which was melting on his tongue, but he could not ignore those insistent voices. He let them put wine in his mouth, and swallowed the pill with it. At least they had the kindness to give him wine, not water. Water would have been undignified for the Harper of Pern. He could never have swallowed water with the pain in his chest.

Something seemed to snap inside him. Ah, the pain in his chest. It was easing, as if the snap had been the loosening of the tight band that constricted his heart.

He sighed at the relief. One didn't fully appreciate the absence of pain, he thought.

"Take a sip of the wine, Master." He felt the cup at his lips again.

Wine, yes, that would complete his cure. Wine always did revive him. Only he still wanted to sleep. He was so very tired.

"And another!"

You may sleep later. You must listen to us and stay. Harper, listen! We love you. You must stay.

The Harper resented their insistence.

"How long does it take the man to get here?" That was Lessa's voice, sounding fiercer than he'd ever heard her. Why did she also sound as if she were weeping? Lessa weeping?

Lessa is weeping for you. You do not want her to

weep. Stay with us, Harper. You cannot go. We will not let you go. Lessa should not weep.

No, that was right, Lessa should not weep. Robinton didn't really believe that she was. He forced his eyes to open and saw her bending over him. She was weeping! The tears were dropping from her cheeks to his hand which lay limp and upturned as if to receive the tears.

"You mustn't weep, Lessa. I will not have you weeping." Great Shells, he was losing his voice control. He cleared his throat. This would never do.

"Don't try to talk, Robinton," Lessa said, gulping back her sobs. "Just rest. You've got to rest. Oldive is coming. I told them to time it. Just rest. More wine?"

"Have I ever refused wine?" Why was his voice so faint?

"Never," and Lessa was laughing and crying at the same time.

"Who's been nagging me? They wouldn't let me go. Make them let me rest, Lessa. I'm so tired!"

"Oh, Master Robinton, please!"

Please what?

Harper, stay with us. Lessa will weep.

"Oh, Master Oldive. Over here!" That was Lessa again, leaving his side.

Robinton tried to reach for her.

"Don't exert yourself!" She was holding him down, but she was staying beside him. Dear Lessa! Even when he was angry with her, he loved her nonetheless. Perhaps more, because she was angry so often and anger intensified her beauty.

"Ah, Master Robinton." Oldive's soothing voice made him open his eyes. "The chest pain again? Just nod. I'd rather you didn't make the effort to speak."

"Ramoth says he has great pain and is very tired."

"Oh? Convenient having the dragon listen, too."

Master Oldive was putting cold instruments to his chest and on his arm. Robinton would have liked to protest.

"Yes, I know they're cold, my dear Harper, but necessary. Now listen to me, your heart has been overstrained. That was the pain in your chest. Lessa gave you a pill which has relieved that pain for the moment. But the immediate danger is past. I want you to try to sleep. You are going to need a lot of rest, my good friend. A lot of rest."

"Then tell them to be quiet and let me sleep."

"Who's to be quiet?" Oldive's voice was soothing, and Robinton was vaguely annoyed because he suspected Oldive didn't believe he'd heard them keeping him awake. "Here, take this pill and a sip of wine. I know you've never refused wine."

Robinton smiled weakly. How well they knew him, Oldive and Lessa.

"It's Ramoth and Mnementh talking to him, Oldive. They said he had nearly gone . . ." Lessa's voice broke on the last note.

Nearly gone, was I? Is that what it feels like to be so close to death? Like being very tired?

You will stay now, Harper. We can let you sleep. But we will be with you. We love you.

Dragons talking to me? Dragons keeping me from death? How kind they are for I did not want to die yet. There is so much to be done. Problems to be solved. There'd been a problem on my mind . . . about dragons, too . . .

"Who flew Caylith?"

Did he manage to say that out loud? He didn't even hear his own voice in his ears.

"Did you hear what he said, Oldive?"

"Something about Caylith."

"Wouldn't you know he'd worry about that at a time like this?" Lessa sounded more like herself, acerbic. "Barnath flew Caylith, Robinton. Now, will you sleep?"

Sleep, Master. We will listen.

The Harper drew a deep breath into his lungs and relaxed gratefully into sleep.

CHAPTER XV

Evening at Jaxom's Cove and Late Evening at Ista Weyr, 15.8.28

SHARRA WAS SHOWING Brekke and Jaxom how to play a children's game in the sand with pebbles and sticks when Ruth, sleeping just beyond them with the fire-lizards, woke up. He reared to a sitting position, stretching his neck and keening the long piercing note that marked a dragon's passing.

"Oh no!" Brekke reacted just a shade faster than Jaxom. "Salth is gone!"

"Salth?" Jaxom wondered who that was.

"Salth!" Sharra's face drained of color. "Ask Ruth where!"

"Canth says he was trying to fly Caylith and burst his heart!" Brekke answered the question, her shoulders sagging in new grief and a poignantly remembered tragedy. "The fool! He must have known that the younger dragons would be faster, stronger than poor old Salth!"

"Serves T'kul right! And don't soar over me, Brekke." Sharra's eyes flashed as Brekke turned to reprimand her. "Remember, I've had to deal with T'kul and the rest of those Oldtimers. They are *not* like your Northern dragonfolk at all. They're . . . they're impossible! I could burn your ears with tales! If T'kul was fool enough to set his bronze to fly a young queen, with the competition there'd be for the Istan Weyrleadership, then he deserves to lose his beast! I'm sorry. Harsh words for you, Brekke, and Jaxom, but I know what those Southerns are like. You don't!"

"I knew there'd be real trouble sometime, exiling them like that," Brekke said slowly, "but . . ."

"From what I've heard, Brekke," Jaxom said from a compulsion to erase the desolate look from her face, "that was the only way to handle them. They weren't honoring their responsibilities to the people beholden to them. They were greedy, over and above proper tithing. Further," and he brought out his strongest point, "I heard Lytol criticizing those dragonriders!"

"I know, Jaxom. I know all that but they did come forward from their own time to save Pern . . ." Jaxom wondered if she realized she was wringing her hands till the knuckles showed white.

"To save Pern, yes, and then they demanded that we remember that every time we drew breath in their presence," Jaxom went on, recalling all too clearly the arrogant and contemptuous manner with which T'ron had treated Lytol.

"We ignore the Oldtimers," Sharra said, with a shrug. "We go about our business, keep our Hold green clear, pen up our animals during Fall. We just run a quick search with the flamethrowers to be sure the grubs have done their work."

"Don't they ride a Fall?" Brekke asked in surprise.

"Oh, now and again. If they feel like it, or if their dragons get too upset . . ." Sharra's contempt was trenchant. Then she noticed the dismay on the other two faces and added, "Oh, what's happened is not the *dragons'* fault, mind you. And I don't suppose that it's really the riders' either. I do think they should at least try to act what they are. To be sure, most of the Oldtimers stayed north. So just a few are giving dragonmen a poor reputation in Southern. Still . . . if they'd met us halfway . . . we would have helped."

"I should go, I think," Brekke said, rising and facing west. "T'kul is half a man now. I know how that

feels . . ." Her voice petered out and her face drained
of all color as she stared to the west, her eyes getting
larger until a cry of horror burst from her lips. "Oh
no!" Her hand went to her throat and she turned it
palm outward as if warding off an attack.

"Brekke, what is it?" Sharra leaped to her feet, her
arms about the woman.

Ruth whimpered and nudged against Jaxom for reassurance.

*She is very afraid. She is speaking to Canth. He is
unhappy. It is terrible. Another dragon is very weak.
Canth is with him. It is Mnementh who talks now.
T'kul fights F'lar!*

"T'kul fights F'lar?" Jaxom reached out to Ruth's
shoulder for balance.

The fire-lizards picked up the agitation, dipping and
swooping, chittering in harsh cacophony that made
Jaxom wave his arms at them to be silent.

"This is ghastly, Jaxom," Brekke cried. "I must go.
They must see that T'kul is not responsible for what
he's doing. Why don't they just overpower him? There
must be someone with wits at Ista! What is D'ram doing? I'll get my flying things." She ran back to the
shelter.

"Jaxom." Sharra turned to him, one hand raised,
appealing for his reassurance. "T'kul hates F'lar. I've
heard him blame F'lar for everything that happens in
Southern. If T'kul's dragonless, he'd be insane. He'd
kill F'lar!"

Jaxom drew the girl close to him, wondering which
of them needed comfort more. T'kul trying to kill
F'lar? He asked Ruth to listen hard.

I hear nothing. Canth is between. *I only hear
trouble. Ramoth is coming . . .*

"Here?"

No, where they are! Ruth's eyes deepened to the
purple of worry. *I do not like this.*

"What, Ruth?"

"Oh, please Jaxom, what's he saying? I'm scared."

"He is, too. And so am I."

Brekke came back through the woods, her flying

gear in one hand, in the other her small pack of medicines, half-closed, and in danger of spilling its contents. She halted just before stepping onto the sands, blinked, frowning with impatience and dismay.

"I can't get there! Canth must stay with B'zon's Ranilth. We can't lose two bronzes today!" She looked this way and that as if the beach could sprout an answer to her dilemma. She bit her underlip and then exclaimed in frustration. "I've got to go!"

The second shock struck both Brekke and Jaxom at the same time as Ruth bugled in fear.

"Robinton!" Brekke reeled and would have fallen if Sharra and Jaxom had not jumped to her support. "Oh, no, not Robinton? How?"

The Master Harper.

"Not dead?" Sharra cried.

The Master Harper is very ill. They will not let him go. He will have to stay. As you did.

"I'll take you, Brekke. On Ruth. Just let me get my flying gear."

Both women reached out to restrain him.

"You can't fly yet, Jaxom. You can't go *between!*" The fear in Brekke's eyes was for him now.

"You really can't, Jaxom," Sharra said, shaking her head and pleading with her eyes. "The cold of *between* . . . you're just not well enough yet. Please!"

They are afraid for you now, Ruth said, sounding confused. *Very afraid. I do not know why it is wrong for you to ride me but it is!*

"He's right, Jaxom, it would be disastrous," Brekke said, her body slumping with defeat. Wearily she raised her hand to her head, and pulled off the now unnecessary helmet. "You mustn't attempt going *between* for at least another month or six sevendays. If you did, you'd risk headaches for the rest of your life and the possibility of blindness. . . ."

"How do you know that?" Jaxom demanded, struggling with fury at having been kept ignorant of such a restriction, with frustration at not being able to help either Brekke or the Harper.

"I know that," Sharra said, turning Jaxom to face

her. "One of the dragonriders at Southern took fire-head. We didn't know the dangers of going *between*. He went blind first. Then mad with the pain in his head and . . . died. So did his dragon." Her voice caught, remembering that tragedy, and her eyes were misted with tears.

Jaxom could only stare at her, stunned.

"Why wasn't I told that before?"

"No reason to," Sharra said, her eyes never leaving his, pleading with him for understanding. "You're getting stronger daily. By the time you realized the restriction existed, it might not have been necessary to warn you anymore."

"Another four or six sevendays?" He ground the words out, conscious that he was working his fists and that his jaw muscles ached with the effort to control his temper.

Sharra nodded slowly, her face expressionless.

Jaxom took a deep breath, forcing emotion down. "That does make it awkward, doesn't it, because right now we need a dragonrider." He looked toward Brekke. Her head was turned slightly to the west. Jaxom could sense her longing to be where she was urgently needed, the restraint that kept her from claiming Canth's help when he was needed elsewhere. "We have a dragonrider!" he exclaimed, whooping. "Ruth, would you take Brekke to Ista without me?"

I would take Brekke anywhere. The little white dragon raised his head, his eyes wheeling quickly as he stepped forward, toward Brekke.

Brekke's face cleared miraculously of sorrow and helplessness. "Oh, Jaxom, would you really let me?"

He was well repaid by the overwhelming gratitude in that breathless question.

He took her arm, hurrying her to Ruth's side.

"You must go. If Master Robinton . . ." Jaxom choked on the rest of that sentence, panic at the thought closing his throat.

"Oh, thank you, Jaxom. Thank you, Ruth." Brekke fumbled with the strap of her helmet. She struggled with her jacket before she could get her arm into the sleeve, and buckled the riding belt in place. When she was ready Ruth dipped his shoulder for Brekke to mount, then turned his head to be sure she was safely seated.

"I'll send Ruth directly back, Jaxom. Oh, no, don't let him go! Don't let him sleep!" The last two sentences were directed to distant minds.

We will not let him go, Ruth said. He briefly nosed Jaxom on the shoulder and then sprang up, showering his friend and Sharra with dry sand. He was barely wing height above the waves before he winked out.

"Jaxom?" Sharra's voice was so unsteady that he turned to her in concern. "What can have happened? T'kul couldn't have been mad enough to attack the Harper, too?"

"The Harper may have tried to stop the fight, if I know him. Do *you* know Master Robinton?"

"I know more *of* him," she said, biting her underlip. She expelled her breath in a deep shudder, struggling to control her fears. "Through Piemur, and Menolly. I've seen him, of course, in our Hold and heard him sing. He's such a wonderful man. Oh, Jaxom! All those Southerners have run mad. *Mad!* They're sick, confused, lost!" She dropped her head against his shoulder, surrendering to her anxieties. Tenderly, he drew her against him.

He lives! Ruth's reassurance rang faint but true in his head.

"Ruth says he lives, Sharra."

"He must continue to live, Jaxom. He must! He must!" Her fists beat on his chest to emphasize her determination.

Jaxom caught her hands, holding them flat, and smiled into her wide, flashing eyes.

"He will. I'm sure he will, if it's in our power to think him so."

Jaxom was intensely aware, at this highly inappropriate moment, of Sharra's vibrant body pressing against his. He could feel her warmth through the thin fabric of her shirt, the long line of her thighs against his, the fragrance of her hair, scented with sun and a blossom she had tucked behind her ear. The startled look that crossed her face told him that she, too, was aware of the intimacy of their positions—aware and, for the first time since he had known her, confused.

He eased his grip on her hands, ready to release her completely if necessary. Sharra was not Corana, not a simple hold girl obedient to the Lord of her Hold. Sharra was not a bed partner for a passing indulgence of desire. Sharra was too important to him to risk destroying their relationship with an ill-timed demonstration. He was also aware that Sharra thought that his feelings for her stemmed from a natural gratitude for her nursing. He'd thought of that possibility in himself and decided that she was wrong. He liked too many things about her, from the sound of her beautiful voice, to the sure touch of her hands: hands he was aching to have caress him. He'd learned a good deal about her in the past few days, but he was aware of a hungry curiosity in himself to know much, much more. Her reaction to the Southerners had surprised him; she often surprised him. Part of her attraction, he supposed, was that he never knew what she'd say or how she'd say it.

Suddenly he broke their partial embrace and, circling her shoulders lightly with his arm, guided her to the mats where they'd been so blithely playing a child's game. He put both hands on her shoulders and gave her a gentle downward push.

"We may have a long wait, Sharra, before we know for certain the Harper's all right."

"I wish I knew *what* was wrong! If that T'kul has harmed our Harper . . ."

"What about his harming F'lar?"

"I don't know F'lar, although I'd naturally be very sorry if he were hurt by T'kul." She absently folded her legs as he sat down beside her, just close enough so that their shoulders nearly touched. "And, in a sense, F'lar ought to fight T'kul. After all, *he* sent the Oldtimers into exile so *he* ought to finish it."

"And he'll finish it by killing T'kul?"

"Or being killed by him!"

"We'd be in a far worse state," Jaxom replied with more heat than he intended at her callous dismissal of F'lar's fate, "if the Benden Weyrleader gets killed! He *is* Pern!"

"Really?" Sharra was willing to be converted. "I've never seen him . . ."

There are many dragons here and many many people, Ruth told him, his tone still faint but clear. *Sebell is coming. Menolly cannot.*

"Is Ruth talking to you?" Sharra asked anxiously, leaning forward and grasping his arm. He covered her fingers with his, silencing her in that gesture. She bit her underlip and studied his face. He tried to reassure her with emphatic nods.

Her fire-lizards are here. The Harper sleeps. Master Oldive is with him, too. They *wait outside. We will not let him go. Should I return to you now?*

"Who are *they?*" Jaxom asked though he was fairly sure of the identity.

Lessa and F'lar. The man who attacked F'lar is dead.

"T'kul's dead, and F'lar is not hurt?"

No.

"Ask him what is wrong with the Harper," Sharra whispered.

Jaxom wanted to know, too, but there was a long pause before Ruth answered, and the little dragon sounded confused.

Mnementh said Robinton's chest hurt and he wanted to sleep. Wine helped him. Mnementh and Ramoth knew he should not sleep. He would go. May I come back now?

"Does Brekke need you?"

There are many dragons here.

"Come home, my friend!"

I come!

"His chest hurt?" Sharra repeated when Jaxom told her what Ruth had said. She frowned. "It could be the heart. The Harper is not a young man and he does a great deal!" She looked about her for her fire-lizards. "I could send Meer . . ."

"Ruth says there's an awful lot of people and dragons at Ista right now. I think we'd better wait."

"I know," and Sharra gave a long sigh. She picked up a handful of sand and let it run through her fingers. Then she gave Jaxom a sad smile. "I know how to wait, but that doesn't mean I like to!"

"We know he's alive, and F'lar . . ." Jaxom gave her a sly look.

"I didn't mean any disrespect to your Weyrleader, Jaxom, I want you to know that . . ."

Jaxom laughed, having managed to tease her. She let out an exclamation of annoyance and threw the handful of sand toward him, but he ducked and the sand went over his shoulder, some of it falling in the gentle waves that lapped up the shore.

Brushed out of existence by the next wave, no ripples lasted in this water. There was a fallacy in the Harper's analogy then, Jaxom thought, amused by this irrelevant thought.

Meer and Talla suddenly squawked, both heads turned toward the western arm of the cove. They raised their wings and crouched on their haunches, ready to spring into the air.

"What is it?"

As quickly as they had become alert, the two fire-lizards relaxed, Meer preening one wing as if she hadn't been startled the moment before.

"Is someone coming?" Sharra asked, turning to Jaxom with amazement.

Jaxom jumped to his feet, scanning the skies. "They wouldn't object to Ruth's return."

"It must be someone they know!" The possibility was as improbable to Sharra as it was to Jaxom. "And he's not flying in!"

They both heard the noises of something large moving through the forest on the point. A muffled curse indicated the visitor was human but the first head that penetrated the screen of thick foliage was undeniably animal. The body that followed the head belonged to the smallest runner beast Jaxom had ever seen.

The muffled curses resolved into intelligible words. "Stop snapping the branches back in my face, you ruddy, horn-nosed, flat-footed, slab-hided dragon-bait! Well, Sharra, so this is where you got to! I was told, but I was beginning to doubt it! Hear you've been ill, Jaxom? You don't look it now!"

"Piemur?" Although the appearance of the young harper was the unlikeliest of events, there was no mistaking the characteristic swagger in the short, compact figure that limped jauntily down the beach. "Piemur! What are you doing here?"

"Looking for you, of course. Have you any idea how many coves along this stretch of nowhere in the world answer the description Master Robinton gave me?"

"Well, the Weyr's all organized," F'lar told Lessa in a quiet voice as he joined her in the foreroom of the weyr which had been hastily vacated by its occupants so that the Master Harper of Pern could be accommodated. Master Oldive would not have him moved even as far as Ista Hold. The Healer and Brekke were with him now in the inner room as he slept, propped up in the bed, Zair perched above him, his glowing eyes never leaving the face of his friend.

Lessa held out her hand, needing her weyrmate's touch. He pulled a stool beside hers, gave her a quick kiss and poured himself a cup of wine.

"D'ram has the Weyrfolk organized. He's sent the older bronzes to help Canth and F'nor bring Ranilth back. The poor old thing will live only a few more Turns . . . if B'zon does."

"Not another one today!"

F'lar shook his head. "No, he's just dead asleep. We've got the disappointed bronze riders drunk as winemakers' apprentices, and from every indication Cosira and G'dened are . . . so involved they haven't any notion of what else has been happening here in Ista."

"That's as well," Lessa replied, grinning from ear to ear.

F'lar stroked her cheek, grinning right back at her. "So when does Ramoth rise again, dear heart?"

"I'll remember to let you know!" As she saw F'lar glance in the direction of the inner room, she added, "He'll be all right!"

"Oldive wasn't hedging about his full recovery?"

"How could he? With every dragon on Pern listening in? Now that," she paused in thoughtful reflection, "was totally unexpected. I know the dragons will call him by name but . . . linking?"

"More incredible to me was Brekke arriving on Ruth, alone!"

"Why ever not?" Lessa asked, piqued. "She's been a rider! And she's had a special touch with dragons ever since she lost Wirenth!"

"I can't quite see you offering her Ramoth under similar circumstances. Now don't soar over me, Lessa. That was a fine gesture of Jaxom's. Brekke told me that he hadn't realized till that moment that he couldn't fly *between*. It must have been a bitter discovery for him and it's greatly to his credit that he could respond so generously."

"Yes, I see your point. It's a relief to have her here, too." Lessa glanced toward the curtain and sighed.. "You know, I could almost get to like fire-lizards after today."

"What brought about this change of heart?" F'lar stared at her in surprise.

"I didn't say I had. I said I could almost—watching Brekke direct Grall and Berd to bring her things, and that little bronze of Robinton's. The creatures can get vicious when their friends are hurt but he just crouched there, watching Robinton's face and crooning till I thought he'd shake his bones loose. Not that I didn't feel much the same myself. When I think . . ." Lessa broke off, her face blotchy with tears.

"Don't think of it, dear heart." F'lar squeezed her hand. "It didn't happen."

"When Mnementh called me, I don't think I've ever moved so fast. I fell off the ledge onto Ramoth's back. Bad enough trying to get here before T'kul tried to kill you, but to find Robinton . . . If only you'd killed T'ron at Telgar Hold . . ."

"Lessa!" He gripped her fingers so tightly she winced. "T'ron's Fidranth was very much alive at Telgar Hold. I couldn't cause *his* death no matter what insult T'ron had given me. T'kul I could kill with pleasure. Though I admit, he nearly had me. Our Harper's not the only one who's Turning old."

"So, thank goodness, are whoever's still left of the Oldtimers in Southern. And now, what are we to do with them?"

"I will go south and take charge of the Weyr," D'ram said. He'd entered, quiet with weariness, while they were talking. "I am, after all, an Oldtimer . . ." He gave a deep sigh. "They will accept from me what they would not endure from you, F'lar."

The Benden Weyrleader hesitated, appealing as this offer was. "I know you're willing, D'ram, but if it's going to overset you . . ."

D'ram raised his hand to cut off the rest of the sentence. "I'm fitter than I thought. Those quiet days in the cove worked a miracle. I will need help . . ."

"Any help we can give . . ."

"I'll take you at your word. I'll need some greens, preferably from R'mart at Telgar, or G'narish at Igen, for there are none to spare here at the moment. If they, too, are Oldtime, it will be easier for the Southerns. I'll need two younger bronzes, and enough blues and browns to make up two fighting wings."

"The Southern dragonriders haven't fought Thread in Turns," F'lar said with contempt.

"I know that. But it's time they did. That would give the dragons who remain purpose and strength. It would give their riders hope and occupation." D'ram's face was stern. "I learned things from B'zon today that grieve me. I have been so blind . . ."

"The fault is not yours, D'ram. Mine was the decision to send them south."

"I have honored that decision because it was the right one, F'lar. When . . . when Fanna died . . ." he got the words out in a rush, "I should have gone to the

Southern Weyr. It would not have been disloyal to you if I had and it might have . . ."

"I doubt it," Lessa said, angry that D'ram was blaming himself. "Once T'kul plotted to steal a queen egg . . ." and she gestured her condemnation of the man.

"If he had come to you . . ."

Lessa's harsh expression did not alter. "I doubt that T'kul would have come," she said slowly. An expression of distaste crossed her mobile features and she made a sound of annoyance before she looked at D'ram again; this time her expression was rueful. "And I'd have probably sent him about his business. But you," she pointed her finger at D'ram, "wouldn't have. And I imagine that F'lar would also have been more tolerant." She grinned at her Weyrmate. "It wasn't in T'kul's nature to beg," she went on more briskly. "Nor in mine to forgive! I will never forgive the Southerns for stealing Ramoth's egg! When I think they brought *me* to the point where I was willing to set dragon against dragon! That I can never forgive!"

D'ram drew himself up. "Do you disagree, Weyrwoman, with my decision to go south?"

"Great Shells, no!" She was astonished, and then shook her head. "No, D'ram, I think you're wise and kind, more generous than I could ever be. Why, that idiot T'kul might have killed F'lar today! No, you must go. You're quite right about their accepting you. I don't think I ever realized what might be happening in the South. I didn't want to!" she added in candid acknowledgment of her own shortcomings.

"Then I may invite additional riders to join me?" D'ram looked first at her and then at F'lar.

"Ask anyone you want from Benden, except F'nor. It wouldn't be fair to ask Brekke to return to Southern."

D'ram nodded.

"I think the other Weyrleaders will help. This matter touches the honor of all dragonriders. And . . ." F'lar broke off, cleared his throat, "and we do not want the Lord Holders precipitously taking charge in the South on the grounds that we cannot maintain order in the Weyrs."

"They'd never . . ." D'ram began, frowning with indignation.

"They well might. For other very valid reasons—to their ways of thinking," F'lar replied. "I know," he paused to emphasize that surety, "that the Southerns under T'kul and T'ron would never permit the Lord Holders to extend their holdings one dragon-length. Toric's settlement has been steadily growing over the past Turns, a few people now and then, craftsmen, the dissatisfied, a few young holder sons without hope of land in the North. All very quietly, so as not to alarm the Oldtimers." F'lar rose, restlessly pacing. "This isn't common knowledge . . ."

"I knew that there were traders north and south," said D'ram.

"Yes, part of the problem. Traders talk, and word has passed back that there's a lot of land south. Granted some of this may be exaggeration but I've reason to believe that the Southern Continent is probably as large as this one—and one protected against Thread by thorough grubbing." He paused again, rubbing forefinger and thumb down the lines from nose to chin, scratching absently under his jaw. "This time, D'ram, the dragonriders will have first choice of land. In the next Interval, I do not intend that any dragonrider will be beholden to the generosity of Hold and Craft. We will have our own places, without prejudice. I, for one, will never beg wine or bread or meat from anyone!"

D'ram had listened, at first with surprise and then with a gleam of delight in his tired eyes. He straightened his shoulders and with a curt nod of his head, looked the Benden Weyrleader straight in the eye.

"You may rely on me, F'lar, to secure the South for that purpose. A grand purpose! By the First Shell, that's a superb notion. That lovely land, soon dragon-rider land!"

F'lar gripped D'ram's arm, affirming the trust. Then his face broke into a sly smile. "If you hadn't volunteered to go South yourself, D'ram, I was going to suggest it to you! You're the only man to handle the situation. And I don't envy you!"

D'ram chuckled at the Benden Weyrleader's admission and returned the arm grip firmly. Then his expression cleared.

"I have grieved for my weyrmate as is proper. But I still live. I liked being in that cove, but it wasn't enough. I was relieved when you came after me, and kept me busy, F'lar. It doesn't answer to give up the only life I've known. I couldn't. *Dragonmen must fly/When Threads are in the sky!*" He sighed once more, inclined his head respectfully to Lessa and then, turning smartly on his heel, strode from the weyr, his step firm, his stance proud.

"D'you think he can manage it, F'lar?"

"He's more likely to pull it off than anyone . . . except possibly F'nor. But I can't ask that of him. Or of Brekke!"

"I should think not!" She spoke sharply and, with a little cry as if regretting her asperity, she ran to embrace him. He put his arms about her, absently stroking her hair.

There are too many deep lines in his face, now, thought Lessa, lines that she hadn't noticed before. His eyes were sad, his lips thin with worry as he gazed after D'ram. But the muscles in his arm were as strong as ever, and his body lean and hard with the active life he led. He'd been fit enough to preserve his skin against a madman. There'd only been one time when weakness had frightened F'lar—just after that knife fight at Telgar, when his wound had been slow to heal and he'd been sick with fever from foolishly going *between*. He'd learned a lesson then and had started delegating some of the strain of leadership to F'nor and T'gellan in Benden, to N'ton and R'mart in Pern, and to Lessa herself! Keenly sensible of her deep need of him, Lessa embraced F'lar fiercely.

He smiled down at her sudden demonstration, the tired lines smoothed away.

"I'm with you, dear heart, don't worry!" He kissed her soundly enough to leave her no room for doubt of his vitality.

The sound of boot heels thudding rapidly down the short corridor interrupted them and they moved apart. Sebell, face flushed from running, charged into the room, checking his pace when Lessa signaled him urgently to be quieter.

"He's all right?"

"He's asleep now, but see for yourself, Sebell," Lessa replied and gestured toward the curtained sleeping chamber.

Sebell rocked on his heels, wanting to reassure himself with a glimpse of his Master and anxious with fear he might disturb him.

"Go on, man." F'lar waved him forward. "Just be quiet."

Two fire-lizards winged into the room, squeaked when they saw Lessa and disappeared.

"I didn't know you had two queens."

"I don't," Sebell said, glancing over his shoulder to see where they'd gone. "The other one's Menolly's. She wasn't allowed to come!" His grimace told both Weyrleaders how Menolly had reacted to that restriction.

"Oh, tell them to come back. I don't eat fire-lizards!" Lessa said, curbing her irritation. She didn't know which annoyed her more, the fire-lizards themselves, or the way people cringed about her when the subject came up. "And that little bronze of Robinton's showed a commendable amount of common sense today. So tell Menolly's queen to come back. If the fire-lizard sees, she'll believe!"

Smiling with intense relief, Sebell held up his arm. Two queens popped in, eyes huge and whirling madly in their perturbation. One of them, Lessa didn't know whose, since they all looked alike to her, chirped as if in thanks. Then Sebell, careful not to disrupt their balance and set them squeaking, walked with exaggerated care toward the sick man's quarters.

"Sebell takes over the Harper Hall?" Lessa asked. "Well able for it, too."

"If only the dear man had had the sense to delegate more to Sebell before this . . ."

"It's partly my fault, Lessa. Benden has asked much of the Harper Hall." F'lar poured himself a cup of wine, looking at Lessa to see if she wanted some as well, and poured another when she nodded. They made an unspoken toast. "Benden wine!"

"The wine that kept him alive!"

"Miss a cup of wine? Not Robinton!" She drank quickly to ease the pressure in her throat.

"And he'll drink many more skins limp," the quiet voice of Master Oldive said. He glided to the table, a curious figure with arms and legs apparently too long for his torso until his back was visible, with its hump. His handsome face was serene as he poured himself a cup of wine, regarding the rich crimson color a moment before he raised it, as Lessa had, and drank it down. "As you said, this helped keep him alive. It's seldom that a man's vice sustained life in his body!"

"Master Robinton will be all right?"

"Yes, with care and rest. He has rallied well. His pulse and heart are beating evenly again, if slowly. He cannot be fretted by any worries. I warned him repeatedly to reduce his activities. Not that I thought he'd listen! Sebell, Silvina and Menolly have done all they could to assist, but then Menolly took ill . . . There is so much to be done for his Hall and for Pern!" Oldive smiled, his long face lighting gently as he took Lessa's hand and put it in F'lar's. "You can do no more here, Weyrleaders. Sebell will wait to reassure Robinton when he rouses that all is well in his Hall. Brekke and I, and the good people of this Weyr, will nurse the Master Harper. You two need rest as well. Go back to your Weyr. This day has taken its toll of many. Go!" He gave them a shove toward the passage. "Go along now!" He spoke as to recalcitrant children, but Lessa was weary enough to obey and concerned enough to override the objections she saw rising in F'lar's eyes.

We do not leave the Harper alone, Ramoth said as F'lar helped Lessa mount her queen. *We are with him.*

All of us are with him, Mnementh said, his eyes slowly turning in quiet reassurance.

CHAPTER XVI

At the Cove Hold, 15.8.28–15.9.7

WHEN JAXOM AND SHARRA blurted out to Piemur the events at Ista Weyr, including the news of the Harper's illness, the young journeyman treated them to a colorful description of his Master's follies, shortcomings, stupid loyalties and altruistic hopes that quite stunned the listeners until they saw the tears leaking down Piemur's cheeks.

At that moment, Ruth returned, scaring Piemur's runner beast into the forest. Piemur had to coax the animal, cheerfully called Stupid, to come out again.

"He's really not stupid, you know," Piemur said, wiping sweat and tears from his face. "He knows that yon," Piemur jerked his thumb surreptitiously in Ruth's direction, "like his sort for eating." He tested the knot on the rope with which he had secured Stupid to a tree trunk.

I wouldn't eat him, Ruth replied. *He's small and not very plump.*

Laughing, Jaxom passed the message to Piemur, who grinned and bowed his gratitude to Ruth.

"I wish I could make Stupid understand that," Piemur said with a sigh, "but it's difficult for him to make distinctions between friendly dragons and hungry ones. As it is, his tendency to disappear into the nearest thicket when dragons come within his senses has saved my skin any number of times. You see, I'm not supposed to be doing exactly what I've been doing. Most of all, I'm not supposed to be caught doing it."

"Go on," Jaxom urged when Piemur stopped to assess the effect of his cryptic statement. "You wouldn't have told us this much if you didn't intend to say more. You did mention that you'd been looking for us?"

Piemur grinned. "Among other things." He stretched out on the sand, grunting and making a show of settling himself. He took the cup of fruit juice Sharra handed him, quaffed the contents and held it out to be refilled.

Jaxom regarded the young man patiently. He was used to Piemur's mannerisms from the days they had spent together in Master Fandarel's and the Harper Hall.

"Did you never wonder why I left the classes, Jaxom?"

"Menolly told me you'd been posted elsewhere."

"And everywhere," Piemur replied with a broad sweep of his arm, his fingers flicking southward in emphasis. "I'll wager that I've seen more of this planet than any living thing . . . including dragons!" He gave a decisive nod of his head to show the others they should be impressed. "I haven't quite . . ." he paused to stress the qualifier, "gone all around this Southern Continent, nor have I gone across it, but I intimately know everywhere I have been!" He pointed to the worn boots on his feet. "New they were, a scant four sevendays ago when I started east. Oh, the tales these boots could tell!" He squinted at Jaxom thoughtfully. "It's one thing, my Lord Jaxom, to soar serenely over land, seeing all from an exalted height. Quite another, I assure you, to stomp on it, through it, under it, around it. You *know* where you've been then!"

"Does F'lar know?"

"More or less," Piemur replied with a grin. "A little less than more, I'd wager. You see, about three

Turns back, Toric started trading North with some fine samples of iron ore, copper and tin—all of which, as you might have heard Fandarel complain, Jaxom, are getting in short supply north. Robinton thought it prudent to investigate Toric's sources of supply. He was smart enough to send me over . . . You're sure he's going to be all right? You're not holding anything from me?" Piemur's anxiety cut through his brash manner.

"You know as much as we know, as much as Ruth knows." Jaxom paused to inquire of his dragon. "And Ruth says he sleeps. He also says the dragons won't let him go."

"The dragons won't let him go, huh? Don't that beat all!" Piemur shook his head from side to side. "Not that I'm surprised, mind you," he added with customary briskness. "The dragons know who're their friends. Now, as I was saying, Master Robinton decided it would be very smart of us to know more about the South, since he had a notion F'lar had an eye for this continent during the next Interval."

"How is it that you know so much about what F'lar and Robinton think?" Sharra asked.

Piemur chortled, wagging a finger at her. "That's for me to know and you to guess. But I'm right, aren't I, Jaxom?"

"I don't know what F'lar's plans might be but he's not the only one interested in the South, I'd wager."

"Truly spoken! But he's the only one that matters, don't you see?"

"No, frankly I don't see," Sharra said. "My brother's Lord Holder . . . Well he is," she added with some heat when Piemur started to contradict her. "Or would be, if his Hold had been acknowledged by the Northern Lord Holders. He risked settling south with F'nor when he timed it back. No one else was willing to try. He's put up with the Oldtimers, and made a fine, big, Threadfree Hold. No one can gainsay his right to hold what he has . . ."

"Nor do I!" Piemur assented quickly. "But . . . for all Toric's attracted a lot of new people from the

North, he can only Hold so much! He can only protect and work so much. And there is so much more
of the Southern Continent than anyone realizes. Except me! I'll bet I've already walked the breadth of
Pern from Tillek Head to Nerat Tip on this continent and not gone its length." Piemur's tone changed
abruptly from derision to awe. "There was this bay,
you see, the opposite shore all but hid in the heat
haze. Stupid and I had been struggling through
really bad sand for two days. I'd only enough water
to go back the way we'd come because I'd thought
that the sand would have to give way to decent land
soon. . . . I sent Farli out, first to the far shore, then
down to the mouth of the bay, but all she brought
back to me was more sand. So I knew I'd have to
turn back. But," he turned to his listeners, "you see,
there's probably as much land beyond that bay as I'd
already transversed from Toric's Hold and I'd still
not come full circle! Toric could not begin to hold
the half of what I've seen. And that's only the western side. East now, it's taken me a full three sevendays to reach you from Toric's and we'd had to
swim part of the way. Good swimmer, that Stupid of
mine! As willing as a new day and never complains.
When I think of how careful my father was to feed
his runner stock on only the best fodder, and what
Stupid makes do on with twice the work out of
him . . ." Piemur broke off to shake his head at the
inequity.

"So," he returned briskly to his narrative, "I've
been exploring as I was told to, and heading in your
general direction, as I was told to, only I expected
to be here long before this! My word, but I'm
tired, and no one knows how much further I've got
to travel before I get where I'm going."

"I thought you were coming here."

"Yes, but I've to go on . . . eventually." He raised
his left leg, the one which he'd been favoring, and
squinched his face up in a grimace of pain. "Shards,
but I can't go another step for a while! This leg's been
walked half off, now, hasn't it, Sharra?"

Still elevating the leg, he swiveled in the sand toward the healer who was looking quite concerned. Deftly she unwound the shreds of what had probably been Piemur's cloak, and uncovered a long but recently healed scar.

"I can't walk any farther on that, now can I, Sharra?"

"No, I don't think you should, Piemur," Jaxom said, critically examining the healed wound. "Do you, Sharra?"

She looked from one to the other and then began to shake her head, her eyes dancing.

"No, positively not. It needs soaking in warm salt water, and plenty of sun, and you're a terrible rascal, Piemur. Just as well you're not a posted harper! You'd scandalize any sensible Holder!"

"Have you kept any Records of your traveling?" Jaxom asked, keenly interested and just a shade jealous of Piemur's freedom.

"Have *I* kept Records?" Piemur snorted derisively. "Most of what Stupid packs *is* Records! Why do you think I'm wearing rags? I haven't room to carry spare clothes." His voice lowered and he leaned urgently toward Jaxom. "You don't just possibly happen to have any of Bendarek's leaves down here, do you? There are a couple of—"

"Plenty of leaves. Drawing tools as well. C'mon!"

Jaxom was on his feet, Piemur not a second behind him with only a trace of a limp, following him to the shelter. Jaxom had not intended Piemur to see his bumbling attempts to map their immediate vicinity. But he'd forgot the young harper's keen eyes missed little, and Piemur had spotted the roll of neatly connected leaves and, without so much as a by-your-leave, laid it open. He soon was nodding his head and muttering under his breath.

"You haven't been wasting your time here, have you?" Piemur grinned, an oblique compliment to Jaxom's work. "You used Ruth as measure? Fair enough. I've taught my queen, Farli, to pace her flight. I count by the second, watch for her dip at the end

292

of the run and record the distance by seconds. I figure it up later when I'm charting. N'ton double-checked the measure when he worked with me, so I know it's reasonably accurate, as long as I allow enough for a wind factor." He whistled as his gaze fell on the tall stack of fresh sheets. "I might need 'em, I might, to map what I've traveled over. If you'd give me a hand . . ."

"You do have to rest that leg, don't you?" Jaxom kept his face expressionless.

Piemur caught his eye in surprise and then they both burst out laughing until Sharra, joining them, wanted to share the joke.

The next few days passed most agreeably for the three, starting with Ruth's assurances about the Harper's continued improvement. The first morning, noticing that Stupid had cropped all the ground greens in the area, Piemur asked if there was any grassland nearby. So Jaxom and Piemur flew Ruth to the river meadows that lay south and east of the cove, a good hour's flying inland. Ruth willingly helped harvest the tall waving grain grasses which Piemur pronounced fine fodder that might even put poor Stupid into condition. Ruth told Jaxom that he'd never seen such a hungry-looking runner.

"We're not fattening him up for you," Jaxom said, laughing.

He is Piemur's friend. Piemur is my friend. I do not eat the friends of friends.

Jaxom couldn't resist repeating this rationalization to Piemur, who howled with laughter and thumped Ruth with the same rough affection he used on Stupid.

They packed half a dozen heavy sheaves of grass on Ruth and were airborne when Piemur asked Jaxom if he'd been to the peak yet.

"Can't fly *between*." Jaxom didn't bother hiding his frustration from Piemur.

"Too bloody right you can't. Not with fire-head!"

Jaxom blinked at Piemur's unequivocal agreement.

"Don't worry! You'll get there soon enough." Piemur squinted at the symmetrical peak, shading his eyes with one hand. "May look near, but it's several, four-five maybe, days' travel. Rough country, I'd guess. You've . . ." he paused to give Jaxom an unexpected blow in the midriff which robbed him of breath, "got to get fit first! I heard you puffing, hacking down that grass. Huh!"

"Wouldn't it be easier to bring Stupid here and let him graze? There aren't any dragons about, except Ruth. And he's agreed not to eat Stupid!"

"Once he sees wild ones, he won't come back. He's too stupid to know he's much safer with me with a dragon to bring him food, instead of eating him as food."

Stupid was delighted with the contribution to his diet and whistled with pleasure as he munched away at the piled grass.

"Just how intelligent is Stupid?" Sharra asked, stroking the creature's rough dun-colored neck.

"Not as smart as Farli, but not really stupid. Limited is a fairer assessment of his scope. Within those limitations, he's pretty bright."

"For instance?" asked Jaxom. He'd never thought much of runner beasts.

"Well, for instance, I can send Farli ahead, telling her to fly so many hours in the direction I've pointed, land and pick up anything lying on the ground. Generally she brings back grasses or bush twigs, and sometimes stone and sand. I can send her to look for water. That's what fooled me about the Big Bay. She'd found water, all right, so Stupid and I humped after her. I didn't specify drinking water." Piemur shrugged and laughed. "But Stupid and I have to go on foot, and he's right smart about ground. Kept me from sinking in mud and those shifting sands time and again. He's clever about finding the easiest route over rough going. He's also good at finding water . . . drinking-type water. So I should have listened to him when he didn't want to cross the sands to the Big Bay. He knew there wasn't any real water over there, although Farli insisted there was. I trusted Farli that time. Generally speaking, the two make one good reliable guide between them. We're a team—Stupid, Farli and I.

"Which reminds me, I found a fire-lizard clutch, a queen's, five . . ." Farli chittered at him, "all right, maybe six or seven coves back. I kind of lost track there, but she'll remember where. . . . In case someone wants some. You know if green fire-lizards weren't as stupid as they are, we'd be up to our ears in little green ones. And they're downright useless."

Sharra grinned. "I remember the day I found my first clutch in the sands. *I* didn't know the difference between green and gold nests. Oh, how I watched that clutch . . . for days. Never told a soul. I was going to Impress all of them . . ."

"Four or five?" Piemur asked with a laugh.

"Six, in fact. Only I didn't realize that a sand snake had got the lot from beneath long before I found the nest."

"How is it, then, that sand snakes don't get a queen's eggs?" Jaxom asked.

"She's never far from her clutch," Sharra said. "She'd spot a snake tunnel right away and kill it." She gave a shudder. "I hate snakes worse than I hate Thread."

"Much the same thing, isn't it?" Piemur asked, "except for the direction of attack." He gestured with both hands, one coming down, the other coming up on an imaginary victim.

During the hot part of the day, Jaxom, Sharra and Piemur began to turn his Records, measurements and rough sketches into proper detailed maps. Piemur wanted to get the report back to Sebell, or Robinton or F'lar if so directed, as soon as possible.

In the cool of the next morning, with Stupid as pack animal and Ruth overhead, the three friends backtracked to Piemur's queen clutch. Twenty-one eggs were in the nest, all nicely hardened to within a day or two of Hatching. Their approach had sent the wild fire-lizard queen to cover so they were able to excavate the eggs, packing them carefully in the carrier they had strapped to Stupid's back. Jaxom asked Ruth to alert Canth that they had fire-lizard eggs.

Canth says that they are coming tomorrow anyway, Ruth replied. *The Harper ate well.*

Ruth gave them such snippets of information about Master Robinton periodically. It was as good as being in the same Hall with the invalid, without having to hear him complain, Piemur observed.

They returned to the shelter cove through the forest. The fruit trees near the clearing had been picked clean and if F'nor were coming, he'd surely appreciate some fresh fruit to take back to Benden Weyr.

"Should you be around when F'nor comes?" Jaxom asked the young harper.

"Why not? He knows what I've been doing. You know, Jaxom, when you see how beautiful this continent is, you wonder why our ancestors went north . . ."

"Maybe the South was too big an area to keep Threadfree until the grubs had been seeded," Sharra suggested.

"Good point!" Then Piemur snorted with derision. "Those old Records are worse than useless; they leave out the most important things. Like telling farmers to watch for the grubs in the North and not mentioning why! Like leaving the Southern Continent alone, and not why! Though if there were half as many earth-shakes then as there are now, I can't fault them for common sense. When I was on the way to Big Bay, I bloody near got killed in a shake. Nearly lost Stupid from fright. If it hadn't been for Farli keeping her eye on him, I never would have caught up with the stupid idiot!"

"Earth-shakes happen in the North," Jaxom said, "in Crom and High Reaches and sometimes Igen and the Telgar Plain."

"Not the kind I've been through," Piemur said, shaking his head at the memory. "Not where the earth drops beneath your feet and two paces beyond you lifts above your head half a dragonlength."

"When did that happen? Three, four months ago?"

"That's when!"

"Earth only trembled at Southern, but that's scary enough!"

"Ever seen a volcano pop up out of the ocean and spew fiery rock and ash about?" asked Piemur.

"No, and I'm not sure you have, either, Piemur," Sharra said, eyeing him suspiciously.

"I have, and N'ton was with me, so I've a witness."

"Don't think I won't ask him."

"Where was it, Piemur?" Jaxom asked, fascinated.

"I'll show you on the map. N'ton's been keeping his eye on the place. Last time we met, he said the volcano had stopped smoking and it had built a regular island about itself as neat as . . . as neat as that mountain of yours!"

"I'd prefer to see it with my own eyes," Sharra said, still skeptical.

"I'll arrange it," the harper replied with good humor. "That's a likely tree!" he added and, leaping in the air, grabbed the lowest branch and swung himself neatly up. He began to sever the stems that held the redfruit, dropping them carefully into the waiting hands of Jaxom and Sharra.

It had taken them only two hours to walk to the fire-lizards' clutch along the beach. But it took them almost three times as long to hack a narrow path back to the shelter through the thick undergrowth. Jaxom began to appreciate the arduousness of Piemur's journey as he slashed valiantly away at the sticky-sapped bushes. His shoulders ached and he'd branch-spiked shins and skinned toes by the time they emerged near the shelter. Jaxom had lost all sense of direction. But Piemur had an uncanny sense and with Ruth and three fire-lizards, had kept them on a direct line to their goal.

Once there, only Jaxom's pride kept him from collapsing on his bed and sleeping off his exertions. Piemur was all for a swim to wash off the sweat and Sharra thought that broiled fish would make a good supper, so Jaxom struggled to keep going.

That might have been why, he thought later, he had such vivid dreams when he finally did crawl into bed to sleep. The mountain, smoking and spewing out fire-ash and glowing rock, dominated the dream, which was full of streams of running people. To Jaxom that was very sensible but he was also part of those people rushing away and it seemed that he couldn't run fast enough. The red-orange glowing river that poured over the lip of the mountain threatened to engulf him and he couldn't make his legs move fast enough.

"Jaxom!" Piemur shook him awake. "You're dreaming! You'll wake Sharra." Piemur paused, and in the dim twilight of predawn, the sound of Sharra's moaning was clearly audible. "Maybe I should. She sounds like she's having a bad dream, too."

Piemur started to crawl out of his sleeping furs when they heard Sharra sigh deeply, and fall into a quieter sleep.

"I shouldn't have talked about that volcano. I relived that eruption. At least, I think that's what I was dreaming." Piemur sounded confused. "Probably too much fish and fruit! I made up for lost meals tonight." He sighed and made himself comfortable again.

"Thanks, Piemur!"

"For what?" Piemur asked in the middle of a yawn.

Jaxom turned over, found a good position and dropped easily back into a dreamless sleep.

Ruth's bugle woke all three the next morning.

"F'nor's coming," Jaxom said, having heard Ruth's message.

F'nor brings others, Ruth added.

Jaxom, Sharra and Piemur had reached the cove when four dragons erupted into the air, the other three dwarfed by brown Canth. Shrieking in surprise, the fire-lizards who had been draped about Ruth abruptly disappeared, leaving only Meer, Talla and Farli.

It is Piemur, Jaxom heard Ruth tell Canth. And then F'nor began to wave wildly, clasping two hands above his head in a signal of victory.

Canth deposited his rider on the sand. Roaring a

command at the other dragons, he waddled happily into the water where Ruth was quick to join him.

"Well met, Piemur," F'nor cried, unloosening his flying gear as he walked toward the others. "Began to wonder if you'd gotten lost!"

"Lost?" Piemur looked outraged. "That's the trouble with you dragonfliers. You've no respect for ground distances! You've got it too easy. Up, up and away! Wink out and you're where you want to be. No effort at all involved." He made a sound of disgust in his throat. "Now *I* know where *I've* been, every bloody finger's length of it!"

F'nor grinned at the young harper and pummeled his back with such vigor Jaxom was surprised to see Piemur unmoved. "You'll amuse your Master then, with the full and properly embroidered tale of your travels . . ."

"You're to bring me to Master Robinton?"

"Not yet. He's coming to you!" F'nor pointed to the ground.

"What?"

F'nor was searching in his belt pouch and brought out a folded leaf. *"This* is my reason for coming today! And don't let me forget the fire-lizard eggs, will you?"

"What's that?" Jaxom, Sharra and Piemur clustered close about the brown rider as he made a show of unfolding the sheet.

"This . . . is a hall for the Master Harper, to be built in this cove!"

"Here?" the three demanded in chorus.

"How'll he get here?" Jaxom asked. "He surely wouldn't be allowed to fly *between*." He couldn't help the edge of resentment in his voice. F'nor cocked an eyebrow at him.

"Master Idarolan has put his fastest, largest vessel at the Master Harper's disposal. Menolly and Brekke are accompanying him. On a sea voyage there is nothing that can disturb or worry the Harper."

"He gets seasick," remarked Jaxom.

"Only in small boats." F'nor looked at them with a

very solemn expression. "So. We'll set to work at once. I've brought tools and extra help," and he gestured toward the three Weyrlings who had joined them. "We'll enlarge that shelter to a proper small hold," he said as he glanced down at the leaf. "I'll want every bit of that underbrush cleared off . . ."

"Then you'll fry the Harper in the sun which is unpleasant," Sharra pointed out.

"I beg your pardon . . ."

Sharra took the leaf from him, frowning critically at it. "Small hold? This is a bloody hall," she said, "and not the least bit suitable to this continent. Furthermore," and she dropped to the sand, picking up a long shell fragment with which she began another sketch. "First, I wouldn't build where the old shelter is—too close to the cove in rough seas and they have them here. There's a rise . . . with mature fruit trees screening it, over there . . ." She pointed to the east of the shelter.

"Mature trees? For Thread to eat?"

"Oh, you dragonriders! This is Southern, not the North. It's all been grubbed. Thread sears a leaf every sevenday or so, but the plant heals itself. Meanwhile, you're coming into the hot season and, believe me, you'll want as much green about you as possible to keep cool. You want to build off the ground, on pilings. There's plenty of reef rock for foundations. You want wide windows, not these tiny slits, to catch every breeze. All right, you can shutter them if you want to but I've lived south all my life, so I know how you should build here. You want windows, and corridors straight through the interior for breezeways . . ." As she spoke, she was delineating the revised hold with strokes that were strong enough to stay in the hot dry sand. "And you want an outdoor hearth for so many. Brekke and I did most of our baking here in stone pits," she pointed to the spot on the cove, "and you don't really need a bathing room with the cove a few steps from the door."

"You don't object to piped water, do you?"

"No, that would be handier than lugging it from

the stream. Only put another tap in the cooking area as well as one in the house. Perhaps even a tank by the hearth so we can have heated water, too . . ."

"Anything else, Masterbuilder?" F'nor was more amused and admiring than sarcastic.

"I'll let you know when the thought occurs to me," she replied with dignity.

F'nor grinned at her and then frowned down at her drawing. "I'm not really certain how the Harper will like having so much greenery near him. You are, I know, used to being out during Threadfall . . ."

"So's Master Robinton," Piemur said. "Sharra's right about the heat and the building down here. We can always cut forest down, F'nor, but you can't build it back up so easily."

"A point. Now you three, B'refli, K'van and M'tok, loose your dragons. They can swim and sun with Ruth and Canth. They won't be needed until we've cut some wood. K'van, let me have your sack. You've got the axes, haven't you?" F'nor passed out the tools, ignoring Piemur's mutterings about slogging through days of forests only to end up cutting one down. "Sharra, take us to your preferred site. We'll clear some of those trees and use 'em for supports."

"They're stout enough," Sharra agreed and led the way.

Sharra was correct about the trees: F'nor marked off the proposed site of the hall and the trees to be cut. This was a lot easier said than done. The axes didn't seem to bite the wood, rather bounced off. F'nor was surprised, muttering about dull axes and brought out his sharpening stone. Having achieved a suitably sharp edge at the expense of a slit finger, he tried again with slightly more success.

"I don't understand it," he said, peering at the cuts in the trunk. "This wood shouldn't be that tough. It's a fruitwood, not a northern hardwood. Well, we've got to clear the site, boys!"

The only one who didn't have a fine set of blisters by midday was Piemur, who was used to hacking.

More discouraging was the lack of progress—only six trees were down.

"Not for lack of trying, is it?" F'nor said, mopping the sweat from his forehead. "Well, let's see what Sharra's got for us to eat. Something smells good."

They had time for a swim before Sharra's meal was ready, the salt water stinging in their blisters which Sharra slathered with numbweed. When they'd eaten the broiled fish and baked roots, F'nor set them to sharpening their axes. They spent the rest of the afternoon lopping off branches before they asked the dragons to haul the timbers to one side. Sharra cleared underbrush and, with Ruth's help, brought black reef rock to mark out the piles of the foundation.

As soon as F'nor took his recruits back to the Weyr for the night, Jaxom and Piemur collapsed on the sand, rousing only long enough to eat the dinner Sharra served them.

"I'd sooner tramp around the Big Bay," Piemur muttered, wincing as he stretched his shoulders this way and that.

"It's for Master Robinton," Sharra said.

Jaxom regarded his blisters thoughtfully. "At the rate we're going it'd better take him months to get here!"

Sharra took pity on their aching muscles and rubbed salve that smelled aromatic and burned pleasantly into the soreness. Jaxom liked to think that she spent more time massaging his back than Piemur's. He'd been glad to see the young harper and was fascinated by the Records and the charts he was drawing from his travels, but he did wish that Piemur had taken a day or two longer before he'd reached the camp. There was no way he could consolidate his hold on her attentions with a third party about.

There was even less opportunity by the following morning. Sharra woke them to announce that F'nor had arrived, with more helpers.

Jaxom should have been more suspicious of her bland expression, and the calls and orders that he heard outside the shelter. But he was totally unprepared for the sight that met his eyes when he and Piemur, moving stiffly, emerged from the shelter.

The cove, the clearing, the sky—all were full of dragons and men. As soon as a dragon was unloaded, he took off to allow another to land. The waters of the cove were full of splashing, playing dragons. Ruth was standing on the eastern tip of the cove, head turned skyward, bugling welcome after welcome. A full fair of fire-lizards chattered at one another on the roof of the shelter.

"Sear and scorch it, will you look at that?" Piemur called at Jaxom's side. Then he chuckled and rubbed his hands. "One thing for sure, no chopping today!"

"Jaxom! Piemur!" The two swung round at F'nor's cheerful greeting and saw the brown rider striding toward them. Following close on his heels were the Mastersmith Fandarel, Masterwoodsman Bendarek, N'ton and, from his shoulder knots, a wingleader from Benden. Jaxom thought he was T'gellan.

"Did I give you the two drawings last night, Jaxom? I can't find them . . . Ah, here they are!" F'nor pointed to the sheets on the small table— Brekke's original drawing and the alterations suggested by Sharra. The brown rider retrieved the sheets and showed them to the Craftmasters. "Now, here, Fandarel, Bendarek, this is our idea . . ."

Acting as one, the two men lifted the sheets from F'nor's hands and scrutinized first one then the other. Both shook their heads slowly from side to side in disapproval.

"Not very efficient, F'nor, but well meant," the huge Smith said.

"Weyrleader R'mart allowed me sufficient riders to bring in well-seasoned hardwoods for the frame," Bendarek told the Smith.

"I have piping for water and other conveniences, metals for a proper hearth and fitments, kitchen implements, windows . . ."

"Lord Asgenar insisted that I bring stonesmiths. Proper foundations and flooring must be well laid . . ."

"First we must correct this design, Master Bendarek . . ."

"I quite agree. This is a nice enough little cot but not at all suitable accommodation for the Masterharper of Pern."

The two Craftmasters became so involved in amplifying the rough sketches that, oblivious to the other occupants of the room, they moved as one toward the table Jaxom had contrived for his charts. Piemur leaped forward and rescued his pouch of notes and sketches. The Masterwoodsman, ignoring any such interruptions to his thoughts, took a clean sheet, slipped a writing tool from a pocket and began, with neat lines, to draw what he had in mind. The Smith, taking a sheet of his own, began to delineate his ideas.

"Honest, Jaxom," F'nor said, his eyes crinkling with amusement, "all I did was ask F'lar and Lessa if I could draft a *few* more helpers. Lessa gave me a stern look; F'lar said I was to recruit as many free riders as I needed and, at dawn, the rim of the Weyr was packed solid with dragons and half the Craftmasters of Pern! Lessa must have bespoken Ramoth, who evidently told everyone in Pern . . ."

"You gave them the excuse they needed, F'nor," Piemur said, surveying the traffic on the once-quiet beach, the throngs of riders and craftsmen piling dragonloads on the already crowded perimeters.

"Yes, I know, but I hadn't expected such a response. And how could I tell 'em they couldn't come?"

"I think," said Sharra, who had joined them, "that this is quite a tribute to the Masterharper." Her eyes caught Jaxom's and he knew that she was aware of his ambivalent feelings about this invasion of their private, peaceful cove.

Then Jaxom saw F'nor watching him and managed a weak smile. "Yesterday's blisters will have a chance to heal, I guess. Right, Piemur?"

Piemur nodded, his jaw muscles working as he observed the activity on the beach. "I'd better find Stupid. All this confusion has probably scared him

deep into the forest. Farli!" He held up his arm for
his fire-lizard, who swooped down from the roof.
"Find Stupid, Farli. Lead me to him!"

The fire-lizard looked over her left shoulder and
chirped, and Piemur strode off in that direction without a backward glance.

"That young man's been alone too long," F'nor
said.

"Yes!"

"You know how he feels?" F'nor asked, grinning
at Jaxom's terse reply. He clapped him on the shoulder. "I wouldn't let it get to me, if I were you, Jaxom.
With the amount of help we've got, the hold will be
up in next to no time. You'll have your peace and
quiet back."

"Idiots!" Sharra exclaimed suddenly.

Jaxom, avoiding F'nor's quizzical expression,
looked at her. She'd been half-listening to the conversation between the two Masters.

"Now I have to have it out with *them!*" Her fists
were clenched with exasperation as she strode purposefully up to the two Craftsmen. "Masters, I must
point out something you have clearly overlooked.
This is hot country. You're both used to cold winters
and freezing rains. If you build this hold on those
lines, people will stifle in the full heat of summer
which is almost upon us. Now, where I live in Southern Hold, we build thick walls to keep the heat out
and the cool in. We build off the ground so air cir-
culates under the floor and keeps that cool. We build
lots of windows—wide ones—and you've brought
enough metal shutters, Master Fandarel, to outfit a
dozen holds. Yes, I know, but Thread doesn't fall
every day and the heat does. Now . . ."

F'nor made a clicking noise against his teeth. "She
sounds like Brekke. And if she acts at all like
my weyrmate when she's in that sort of mood, I'd
rather be elsewhere. *You,*" F'nor poked Jaxom in the
chest, "can show us where to hunt. Food was brought
along but since you're in effect the resident Lord

Holder, it's up to you to play host with some roasting meat . . ."

"I'll just get my flying gear," Jaxom said with such a tone of relief that the three dragonriders laughed.

Jaxom quickly slipped long trousers over the short pants he'd been wearing for sunning and swimming, threw his jacket over his shoulder and joined the three riders by the doorway.

"I think we can mount on the left-hand arm of the cove, near Ruth," said F'nor.

Something whizzed by Jaxom's ear and instinctively ducking, he looked back as Meer came to a hover, clutching a piece of black reef rock in his front paws. Jaxom heard Sharra thanking her fire-lizard for his prompt return.

He hastily left before she could think of any errands for him. F'nor had hunting ropes for each of them which they checked and coiled over their shoulders. As they made their way past piles of assorted woods in various lengths and widths, past metal shutters and unlabeled bales, men hailed the riders and inquired how Jaxom was feeling.

Before they completed the short walk to the cove tip, Jaxom had identified men from every Weyr except Telgar—which was expecting Thread that day —and representatives of every craft in Pern, mostly journeyman rank and higher. Isolated as he'd been for so many sevendays, it hadn't occurred to Jaxom that his illness might have been a subject of widespread interest through Weyr, Craft, and Hold. He was embarrassed as well as gratified, but that did not ease his sense of being overwhelmed, or this violation, however well-intentioned, of the privacy and peace of his cove.

What had F'nor called him? Resident Lord Holder? He gave himself a shake just as Ruth, dripping wet, landed lightly beside him.

So many people. So many dragons! This is fun! Ruth's eyes were whirling with excitement and pleasure.

The white dragon, now dwarfed by two huge

bronzes and a nearly as large brown dragon, was so delighted with all this excitement that Jaxom could not remain disgruntled.

Laughing, he thumped Ruth affectionately on the shoulder and sprang to his neck. The other riders were also mounted so, raising his arm, fist closed, he pumped it to indicate ascent. Still laughing, he braced himself as Ruth launched straight upward, leaving the heavier beasts sandbound while he was in free air. Politely Ruth circled while the others became airborne and then, heading southeast, he led the way.

He headed toward the farthest of the river meadows that he and Sharra had found. Wherries and runner beasts generally made their way there about midmorning, to wallow in the water and the cool mud. There would also be sufficient open space for the bigger dragons to maneuver and permit their riders good casts.

Sure enough, herd and flock were wandering about the river meadows, where the land sloped from the trees to the flood edges of the river in a series of banks where successive rainy seasons had made it impossible for trees to root. Grass abounded now, about to turn sere as the hotter weather burned it relentlessly to hay.

We are to hunt singly. F'nor asks that we get a large wherry. They will try for a buck apiece. That should be enough for today.

"If it isn't," Jaxom replied, "we can always go after one of the big fish."

In fact, Jaxom quite looked forward to the opportunity. He had never had occasion to use a spearheaded rope but . . . He spotted a wherry, a fine big one, fanning its tail spines as it stalked majestically after the wherry-fens. Jaxom tightened his legs on Ruth's neck, tested the weighted loop end of the rope in his hands. He pictured the wherry-male to Ruth, who turned his head obediently to point. Then Ruth dove, his wings back to give Jaxom room to throw, his tucked-up legs nearly touching the meadow grass. Jaxom leaned forward over Ruth's near side and threw the loop deftly about the wherry's big ugly head. The creature reared back, helpfully tightening the noose. As Jaxom dug his heels into Ruth, the dragon soared upward. With a deft yank, Jaxom neatly broke the wherry's neck.

It was a heavy bird, Jaxom realized as the dead weight pulled his arms almost from the sockets. Ruth took some of the strain as he caught the rope with his forepaw.

F'nor says good catch. He hopes he can do as well!

Jaxom guided Ruth to the edge of the meadow furthest from the other hunters. Then, letting the carcass down lightly, Ruth landed and Jaxom began to secure the snatch across Ruth's back. They were airborne again in time to see T'gellan valiantly pursuing the buck he'd missed on his first throw. F'nor and N'ton had their beasts neatly dangling. F'nor pumped his arm in triumph as he and N'ton circled back to the cove. As Ruth followed, Jaxom saw T'gellan succeed in his second throw; none too soon for they'd had to soar to miss the edge of the forest and nearly entangled the depending buck in the trees. A good quick hunt, though, which meant the quarry would forget quickly the small excitement. Undoubtedly they'd have to hunt again tomorrow. Jaxom couldn't see even that enormous work force finishing the Harper's new hold in a day! Maybe tomorrow they could go after the big fish.

They had not been gone long, although their return trip took slightly more time, burdened as they were. A massive clearing had been made in the center of the grove. Just as Jaxom wondered how on earth even that many men had been able to fell the necessary trees, he saw a dragon lift one out of the ground by the roots, and carry it to the beach of the next cove east where the tree was neatly stacked on others. As Ruth and he neared the site, Jaxom saw that pillars of black reef rock were in place and several crossbeams of the treated, seasoned hardwoods Master Bendarek had brought were being secured in position. A wide avenue in a graceful curve had also been cleared and sand dumped from firestone sacks transported on dragonback. Other workmen on the edges of the clearing were involved in a variety of tasks—sawing, planing, nailing, fitting—while another file of men carried black reef rock from piles on the cove edge.

On the eastern tip, Jaxom could see that pits had been dug for roasting, metal spits erected and fires started. Tables had been placed in the shade on which Jaxom could see the piled mounds of red, orange and green fruits.

Ruth hovered over the clearing, gently landing. Two men by the fire-pits leaped to Jaxom's assistance as he offloaded the wherry. Ruth immediately vaulted out of the way so that Jaxom could guide the other carcasses dangling from the hunting ropes of the bigger dragons.

F'nor, stripping off his flying gear, walked slowly up to Jaxom, squinting against the brilliant glare from the sands as he surveyed the activity in the once peaceful cove. He sighed deeply but began to nod his head as if unexpectedly satisfied by something.

"Yes, it'll work out all right," he said, more to himself than to Jaxom because he turned then, smiling, and gripped Jaxom by the shoulder. "Yes, they'll make the transition easily."

"Transition?"

F'nor clearly didn't mean the present building frenzy.

"Dragonfolk going back to the land, the hold. How much exploring have you been able to do around here?"

"The coves, as far back as those river meadows, and some of the immediate interior the day before yesterday with Piemur."

As one, the two men turned toward the cone of the volcano that lay, cloud clad, in the distance.

"Yes, it does sort of draw your eye, doesn't it?" F'nor grinned. "You'll get there first, Jaxom. In fact, I'd prefer it if you and Piemur began some serious explorations with that as your goal. Yes, that pleases you, doesn't it? Better for you, too, and Piemur. Now, before I forget it again, where's that fire-lizard clutch you reported?"

"There're twenty-one eggs and I'd like to have five of them, if I may . . ."

"Of course!"

"To be taken to Ruatha!"

"By evening,"

"You know, that's curious." Jaxom craned his body about, looking everywhere.

"What?"

"Usually there're a lot more fire-lizards around. I don't count more than a double handful. And they're all banded."

CHAPTER XVII

Fort Hold, Benden Weyr, at Cove Hold,
and at Sea aboard the *Dawn Sister*,
15.10.1–15.10.2

WHEN THE THREE fire-lizards had made the first
overtures of greeting, the three men, grinning at the
enthusiasm shown by their friends, made themselves
comfortable around the table in the small room at Fort
Hold where Lord Groghe held his private meetings.
Sebell had been there frequently, but never as spokesman for his Crafthall and never when Lord Groghe
had summoned the Fort Weyrleader as well, in what
was obviously a matter of some importance.

"Not sure how to begin," Lord Groghe said as he
poured the wine. Sebell thought that was a very good
way to begin, especially since the Lord Holder had
honored them with Benden wine. "Might as well
plunge. Problem's this . . . I backed F'lar when he
fought T'ron," Groghe nodded at the current Fort
Weyrleader, "because I knew he was right. Right to
exile those misfits where they'd do no one any harm.
While the Oldtimers were in the Southern Weyr, made
sense to leave them alone, just as long as they left us
alone—which they mostly did." Lord Groghe peered
from under his heavy brows first at N'ton and then at
Sebell.

Since both men were aware that there had been occasional depredations in Fort Hold which could only be attributed to the dissident Oldtimers, they nodded acknowledgment of that point. Lord Groghe cleared his throat, and folded his hands across his thick middle.

"Point is, they're mostly dead, or waiting to die. No trouble anymore. D'ram, being sort of F'lar's representative, is bringing in dragonfolk from other Weyrs, to make it a proper Weyr again, fighting Thread and all that! I approve!" He favored the Harpercraftmaster and then the Weyrleader with long meaningful glances. "Hmmm. Well, that's all to the good, isn't it? Protecting the South against Thread! Thing of it is, with the Southern Weyr working again, as it were, that Southern land is safe. Now I know there's a hold established there. Young Toric. Wouldn't want to interfere with *his* Holding. No way! He's earned it. But a working Weyr can protect more than one small hold, now, can't it?" He pinned his gimlet stare on N'ton, who contrived to maintain an attitude of courteous interest, forcing Lord Groghe to continue without any help.

"Well, hmmm. Trouble is, you bring up a fair of young 'uns to know how to hold proper and that's what they want to do. Hold! Terrible fights they get into. Terrible quarrels. Fostering 'em don't help much. Just got to foster others and *they* quarrel and fight. Scorch it! They all need holds of their own." Lord Groghe banged his fist on the table emphasizing this point. "I can't split my land more'n it is and I'm Holding every square length that isn't bare rock. Can't put out men who're beholden to me as their fathers and grandfathers and greats were? That's not proper Holding on my side. And I won't turn 'em out to please my kin. Not that it would.

"Thing of it is, while the Oldtimers were south, wouldn't have dreamed of suggesting it. But they aren't in command anymore. D'ram is and he's F'lar's man and he'll make it a proper Weyr so there could be more holdings, couldn't there?"

Lord Groghe glanced from Harper to Weyrleader,

daring them to contradict him. "There's plenty of un-held land in the South, isn't there? No one really knows how much. But I heard Masterfisherman Idarolan say one of his ships cruised for days along a coastline. Hmmm yes, well." Then he started to chuckle, a mirth that increased into a wheeze that shook the large well-fleshed frame of the Lord Holder. He was reduced to speechlessness and impotently pointed his thick fore-finger first at one and then the other, trying to indicate something by gesture which his laughter kept him from explaining by word.

Helplessly, N'ton and Sebell exchanged grins and shrugs, unable to perceive what amused Lord Groghe or what he wanted to convey to them. The monu-mental mirth subsided, leaving Lord Groghe weak to the point of wiping tears from his eyes.

"Well trained! That's what you pair are! Well trained!" he gasped, pounding his chest with his fist to stop his wheezing. He coughed long and then, as abruptly as the laughter had seized him, he turned solemn. "Can't fault either of you. Won't. Shouldn't give up Weyr secrets easily anyhow. Appreciate that. Do me one favor. Tell F'lar. Remind him that it's bet-ter to attack than defend. Not but what he doesn't al-ready know that! I think," Lord Groghe stabbed at his chest with his thumb, "he'd better be prepared . . . soon. Trouble is, everyone in Pern knows that the Masterharper is going south to get well. Everyone wishes Master Robinton the best of luck. Yet everyone is beginning to wonder about that Southern Continent now it's not closed anymore."

"Southern is too big to be adequately protected against Thread which still falls there," N'ton said.

Lord Groghe nodded, mumbling that he was aware of that. "Point is, people know you can live without hold and survive Threadfall!" The Lord Holder's eyes narrowed as he glanced at Sebell. "That Menolly girl of yours did it! Hear tell Toric in Southern got little help from those Oldtimers during Falls."

"Tell me, Lord Groghe," Sebell asked in his quiet way, "have you ever been out in Fall?"

Lord Groghe shuddered a bit. "Once. Ohhh, well, yes, I take your point, Harper. I take your point. Still, one way to separate boys from men!" He gave a sharp nod of his head. "That's my notion. Separate boys from men!" He gazed up at N'ton, a sly look in his eyes though his expression continued bland. "Or don't the Weyrs want the boys separated?"

N'ton laughed, to the Lord's surprise. "It's time we separated more than the boys, Lord Groghe."

"Huh?"

"We will convey your message to F'lar today." The Fort Weyrleader raised his cup to the Lord Holder as a seal on that promise.

"Can't ask fairer than that! What news, Master Sebell, of Master Robinton?"

Sebell's eyes lit with amusement. "He's four days out of Ista Hold, resting comfortably."

"Ha!" Lord Groghe begged to disbelieve that.

"Well, I'm told he's comfortable," Sebell replied. "Whether he is of the same opinion or not."

"Going to that pretty place where young Jaxom's trapped, huh?"

"Trapped?" Sebell regarded Lord Groghe with mock horror. "He's not trapped, only restricted from flying *between* for a while longer."

"Been at that cove. Beautiful. Whereabouts is it exactly?"

"In the South," Sebell answered.

"Humph. All right, you won't tell? You won't tell! Don't blame you. Beautiful place. Now, off with the pair of you and tell F'lar what I've said. Don't think I'll be the last but it'd be a help to be the first. Help to him. Help to me! Dratted sons of mine drive me to drinking!" The Lord Holder rose and so did the two younger men. "Tell your Master I was asking for him when you see him next, Sebell."

"I will, sir!"

Lord Groghe's little queen, Merga, chirped brightly at Sebell's Kimi and N'ton's Tris as the three men walked to the Hall door. To Sebell, it indicated that Lord Groghe was well pleased with the interview.

Neither man made any comment until they were well down the wide ramp that led from the courtyard of Fort Hold to the main paved roadway of the complex Hold.

Then N'ton heard Sebell's soft and satisfied chuckle. "It worked, N'ton, it worked."

"What worked?"

"The Lord Holder's asking the Weyrleaders' permission to go south!"

"Why shouldn't they?" N'ton seemed perplexed.

Sebell grinned broadly at his friend. "By the Shell, it worked with you, too! Do you have time to take me to Benden Weyr? Lord Groghe's right. He might be the first though I doubt it, knowing Lord Corman's ways, but he won't be the last."

"What worked with me, Sebell?"

Sebell's grin deepened and his brown eyes danced. "Now I'm well trained not to give away craft secrets, my friend."

N'ton made a noise of disgusted impatience and stopped in the middle of the dusty pavement. "Explain or you don't go."

"It should be so obvious, N'ton. Do think on it. While you take me to Benden. If you haven't figured out what I mean, I'll tell you there. I'll have to inform F'lar what's been done anyhow."

"Lord Groghe, too, eh?" F'lar regarded the two younger men thoughtfully.

He'd just returned from fighting Thread over Keroon and a surprising after-Fall interview with Lord Corman, punctuated with much honking of the Lord's large and perpetually runny nose.

"Threadfall over Keroon today?" Sebell asked and when F'lar grimaced sourly, the young Craftmaster grinned at N'ton. "Lord Groghe wasn't first!"

Giving vent to the irritation he felt, F'lar slapped his riding gauntlets down on the table.

"I apologize for barging in when you must wish to rest, Weyrleader," Sebell said, "but if Lord Groghe has thought of those empty lands to the south, others have, too. He suggested that you'd better be warned."

"Warned, huh?" F'lar brushed the forelock out of his eyes and grimly poured a cup of wine for himself. Recalling courtesy, he poured wine for N'ton and Sebell.

"Sir, the matter's not yet out of hand."

"Hordes of holdless men wanting to swarm south, and it's not out of hand?"

"They have to ask Benden's permission first!"

F'lar was in the act of swallowing wine and nearly choked in surprise.

"Ask Benden's permission? How does that come about?"

"Master Robinton's doing," N'ton said, grinning from ear to ear.

"Excuse me, I don't seem to be following you," F'lar said, sitting down. He dabbed the splattered wine from his lips. "What has Master Robinton, who is, I trust, safely at sea, to do with Groghe, Corman and who knows who else wanting Southern lands for their many sons?"

"Sir, you know that I've been sent about Pern—north and south—by the Masterharper? Lately I've had two important tasks to accomplish above and beyond my normal duties. First I was to take the temper of every small Hold as regarded duty to Hold and Weyr. Secondly I was to reinforce the belief that it is to Benden Weyr everyone on Pern must look!"

F'lar blinked, shook his head as if to clear his mind and then leaned forward to Sebell.

"Go on. This is very interesting."

"Benden Weyr only could appreciate the changes that had occurred to Hold and Craft during the Long Interval, because only Benden had changed *with* the Turns. You, as Benden Weyrleader, saved Pern from Thread when no one else felt Thread would ever fall again. You also protected your Time from the excesses of those Oldtimers, who could not accept the gradual changes of Hold and Craft. You upheld the rights of

Hold and Craft against your own kind and exiled those who would not look to you for leadership.

"Hmm. I hadn't ever heard it put quite like that," F'lar said.

To N'ton's amusement, Benden's Weyrleader squirmed, partly embarrassed but mostly gratified by the summation.

"And so the South became closed off!"

"Not precisely closed off," F'lar said. "Toric's people always came and went." He grimaced at the present repercussions of that liberty.

"They came north, true, but traders or anyone else only went south with the permission of Benden Weyr."

"I don't remember saying that at Telgar Hold the day I fought T'ron!" F'lar struggled to recall clearly what had happened that day other than a wedding, a fight and a Threadfall.

"You didn't actually say so in so many words," Sebell replied, "but you asked for and received the support of three other Weyrleaders, and every Lord Holder and Craftmaster . . ."

"And Master Robinton construed that to mean Benden gives all orders regarding Southern?"

"More or less." Sebell made that admission cautiously.

"But not in so many words, eh, Sebell?" F'lar asked, appreciating afresh the devious mind of the Harper.

"Yes, sir. It seemed the course to take, sir, considering your own wish to secure some part of the Southern Continent for the dragonfolk during the next Interval."

"I'd no idea that Master Robinton had taken a chance remark of mine so much to heart."

"Master Robinton has always had the best interests of the Weyrs clearly in mind."

Grimly F'lar thought of the painful estrangement when the Harper had intervened on the day the egg had been stolen. But again, though it hadn't seemed so at the moment, the Harper had acted in the best interests of Pern. If Lessa had carried out her intention of setting the Northern dragons against the poor old beasts at Southern . . .

"We owe the Masterharper much."

"Without the Weyrs . . ." Sebell spread his hands wide to indicate that there was no other option.

"Not all the Holds would agree to that," F'lar said. "There is still that notion that the Weyrs do not destroy the Red Star because the end of Thread would mean the end of their dominance in Pern. Or has Master Robinton cleverly changed that notion, too?"

"Master Robinton didn't have to," Sebell said with a grin. "Not after F'nor and Canth tried to go to the Red Star. The notion is *Dragonmen must fly/When Threads are in the sky.*"

"Isn't it current knowledge now," F'lar tried to keep the contempt from his tone, "that the Southerners rarely stirred themselves to fly Thread in the South?"

"That is, as you believe, now known. But, sir, I think you fail to appreciate that it is one thing to *think* about being holdless in the Fall, and quite another matter to endure it."

"You have?" F'lar asked.

"I have." Sebell's expression was solemn. "I would prefer above all else to be within a Hold." He shrugged his shoulders. "I know that it's a question of changing the habits of my early years, but I definitely prefer to be sheltered during Fall. And to me that will always imply protection by dragons!"

"So, in the final analysis, I've got the problem of Southern right back in my lap?"

"What's the problem with Southern now?" Lessa asked, entering the weyr just then. "I thought it was understood that *we* have first rights in Southern!"

"That," F'lar chuckled, "does not appear to be in contention. Not at all. Thanks to good Master Robinton."

"Then what is the problem?" She nodded at Sebell and N'ton by way of greeting, then looked sternly at her weyrmate for his answer.

"Only which part of the Southern Continent we'll open to the holdless younger sons of the North before they become a problem in themselves. Corman spoke to me after Fall."

"I saw you two talking. Frankly, I've been wondering when the subject would come up now that we've had to interfere with the Oldtimers again." Lessa loosened her riding belt, and sighed. "I wish I knew more. Has Jaxom done nothing with his time down at the cove?"

Sebell extracted a bulky packet from his tunic. "He has, among others. Perhaps this will ease your mind, Lessa." With an air of quiet triumph, Sebell unfolded the carefully joined leaves of a large chart, portions of which remained white. A clearly defined coastline was occasionally expanded inland with colored and shaded areas. In the margins were dates and the names of those who had surveyed the various sections. The thumb of land pointing at Nerat Tip was completely filled in and familiar to the Weyrleader as Southern Weyr and Hold. On either side of that landmark was an incredible sweep of continent, bounded on the west by the delineation of a great sandy waste on two sides of a huge bay. On the east, ever further from the thumb of Southern, a longer coastline stretched, dipping sharply south, punctuated at its most easterly point by the drawing of a high, symmetrical mountain and a small, starred cove.

"This is what we know of the Southern Continent," Sebell said after a long interval while the dragonriders studied the map. "As you see, we still haven't managed to chart the entire coast, let alone the interior. This much has taken three full Turns of discreet survey to do."

"By whom?" Lessa inquired, now deeply interested.

"By many people, myself included, N'ton, Toric's holders, but most of it by a young harper named Piemur."

"So that's what happened to him when his voice changed," Lessa said in surprise.

"By the scale of this map," F'lar said slowly, "you could fit the North of Pern in the western half of the Bay."

Sebell laid his left thumb on the protuberance of

Southern and planted the rest of his hand, fingers splayed on the western section of the map. "This area could easily occupy the Lord Holders." He heard Lessa's sharp intake of breath and smiled at her, spreading his right hand over the eastern portion. "But this, Piemur tells me, is the best part of the South!"

"Near that mountain?" Lessa asked.

"Near that mountain!"

Piemur, leading Stupid while Farli circled above him, reappeared from the forest just as full dark was falling on the cove. He swung a plaited string of ripe fruit to the ground in front of Sharra.

"There! That's to make up for cutting out this morning," he said, a tentative grin on his face as he squatted on his haunches. "Stupid wasn't the only one scared of that mob this morning." He made a show of wiping his forehead. "I haven't seen that many people in . . . since the last gather I attended a South Boll. *That* was two Turns ago! I was afraid they'd never leave! They'll be back tomorrow?"

Jaxom grinned at his plaintive question and nodded. "I wasn't much better than you, Piemur. I got away by having to hunt. Then I tracked down that clutch and spent the afternoon rigging fishnet." He gestured toward the next cove.

Piemur nodded. "Funny thing that, not wanting to be among people. Felt as if I couldn't breathe with so many using the same air supply. And that's downright foolish." He looked about him, at the black bulks of supplies lining the cove. "We're not stuffed in a Hold, with fans going!" He shook his head. "Me, Piemur, harper, a social fellow. And I turn and run from people . . . faster than Stupid did!" He gave a snort of laughter.

"If it'll make you two feel any better, I was a bit overwhelmed myself," Sharra said. "Thank you for the fruit, Piemur. That . . . that horde ate all we had. I think there's some roast wherry left, and a few rib bones from the buck."

"I could eat Stupid, only he'd be too tough." Piemur

breathed a sigh of relief and eased himself down to the sand.

Sharra chuckled as she went to get him something to eat.

"I don't like to think of a lot of people here," Jaxom told Piemur.

"Know what you mean." The young harper grinned. "Jaxom, do you realize that I've been places no man has ever stepped before? I've seen places that scared me to leaking, and other spots that I had trouble leaving because they were so beautiful." He exhaled in resignation. "Oh, well, I got there first." Suddenly he sat up, pointing urgently into the sky. "There they are! If only I had a far-viewer!"

"Who are?" Jaxom slewed himself around to see where Piemur was pointing, expecting dragonriders.

"The so-called Dawn Sisters. You can only see them dusk and dawn down here and much higher in the sky. See, those three very bright points! Many's the time I've used them as guides!"

Jaxom could scarcely miss the three stars, gleaming in an almost constant light. He wondered that he hadn't noticed them before now.

"They'll fade soon," Piemur said, "unless one of the moons is out. Then you see them again just before dawn. Must ask Wansor about that when I see him. They don't act like proper stars. The Starsmith's not scheduled to come down and help build the Harper's hold, is he?"

"He's about the only one who isn't," Jaxom replied. "Cheer up, Piemur. The way they worked today, it won't take long to finish that hold. And what do you mean about the Dawn Sisters?"

"They just don't act like proper stars. Didn't you ever notice?"

"No. But we've been in most evenings and certainly every dawn."

Piemur pointed with several stabs of his right arm at the Dawn Sisters. "Most stars change position. They never do."

"Sure they do. In Ruatha they're almost invisible on the horizon . . ."

Piemur was shaking his head. "They're constant. That's what I mean. Every season I've been here, they're always in the same place."

"Can't be! It's impossible. Wansor says that stars have routes in the sky just like—"

"They stay still! They're always in the same position."

"And I tell you that's impossible."

"What's impossible? And don't snarl at each other," Sharra said, returning with a tray piled high with food and a wineskin slung over her shoulder. Giving Piemur the food, she filled cups all around.

Piemur guffawed as he reached for a buck rib. "Well, I'm going to send a message to Wansor. *I* say it's bloody peculiar behavior for stars!"

A change in the breeze awakened the Master Harper. Zair chirped softly, curled on the pillows above Robinton's ear. A sunscreen had been rigged above the Harper's head but it was the airless heat that roused him.

For a change, no one was seated in watch over him. The respite of surveillance pleased him. He had been touched by the concern of everyone, though at times the attention bade fair to smother him. He'd curbed his impatience. He had no choice. Too weak and tired to resist the ministrations. Today must be another small indication of his general improvement: leaving him alone. He reveled in the solitude. Before him, the jib sheet flapped idly and he could hear the mainsail, behind him—aft, he corrected himself abruptly—rumbling windless as well. The gentle rolling swells seemed to be all that drove the ship forward. Waves, curls of foam on their crests, were mesmeric in their rhythm and he had to shake his head sharply to break their fascination. He raised his glance above the swell and saw nothing but water, as usual, on all sides. They would not see land for days more, he knew, though Master Idarolan said they were making good speed on their southeasterly course now that they had picked up the Great South Current.

The Master Fisherman was as pleased with this expedition as everyone else connected with it. Robinton snorted to himself with amusement. Everyone else apparently was profiting by his illness.

Now, now, Robinton chided himself, don't be sour. Why did you spend so much time training Sebell if not to take over when it became necessary? Only, Robinton thought, he hadn't ever expected that to happen. He wondered fleetingly if Menolly was faithfully reporting the daily messages from Sebell. She and Brekke could well be conspiring to keep any worrying problem from him.

Zair stroked his cheek with his soft head. Zair was the best humor-vane a man could have. The fire-lizard knew, with an instinct that outshone his own reliable sense of atmosphere, the emotional climate of those about Robinton.

He wished he could throw off this languor and use the journey time to good effect—catching up on Craft business, on those songs he had in mind to write, on any number of long-delayed projects that the press of immediate concerns had pushed further and further from completion. But Robinton had no ambition at all; he found himself content to lie on the deck of Master Idarolan's swift ship and do nothing. The *Dawn Sister,* that's what Idarolan called her. Pretty name. That reminded him. He must borrow the Fisherman's far-viewer this evening. There was something odd about those Dawn Sisters. They were visible, higher up than they ought to be, in the sky at dusk as well as dawn. Not that he'd been allowed to be awake at dawn to check. But they were mostly in the sky at sunset. He didn't think that stars should act that way. He must remember to write Wansor a note.

He felt Zair stir, heard him chirp a pleasant greeting before he heard the soft step behind him. Zair's mind imagined Menolly.

"Don't creep up on me," he said with more testiness than he intended.

"I thought you were asleep!"

"I was. What else do I do all day?" He smiled at her to take the petulance from his words.

Surprisingly, she grinned and offered him a cup of fruit juice, lightly laced with wine. They knew better now than to offer him plain juice.

"You sound better."

"Sound better? I'm as peevish as an old uncle! You must be heartily tired of my sulks by now!"

She dropped beside him, her hand on his forearm.

"I'm just so glad you're able to sulk," she said. Robinton was startled to see the glimmer of tears in her eyes.

"My dear girl," he began, covering her hand with his.

She laid her head on the low couch, her face turned from him. Zair chirped in concern, his eyes beginning to whirl faster. Beauty erupted into the air above Menolly's head, chittering in echoed distress. Robinton set down his cup and raised himself on one elbow, leaning solicitously over the girl.

"Menolly, I'm fine. I'll be up and about any day now, Brekke says." The Harper permitted himself to stroke her hair. "Don't cry. Not now!"

"Silly of me, I know. Because you are getting well, and we'll see to it that you never strain yourself again . . ." Menolly wiped her eyes impatiently with the back of her hand and sniffled.

It was an endearingly childlike action. Her face, now blotchy from crying, was suddenly so vulnerable that Robinton felt his heart give a startling thump. He smiled tenderly at her, stroked tendrils of her hair back from her face. Tilting her chin up, he kissed her cheek. He felt her hand tighten convulsively on his arm, felt her lean into his kiss with an appeal that set both fire-lizards humming.

Perhaps it was that response from their friends, or the fact that he was so startled that caused him to stiffen, but Menolly swiveled away from him.

"I'm sorry," she said, her head bent, her shoulders sagging.

"So, my dear Menolly, am I," the Harper said as gently as he could. In that instant, he regretted his age, her youth, how much he loved her—the fact that he never could—and the weakness that caused him to admit so much. She turned back to him, her eyes intense with her emotion.

He held up his hand, saw the quick pain in her eyes, as the merest shake of his fingers forestalled all she wanted to say. He sighed, closing his eyes against the pain in her loving eyes. Abruptly he was exhausted by an exchange of understanding that had taken so few moments. As few as at Impression, he thought, and as lasting. He supposed he had always known the dangerous ambivalence of his feelings for the young SeaHold-bred girl whose rare talent he had developed. Ironic that he should be weak enough to admit it, to himself and to her, at such an awkward moment. Obtuse of him not to have recognized the intensity and quality of Menolly's feelings for him. Yet, she'd seemed content enough with Sebell. Certainly they enjoyed a deep emotional and physical attachment. Robinton had done everything in his subtle power to insure that. Sebell was the son he had never had. Better that!

"Sebell . . ." he began, and stopped when he felt her fingers tentatively closing over his.

"I loved you first, Master."

"You've been a dear child to me," he said, willing himself to believe that. He squeezed her fingers in a brisk grip which he broke and, elbowing himself off the pillows, retrieved the cup he had set down and took a long drink.

He was able, then, to smile up at her, despite the lingering ache in his throat for what could never have been. She did manage a smile in return.

Zair flew up and beyond the sunscreen, though Robinton couldn't imagine why the approach of the Masterfisher would startle the creature.

"So, you wake. Rested, my good friend?" the Seamaster asked.

"Just the man I wanted to see. Master Idarolan,

have you noticed those Dawn Sisters at dusk? Or has my eyesight deteriorated with the rest of me?"

"Oho, the eye is by no means dimmed, good Master Robinton. I've already sent word back to Master Wansor on that account. I confess that I have never sailed so far easterly in these Southern waters so I'd never observed the phenomenon before, but I do believe that there is something peculiar about the positioning of those three stars."

"If I'm allowed to stay up past dusk this evening," the Harper glared significantly at Menolly, "may I have the loan of your distance-viewer?"

"You certainly may, Master Robinton. I'd appreciate your observations. I know you've had a good deal more time to study Master Wansor's equations. Perhaps we can figure out between us this erratic behavior."

"I'd like nothing better. In the meantime, let us complete that game we started this morning. Menolly, have you the board handy?"

CHAPTER XVIII

At the Cove Hold the Day of Master Robinton's Arrival, 15.10.14

WITH SO MANY eager hands and skilled craftsmen, Cove Hold took only eleven days to complete, though the stonemen shook their heads a bit over rushing the drying of hardset. Another three days were spent on the interior. Lessa, Manora, Silvina and Sharra consulted long, and with much shifting of the furnishings finally achieved what they considered the effective use —not efficient, Sharra told Jaxom with a wicked grin, but effective—of the offerings which poured in from every hold, craft and cot.

Sharra's voice began to take on a tone that mixed suffering and pride. She'd spent the day unpacking, washing and arranging things. "What did you fall into?" she asked Piemur, noticing newly acquired scratches on his face and hands.

"Doing things his way," Jaxom replied, though he'd a few marks on his neck and forehead as well.

With so many to build the Hold, N'ton, F'nor, and F'lar, when he could arrange the time, had joined Piemur and Jaxom to increase their knowledge of the lands immediately adjacent to the Cove.

Piemur rather arrogantly told F'lar that dragons had to *be* to a place first to get there again *between* —or else get a sharp enough visualization from someone who had. But he, with his two feet and Stupid's four, had to be first so that mere dragonriders could then follow. The dragonriders ignored the somewhat disparaging remarks, but Piemur's attitude was beginning to get on Jaxom's nerves.

No matter the method of accomplishment, temporary camps at a good day's flight by dragon from Cove Hold were established in a wide arc fanning out from the new Hold. Each camp consisted of a small tile-roofed shelter and a stone bunker to secure emergency supplies and sleeping furs. By a tacit agreement, they had gone two days' flight on a direct bearing to the mountain and built a secondary camp.

The restriction on Jaxom flying *between* would shortly be removed. He had only to wait now, F'lar told him, until Master Oldive gave him a final examination. Since Master Oldive would soon be in Cove Hold to check Robinton's recovery, Jaxom wouldn't have long to wait.

"And, if I can go *between,* so can Menolly," Jaxom said.

"Why would you have to wait until Menolly can go *between?*" Sharra asked, with an edge to her voice that Jaxom hoped might be a twinge of jealousy.

"She and Master Robinton found this Cove first, you know." He wasn't glancing in the direction of the Cove when he spoke, but toward the omnipresent mountain.

"By sea," Piemur said with some disgust for such a mode of transport.

"I have to admit, Piemur," Sharra said after regarding him for a long moment, "that feet were used before wings and sail. I, for one, am thankful that there are other ways of getting from one place to another. And it's no disgrace to use them."

She then turned and walked off, leaving Piemur to stare after her in surprise.

The incident cleared the air and Jaxom was relieved to note that Piemur ceased his snide remarks about flying and riding.

Attesting to the accuracy of Piemur's charting was

the fact that, once the Great South Current curved shoreward, Master Idarolan was able to identify his position by the contour of the now visible coast and to predict the arrival of the *Dawn Sister* at Cove Hold. She was twenty-two days out of Istan water before she rounded the west point of the Cove one bright morning, an event that was celebrated by a special, select welcoming committee.

Oldive and Brekke had forbidden a large reception and party. There was no point in undoing all the benefit of the long, restful voyage with the strain and fatigue of a feast. So Master Fandarel represented the hundreds of craftsmen and masters who had produced the beautiful Cove Hold. Lessa stood for all the Weyrs whose dragons had transported men and material, and Jaxom was the logical spokesman for the Lord Holders who had contributed the men and supplies.

These last moments, as the graceful three-masted ship headed up the Cove toward the stubby stone pier, seemed the hardest to endure. Jaxom strained his eyes as the ship glided closer and closer on the calm waters, and let out a jubilant whoop that made the fire-lizards squeak in surprise when he discerned the figure of the Harper standing in the prow, waving to those on shore. The fire-lizards executed aerial dances of great intricacy above the ship.

"Look, he's almost black with sun," Lessa cried, clutching Jaxom's arm in her excitement.

"Don't worry, he'll have had a good long rest," Fandarel said, grinning from ear to ear in anticipation of his friend's delight and pleasure in the new Hall. It was just out of sight from the pier.

The ship suddenly wheeled as Master Idarolan swung the tiller starboard, to slip his vessel deftly broadside to the dock. Seamen leapt to the pier, snubbing lines on the bollards. Jaxom jumped forward to lend a willing hand. The ship creaked as her timbers resisted the sudden halt. Bound bolsters were run over the side to prevent the ship rubbing against stone.

Then a plank was dropped from an opening in the ship's rail to the pier.

"I've brought him safely to you, Benden, Mastersmith, Lord Holder," boomed the voice of the Master Seaman as he jumped to the cabin housing.

A spontaneous cheer burst from Jaxom's throat, echoed by a roar from Fandarel and a cry from Lessa. Jaxom and Fandarel stood on either side of the springy plank to grip Robinton's hands as he all but slid ashore.

Ramoth and Ruth bugled overhead, startling the fire-lizards into wilder extravagances of motion. Lessa embraced the Harper by standing on tiptoe and imperiously pulling his head down so she could kiss him soundly. Tears sparkled on her cheeks and, to Jaxom's surprise, he realized his own eyes were wet, too. He stood politely back while Fandarel gently thumped the Harper off balance, sticking out a hamlike hand to steady his friend. Then he turned to assist Brekke and Menolly down the bouncing plank. Everyone began talking at once. Brekke looked anxiously from Robinton to Jaxom, demanding if the latter had had any headaches or eye spots, then urging the Harper to get out of the fierce sun as if he hadn't been baking in it on board ship day after day.

Good-naturedly everyone seized bundles from those the seamen were passing from ship to shore—everyone except Robinton, who was only allowed to carry his gitar.

Brekke began to walk up the shore toward the old shelter when Fandarel, laughing hugely in anticipation, placed his big hand on her back and gently propelled her toward the sanded path that led to the new Cove Hold. When Brekke began to protest, Lessa hushed her and pointed decisively at the path, taking her arm and half-pulling her along.

"I'm sure the shelter was that way . . ."

"It was," replied Master Fandarel, striding along beside the Harper. "We found a better site, more suitable for our Harper!"

"More efficient, my friend?" Robinton asked, laughing as he clapped his hand on the Smith's bulging shoulder.

"Much more efficient. Much!" The Smith nearly choked with his laughter.

Brekke had reached the bend of the path and stared incredulously at the sight of the new Hold. "I don't believe it!" She glanced quickly from Lessa to the Smith to Jaxom. "What have you done? How have you done it? It just isn't possible!"

Robinton and Fandarel had reached the two women, the Smith beaming so broadly that every tooth in his head showed and his eyes were mere squints in the folds of his cheeks.

"I thought Brekke said the shelter was small," Robinton said, peering at the structure and smiling hesitantly. "Otherwise I'd have asked for . . ."

Lessa and Fandarel could bear the suspense no longer and, each taking one of the Harper's arms, urged him toward the wide porch steps.

"Just you wait until you see what's inside," Lessa said with a crow of satisfaction.

"Everyone on Pern helped, either sending craftsmen or material," Jaxom told Brekke, taking her limp arm and escorting her on. He beckoned Menolly to hurry and join them.

Menolly glanced about and saw only the peaceful cove, carefully raked sand, trees and flowering shrubs which bordered the beach looking as unscathed as the day she and Jaxom had arrived. Only the bulk of the Hold, with its peripheral path of sand and shells, gave evidence of any change. "I just don't believe it."

"I know, Menolly. They took pains to keep it lovely. And just wait till you see inside Cove Hold . . ."

"It's already been named?" That seemed to irritate her, but Jaxom could appreciate her reaction.

"Well, it is a hold in a cove, so 'Cove Hold.'"

"It's all so beautiful," Brekke said, turning her head this way and that to see everything. "Menolly, don't be annoyed. It's such a marvelous surprise. When I think what I thought we were coming to . . ." She laughed, a happy sound. "I must say, this *is* much more the suitable thing!"

They had reached the steps of black reef rock, filled with white hardset, making it sturdy and attractive at the same time. A creamy orange tile roof extended over the porch which ringed the Hold almost to the surrounding trees, their blooms adding spicy fragrance to the air. The metal shutters were folded back from the unusually wide windows so that they could see through the house and catch glimpses of the furnishings within. The Harper's voice was raised in delight and amazement as he moved about the main room. As Jaxom, Brekke and Menolly entered, Robinton had been peering into the room set aside as his study, and his expression was dazed as he realized that Silvina had sent down everything from his crowded workroom in the Harper Hall. Zair echoed his confusion, chittering high and excitedly from his perch on a crossbeam. Beauty and Berd flew to join him, and suddenly, Meer, Talla and Farli appeared. They all seemed to be comparing notes, Jaxom thought.

"That's Farli! I thought I'd heard that Piemur was here. But where is he?" The Harper sounded surprised and a trifle hurt.

"Sharra and he are tending the spits," Jaxom said.

"We didn't want too many people about, tiring you . . ." Lessa added in a soothing tone.

"Tiring me? Tiring me! I need a little tiring! PIEMUR!"

If his tanned and relaxed face had not been proof enough of his return to health, the bellow he let loose, as vigorous and deafening as ever, left no further doubts of his vitality.

Clearly audible was the distant startled reply: *"Master?"*

"REPORT, PIEMUR!"

"Thank goodness we put him on a ship to rest," Brekke said, smiling at the Weyrwoman. "Can you imagine the time we'd have had with him on land?"

"What you two cannot appreciate is how much my

momentary disability has set back some very important—"

"Momentary disability?" Fandarel's eyes protruded in amazement. "My dear Robinton—"

"Master Robinton?" Menolly took a cup from the crowded cabinet, a beautiful glass goblet, its base stained harper blue, its cup incised with the Master's name and a harp. "Have you seen this?" She held it out to him, her eyes round with approval.

"My word, harper blue!" Robinton took and examined the beautiful thing.

"From my crafthall," Fandarel said, beaming. "Mermal thought to tint the entire glass blue but I argued that you would prefer to see the red of Benden wine in a clear cup."

Robinton's eyes gleamed with appreciation and gratitude as he examined the cup carefully. Then his long face fell into a sorrowful expression.

"But it's empty," he said in a plaintive, mournful tone.

At that moment a commotion started in the kitchen corner of the Hold. The curtain was flung roughly aside as Piemur, all but losing his balance in an effort not to careen into Brekke, lurched into the room.

"Master?" he gasped.

"Ah, yes, Piemur," the Harper drawled, eyeing his young journeyman as if he had momentarily forgotten why he had summoned the young man. The two regarded each other steadily, a puzzled frown on the Harper's face while Piemur's chest heaved as he panted, blinking sweat from his eyes. "Piemur, you've been here long enough to know where they store the wine? I've been given this lovely goblet and it's empty!"

Piemur blinked again and then shook his head slowly and said to the room at large, "There's nothing wrong with him anymore! And if that roast wherry burns . . ." He gave the Harper a thoroughly disgusted look, turned on his heel, whipped aside the curtain and could be heard noisily opening doors.

Jaxom caught Menolly's eye and she winked at him.

Piemur's gruff manner and cracking voice had not disguised his emotion to those who knew him. He stamped back into the main hall, swinging a wineskin, with Benden wax on its stopper.

"Don't swing it, lad," the Harper cried, holding up a restraining hand at such sacrilegious treatment. "Wine must be handled with respect . . ." He took the skin from Piemur and peered at the seal. "Hmmm. One of the better vintages! Tsk, tsk, Piemur, have you learned nothing from me of how to treat wine?" He made a grimace as he expertly cracked the seal and sighed with relief as he saw the condition of the stopper's end. He passed it under his nose, sniffing delicately. "Ah! Yes! Beautiful! Took no harm from its travel! There's a good lad, Piemur, pour for us all, will you, please? I can see this Hold is admirably supplied with cups."

Jaxom and Menolly were already distributing them as Piemur, with the courtesy due good Benden vintages, poured. The Harper, holding his cup high, watched the ceremony with growing impatience.

"Your continued good health, my friend." Fandarel proposed the toast which was repeated firmly by everyone.

"I am truly overwhelmed by all this," the Harper said, giving strength to his claim by taking only a small sip of the excellent wine. He looked from one to another of his friends, nodding his head and then shaking it. "Truly overwhelmed!"

"You haven't seen everything yet, Robinton," Lessa said and took him by the hand. "Brekke, you come see, too. Piemur, Jaxom, bring the bundles."

"Not so fast, Lessa. I'll spill the wine!" The Harper watched his glass as Lessa pulled him behind her.

He was guided through the sliding panel into the small corridor that separated the main Hall from the sleeping quarters. Brekke followed, her face alight with keen interest and curiosity.

The Harper's sleeping room was the largest, occupying the corner opposite his workroom. Four more sleeping rooms had been furnished to accommodate two guests in each but, as Lessa pointed out, the porch itself could comfortably sleep half a Hold of guests. Not that Robinton was to be allowed that many. He expressed pleasure at the bathing room and was suitably impressed by the large kitchen, and dutifully peered at the auxiliary hearth outside. He sniffed as the aroma of roasting meat wafted on the sea breeze.

"Where's that being done, might I ask?"

"We've steaming and roasting pits on the beach," Jaxom said, "to use when there's a horde here."

The Harper laughed, agreed that horde was probably the proper term.

"Try your chair," Fandarel said, striding to the armed chair when they returned to the main room. He turned it about for the Harper to see. "Bendarek made it exactly to your measure. See if it suits. Bendarek will be anxious to hear."

The Harper took time to examine the beautifully carved, high-backed chair, covered with wherhide dyed a deep harper blue. He sat down, put his hands along the armrests, found they were precisely the length of his forearm, and that the seat of the chair admirably fit his long legs and torso.

"It *is* beautiful, tell Master Bendarek. And a perfect size. How considerate Bendarek is. How overwhelmed I am by this and every other single item in this Hold. It is . . . magnificent. That's the only word for it. I'm speechless. Rendered completely speechless. Never in my wildest flights of fancy did I expect such luxury in unexplored wilds, such beauty, such thoughtfulness, such comfort."

"If you're speechless, Robinton, spare us your eloquence," came a dry voice. All turned to see the Masterfisherman standing in the open main door.

Everyone laughed, and Master Idarolan was beckoned forward and given a cup of wine.

"There are more bundles for you, Master Robinton," the Seaman said, gesturing toward the porch.

"You and your crew are to eat with us, Master Idarolan," Lessa called out.

335

"I was hoping so. Don't noise it about, but occasionally I do get the craving for red meat, not white."

"Master Robinton! Look here!" Menolly's voice was high with surprise. She was looking inside one of the cabinets that lined the walls between windows. "I'd swear it's Dermently's hand! And every single Traditional song and ballad, newly written on leaves and bound in blue wherhide! Just what you've been wanting to have Arnor do for you."

The Harper exclaimed with surprise and nothing would do but he had to open each folder and appreciate the craftsmanship and collection. Then he began to investigate all the cupboards and presses of Cove Hold until the midafternoon heat drove everyone to the beach to swim and cool off. Brekke fretted that the Harper should rest, quietly by himself, but Fandarel dismissed the notion, gesturing to Robinton, who was sporting in the water with the others.

"He is indulging in another type of rest right now. Leave him. Night's soon enough for sleeping!"

The evening breezes sprang up as the sun dipped closer to the western horizon. Rugs and woven mats as well as benches were brought out so that all the guests could be comfortable. When F'lar and F'nor arrived, they were enthusiastically welcomed by the Harper, who wanted to show them his beautiful Hold and was somewhat disappointed that they were already quite familiar with it.

"You forget how many people helped build it, Robinton," F'lar said. "It's probably the best known Hold on the entire world."

At that moment Sharra and the ship's cook—a thin man because that's the only sort, he told her, who could fit in the closet-sized excuse for a galley on the *Dawn Sister*—proclaimed that the feast was ready and were nearly run down by the hungry guests.

When no one could eat another morsel and even the Harper was reduced to small sips of wine, the guests settled into smaller groups: Jaxom, Piemur, Menolly and Sharra in one, the seamen in the largest, and the dragonriders and craftsmen in the third.

"I wonder what they're plotting for us to do now," Piemur said in a sour mutter after staring at the intense expressions of the third group.

Menolly laughed. "More of the same, I expect. Robinton's been going over those charts and reports of yours on shipboard until I thought he'd wear the ink out from looking." She pulled her knees up under her chin, a shy smile lighting her eyes. "Sebell's coming tomorrow with N'ton and Master Oldive." She went on quickly, before anyone could comment: "As I understand it, Sebell, N'ton and F'lar are overseeing Toric's people and that herd of holders' sons coming from the North. They'll chart the western part . . . the dividing line is that black rock river of yours, Piemur!"

Piemur groaned, writhing dramatically on the sand. "That place! May I never see it again!" He lifted one fist skyward to emphasize his determination. "Took me days to find a break in the cliffs on the other shore that we could climb out of. At that I had to ride Stupid off the cliffs into the water and swim him across. The fishes nearly made us their lunch."

"And the rest of us," Menolly continued, "with F'nor and the Harper, will explore this side."

"Inland, I hope?" Piemur asked sharply.

She nodded. "I understand," and she glanced over her shoulder at the Weyrleaders and Craftmasters, "that Idarolan may sail the coast . . ."

"More power to him. I've walked far enough!"

"Oh, hush, Piemur. No one forced you to . . ."

"Oh?"

"Enough, Piemur," Jaxom said, impatiently. "So we're to go inland?" Menolly nodded.

As one they looked over their shoulders toward the mountain, invisible though it was from their recumbent position.

Jaxom grinned at Menolly. "And Master Oldive'll be here tomorrow so I'll be able to go *between* again!"

"Lot of good that'll do you," Piemur said with a snort. "You still have to fly the route straight first."

"That doesn't put me out one little bit."

A fire-lizard squabble in the trees startled all of them and diverted Piemur from what Jaxom was certain was a renewal of his usual sour theme. Two gold streaks could be seen against the darker green of the foliage.

"Beauty and Farli to settle the matter!" Menolly cried, then looked around, curiously. "There're just our fire-lizards here now, Jaxom. Has all the activity frightened the Southern ones away?"

"I doubt it. They come and go. I suspect some of them are in the trees, fussing because they don't dare come near Ruth."

"Did you ever find out more about their men?"

Jaxom was chagrined to say that he hadn't even tried. "There's been too much else happening."

"I'd have thought you'd have given it one go." Menolly sounded irritated.

"What? And deprive you of the pleasure?" Jaxom affected surprised hurt. "I wouldn't dream of it . . ." He stopped abruptly, remembering those very peculiar dreams, as if he'd been seeing something out of hundreds of eyes. He also recalled what Brekke had said, the first day Ruth had flown Thread: "It was difficult to see the same scene through three pairs of eyes." Had he in fact been seeing, in his dreams, a scene from many fire-lizard eyes?

"What's wrong, Jaxom?"

"Maybe I did dream of it, after all," he said, with a hesitant laugh. "Look, Menolly, if you dream tonight, remember it, huh?"

"Dream?" Sharra asked, curious. "What kind of dreams?"

"Have you been having some?" Jaxom turned toward her. Sharra had assumed her usual intricate fold of leg, a posture which evidently fascinated and confounded Menolly.

"Certainly. Only . . . like you, I don't remember them, except that I couldn't seem to see clearly. As if my dream eye gets unfocused."

"That's a nice concept," Menolly said. "A dream eye unfocused."

338

Piemur groaned and flailed at the sand with his fists. "Here comes another song!"

"Oh, do be quiet!" Menolly regarded him with impatience. "All that lone traveling has changed you, Piemur, and I for one don't like the change."

"No one says you have to," Piemur snapped at her and, with a fluid motion, was on his feet and striding into the forest, angrily batting the underbrush out of his way.

"How long has he been so touchy?" Menolly asked Jaxom and Sharra.

"Since he arrived here," Jaxom said, shrugging to indicate that they hadn't been able to change him.

"Remember, he's been very worried about Master Robinton," Sharra said slowly.

"We've all been worried about Master Robinton," Menolly said, "but that's no reason to change one's temperament!"

There was an awkward silence. Sharra unfolded her legs and rose abruptly.

"I wonder if anyone remembered to feed Stupid this evening!" She walked off, not quite in the same direction as Piemur.

Menolly looked after her for a long moment. Her eyes were dark with concern as she turned back to Jaxom and then a wicked gleam changed them to their normal sea-blue.

"While they're out of earshot, Jaxom," she glanced about to be sure no one had come up behind her, "I'd better mention that it's been pretty well established now that no one at Southern Weyr returned Ramoth's egg."

"Oh? Really?"

"Oh! Really!"

She rose then, cup in hand, and strode across to the wineskin hanging from a tree branch.

Was she warning him? Not that it made any difference. His adventure had served a purpose at the time. Now that the Southern Weyr was being integrated into the others, there was less need than ever to admit his part in the affair.

Menolly wandered over to collect her gitar from the table and then seated herself at the bench, strumming softly to herself. A new song, about dream eyes, Jaxom wondered. Then he looked off in the direction Sharra had gone. Had he any legitimate reason for following her? He sighed. He liked Piemur, despite his acid tongue. He'd been glad to see the young Harper, grateful for his company and assistance. He just wished that Piemur had taken a day longer, even half a day longer, to reach the Cove. Since his arrival, Jaxom had had no time at all alone with Sharra. Was she avoiding him? Or was it just the circumstances of the building and getting Cove Hold ready for Master Robinton? He must figure out some way to separate Sharra from the others! Or else visit Corana!

CHAPTER XIX

Morning at the Cove Hold, Star-gazing in Late Evening, Next Morning, Discovery at the Mountain, 15.10.15–15.10.16

BY THE TIME Jaxom and Piemur had reluctantly struggled from their furs the next morning, Sharra told them that the Harper had risen at the first light of day, taken a bracing swim, made himself a breakfast and been long in his study, muttering over the charts and making copious notes. He now wished to have a few words with Jaxom and Piemur, if they didn't mind.

Master Robinton acknowledged their entry with a sympathetic grin for their deliberate and slow movements, the aftereffects of a very convivial evening. He then began asking for explanations of their latest additions to the main chart. When he had satisfied himself on that point, he asked how they had arrived at their conclusions. When they'd told him, he leaned back from the desk, fiddling with his drawing stick with such an unreadable expression on his face that Jaxom began to worry about what the Harper might be planning.

"Have either of you happened to notice the trio of stars we have been calling—erroneously, I might add —the Dawn Sisters?"

Jaxom and Piemur exchanged glances.

"Do you have a far-viewer with you, sir?" Jaxom asked.

The Harper nodded. "Master Idarolan has one aboard his ship. I construe that question to mean that you've noticed that they also appear at dusk?"

"And whenever there's enough moonlight . . ." Piemur added.

"And always in the same place!"

"I see you did profit by your classes," the Harper said, beaming at both of them. "Now, I've asked Master Fandarel if we could prevail on Master Wansor to visit here for a few days. Why, might I ask, are you two grinning as if you'd eaten all the bubbly pies at a gather?"

Piemur's grin deepened at this reference to his apprentice pastime.

"I don't think anyone on Pern would refuse to come here, given the whisper of an invitation," he said.

"Does Master Wansor have his new far-viewer finished?" Jaxom asked.

"I certainly hope that he does . . ."

"Master Robinton . . ." Brekke stood in the doorway, a curious expression on her face.

"Brekke," the Harper held up a warning hand, "if you have come to tell me that I have to rest, or drink a potion of your making, I beg you, don't! I have far too much to do."

"All I have is a message which Kimi has just brought from Sebell," she said, handing him the small tube.

"Oh!"

"As to your resting, I've only to watch Zair to know when that's necessary!" Her glance, as she turned to leave the study, fell on Jaxom and Piemur. There was no doubt in Jaxom's mind that he and Piemur were under tacit orders not to overstrain the Harper's strength.

Master Robinton raised his eyebrows in surprise as he read the message. "Oh, dear. Toric was invaded by a shipload of holders' sons last evening. Sebell feels he should wait till they've settled into temporary quarters." He chuckled and, when he saw the expressions of Jaxom and Piemur, then added, "I infer that all did not progress as smoothly as the holder boys could wish!"

Piemur snorted, with the contempt born of his Turns' exploring and his knowledge of Toric and his Hold's accommodations.

"Once you can go *between,* Jaxom," Robinton continued, "our investigation can proceed more rapidly. I've in mind to set you and the girls out as teams."

"Harper and Holder?" Jaxom asked, seizing the opportunity he'd been waiting for.

"Harper and Holder? Oh, yes, of course. Piemur, you and Menolly have worked well together, I know. So Sharra can go with Jaxom. Now . . ." Oblivious to the sharp look Piemur gave Jaxom, the man went on. "One sees things from the air in a perspective not always possible at ground level. The reverse, of course, applies. So any exploration should involve both methods. Jaxom, Piemur knows what I'm looking for . . ."

"Sir?"

"Traces of the original habitation of this continent. I can't for the life of me imagine why our long-dead ancestors left this fruitful and beautiful continent for the colder, duller North, but I assume that they had good reasons. The oldest of our Records states: *When man came to Pern, he established a good Hold in the South.* We used to think," the Harper smiled apologetically for that error, "that Fort Hold was meant, since it is south in the Northern Continent. But that particular document goes on to state ambiguously: *but found it necessary to move north to shield.* That never made any sense, but so many of the old Records have deteriorated past deciphering, much less coherence.

"Well, then Toric discovered an iron mine, worked in the open fashion. And N'ton and I sighted unnatural formations set in a mountainside which, when we had finally reached the spot on foot, were clearly mine shafts.

"If the ancients had been long enough in the Southern Continent to discover ore and mine it, there must be other traces of their habitation somewhere here in the South."

"In hot weather and rainy forest, nothing survives very long," Jaxom said. "D'ram built a shelter here a scant twenty-five Turns back and not much remains of it. And what F'lessan and I stumbled on in Benden Weyr had been sealed up, protected from weather."

"Nothing," Piemur said emphatically, "could dent, scratch or mar the pit supports we found in that mine. And not even the best stoneman can carve through solid rock like cheese. Yet the ancients did."

"We have found some traces. There must be more."

Jaxom had never heard the Harper so adamant, but he couldn't suppress a sigh as he glanced at the size of the map before him.

"I know, Jaxom, the scope is daunting, but what a triumph when we find the place. Or places!" Master Robinton's eyes shone with anticipation. "Now," he went on briskly, "once Jaxom is pronounced fit enough to fly *between*, we will progress southward, using that symmetrical mountain as our guide. Any objections?" The man barely waited for an answer. "Piemur will start out on the ground with Stupid. Menolly can accompany him, if she wishes, or can wait for Jaxom to take her and Sharra on Ruth to the secondary camp. While the girls survey the immediate vicinity, which I understand has not been done, you, Jaxom, can fly ahead with Ruth to set up another camp to which you can fly *between* the next day. And so on.

"I think you must have been drilled at Fort Weyr," the Harper said, looking at Jaxom, "to be able to observe and distinguish ground formations from the air? However, I want to impress on you both that though this is a joint effort, Piemur is far more experienced, Jaxom, and you will please bear this in mind when problems occur. And send me your reports for this . . ." he tapped the chart, "every evening! Off with you both, now, and organize your equipment and supplies. And your partners!"

Though explaining the situation to Menolly and Sharra and organizing their supplies and equipment took very little time, the explorers did not leave Cove Hold that day.

Master Oldive arrived on Lioth with N'ton and was lavishly welcomed by the Harper, more sedately by Brekke and Sharra, and with some reservations by Jaxom. Robinton immediately insisted on showing the Healer the beautiful new hold before, as Robinton expressed it, Oldive had to see his old carcass.

"He's not fooling Master Oldive," Sharra said, her rich voice for Jaxom's ear alone as they watched the Harper striding vigorously about the holding, Master Oldive murmuring appropriate comments. "Not one fingertip is he fooling the Healer."

"That's a relief," Jaxom said. "Otherwise the Harper'll be coming with us."

"Not *between,* he won't."

"No, he'd ride Stupid."

Sharra laughed, but her amusement ended as they both watched the Healer firmly steer the Harper into his sleeping quarters and quietly close the door.

"No," Sharra said, shaking her head slowly, "Master Robinton wasn't fooling Master Oldive!"

Jaxom was very glad he didn't have to try to fool the Master Healer when it came his turn to be examined. The ordeal for him was brief—a few questions, Master Oldive's inspection of his eyes, tapping on his chest, listening to his heart and the pleased smile on the Healer's mobile face gave Jaxom the favorable verdict.

"Master Robinton will be all right, too, won't he, Master Oldive?" Jaxom couldn't resist asking.

When the Harper had emerged from his room, he had been too quiet, rather thoughtful, and the bounce had gone out of his step. Menolly had poured him a cup of wine which he had accepted with a wistful smile and a deep sigh.

"Of course, Master Robinton will be all right," Master Oldive said. "He's much improved. But," the Healer held up one long forefinger, "he must learn to pace himself, conserve his energy and ration his strength or he will bring on another attack. You young people

345

can assist, with your strong legs and stouter hearts, without seeming to curtail his activities."

"Indeed we will. In fact, we do!"

"Good. Continue and he will soon be completely recovered. *If* he keeps in mind the lesson he learned from this seizure." Master Oldive glanced through the open window, mopping his forehead a little. "This beautiful place was a grand idea." He favored Jaxom with a sly smile. "The heat makes the Harper drowsy midday and forces him to rest. The prospects on all sides delight the eyes, and the scent of the air pleases the nose. How I envy you this spot, Lord Jaxom."

The beauties of Cove Hold had evidently worked their charm on the Masterharper as well, for he had recovered his good spirits even before the arrival of Master Fandarel and Master Wansor from Telgar. Robinton's delight was doubled when Fandarel and Wansor proudly exhibited the new distance-viewer that had occupied the Starsmith's time for the past half-Turn. The instrument, a tube as long as Fandarel's arm, and thick enough so that he needed two hands to surround it, was carefully encased in leather, with a curious eye-piece set, not on its end where Jaxom thought it ought to be, but on its side.

Master Robinton commented on that variation as well, and Wansor muttered something about reflective and refracting, ocular and objective and that this was the arrangement he thought best for the purposes of viewing distant objects. Whereas the instrument found in Benden Weyr made small things larger, the principles employed here were somewhat similar.

"That is neither here nor there but we are very pleased to use the new far-viewer in Cove Hold," Wansor went on, mopping his brow for he'd been so busy explaining his new device that he'd not bothered to remove his wherhide flying clothes.

Master Robinton winked at Menolly and Sharra and the two girls divested the lecturing Starsmith of his outer garments while he explained, almost oblivious to their assistance, that this was his first visit to the Southern Continent and yes, he had of course heard of the aberrant behavior of the three stars known as the Dawn Sisters. Until recently he had put the anomaly down to the inexperience of the observers. But, with Master Robinton himself noting their peculiarities, Wansor felt justified in bringing his precious instrument to the South to investigate the matter himself. Stars did not remain in fixed positions in the sky. All his equations, not to mention such experienced observers such as N'ton and Lord Larad, had verified this characteristic. Furthermore the Records handed down from the ancients, though they were in a shocking state, mentioned that stars undeniably followed a pattern of movement. Stars obeyed laws. Therefore when three stars had been observed to be in defiance of these natural laws, there had to be some explanation. He was hoping to find it this evening.

Not without a good deal of discussion, the site for this viewing was placed on the slight elevation of the stony eastern tip of Cove Hold, beyond the spot where the roasting and baking pits had been dug. Master Fandarel drafted Piemur and Jaxom to help him erect a frame on which he placed a swivel to mount the new viewer. Wansor, naturally, supervised this project until he was so in the Smith's way that the good man sat his Craftmaster on the edge of the promontory, near the trees, where he had a full view of all the activities but was no longer in his way. By the time the frame had been completed, Master Wansor was fast asleep, his head cushioned on his hands, snoring in a soft rhythm.

Finger against his lips to indicate the little man was not to be disturbed, Fandarel led Jaxom and Piemur back to the main beach. They all took a refreshing swim before joining the others in the afternoon rest. Rather than miss a single moment of the dusky display of the Sisters, everyone ate on the promontory. Master Idarolan brought out his ship's viewer, and the Smith quickly constructed a second frame from the materials left over from making Wansor's.

Sunset, which had previously come upon them all

too quickly, seemed delayed and delayed. Jaxom thought that if Wansor adjusted either the viewer or his bench, or his position on the bench, one more time, he would probably display some aberrant behavior of his own. Even the dragons who'd been playing in the water as if the sport had just been invented, were sprawled quietly on the beach, the fire-lizards sleeping about Ruth or perched on their friends' shoulders.

The sun finally went down, spreading its brilliant aftercolors across the western horizon. As the eastern sky darkened, Wansor put his eye to his instrument, let out a startled cry and nearly fell backward off his bench.

"It can't be. There is no possible logical explanation for such an arrangement." He righted himself and looked once again through the viewer, making delicate adjustments to the focus.

Master Idarolan had his eye pressed to his own viewer. "I see only the Dawn Sisters in their usual alignment. Just as they have always been."

"But they can't be. They are close together. Stars do not congregate so closely. They are always far distant."

"Here, let me have a look, man." The Smith was almost dancing in eagerness to have a glimpse through the instrument. Wansor reluctantly gave way to him, repeating the impossibility of what he had just seen.

"N'ton, your eyes are younger!" The Seaman passed his viewer to the bronze rider, who quickly accepted it.

"I see three round objects!" Fandarel announced in a booming voice. "Round metallic objects. Manmade objects. Those are not stars, Wansor," he said, looking at the distressed Starsmith, "those are things!"

Robinton, almost shoving the Smith's bulk to one side, bent his eye to the viewer, gasping.

"They are round. They do shine. As metal does. Not as stars do."

"One thing sure," Piemur said irreverently in the awed silence, "you have now found traces of our ancestors in the South, Master Robinton."

"Your observation is eminently correct," the Harper said in such a curiously muffled tone Jaxom wasn't certain if the man was suppressing laughter or anger, "but not at all what I had in mind and you know it!"

Everyone was given a chance to peer through Wansor's device, since Master Idarolan's was not powerful enough. Everyone concurred with Fandarel's verdict: the so-called Dawn Sisters were not stars. Equally indisputable was that they were round, metallic objects that apparently hung in a stationary position in the sky. Even the moons had been observed to turn a different side to Pern in the course of their regular cycles.

F'lar and Lessa as well as F'nor were asked to come with all urgency before the nightly appearance of the Dawn Sisters was over. Lessa's irritation at such a summons evaporated when she saw the phenomenon. F'lar and F'nor monopolized the instrument for the short space of time that the peculiar objects remained visible in the slowly darkening sky.

When Wansor was seen trying to work equations in the sand, Jaxom and Piemur hurriedly brought out a table and some drawing tools. The Starsmith wrote furiously for some minutes and then studied the result he'd achieved as if this presented a more inscrutable puzzle. Bewildered, he asked Fandarel and N'ton to check his figures for error.

"If there's no error, what is your conclusion, Master Wansor?" F'lar asked him.

"Those . . . those things *are* stationary. They stay in the same position over Pern all the time. As if they were following the planet."

"That would prove, would it not," Robinton said, unperturbed, "that they are manmade."

"My conclusion precisely," but Wansor did not appear to be reassured. "They were made to stay where they are all the time."

"And we can't get from here to there," F'nor said in a regretful murmur.

"Don't you dare, F'nor," Brekke said with such fervor that F'lar and the Harper chuckled.

"They were made to stay there," Piemur began,

"but they couldn't have been made here, could they, Master Fandarel?"

"I doubt it. The Records give us hints of many marvelous things made by men but no mention was ever made of stationary stars."

"But the Records say that men came to Pern . . ." Piemur looked at the Harper for confirmation. "Perhaps they used those things to travel from some other place, some other world, to get here. To Pern!"

"With all the worlds in the heavens to choose from," Brekke began, breaking the thoughtful silence that followed Piemur's conclusion, "had they no better place to come to than Pern?"

"If you'd seen as much of it as I have lately," Piemur said, his spirit undaunted for any appreciable length of time, "you'd know that Pern's not all that bad a world . . . if you ignore the danger of Thread!"

"Some of us never can," F'lar replied in a wry tone.

Menolly gave Piemur a sharp jab in the ribs, but F'lar only laughed when Piemur suddenly realized the tactlessness of his remark.

"This is a most amazing development," Robinton said, his eyes sweeping the night sky as if more mysteries were to be revealed. "To see the very vehicles that brought our ancestors to this world."

"A good topic for some quiet reflections, eh, Master Robinton?" Oldive asked, with a sly grin on his face and an emphasis on the *quiet*.

The Harper made an impatient dismissal of that suggestion.

"Well, sir, you could hardly go there," the Healer said.

"I cannot," Master Robinton agreed. Then startling everyone, he suddenly thrust his right arm in the direction of the Three Sisters. "Zair, the round objects in the sky? Can you go there?"

Jaxom held his breath, felt the rigidity of Menolly's body beside him and knew she wasn't breathing either. He heard Brekke's sharp, quickly muffled cry. Everyone watched Zair.

The little bronze stretched his head toward Robinton's lips and made a soft quizzical noise in his throat.

"Zair? The Dawn Sisters?" Robinton repeated his words. "Would you go there?"

Now Zair cocked his head at his friend, clearly not understanding what was asked of him.

"Zair? The Red Star?"

The effect of that question was instantaneous. Zair vanished with a squawk of angry fear, and the fire-lizards nestling by Ruth woke and followed his lead.

"That does seem to answer both questions," F'lar said.

"What does Ruth say?" Menolly whispered in Jaxom's ear.

"About the Dawn Sisters? Or Zair?"

"Either."

"He's been asleep," Jaxom replied after consulting his dragon.

"He would be!"

"So? What did Beauty image before she winked out?"

"Nothing!"

Despite an evening of earnest debate and discussion, the humans solved nothing either. Robinton and Wansor would probably have kept the conversation up all night if Master Oldive hadn't slipped something into Robinton's wine. No one had actually seen him, but one moment Master Robinton was arguing forcefully with Wansor, the next he had wilted at the table. No sooner was his head down than he began to snore.

"He cannot neglect his health for talking's sake," Master Oldive remarked, signaling to the dragonriders to help him carry the Harper to his bed.

That effectively ended the evening. The dragonriders returned to their Weyrs, Oldive and Fandarel to their respective Halls. Wansor remained. A full wing of dragons could not have dragged him from Cove Hold.

It had been tactfully decided not to broadcast the true nature of the Dawn Sisters, at least until such time as Wansor and other interested starcrafters had had a chance to study the phenomenon and reach some conclusion that would not alarm people. There'd been enough shocks of late, F'lar commented. Some might construe those harmless objects to be a danger, much as the Red Star was.

"Danger?" Fandarel had exclaimed. "Were there any danger from those things, we should have known it many Turns past."

To that, F'lar agreed readily enough but, with everyone conditioned to believe that disaster fell from skyborne things, it was better to be discreet.

F'lar did agree to send anyone who could be spared from Benden to help search. It was, the Weyrleader felt, more important than ever to discover just what this land contained.

As Jaxom pushed his legs into his sleeping blanket, he tried not to be annoyed with the thought of another invasion in Cove Hold, just when he thought he and Sharra would be left alone for a while.

Had she been avoiding him? Or was it simply that circumstances had intervened? Such as Piemur's premature arrival in Cove Hold? The worry over Master Robinton, the need to explore which left them too tired to do more than crawl into their furs, the arrival of half of Pern to complete the Hold for the Harper, then his arrival, and now this! No, Sharra had not been avoiding him. She seemed . . . *there*. Her beautiful rich laugh, a tone below Menolly's, her face often hidden by the strands of dark hair which kept escaping thong and clip . . .

He wished, intensely, that Cove Hold would not be overrun again—a wish that did him little good since he had no control over what was going to happen here. He was Lord of Ruatha, not of the Cove. If the place belonged to anyone, it was Master Robinton's and Menolly's by virtue of their being storm-swept into it.

Jaxom sighed, his conscience nagging at him. Master Oldive had rated him fully recovered from the effects of fire-head. So he could go *between*. He and Ruth could return to Ruatha Hold. He ought to return to

Ruatha Hold. But he didn't want to—and not just because of Sharra.

It wasn't as if he were needed in Ruatha. Lytol would manage the Hold as he'd always done. Ruth was not required to fight Thread either at Ruatha or at Fort Weyr. Benden had been lenient but F'lar had made it plain that the white dragon and the young Lord of Ruatha were not to be at risk.

There had been no prohibition, had there, Jaxom suddenly realized, to his exploring. In fact no one had suggested that he ought to return to Ruatha now.

Jaxom took some comfort in that thought, if he took none at all in the knowledge that tomorrow F'lar would be sending in riders—riders whose dragons could fly considerably faster and farther than his Ruth, riders who'd be able to reach the mountain before him. Riders who might just discover those traces which Robinton hoped existed somewhere in the interior of the Southern Continent. Riders who might also see in Sharra the beauty and gentle warmth of spirit that attracted Jaxom.

He tried, turning on the rushes yet again, to find a comfortable position, to find sleep. Maybe Robinton's plan for himself, Sharra, Menolly and Piemur would not undergo revision. As Piemur constantly reminded them all, dragons were great for flying over, but you still had to traverse the ground on foot to really know it. F'lar and Robinton might well want the dragonriders to spread out, cover as much territory as possible, and let the original explorers continue on to the mountain.

Jaxom then admitted to himself that he wanted to be first to the mountain! That serenely symmetrical cone had drawn him, sick and fevered, back to the Cove, had dominated his waking hours and intruded with nightmarish drama into his dreams. He wanted to be first to reach it, irrational as the notion might be.

Somewhere in the middle of these reflections, he did fall asleep. Again those overlapping scenes figured in his dreams: again the mountain erupted, one whole side shattering and spewing pulsingly red-orange flaming rocks and hot flows of molten lava down its side. Again Jaxom was both frightened refugee and dispassionate observer. Then the red wall began bearing down on him, so close to his heels that he could feel its hot breath on his feet . . .

He woke! The rising sun was slanting through the trees to caress his right foot which protruded from a rent in the light blanket. Rising sun!

Jaxom felt for Ruth. His dragon was still asleep in the clearing for the old shelter where a sandy wallow had been made to accommodate him.

Jaxom glanced across to Piemur, who slept in a neat ball, both hands resting under his right cheek. Slipping out of his bed, Jaxom noiselessly opened the door and, carrying his sandals, tiptoed out through the kitchen. Ruth stirred briefly, dislodging a fire-lizard or two from his back, as Jaxom passed him. Jaxom paused, struck by some puzzle. He stared at Ruth, then at the fire-lizards. None of those nestled against his friend were banded. He must ask Ruth when he woke if the Southern fire-lizards always slept with him. If they did, those dreams could be fire-lizard dreams—old memories triggered by the presence of men! That mountain! No, from this side a perfect cone appeared to the naked eye, unblemished by eruptive damage!

As soon as he reached the beach, Jaxom glanced up to see if he could sight the Dawn Sisters. But it was, unfortunately, already too late to catch their morning appearance.

The two viewers, Wansor's carefully covered with wherhide against morning dew and Idarolan's in its leather case, were still mounted on their frames. Grinning at the futility of his action, Jaxom nonetheless couldn't resist uncovering Wansor's viewer and peering skyward. He recovered the instrument carefully and stood looking southeast, toward the mountain.

In his dream the cone had blown out. And there were two sides to that mountain. Suddenly decisive, he removed the Seaman's viewer from its case. Though he might get more definition from Wansor's, he wouldn't presume to alter that careful focus. Besides, Idarolan's was strong enough for what he needed. Not that it could show the damage that Jaxom had half-hoped to see. Thoughtfully he lowered the instrument. He could go *between* now. Further, he was under Master Robinton's orders to explore the Southlands. More important, he wanted to be first to that mountain!

He laughed. This venture was scarcely as dangerous as the return of the egg. He and Ruth could go *between* and return before anyone in Cove Hold was aware of their intention. He took the viewer from its mounting. He'd need this with him. Once he and Ruth were airborne, he'd have to get a good long look at the mountain to find a point to which Ruth could move safely *between*.

He pivoted on his heel and lurched backward in surprise. Piemur, Sharra and Menolly were standing in a row, watching him.

"Do tell, Lord Jaxom, what you saw in the Seaman's viewer? A mountain, perhaps?" Piemur asked, showing all his teeth in that smug grin.

On Menolly's shoulder, Beauty chirped.

"Did he see enough?" Menolly asked Piemur, ignoring Jaxom.

"I'd say he had!"

"He wouldn't have planned to go without us, would he?" Sharra asked.

They regarded him with mocking expressions.

"Ruth can't carry four."

None of you are fat. I could manage, Ruth said.

Sharra laughed, covered her mouth to silence the sound and pointed an accusing finger at him.

"I'll bet anything Ruth just said he could!" she told the other two.

"I'll bet you're right." Menolly didn't take her eyes from Jaxom's face. "I think it really is best if you have some help on this venture." She drawled the last two words significantly.

"This venture?" Piemur echoed the words, alert as ever to nuances of speech.

Jaxom clenched his teeth, glaring at her. "You're sure you could carry four?" he asked Ruth.

The dragon emerged on the beach, his eyes glowing with excitement.

I have had to fly straight for many days now. That has made me very strong. None of you are heavy. The distance is not great. We are going to see the mountain?

"Ruth is obviously willing," Menolly said, "but if we don't make a move soon . . ." She gestured toward Cove Hold. "C'mon, Sharra, we'll get the flying gear."

"I'll have to rig flying straps for four."

"Then do it." Menolly and Sharra raced off down the sand.

Hunting ropes were handiest and Jaxom and Piemur had them in position when the girls returned with jackets and helmets. Jaxom hefted the Seaman's viewer and mentally promised that they'd be back so quickly that the man wouldn't have had time to notice its disappearance.

Ruth did have to strain to get himself off the beach, but once airborne, he assured Jaxom that he was flying easily. He veered southeast as Jaxom focused on the distant peak. Even at this altitude, he could discern no damage in the cone. He lowered the viewer fractionally until, clear and detailed, there was a distinctive ridge in the foreground of the mountain.

Jaxom asked Ruth if he visualized the objective. Ruth assured him he could. And took them *between* before Jaxom could have second thoughts on this venture. Abruptly, they were above the ridge, gasping. Breathless because of the incredible shock of cold *between* after months of baking in tropical suns, and because of the spectacular panorama before them.

As Piemur had once said, distance was deceptive. The mountain rose on the shoulders of a high plateau already thousands of dragonlengths above the sea. Far below them a broad sparkling inlet cut high cliffs: grassy on the mountain's side, densely forested on theirs. To the south, a towering range of mountains, snow-capped and misty in the distance, lay as a barrier east and west.

The mountain, still a good distance from them, dominated the scene.

"Look." Sharra suddenly pointed to their left, seaward. "More volcanoes. Some are smoking!"

Studding the open sea, a long chain of peak tops bent northeast, some with substantial islands at their feet, others mere cones poking from the water.

"A loan of the viewer, Jaxom?" Piemur took the instrument and peered. "Yes," he replied casually after a long look, "a couple of them are active. Far out though. No danger." Then he swung the viewer toward the barrier range, slowly shaking his head after a moment. "It could be the same barrier range I saw in the west." He sounded dubious. "Take months to get there! And cold!" He turned the viewer in a short arc. "Useful thing, this. That water goes deep inland. Idarolan could likely sail up if he has a mind to." He handed the viewer back to Jaxom and stared ahead at the mountain.

"That is the most beautiful sight," Sharra said on a long sigh.

"Must be the other side that blew out," Jaxom said, more to himself than to the others.

"The other side?" Sharra and Menolly spoke at once. And Jaxom could feel Piemur stiffening behind him.

"Did you dream, too, last night?" Jaxom asked.

"What on earth did you think had awakened us in time to hear you creeping out?" Menolly asked, a bit sharply.

"Well, let's go see the other," Piemur said as if he were merely suggesting a swim.

"Why not?" Sharra replied with the same carelessness.

I would like to see the place of my dreaming, Ruth said and, without any warning, he dropped from the ridge height.

Jaxom heard Menolly and Sharra exclaim in surprise and he was glad that he'd rigged flying straps for them. Ruth expressed apologies which Jaxom had no time to relay as the white dragon swooped into a current of warm air that bore them up and over the broad inlet.

When his flying had leveled, Jaxom used the viewer and found a distinctive rock formation on the northern shoulder. He gave Ruth the visualization.

They were *between:* they were hovering above the rock formation and the mountain seemed to bend frighteningly toward them for the space of several breaths. Ruth recovered his flying speed and veered further north, beating strongly in a wide arc toward the eastern face of the mountain.

Momentarily they were all blinded by the full brilliance of the rising sun which had been occluded by the mountain's bulk. Ruth shifted to a southerly heading. Before them lay the most incredible sweep of land that Jaxom had ever seen—far broader, and deeper than Telgar's flatlands, or the desert of Igen. His eyes were drawn quickly from that spectacular vista to the mountain.

The view was suddenly all too familiar to Jaxom, the product of so many uneasy nights and unfocused dreams. The eastern lip of the mountain was gone! The gaping mouth seemed to snarl, its left-hand corner pulled down. Jaxom's eyes followed that line and he saw, crouching on the southeastern flank, three more volcano mouths, like malevolent offspring of the larger. The lava flowed down, south, toward the rolling plains.

Ruth continued to glide instinctively away from the mountain, toward the kinder valley.

As much as Jaxom had admired and feasted his eyes on the northern aspect of that volcano, now he turned from the malevolent teeth of the blown side, the side of his nightmares.

Jaxom all but anticipated Ruth's words: *This place I know. They say this is where their men were!*

Out of the sun, fairs of fire-lizards dove and veered out of Ruth's flightline. Beauty, Meer, Talla and Farli, who had ridden their friends' shoulders to this incredible place, took off to join the newcomers.

"Look, Jaxom! Look down!" Piemur yelled in his ear while tugging at his shoulder and pointing frantically to a spot below Ruth's left foreleg. The early sun threw the outlines in bold relief. Regular outlines, mounds, and then straight lines dissecting, forming curious squares where no such regular formations should be.

"That's what Master Robinton is looking for!" He grinned back over his shoulder at Piemur, who had turned to attract the girls' attention to the ground.

Then Jaxom gasped, pressuring Ruth with his legs to turn northeast. He felt Piemur clutch at his shoulders as the Harper, too, saw what he'd seen. Where the haze from the distant smoking volcanoes in the sea was joined by a gray haze from the skies—Thread!

"Thread!"

Thread! Before Jaxom could direct him, Ruth had taken them smartly *between*. In the next instant they were hovering above the Cove, its beaches accommodating the bulks of five dragons. Master Idarolan's fishermen were scurrying from shore to ship, placing slates on a frame rigged to protect the wooden decks from Threadfall!

Canth asks where have we been? I must chew firestone immediately. The fire-lizards are to help protect the ship. Everyone is annoyed with us. Why?

Jaxom asked Ruth to land them near the firestone pile on the beach and to start chewing.

"I've got to find Stupid!" Piemur dropped to the sand and was off in a run toward the forest.

"Give me Master Idarolan's viewer," Menolly said to Jaxom. "I got a look at his face and though I don't say it's his viewer he's angry about . . ."

"I'll brave the storm in Cove Hold," Sharra told Jaxom, grinning at him and gripping his arm in reassurance. "Don't look so depressed! I know I wouldn't have missed this morning's jaunt. Not even if I get scolded by Lessa."

We have been exploring south as we were told to do by the Harper! Ruth announced suddenly, lifting his head and staring in the direction of the other dragons. *We are back here in time to fight Thread. We have done nothing wrong.*

Jaxom flinched, surprised at the determination in Ruth's tone, particularly since Jaxom was certain the white dragon was answering Canth since the brown dragon was looking in their direction and his eyes were whirling. Jaxom saw Lioth next to Canth, Monarth and two other Benden browns whom he did not know on sight.

Yes, I will fly across your pattern, Ruth said, again responding to words Jaxom didn't hear. *As I have done before. I have enough stone to flame. Thread is nearly on the Cove.*

He craned his neck toward Jaxom, and his rider sprang to his neck, truly relieved that the imminence of Thread delayed a confrontation with either F'nor or N'ton. Not, Jaxom realized, that he was in the wrong with either rider.

We have done what the Harper told us to do, Ruth said as he launched himself into the sky. *No one told us* not *to fly to the mountain today. I am glad we did. I will not be bothered with dreams now that I have seen the place.* Then Ruth added with some surprise: *Brekke does not think you are strong enough to fly Thread the first day you are allowed* between. *You are to tell me if you tire!*

Nothing would have induced Jaxom to admit fatigue after that, had they flown the entire four-hour Fall. As it was, they met Thread three coves east. Met and destroyed it, Ruth and Jaxom weaving over, under, through the other five who set the triangle pattern east and west. Jaxom hoped that Piemur had got Stupid to safety. After a moment, Ruth replied that Farli said the beast was on the porch of Cove Hold. She was ready to flame any Thread that attacked the Hold.

Jaxom noticed, as they wheeled above the Cove itself, that the tall masts of the *Dawn Sister* seemed to have sprouted fire and then realized that it must be the other fire-lizards protecting the ship. There seemed to be rather a lot of them flaming! Had the Southerners joined forces with the banded ones? Had they decided for some reason to help men?

He hadn't time for more speculation in the dive, swoop and flame of Threadfall. He was very tired by the time the silver rain had dwindled to nothing and

Canth bugled return. Ruth swept east and Jaxom saw F'nor give the signal: *Well done.* Then they glided back to the Cove.

Jaxom landed Ruth on the narrower portion of the western beach to allow the bigger dragons more space. He slid from Ruth's back, thumping the sweat-dampened neck, sneezing when the reek of firestone blew in his face. Ruth gave a little cough.

I am getting better and better at chewing. No flame left. He raised his head then, looking toward Canth, who had landed near them. *Why is F'nor annoyed? We have flown well. No Thread escaped us.* Ruth craned his neck back at his rider, his eyes beginning to whirl faster, flicks of yellow appearing. *I do not understand.* He snorted once, the firestone fumes making Jaxom cough.

"Jaxom! I want a word with you!"

F'nor strode across the sand to him, unbelting his jacket and stripping off his helmet in sharp angry gestures.

"Yes?"

"Where were the lot of you this morning? Why did you leave with no word to anyone? What have you to say for yourself arriving so close to Thread? Did you forget Thread was due today?"

Jaxom regarded F'nor. The brown rider's face was suffused with anger and fatigue. The same cold rage that had erupted within Jaxom that day so long ago in his own Hold began to possess him. He straightened his shoulders and raised his head higher. His eyes were level with F'nor's, a fact he had not previously noted. He could not, he would not, permit himself to lose control of his temper as he had that morning in Ruatha.

"We were ready for Thread when it fell, brown rider," he responded calmly. "My duty as the rider of a dragon was to protect Cove Hold. I did. My pleasure and privilege was to fly with Benden." He gave a slight bow and had the satisfaction of seeing the anger in F'nor's face give way to surprise. "I'm sure the others have by now reported to Master Robinton what we discovered this morning. Into the water with you, Ruth. I'll be glad to answer all your questions, F'nor, when I've cleaned Ruth up." He gave F'nor, who was staring at him in honest amazement, a second bow and then stripped off hot and sweaty flying gear, leaving on only the shortened trousers that were more suitable to the heat.

F'nor was still staring at him when he ran and dove neatly into the water, coming up beside his wallowing white friend.

Ruth twisted, blowing water in a fountain above his head, his half-lidded eyes gleaming greenly just under the surface.

Canth says that F'nor is confused. What did you say that confuses a brown rider?

"What he didn't expect to hear from a white rider. I can't wash you when you're rolling over all the time."

You are angry. You will tear my hide scrubbing so hard.

"I am angry. Not at you."

Should we go to our lake? Ruth's question was tentative and he turned his head toward his rider in an anxious manner.

"What do we need with a freezing lake when we've an entire warm ocean? I'm just annoyed with F'nor. It isn't as if I were still sick, or a child that needed a guardian. I've fought Thread with you, and without you. If I'm old enough to do that, I don't need to account for any of my movements to any one for any reason."

I forgot that Thread would fall today!

Jaxom couldn't help but laugh at Ruth's humble admission.

"So did I. But don't you ever let on to anyone."

Fire-lizards descended now to assist, needing a bit of scrub themselves to judge by the reek their wet hides exuded. They scolded Ruth much more unkindly than Jaxom did if he wallowed too deeply in the waves when they wanted to rinse him. Among the fair were Meer, Talla and Farli. Jaxom bent to his task. He was tired but he decided that as long as he kept himself going, he'd be able to finish bathing Ruth. Then he'd have all afternoon to rest.

He didn't. He also didn't have to bathe Ruth all by himself because Sharra joined him.

"Would you like me to take the other side again?" she asked as she waded up to him.

"I'd appreciate it no end," he said with a grin and sigh.

She tossed him a handled brush. "Brekke brought these with her. Thought they'd help clean dragons, and things. Good stiff bristles. You'll like that, won't you, Ruth?"

She scooped handsful of sand from the cove floor, dribbling the wet stuff on Ruth's neck and then applying the brush with vigor. Ruth whistled through the water with pleasure.

"What happened to you while I was fighting Thread?" he asked her, pausing before attacking Ruth's rump.

"Menolly's still answering questions." Sharra regarded him over Ruth's recumbent body, her eyes dancing, her smile full of mischief. "She talked so fast he couldn't interrupt, and she was still talking when I left. I didn't realize anyone could outtalk the Master Harper. Anyway, he stopped fuming very early on. Did you get scorched by F'nor?"

"We exchanged . . . opinions."

"I'll just bet you did the way Brekke was carrying on. I told her that you'd got pretty fit while she was away. She acted as if you'd risen from your deathbed to ride Fall!" Sharra made a scornful sound.

Jaxom leaned over Ruth's back, grinning at her, thinking how pretty she was with the mischief in her eyes, and beads of water on her face where Ruth had splashed her. She glanced up at him, raising one eye in query.

"Did we really see what I thought we saw this morning, Sharra?"

"We surely did!" She pointed her brush at him, her expression severe. "And you're very lucky that we were along to vouch because I don't think anyone would have believed just you." She paused, the twinkle back in her eyes. "I'm not entirely sure they believe us anyhow."

"Who doesn't believe us?"

"Master Robinton, Master Wansor and Brekke. Weren't you listening to me?"

"No," he said, grinning, "I was looking at you."

"Jaxom!"

He laughed as the blush deepened the tan on her face and neck.

I have a severe itch where you are leaning against me, Jaxom.

"There now, you see?" Sharra said, slapping his hand with the bristles. "You're neglecting Ruth in a shocking fashion."

"How'd you know Ruth was speaking to me?"

"Your face always gives you away."

"Say, where's the *Dawn Sister* going?" Jaxom asked, noticing the ship, her sails billowing out in the breeze, standing out to sea.

"Fishing, of course. Threadfall always brings out schools. And our escapade this morning is going to bring people down here in droves. We'll need the fish to feed 'em."

Jaxom groaned, closing his eyes and shaking his head in dismay.

"That . . ." Sharra paused for emphasis, "is our punishment for the unauthorized jaunt this morning."

They were both dumped into the water as Ruth unexpectedly lunged out.

"Ruth!"

My friends are coming! The white dragon bugled happily as Jaxom saw, bleary-eyed from the ducking, a half-wing of dragons appearing in the sky.

There is Ramoth and Mnementh, Tiroth, Gyamath, Branth, Orth . . .

"All the Weyrleaders, Sharra!"

She was spitting and choking over the water she'd swallowed.

"Great!" She didn't sound happy. "My brush!" She began searching about her.

And Path, Golanth, Drenth and he's here on our watchdragon!

"There's Lytol! Stand still, Ruth. We've still got your tail to clean."

I must give a proper greeting to my friends, Ruth replied, pulling his tail out of Jaxom's grasp to sit up on his haunches and warble to the second group of dragonriders appearing over the Cove.

"He may not be clean," Sharra said with some acerbity as she began to wring her long hair dry, "but I am."

I am clean enough. My friends will want to swim, too.

"Don't count on another swim, Ruth. It's going to be a busy day!"

"Jaxom, did you get a chance to eat anything yet?" Sharra asked. When he shook his head, she grabbed his hand. "C'mon, quickly, the back way, before someone catches us."

He paused long enough on the shore to collect his flying gear, then they both ran up the old path to the kitchen entrance of Cove Hold. Sharra breathed an exaggerated sigh of relief to discover the place empty. Ordering him to sit, she poured a cup of klah, and served him slices of fruit and warm cereal from the pot on the back of the warming hearth.

They both heard the calls and exclamations from the new arrivals, Robinton's deep baritone dominating as he called greetings from the porch.

Jaxom half-rose from his bench, gulping down another mouthful, but Sharra pushed him back.

"They'll find you soon enough. Eat!"

"Ruth is on the beach," Lytol's voice was audible suddenly, "but I don't see Jaxom anywhere . . ."

"I know he's about . . ." Robinton began.

A bronze arrow whizzed into the kitchen, chittered and zipped away.

"He's through that door, Lytol, in the kitchen," Robinton said with a laugh.

"I could almost agree with Lessa," Jaxom said in a mutter of disgust. He scraped a huge spoonful out of his bowl, cramming it into his mouth. He had to rise, catching the overflow at the corners of his mouth as Lytol came striding in.

"Sorry, sir," Jaxom mumbled through his food. "Had no breakfast!"

Lytol stood, his eyes so intent that Jaxom grinned in nervous embarrassment. He wondered if Lytol could already know of his excursion that morning.

"You look a great deal better than when I last saw you, lad. Good day to you, Sharra." His greeting was absent-minded courtesy as he crossed the remaining distance to clasp Jaxom's arm strongly in his. A smile pulled at his lips before he stepped back. "You're tanned, you look fit. Now what is this trouble you created today?"

"Create it? Me? No, sir." Jaxom couldn't help grinning now. Lytol was delighted, not annoyed. "That mountain's been there a long time. I didn't create it. But I did want to see it, close up, first!"

"Jaxom!" The Harper's bellow was impossible to ignore.

"Sir?"

"Come here, Jaxom!"

In the hours that followed, Jaxom was grateful that Sharra had thought to feed him breakfast. He didn't get much time for more food. The moment he entered the main Hall, questions were thrown at him by the Weyrleaders and Craftmasters assembled. Piemur had been very busy during Fall because Master Robinton had already completed a sketch of the southeastern face of the mountain to show the incredulous visitors, and a rough, small-scale map of this section of Southern. From the almost rhythmic way Menolly described their jaunt, Jaxom decided she had already repeated the account many times.

What Jaxom remembered most of that session was feeling sorry that the Master Harper was unable to see the mountain first hand. But, if Jaxom had waited until Master Oldive permitted the Harper to fly *between* . . .

"I know you've just flown Fall, Jaxom, but if you'd

just give Mnementh the visualization . . ." F'lar began.

N'ton burst out laughing, pointing to Jaxom. "The look on your face, lad. F'lar, he's got to lead us! Give him that!"

So Jaxom got back into slightly damp flying gear and roused Ruth from his sandy baking. Ruth was pleased enough with the honor of leading the bronzes of Pern, but Jaxom could barely contain behind a composed expression the thrill he was experiencing. Jaxom and the white dragon, leading the most important people on Pern.

He could have asked Ruth to jump directly to the southeastern side of the Two-Faced Mountain, his private designation. Somehow he wanted everyone to experience the full impact of those two sides—the benign and beautiful.

From the expressions on the riders' faces as they settled briefly on the ridge, he could see that he had achieved the desired effect. He allowed them time to sight the Barrier Range, glistening in the sun, ragged white teeth on the horizon. He gestured seaward where neither morning mists nor Thread now obscured the tail of volcanoes snaking northeasterly out into the sea, smoke just curling from the curve of the world in that direction.

At his request, Ruth soared across the inlet as he had done before, climbing high before he gave the coordinates of the next jump *between*. They came out above the broad expanse of the southeastern side of Two-Face, as dramatic an approach as anyone could have wished.

Mnementh suddenly surged into the fore and, as Ruth relayed to Jaxom, said that they should land. Politely, Ruth and Jaxom circled as the great bronze settled near the intersection of some of the regular lines, as far as possible from the three secondary cones. One by one the great bronze dragons of Pern settled in the grassy sward, their riders and passengers striding through the tall waving grasses to join F'lar, who had hunkered down to dig with his belt knife into the edge of one of those curious lines.

"Covered with Turns of blow dirt and old grasses," he said, giving up his attempt.

"Volcanoes often blow out quantities of ash," T'bor of the High Reaches said. He would know since quite a few old volcanoes were in Tillek which was beholden to the High Reaches Weyr. "If all those mountains blew at once, there'd be half a length of ash before you'd reach anything."

For a split second, Jaxom thought they were being threatened with ash. Sunlight was blotted out and a chittering, fluttering mass swooped down, almost touching Mnementh's head before the hundred fire-lizards lifted up again.

Amid shouts of consternation and surprise, Jaxom heard Ruth's announcement.

They are happy. Men have returned to them!

"Ask them about the three mountains, Ruth? Do they remember the mountains blowing up?"

There was no doubt they did. Suddenly there wasn't an unbanded fire-lizard in the sky.

They remember the mountains, Ruth said. *They remember fire in the air and fire crawling on the ground. They are afraid of the mountains. Men were afraid of the mountains.*

Menolly came running up to Jaxom, her face contorted with concern. "Did Ruth ask those fire-lizards about the mountains? Beauty and the others just had a fit. About those blasted mountains."

F'lar came striding up to them. "Menolly? What was all that fuss with the fire-lizards? I didn't see any banded ones. Were they all Southern ones?"

"Of course men were here. They're not telling us anything we didn't know. But for them to say they remembered?" F'lar was scornful. "I could accept your finding D'ram in the Cove with their aid . . . but that was only a matter of twenty-five Turns in the past. But . . ." For want of appropriate expression of his skepticism, F'lar merely gestured at the dead volcanoes and the long-covered traces of a settlement.

"Two points, F'lar," Menolly said, boldly contradicting the Benden Weyrleader, "no fire-lizard in this time knew the Red Star, but they were, nonetheless, all afraid of it. They also . . ." Menolly paused, and Jaxom was certain she had been about to bring up the fire-lizard dreams about Ramoth's egg. He hastily interrupted.

"Fire-lizards must be able to remember, F'lar. Ever since I've been in the Cove, I've been troubled with dreams. At first I thought it was leftovers from fire-head fever. The other night I found out that Sharra and Piemur have had similar nightmares . . . about the mountain. This side of it, not the one facing the Cove."

"Ruth always sleeps with fire-lizards at night, F'lar," Menolly said, pressing their case. "He could be relaying those dreams to Jaxom! And our fire-lizards to us!"

F'lar nodded, as if granting them this possibility.

"And last night your dreams were more vivid than ever?"

"Yes, sir!"

F'lar began to chuckle, looking from Menolly to Jaxom. "So this morning you decided to see if there was any substance to the dreams?"

"Yes, sir!"

"All right, Jaxom." F'lar thumped him good-naturedly on the back. "I suppose I can't blame you. I'd have done the same thing given the opportunity. Now, what do you . . . and those precious fire-lizards of yours . . . suggest we do now?"

"I am no fire-lizard, F'lar, but I would dig," the Mastersmith said, striding up to them. His face was aglow with perspiration, his hands grass and dirt-stained. "We must dig beneath the grass and soil. We must find out how they managed to make lines straight as rules that last Turn after Turn. Why did they build in mounds, if that's what those things are. Dig, that's what we must do." He pivoted slowly, staring about him at the desultory digging efforts of some of the dragon-riders. "Fascinating. Utterly fascinating!" The Smith beamed. "With your permission, I will ask Masterminer Nicat for some of his craftmasters. We will need skilled diggers. Also I promised Robinton that I would return immediately and tell him what I have seen with my own eyes."

"I'd like to go back, too, F'lar," Menolly said. "Master Robinton is in a swivet. Zair's been here twice. He must be impatient."

"I'll take them back, F'lar," Jaxom said. Suddenly he was as possessed by an irrational desire to leave as he had been eager to come that morning.

F'lar would not permit Ruth to carry weight again, not after the morning's excursion and Threadfall. He sent Master Fandarel and Menolly back to Cove Hold with F'lessan and Golanth, with instructions to the young bronze rider to take the Mastersmith wherever he wished to go. If he was surprised at Jaxom's wish to return, he gave no sign.

He and Ruth were away before the Smith and Menolly had mounted Golanth. They returned to a Cove delightfully empty of people. The warm, sultry air, after the cooler, clear atmosphere of the Plateau, was like an enveloping blanket, enervating Jaxom. He took advantage of his unremarked return and let Ruth take them to his clearing. It was cooler there and, when Ruth had settled himself, Jaxom gratefully curled up in the dragon's forearms. He was asleep in two breaths.

A touch on his shoulder roused him. His flying jacket had fallen from his shoulder and he felt chilly.

"I said I'd wake him, Mirrim," he heard Sharra say, her tone one of annoyance.

"Does it matter? Here, Jaxom, I've brought you some klah! Master Robinton wants to talk to you. You've slept all afternoon. We couldn't figure out where you'd got to."

Jaxom muttered under his breath, wishing with all his heart that Mirrim would go away. He resented her implication that he hadn't any right to sleep in the afternoon.

"Come on, Jaxom. I know you're awake."

"You're wrong. I'm half asleep." Jaxom indulged in a massive yawn before he opened his eyes. "Go away, Mirrim. Tell Master Robinton I'll be in directly."

"He wants you now!"

"He'll get me a lot sooner if you go tell him I'm coming. Now, get out of here!"

Mirrim gave him one more long hard look, brushed past Sharra and stomped up the stairs to the kitchen.

"You are my true friend, Sharra," Jaxom said. "Mirrim irritates me so! Menolly told me that once Path had flown, she'd improve. I haven't noticed any sign."

Sharra was peering at Ruth, who was still fast asleep, not even an eyelid twitching.

"I know what you're going to ask . . ." Jaxom said with a laugh, holding up a hand to forestall her words. "No, nary a dream."

"Nary a fire-lizard either." She smiled at him, shaking her head and retying her hair thong. "You were smart to come here and rest. There's none up at the Hall. Fire-lizards popping in and out, from Cove to the plateau, nearly hysterical! No one can make any sense out of what ours say or the Southern ones tell them. And it's not as if some of the Southern ones hadn't known we were here."

"And Master Robinton thinks Ruth can sort it all out?"

"He just might." She regarded the sleeping white dragon thoughtfully. "Poor darling, he's exhausted with all he's done today." Her rich voice was a tender croon and Jaxom could have wished her words included him. She saw him looking at her and flushed a little. "I'm so glad we got there first!"

"So'm I!"

"Jaxom!"

At Mirrim's shout, she moved back hastily.

"Scorch her!"

He grabbed Sharra's hand and ran with her toward the Hold, nor did he relinquish her hand when they entered the main Hall.

"Was I asleep an afternoon or a whole day?" Jaxom asked her in an undertone as he saw maps, charts, sketches and diagrams pinned on the walls and propped up on tables.

The Harper, his back to them, was bending over the

long dining table. Piemur was occupied in sketching something; Menolly was looking at whatever absorbed the Harper, and Mirrim stood at one side, bored and irritated. Fire-lizards peered down from the crossbeams. Every now and then, one would flick out of the room and another would swoop in the window to take its place. An aroma of roasting fish filled the air as a sea breeze began to clear away the day's heat.

"Brekke's going to be furious with us," Jaxom said to Sharra.

"With us? Why? We're keeping him completely occupied at a sedentary task."

"Stop mumbling, Sharra. Jaxom, come over here and add your mark to what the others have told me," Robinton said, skewing his body about to frown at them.

"Sir, Piemur, Menolly and Sharra have done a lot more exploring than I have."

"Yes, but they don't have Ruth and his way with fire-lizards. Can he help us sort out their conflicting and confusing images?"

"I'm certainly willing to help, Master Robinton," Jaxom said, "but I think you might be asking more of Ruth and those fire-lizards than they can do."

Master Robinton straightened up. "If you'd explain?"

"Granted that the fire-lizards seem to share violent mutual experiences like . . . ." Jaxom pointed in the direction of the Red Star, "and Canth's fall, and now, of course, the mountain. But these are all momentous events . . . not everyday routine."

"You did locate D'ram here in the Cove," Robinton said.

"And lucky at that. If I'd asked about men first, we'd never have got an answer," Jaxom replied with a grin.

"There was scarcely more detail to go on in your first venture."

"Sir?" Jaxom stared in stunned amazement because the Harper's drawl had been so deceptively mild, with just a slight emphasis on "first," yet the implication

had been unmistakable; somehow the Harper knew
Jaxom had rescued the egg. Jaxom shot an accusing
glance at Menolly, whose expression was slightly perplexed as if the Harper's subtle reference surprised
her, too.

"Come to think of it, I had much the same information from Zair," Master Robinton continued smoothly,
"but not the wit to interpret it as cleverly as you did.
My compliments, however belated," he inclined his
head and went on as swiftly as if this were just some
passing matter, "on the way you handled the feat. Now,
if you and Ruth can turn your fine perceptions to
today's problem, we can save ourselves endless hours
of vain effort. As before, Jaxom, time is against us.
This Plateau," Robinton tapped the sketches before
him, "cannot remain a secret. It is the heritage of
everyone on Pern—"

"But it's in the east, Master Robinton, which is to be
dragonrider land," Mirrim said, her tone almost bel-
ligerent.

"Of course it is, my dear child," the Harper said
soothingly. "Now if Ruth could charm the fire-lizards
enough to focus their memories . . ."

"I'll certainly try, Master Robinton," Jaxom said
when the Harper regarded him expectantly, "but you
know how they are about . . ." and he pointed skyward. "They're nearly as incoherent about the eruption."

"As Sharra put it, the dream eye is unfocused,"
Menolly said, grinning at her friend.

"My point exactly," the Harper said, bringing the
flat of his hand down hard on the table. "If Jaxom,
through Ruth, can sharpen the focus, maybe those of
us with fire-lizards can get distinct and helpful images
from their minds, instead of this confusion of perspective."

"Why?" Jaxom asked. "We know the mountain
erupted. We know the settlement had to be abandoned,
that the survivors came north . . ."

"There's a lot we don't know, and we might find
some answers, perhaps even some equipment left

behind, just as the enlarging viewer was left in those deserted rooms at Benden Weyr. Look how that instrument has improved our understanding of our world and the heavens above us. Maybe even some models of those fascinating machines the old Records mention." He pulled the sketches over the map. "There are a lot of mounds, great and small, long and short. Some would have been for sleeping, storage, general living: some quite likely workhalls . . ."

"How do we even know that the ancients did things the way we do?" Mirrim demanded, "storage, and workhalls and such."

"Because, my dear child, neither human nature nor human needs have changed since the earliest Records we have."

"That doesn't mean they left anything in the mounds when they left the Plateau," Mirrim said, frankly dubious.

"The dreams have been consistent in some details," Robinton said with more patience for Mirrim's obstructionism than Jaxom would have accorded him. "The fiery mountain, the molten rock and lava raining down. People running . . ." He paused, looking expectantly at the others.

"People in a panic!" Sharra said. "They wouldn't have had time to take anything with them. Or very little!"

"They could have come back after the worst of the eruption was over," Menolly said. "Remember that time in western Tillek—"

"That's precisely what I had in mind," the Harper said, nodding approval.

"But, Master," Menolly went on, confused, "the ash spewed out of that volcano for weeks. The valley was eventually level with ash," she made a flat gesture with her hand, "and you could see nothing of what had been there for the debris."

"The prevailing wind on that plateau is southeast, and strong," Piemur said, and his gesture was one of sweeping clear. "Didn't you notice how strong it is?"

"That's precisely why something was left for us to

see from the air," the Harper said. "I know it's just an off-chance, Jaxom, but my feeling is that the eruption caught the ancients completely unaware. Why, I can't comprehend. Surely people who could hold the Dawn Sisters in the sky in a stationary position for who knows how many Turns ought to be wise enough to identify an active volcano. My surmise is that the eruption was spontaneous, totally unexpected. The people were caught going about their daily tasks in cot, hold, crafthall. If you can get Ruth to focus those disparate views, perhaps we could identify which of the mounds were important from the numbers of people coming from it, or them.

"I am not able to get to the Plateau to do my own exploring, but nothing prevents my brain from suggesting possibilities of what I'd do if I were there."

"We'll be your hands and legs," Jaxom offered.

"They'll be your eyes," Menolly added, gesturing to the fire-lizards on the crossbeams.

"I thought you'd see it my way," the Harper said, beaming fondly on them all.

"When would you like us to try?" Jaxom asked.

"Would tomorrow be too soon?" the Harper asked plaintively.

"All right by me. Piemur, Menolly, Sharra, I'll need you and your fire-lizards!"

"I can arrange to come, too," Mirrim said.

Jaxom caught Sharra's closed expression and realized that Mirrim's presence would be as unwelcome to her as to himself.

"I don't think that would work, Mirrim. Path would scare the Southern fire-lizards away!"

"Oh, don't be ridiculous, Jaxom," Mirrim replied, brushing aside that argument.

"He's right, Mirrim. Look out in the Cove right now. Not a single fire-lizard that isn't banded," Menolly said. "They all disappear the minute they see any other dragon but Ruth."

"It's ridiculous. I have three of the best-trained fire-lizards in Pern . . ."

"I must agree with Jaxom," the Harper said, smiling

with sincere apology to the Benden dragongirl. "And, though I quite agree that yours are undoubtedly the best-trained fire-lizards in Pern, we don't have time for the Southern ones to get used to Path."

"Path needn't be in evidence—"

"Mirrim, the decision has been made," Robinton said firmly, with no trace of a smile now.

"Well, that's plain enough. Since I'm not needed here . . ." She stalked out of the hall.

Jaxom noticed the Harper's gaze following her, and he felt acutely embarrassed by her display of temperament. He could see that Menolly was also disturbed.

"Is her Path proddy today?" the Harper asked Menolly quietly.

"I don't think so, Master Robinton."

Zair chittered on the Harper's shoulder and his expression changed to chagrin. "Brekke's come back. I was supposed to rest."

He half-ran out of the hall, turning briefly at the door to put his finger to his lips as he quickly ducked into his room. Piemur, his expression bland, took a step sideways to fill the space so precipitously vacated. Fire-lizards zipped into the room. Jaxom spotted Berd and Grall.

"Master Robinton really should have rested," Menolly said, nervously twitching sketches across the table surface.

"He wasn't exerting himself," Piemur pointed out. "This sort of thing is bread and meat to him. He was going out of his skull with boredom and with Brekke fussing over him when you weren't. It isn't as if he was up on the Plateau, digging about . . ."

"I told you, Brekke," F'nor said, his voice carrying from the porch as he and his weyrmate mounted the last step, "you worried for no reason at all."

"Menolly, how long has Master Robinton been resting?" Brekke asked, coming right up to the table.

"Half a skinful," Piemur replied, grinning as he pointed to the wine on the back of the chair, "and he went without a protest."

Brekke gave the young harper a long and searching

look. "I wouldn't trust you for a moment, Harper Pie-mur." Then she looked at Jaxom. "Have you been here all afternoon, too?"

"Me? No indeed. Ruth and I slept until Mirrim woke us."

"Where is Mirrim?" F'nor asked, glancing about.

"She's outside somewhere," replied Menolly in a voice so devoid of tone that Brekke glanced at her apprehensively.

"Has Mirrim been . . ." Brekke pressed her lips in a thin, disapproving line. "Drat that girl!" She looked up at Berd, and he immediately darted from the hall.

F'nor was bending over the maps now, shaking his head with pleased surprise.

"You lot work like twenty, don't you?" He grinned at all of them.

"Well, this part of the twenty has done quite enough work," Piemur said, stretching his arms until his joints cracked. "I want a swim, to wash the sweat from my brow, and the ink from my fingers. Anyone coming?"

Jaxom's acceptance was as enthusiastic as the two girls' and, with F'nor's jocular complaint about being deserted ringing in their ears, they all made for the beach. Jaxom managed to grab Menolly by the hand as Sharra and Piemur pelted around the bend.

"Menolly, how did Master Robinton know?"

She'd been laughing as they raced down the path, but now her eyes darkened.

"I didn't tell him, Jaxom. I didn't have to. I don't know when he figured it out. But the facts all point to you."

"How?"

She ticked off reasons on her fingers. "To start with, a dragon had to return the egg. Only way. Prefer-ably a dragon who was totally familiar with Benden Hatching Ground. The dragon had to be ridden by someone who wanted earnestly to return that egg, and who could find it!" The last qualification seemed to be the most important. "More people will figure out it was you now."

"Why now?"

"No one in the Southern Weyr returned Ramoth's egg." Menolly smiled up at Jaxom, and put her hand to his cheek, giving him an affectionate slap. "I was so proud of you, Jaxom, when I realized what you and Ruth had managed to do! Prouder even because you didn't noise it about. And it was so critical just then for Benden to believe that a Southern rider had relented and restored Ramoth's egg . . ."

"Hey, Jaxom, Menolly, c'mon!" Piemur's roar distracted them.

"Race you?" Menolly said, turning and dashing for the beach.

They weren't to have much time for their swim. Master Idarolan's ship reappeared, the blue full-catch pennant flying from its foremast. Brekke called them to help gut enough fish for the evening's meal. She wasn't certain how many of those now at the Plateau would return to Cove Hold for dinner but cooked fish could be served in rolls the next day, she said, cheerfully ignoring the protests. She sent Mirrim off with supplies for Master Wansor and N'ton, who planned to make an evening of star-watching or, as Piemur said irreverently, the Dusk-Dawn and Midnight Sisters.

"And what do you bet Mirrim tries to stay there the night, too, to see if Path does keep away the Southern fire-lizards?" Piemur asked, a slightly malicious grin on his face.

"Mirrim does have well-trained fire-lizards," Menolly said.

"And they sound just like her when they scold everyone else's friends," Piemur added.

"Now that's not fair," Menolly said. "Mirrim's a good friend of mine . . ."

"And as her best friend you ought to explain to her that she can't manage everyone on Pern!"

As Menolly prepared to take umbrage, dragons began popping into the air over the Cove, and with their bugling no one could hear anything else.

The dragons were not the only ones in good moods. An atmosphere of intense excitement and expectation pervaded the evening.

Jaxom was grateful for his afternoon's nap, for he wouldn't have missed that evening. All seven Weyrleaders were there, D'ram with some private news for F'lar's ears about the affairs in the Southern Weyr, and N'ton, who stayed only part of the evening since he was sky-watching with Wansor. There were also Mastercraftsmen Nicat, Fandarel, Idarolan, Robinton, and Lord Lytol.

To Jaxom's surprise, the three Oldtimer Weyrleaders, G'narish of Igen, R'mart of Telgar and D'ram now of Southern, were less interested in what might lie hidden in the settlement than N'ton, T'bor, G'dened and F'lar. The Oldtimers were far more eager to explore the broad lands and the distant range than dig to unearth their past.

"That *is* past," R'mart of Telgar said. "Past, dead, and very much buried. *We* have to live in the present, a trick, mind you, F'lar, that you taught us." He grinned to remove any sting from what he said. "Besides, wasn't it you, F'lar, who suggested that it's useless to muddle our brains thinking how the ancients did things . . . that it's better to build for ourselves what is useful for our times and Turn?"

F'lar grinned, amused to have his words returned. "I suppose I'm hoping that we'll find undamaged records somewhere, filling in the holes in what came down to us. Maybe even another useful item like the enlarger viewer we discovered in Benden Weyr."

"Look where that got us!" R'mart exclaimed, whooping with laughter.

"Undamaged instruments would be invaluable," Fandarel said, very solemn.

"We might just find you some, Master Robinton," Nicat said thoughtfully, "because only one section of that settlement sustained much damage." He had everyone's attention. "Look," he drew out a sketch of the general site, "the flow of lava is to the south. Here, here, and here, the cones of the mountains broke, and the flow followed the slope of the land, away from much of the settlement. The prevailing wind also carried the ash away from the place. From the little digging I did today, I found only a thin layer of volcanic debris."

"Is there only this one settlement? When they had a whole world to occupy?" asked R'mart.

"We'll find the others tomorrow," the Harper assured them, "won't you, Jaxom?"

"Sir?" Jaxom rose, half-startled by his unexpected inclusion in the main discussion.

"No, to be serious, R'mart, you may be quite correct," F'lar said, leaning forward across the table. "And we really don't know if the eruption made the ancients leave the Plateau immediately afterward."

"We won't know anything until we've entered one of those mounds and discovered what they left behind, if anything," N'ton said.

"Go carefully, Weyrleader," Master Nicat told N'ton, but his glance took in everyone. "Better still, I'll send a craftmaster and a few steady journeymen to direct the excavations."

"Show the tricks of your craft, eh, Master Nicat," R'mart said. "We'd better learn a thing or two about mining, right, Masterminer?"

Jaxom stifled a chuckle at the expression of puzzlement and then indignation on the Masterminer's face.

"Dragonriders mining?"

"Why not?" F'lar asked. "Thread will Pass. There'll be another Interval on us all too soon. I promise you one thing, with the Southern lands open, never again will the Weyrs be beholden to anyone during an Interval."

"Ah, yes, a very sound idea, Weyrleader, very sound," Master Nicat prudently agreed, though he would plainly need time to assimilate such a revolutionary idea.

The dragons lounging on the shore crooned a welcome to someone.

N'ton suddenly rose. "I must join Wansor in our star-watch. That must be Path and Mirrim returning. My duty to you all."

"I'll light your way, N'ton," Jaxom said, grabbing a glow basket and unshielding it.

They were well out of hearing range of the others when N'ton turned to Jaxom. "This is more to your fancy, isn't it, Jaxom, than flying tamely in the queens' wing?"

"I didn't do it on purpose, N'ton," Jaxom said with a laugh. "I just wanted to see the mountain before anyone else did."

"No hunch this time?"

"Hunch?"

N'ton threw a companionable arm about his shoulders, chuckling. "No, I suppose it was inspired by the fire-lizards' images."

"The mountain?"

N'ton gave him a bit of a shake. "Good man!"

They saw the dark bulk of a dragon settling to the beach and then two gleaming circles as Lioth turned his head toward them.

"A white dragon has an advantage at night," N'ton said as he pointed to the visible hide of Ruth a little to one side of his bronze.

I'm glad you've come. I've an itch I cannot reach, said Ruth.

"He's in need of attention, N'ton."

"Leave the glows with me then, I'll pass them on to Mirrim so she can find her way to the point."

They separated as Jaxom moved aside to attend to Ruth. He heard N'ton greet Mirrim, their voices carrying on the quiet night air.

"Of course, Wansor's all right," Mirrim said, sounding peevish. "He's got his eyes glued to that tube of his. He never knew I came, never ate the food I brought, never knew I left. And further," she paused, taking a deep breath, "Path did not scare away the Southern fire-lizards."

"Why would she?"

"*I'm* not allowed to be on the Plateau when Jaxom and the others try to coax some sense out of the Southerners."

"Sense? Oh, yes, seeing if Ruth can focus the fire-lizards' images. Well, I shouldn't worry about it, Mirrim. There are so many other things you can do."

"At least my dragon is not an unsexed runt, good for nothing but consorting with fire-lizards!"

"Mirrim!"

Jaxom heard the coldness in N'ton's voice; it matched the sudden freezing in his own guts. Mirrim's petulant comment resounded over and over in his ears.

"You know what I mean, N'ton . . ."

Just like Mirrim, Jaxom thought, not to heed the warning in N'ton's voice.

"You ought to," she went on with the impetus of grievance. "Wasn't it you who told F'nor and Brekke that you doubted if Ruth would ever mate? Where are you going, N'ton? I thought you were going . . ."

"You don't think, Mirrim!"

"What's the matter, N'ton?" The sudden panic in her voice afforded Jaxom some consolation.

Don't stop, Ruth said. *The itch is still there.*

"Jaxom?" N'ton's call was not loud, meant to reassure, but the sound carried back.

"Jaxom?" Mirrim cried. "Oh, no!" Then Jaxom heard her running away, saw the glow basket jolting, heard her weeping. Just like the girl, speak first, think later and weep for days. She'd be repentant and hanging on about him, driving him *between* with her need to be forgiven her thoughtlessness.

"Jaxom!" N'ton was anxious.

"Yes, N'ton?" Jaxom dutifully continued to scratch Ruth's backbone, wondering why Mirrim's cruel remark did not rankle as it ought. Sexless runt! As he saw N'ton striding toward him, he was aware of a curious sense of relief, of relaxation deep inside him. The memory of those riders, waiting for the Fort green to mate, flashed through his mind. Yes, he'd been relieved then that Ruth had proved disinterested. He could somewhat regret that Ruth would be deprived of that experience; but he was relieved that he would never be called upon to endure it.

"You must have heard her." There was a tinge of hope in N'ton's voice that Jaxom hadn't.

"I heard. Sound carries near water."

"Blast the girl! Scorch the girl! We were going to explain . . . then you took the fire-head, and now this. The opportunity hasn't presented itself . . ." N'ton's explanations came out in a rush.

"I can live with it. Like Mirrim's Path, there are other things we can do."

N'ton's groan came from his guts. "Jaxom!" His fingers closed tightly on Jaxom's shoulder, trying in the contact to express his inarticulate regret.

"It's not your fault, N'ton."

"Does Ruth comprehend what was said?"

"Ruth comprehends that his back itches." Even as Jaxom said it, he found it curious that Ruth was not the least bit upset.

There, you have the exact spot. Harder now.

Jaxom could feel the slightly flaky dryness in the otherwise loose and soft hide.

"I think I guessed, N'ton," Jaxom went on, "that time at Fort Weyr, that something was wrong. I know K'nebel expected Ruth to rise for the green. I thought that Ruth, being born small, maybe would mature later than other dragons do."

"He's as mature as he'll ever be, Jaxom!"

Jaxom was rather touched by the genuine regret in the bronze rider's voice.

"So? He's my dragon and I'm his rider. We are to-gether!"

"He's unique!" N'ton's verdict was fervent, and he stroked Ruth's hide with affectionate respect. "So, my young friend, are you!" He gripped Jaxom's shoulder again, letting the gesture stand for words unsaid. Lioth crooned in the darkness beyond them and Ruth, turn-ing his head toward the bronze dragon, made a courte-ous response.

Lioth is a fine fellow. His rider is a kind man. They are good friends!

"We are ever your friends," N'ton said, giving Jaxom's shoulder a final, almost painful squeeze. "I must get to Wansor. You're sure you're all right?"

"Go along, N'ton. I'll just settle Ruth's itch!"

The Fort Weyrleader hesitated one more moment

before he pivoted and walked quickly toward his
bronze.

"I think I'd better oil that patch, Ruth," Jaxom said.
"I've been neglecting you lately."

Ruth's head came around, his eyes gleamed more
brilliantly blue in the darkness. *You never neglect me.*

"I have too, or you wouldn't be patchy!"

There has been much for you to do!

"There's a fresh pot of oil in the kitchen. Hold
tight."

His eyes accustomed to the tropic darkness, Jaxom
made his way to the Hold, found the pot in the kitchen
press and trotted back. He was conscious of a weariness, in mind and body. Mirrim was the most awkward
person! If he'd let her and Path come . . . Well, he'd
have learned the verdict on Ruth sooner or later. *Why*
wasn't Ruth upset? Maybe if he had been completely
willing for his dragon to experience that part of his
personality, Ruth would have matured. Jaxom railed
at the fact that they had always been kept from being
full dragon and rider: brought up as they were in the
Hold, instead of the Weyr where the mating of dragons was an understood and accepted fact of the weyr
life. It wasn't as if Ruth were immune to sexual experience. He was always present when Jaxom had sex.

*I love with you and I love you. But my back itches
fiercely.*

That was clear enough, Jaxom thought as he hurried through the forest to his dragon.

Someone was with Ruth, scratching his back for him.
If it was Mirrim . . . Jaxom strode forward angrily.

Sharra is with me, Ruth told him calmly.

"Sharra?" Swallowing an irrational surge of anger,
he acknowledged her presence. "I've got the oil. Ruth's
got a bad flaky patch. I've been neglecting him."

"You've never neglected Ruth," she said so emphatically that Jaxom had to smile in surprise.

"Did Mirrim . . ." He began, holding the oil pot
out so she could dip her hand in.

"Yes, and no sympathy from any of us, let me assure you." Her anger translated itself to an overly hard

rub on Ruth's back that made him complain. "Sorry, Ruth. They sent Mirrim back to Benden!"

Jaxom glanced up the beach to where Path had landed and, indeed, the green dragon was gone.

"And you were sent to me?" He found he didn't mind Sharra: her presence was, in fact, a boon.

"Not sent . . ." Sharra faltered. "I was . . . I was called!" She finished her sentence in a rush.

"Called?" Jaxom left off rubbing oil into Ruth's back and looked at her. Her face was a pale blur with dark spots for her eyes and mouth.

"Yes, called. Ruth called me. He said Mirrim . . ."

"He said?" Jaxom interrupted her as her words finally sank in. "You can hear Ruth?"

She needed to hear me when you were sick, Jaxom, Ruth said at the same moment Sharra was saying out loud, "I've been able to hear him ever since you were so ill."

"Ruth, why did you call Sharra?"

She is good for you. You need her. What Mirrim said, even what N'ton said but he was kinder, has made you close up. I do not like it when I cannot hear your mind. Sharra will open it for us.

"Will you do that for us, Sharra?"

This time Jaxom didn't hesitate. He took Sharra's hands, oily as they were, and drew her to him, inordinately pleased that she was so nearly his height and her mouth so close to his. All he had to do was tilt his head slightly.

"I would do anything for you, Jaxom, anything for you and Ruth!" Her lips moved delightfully against his until he made more speech impossible.

A warmth began in his belly, dispelling the cold closeness that distressed his dragon and himself—a warmth that had to do with Sharra's lithe body against his, the scent of her long heavy hair in his nostrils as he kissed her, the pressure of her arms on the skin of his back. And her hands, flat against his waist, were not the hands of a healer, but the hands of a lover.

They made love in the soft warm darkness, delighting in each other and fully responsive to the moment of ecstasy that came, totally aware that Ruth loved with them.

CHAPTER XX

At the Mountain and at Ruatha Hold, 15.10.18–15.10.20

JAXOM COULD NOT FEEL easy looking at the eastern face of the mountain. He arranged himself, Sharra and Ruth so that they did not have to see it. The other five made themselves comfortable in a loose semicircle about Ruth.

The seventeen banded fire-lizards—for at the last moment, Sebell and Brekke asked to be included in the group—settled on Ruth's back. The more trained fire-lizards, the better, reasoned Master Robinton, which, he went on to say, gave him the chance to include Zair.

Word of the ancients' settlement at the high Plateau had spread throughout Pern with a swiftness that had amazed even the Harper. Everyone clamored to see the place. F'lar sent the message that if Jaxom and Ruth were to prod the fire-lizards' memories, they'd better do so quickly, or not at all.

Once Ruth had settled, the Southern fire-lizards began arriving in fairs, led by their queens, dipping toward Ruth who crooned a greeting as Jaxom had suggested he do.

They are pleased to see me, Ruth told Jaxom. *And happy that men come to this place again.*

"Ask them about the first time they saw men."

Jaxom caught an instant image from Ruth of many dragons arriving over the shoulder of the mountain.

"That's not what I meant."

I know, Ruth acknowledged with regret. *I will ask again. Not the time with the dragons, but a long time ago, before the mountain blew up.*

The reaction of the fire-lizards was predictable and discouraging. They flew up from their perches on and about Ruth and did wild sky-dances, chittering and bugling in dismay.

Disappointed, Jaxom turned to see Brekke's hand raised, a look of intense concentration on her face. He relaxed against Ruth, wondering what arrested her attention. Menolly also held up her hand. She was sitting near enough to Jaxom so that he saw her eyes were totally unfocused. On her shoulder, Beauty had assumed a rigid position, her eyes wheeling violently red. Above their circle, the fire-lizards chattered and continued their wild gyrations.

They are seeing the mountain on fire, said Ruth. *They see people running, the fire following them. They are afraid as they were afraid so long ago. This is the very dream we used to have.*

"Can you see the mounds? Before they were covered?" In his excitement, Jaxom forgot and spoke aloud.

I see only people running, this way and that. No, they are running toward . . . toward us? Ruth looked about him as if he half-expected to be overrun, so vivid were the fire-lizard images.

"Toward us, and then where?"

Down to the water? Ruth wasn't sure himself, and turned to look toward the distant, invisible sea.

They are afraid again. They don't like remembering the mountain.

"Any more than they like remembering the Red Star," Jaxom said imprudently. Every fire-lizard disappeared, including the banded ones.

"That did it, Jaxom," Piemur said in deep disgust.

"You can't mention that bloody Red Star in front of fire-lizards. Flaming mountains, but not red stars."

"Undeniably," Sebell said in his deep quiet voice, "there are moments that are branded in the minds of our little friends. When they start remembering, everything else is excluded."

"It is association," Brekke said.

"What we need then," Piemur said, "is another spot that strikes less distressing memories in them. Memories . . . useful . . . to us . . ."

"Not so much that," Menolly considered her words carefully, "as interpretation. I saw something. I think I'm right . . . it wasn't the big mountain that erupted, it was . . ." She turned, and pointed to the smallest of the three. "That's the one that blew in our dreams!"

"No, it was the big one," Piemur contradicted, pointing higher.

"You're wrong, Piemur," Brekke said with quiet certainty. "It was the smallest one . . . everything is to the left in my images. The big mountain is too much higher than the one I'm sure I saw."

"Yes, yes," Menolly said, excited. "The angle is important. The fire-lizards couldn't see that high! Remember they're much, much smaller. And see, the angle. It's right!" She was on her feet, gesturing to illustrate her points. "People came from there, running this way, away from the smallest volcano! They came from those mounds. The largest ones!"

"That's the way I saw it," Brekke agreed. "Those mounds there!"

"So do we start with these?" F'lar asked, the next morning, sighing at the task of unearthing a small hill. Lessa stood beside him, surveying the silent mounds, with the Master Smith, Masterminer Nicat, F'nor and N'ton. Jaxom, Piemur, Sharra and Menolly remained discreetly to one side. "This large one?" he asked, but his eyes swept down the parallel ranks, squinting with resignation.

"We could be digging until the Pass is done," Lessa said, slapping her riding gloves against her thigh as she, too, did a slow thoughtful survey of the sprawl of anonymous earthen lumps.

"A vast area," Fandarel said, "vast! A larger settlement than the combined Holds at Fort and Telgar." He glanced up in the direction of the Dawn Sisters. "They *all* came from those?" He shook his head, staggered by the concept. "Where to start to best effect?"

"Is everyone on Pern coming here today?" Lessa asked as a bronze dragon burst into the air over their heads. "D'ram's Tiroth! With Toric?"

"I doubt we could exclude him if we wished, and it would be unwise to try," F'lar remarked in a droll tone.

"True," she replied and then smiled at her weyrmate. "I rather like him," she added, surprised at her own verdict.

"My brother makes himself likable," Sharra said quietly to Jaxom, a curious smile on her lips. "But to trust him?" She shook her head slowly, watching Jaxom's face. "He is a very ambitious man!"

"He's taking a good look, isn't he?" N'ton remarked, watching the circling dragon's lazy downward glide.

"It's worth looking at," F'nor replied, scanning the broad, mounded expanse.

"Is that Toric aloft?" Master Nicat asked, digging his boot toe into the large mound. "Glad he's here. He sent for me when he found those mine shafts in the Western Range."

"I'd forgot he's already had some experience with the ancients' handiwork," F'lar said.

"He's also got experienced men to help us without having to go back to the Lord Holders," N'ton said with a knowing grin.

"Whom I don't want too interested in these eastern lands," Lessa said firmly.

When D'ram and Toric had dismounted, Tiroth glided down the grassy plain to where the other dragons were lounging on an outcropping of sun-warmed rock. As Toric and the bronze rider walked toward them, Jaxom regarded the Southerner with Sharra's remarks in his mind. Toric was a big man, as big as

390

Master Fandarel in build and height. His hair was sun-streaked, his skin a deep brown and, while his smile was broad, there was a certain arrogant self-possession in the very way he strode that suggested he felt himself the equal of any awaiting him. Jaxom wondered just how that attitude would strike the Benden Weyr-leaders.

"You certainly have discovered the Southern Continent, haven't you, Benden?" he said, gripping F'lar's arm in greeting and bowing as he smiled at Lessa. He nodded and murmured the name of the other leaders and masters present, glancing beyond them with a raking look at the younger people. When Toric's eyes came back to his face, just briefly, Jaxom knew he'd been identified. Resenting the way Toric's glance slid from him, as if he were negligible, he stiffened. Then he felt Sharra's hand lightly on his arm.

"He does that to irritate," she said in a very soft voice, with a ripple of her rich laughter in it. "Most of the time it's effective."

"It puts me in mind of the way my milk-brother used to tease me in front of Lytol, when he knew I couldn't retaliate," Jaxom said, surprising himself with such an unexpected comparison. He saw her approval in her dancing eyes.

"Trouble is," Toric was saying, his voice carrying to them, "that the ancients didn't leave much behind. Not if they could move it elsewhere and use it. Saving people they were!"

"Oh?" F'lar's exclamation invited Toric to explain.

The Southerner shrugged. "We've been through the mine shafts they left. They'd even pulled up the rails for their ore carts, and the brackets where they must have hung lights. One place had a largish shelter at the mouth," he gestured toward the smallest nearby mound, "about that size, carefully shut against the weather and totally bare inside. Again, you could see where things had been bolted to the floor. They'd prized the bolts out, too."

"If this thriftiness applies here," Fandarel said, "then if anything is likely to be found, it will be in those mounds." He pointed to a smaller cluster on the edge of the settlement nearest the lava flow. "They would have been too hot or too dangerous to approach for a long time."

"And if too hot to approach, what makes you think anything survived the heat?" Toric demanded.

"Because the mound has survived to this time," Fandarel replied as if he were only being logical.

Toric regarded him for a moment and then clouted the Smith on the shoulder. He was oblivious to the startled look awarded him by Fandarel, whom men tended to treat with distant respect.

"Point in your favor, Mastersmith," Toric said. "I'll dig gladly with you and hope you're right."

"I'd like to see what's in the smaller humps," Lessa said, wheeling and indicating one. "There are such a lot of them. Maybe they were used as small holds. Surely something would be left behind in the rush to leave."

"What would they have had in such big places?" F'lar asked, kicking at the grassy roundness of the large one nearest him.

"There're hands enough and . . ." Toric took three long strides to the pile of digging implements, "plenty of shovels and picks for everyone to take a dig at the mound of his choice." He picked up a long-handled shovel and tossed it to the Mastersmith, who caught it in a reflex action as he stared, bemused, at the big Southerner. Toric shouldered another shovel, selected two picks and with no more discussion strode toward the cluster of mounds that were the Smith's choice.

"Presuming Toric's theory is correct, is it worth digging here?" F'lar asked his weyrmate.

"What we found in that long-forgotten room at Benden Weyr was obviously a discard of the ancients. And after all, mining equipment they could have used elsewhere. Besides, I want to *see* what's inside." Lessa said that with such determination that F'lar laughed.

"I guess I do, too. And I do wonder what they'd do in this size place! It's big enough to weyr a dragon or two!"

"We'll help you, Lessa," Sharra said, urging Jaxom to pick a tool.

"Menolly, shall we assist F'lar?" F'nor directed the Harper girl toward the tools.

N'ton shook his head as he hefted spade and pick. "Master Nicat, what's your preference?"

The Masterminer looked about him dubiously but his eyes kept returning to the mounds nearest the mountain toward which Toric and Fandarel moved purposefully. "I think our good Mastersmith might have the right of it. But we'll spread the effort. And try those." He pointed with sudden decision toward the sea side of the Plateau, where six smallish mounds made a loose circle.

It was not work to which any of them were accustomed despite the fact that Master Nicat had begun as an apprentice miner in the pits, and Master Fandarel still took long turns at the forges when he worked on something particularly intricate.

Jaxom, sweat pouring from his face and body, had the distinct feeling that he was under surveillance. But when he leaned on the pick for an occasional breather, or lifted colonies of grubs safely to one side, he could see no one looking in his direction. The sensation bothered him.

The big one watches you, Ruth said suddenly.

Jaxom shot a glance under his arm at the mound where Toric and Master Fandarel were working and, sure enough, Toric was looking in his direction. Beside him, Lessa groaned suddenly, jamming her shovel blade into the rough-rooted grass of the mound. She examined her hands, reddened and beginning to blister.

"It's a long time since these have worked so hard," she said.

"Use your flying gloves?" Sharra suggested.

"A few moments in them and my hands would swim in sweat," Lessa replied, grimacing. She glanced at the other work parties and, chuckling to herself, sank gracefully to the mound. "Much as I dislike revealing this site to more people than necessary, I think we shall have to recruit strong hands and backs." She deftly captured a tangle of grubs and deposited them to one side, watching them tunnel back into the rich gray-black soil. She rubbed particles between her thumbs and forefinger. "Like ash. Gritty. Never thought I'd be dealing in ashes again. Did I ever tell you, Jaxom, that I was cleaning the fireplace in Ruatha Hold the day your mother arrived?"

"No," Jaxom said, surprised at this unexpected confidence. "But then, few people ever mention my parents to me."

Lessa's expression became severe. "Now I wonder why I called Fax to mind . . ." she said, glancing in Toric's direction and adding, more to herself than to Jaxom and Sharra, "except he was ambitious, too. But Fax made mistakes."

"Such as taking Ruatha Hold from its rightful Bloodline," Jaxom said, grunting as he swung the pick.

"That was his worst mistake," Lessa said with intense satisfaction. Then she noticed Sharra staring at her and smiled. "Which I rectified. Oh, Jaxom, leave off a moment. Your enthusiasm exhausts me." She mopped at the perspiration on her forehead. "Yes, I think some strong backs will have to be drafted. At least for my mound!" She patted it, almost affectionately. "There's no telling how deep the covering goes. Perhaps," the thought amused her, "the mounds aren't big at all, just so overloaded. We may end up with nothing larger than a wherhole for all our digging."

Jaxom, conscious of Toric's scrutiny, continued to dig, though his shoulders ached and his hands were hot and stiff with blister.

Just then, Sharra's two fire-lizards popped into the air, chirruping at each other as if they didn't understand what their friend was doing. They dropped lightly to the spot where Sharra had just planted her shovel and, with tremendous energy, they began to dig, their strong forepaws lifting the dirt to either side, their hindquarters pushing it farther out of the way. They had tunneled almost an arm's length while Lessa, Sharra and Jaxom watched in amazement.

"Ruth? Would you lend us your aid?" Jaxom called.

The white dragon obediently rose from his sunny perch and glided over to his friend, his eyes beginning to whirl more quickly with curiosity.

"Would you mind digging holes for us, Ruth?"

Where? Here? Ruth indicated a spot to the left of the fire-lizards who had not stopped their efforts.

"I don't think it matters where, we just want to see what the grass covers!"

No sooner had the other dragonriders seen what Ruth was doing than they called on theirs. Even Ramoth felt inclined to lend her aid, with Lessa giving her every encouragement.

"I wouldn't have believed it," Sharra said to Jaxom. "Dragons digging?"

"Lessa wasn't too proud to dig, was she?"

"We're people, but they're dragons!"

Jaxom couldn't help laughing at her incredulity. "You've got a jaundiced view of dragons, living among the Oldtimers' lazy beasts." He caught her about the waist, pulling her toward him before he felt her stiffen. He looked in Toric's direction. "He's not watching, if that's what you're worried about."

"He might not have been," she pointed skyward, "but his fire-lizards are. I'd wondered where they were."

A trio of fire-lizards, a golden queen and two bronzes, were circling lazily above Jaxom and Sharra.

"So? I'll just speak to Master Robinton to mediate . . ."

"Toric has other plans for me . . ."

"Am I not included in your plans?" Jaxom asked, experiencing sudden shock.

"You know you are, which is why . . . we loved each other. I wanted you while I could." Sharra's eyes were troubled.

"Why should he interfere then? My rank is . . ." Jaxom took both her hands in his and retained them when she tried to pull away.

"He doesn't think much of the young Northern men, Jaxom. Not after coping with fairs of younger sons in the past three Turns who are really," Sharra sounded exasperated, "enough to try the patience of a harper. I know you're not like them, but Toric . . ."

"I'll prove myself to Toric, never fear." Jaxom brought her hands to his lips, holding her eyes with his, determined by the force of his will to banish the unhappiness in her eyes. "And I'll do it properly, through Lytol and Master Robinton. You will be my lady, won't you, Sharra?"

"You know I will, Jaxom. For as long as I can . . ."

"For as long as we live . . ." he corrected her, gripping her hands tight enough to make her wince.

"Jaxom! Sharra!" cried Lessa, who had been far too engrossed in Ramoth's industry to notice their quiet exchange.

Jaxom felt Sharra's hands struggle but, having decided to confront Toric in all his arrogance, Jaxom was not about to defer before Lessa. He kept a tight hold on Sharra as they turned toward the Weyrwoman.

"Come and see. Ramoth has struck something solid. And it doesn't look like rock . . ."

Jaxom pulled Sharra up the slight incline to Lessa's side of the mound. Ramoth was sitting back on her haunches, peering over Lessa to look into the trench her forepaws had scored.

"Move your head slightly, Ramoth. You're in my light," Lessa said. "Here, take my shovel, Jaxom, and see what you think. Clear out a bit more dirt."

Jaxom jumped into a trench which reached to midthigh. "Feels solid enough," he said, pressing his weight down before he tapped with the shovel. "Sounds like stone?" But it didn't. The shovel thunked echoingly. Scraping clear a long swath, Jaxom stepped aside for all to see.

"F'lar, come here! We've reached something!"

"So have we!" came the Weyrleader's triumphant reply.

There was a mutual inspection from one dragon-dug trench to the other which exposed much the same material, except that in F'lar's case the rocklike substance had an amber panel set into the curve of the mound.

Finally the Mastersmith raised his huge arms above his head and roared for silence.

"This is not efficient use of time and energy." A loud guffaw, almost contemptuous in agreement, came from Toric. "It is not funny," the Smith said at his most serious. "We will concentrate on Lessa's mound since it is smaller. Then we will work on Master Nicat's and then . . ." He pointed to his own choice as Toric interrupted.

"All in one day?" he asked, again with a tone of supercilious derision that irritated Jaxom.

"We will do as much as we can, certainly, so let us begin!"

Jaxom decided that the Smith chose to ignore Toric's attitude, an example for him to follow.

It also proved inefficient to have more than two dragons working on Lessa's small mound since it was scarcely longer than a dragon. So F'lar and N'ton urged their bronzes to help Master Nicat.

By midafternoon the curving sides of Lessa's mound had been unearthed to the original floor of the valley. Six panels, three on an arc of the curved roof, tantalized, but their surface, once undoubtedly transparent, was now badly scored and darkened. Attempts to see through to the interior were vain. Disappointing, but no openings were found on the long sides so one end was promptly dug out. The dragons, despite the gray-black dust that now dulled their hides, showed no sign of fatigue and considerable interest in this unlikely task. And shortly the access was unearthed.

A door, made of an opaque form of the material used in the roof panels, slid across the opening on rails. The dirt-clogged tracks had to be cleared and dragon-hide oil applied to the runners before the door could be forced wide enough to permit entry. Lessa, all set to enter first, was restrained by the Smith's hand.

"Wait! The air inside is sick with age! Smell! Let fresh air in first. The place has been shut who knows how many Turns!"

The Smith, Toric and N'ton, set their shoulders to the door and forced it fully open. The air that flooded out was fetid, and Lessa stepped back, sneezing and coughing. Dim rectangles of tan light fell on a dusty floor, touched cracked and water-stained walls. As Lessa and F'lar, followed by the others, made their way into the small building, dust swirled under their boots.

"What was it for?" Lessa asked in a hushed voice.

Toric, unnecessarily ducking his head, for the top of the doorway cleared even his height by another hand's breadth, pointed to a far corner, to the now-visible remnants of a wide, wooden frame.

"Someone could have slept on that!" He turned to the other corner, and then with a sudden movement that made Lessa gasp, he stooped and came up with an object which he then made a show of presenting to her. "A treasure from the past!"

"It's a spoon!" Lessa held it up for all to see, then ran her fingers over its shape. "But what's it made of? It's no metal I've ever seen. Certainly it's not wood. It's more like . . . like the panels, and the door, only transparent. But it's strong," and she tried to bend it.

The Smith asked to examine the spoon. "It does seem to be a similar material. Spoons and windows, huh? Hmmmm!"

Overcoming a sense of awe at being inside such an ancient place, everyone began to examine the interior. Shelves and cabinets had once hung on the walls, for marks of paint left outlines. The structure had once been partitioned into sections and there were distinct gouges in the tough material of the floor to indicate that large permanent objects had rested here and there. In one corner, Fandarel discovered circular outlets, leading down. When he checked the exterior, he had to assume that the piping went through the wall and underground. One, he maintained, was undoubtedly for water. But the other four puzzled him.

"Surely they can't all be empty!" Lessa said in a wistful tone, trying to hide a disappointment that everyone, Jaxom thought, was experiencing.

"One can assume," Fandarel said in a brisk voice when they had all left Lessa's building, "that many of these of the same shape were also living quarters for the ancients. They would, I feel, take all their personal things with them. I think we ought then to devote more effort to the larger or the much smaller places."

Then, without waiting to see if anyone concurred with his opinion, the Smith marched straight to the interrupted excavation of Nicat's mound. This building was square and once they had uncovered enough of the top to notice the same roof panels, they concentrated their efforts on the inner end. The tropical night was quickly descending when they finally unearthed the entrance, but they couldn't quite clear the door tracks to open it more than a crack. They were barely able to make out some sort of decorations on the walls. No one had thought to bring glow baskets with them and this second disappointment drained the last of their energy so that no one even suggested sending fire-lizards for glows.

Leaning against the half-open panel, Lessa gave a tired laugh and looked down at her muddied condition. "Ramoth says she's tired and dirty and wants a bath."

"She's not the only one," F'lar promptly agreed. He made a vain effort to close the door, then laughed. "I don't suppose anything will happen overnight. Back to Cove Hold."

"You'll join us, Toric?" Lessa asked, cocking her head to look up at the big Southerner.

"I think not this evening, Lessa. I've a Hold to manage and cannot always please myself," he said. Jaxom saw the Southerner's eyes on him, the implication obvious to Jaxom. "All things being equal, I'll return tomorrow for a time to see if Fandarel's mound proves more profitable. Shall I bring more strong hands and spare your dragons?"

"Spare the dragons? They're enjoying themselves hugely," Lessa said. "*I* need the relief. What do you think, F'lar? Or should we draft some Benden riders?"

"I can appreciate that you'd like to keep this for yourself," Toric went on, smoothly, his eyes on F'lar. "This Plateau will have to be available to everyone,"

F'lar said, ignoring Toric's implication. "And since dragons enjoy earth-moving . . ."

"I'd like to bring Benelek with me tomorrow, F'lar," said the Master Smith, rubbing his gray-mudded hands together and flicking off the dried pellets off his clothes. "And two other lads with good imaginations . . ."

"Imagination? Yes, you'll need a lot of that here to make sense out of what the ancients have left for you," Toric said, the faintest hint of scorn in his tone. "When you're ready, D'ram?"

For some reason Toric's manner toward the old Weyrleader was more respectful than to anyone else. At least to Jaxom's sensitive ears. He was inwardly seething over Toric's insinuation that he did not manage his own Hold but pleased himself. He seethed because it was a valid accusation. Yet why, Jaxom sought to console himself, would anyone have expected him to return tamely to Ruatha, which prospered under Lytol's expert management, when all the excitement in the world was happening here? He felt Sharra's fingers curl around his arm, and he reminded himself of his own analogy between Toric and Dorse.

"I'll have a job getting Ruth clean," he said with a rueful sigh as he undid Sharra's fingers from his arm and clasped them tightly, drawing her with him to Ruth.

As the dragons broke from *between* over the Cove, the Harper's tall figure was visible on the beach, his impatience to hear of their explorations echoed by the fire-lizards who did dizzy spirals about him. When he saw the state the group was in, and how impatient they were to swim clean, he simply divested himself of his clothes and swam from one to another, hearing their reports.

It was an altogether deflated group that sat about the fire that evening.

"There's no guarantee, is there," the Harper said, "that even if we had the energy to excavate all those hundreds of mounds, we'd find anything of value left behind."

Lessa held up her spoon with a laugh. "No intrinsic

value, but it does give me a tremendous thrill to hold something my hundred-times ancestress might have used!"

"Efficiently made, too," Fandarel said, politely taking the small object and examining it again. "The substance fascinates me." He bent toward the flames to scrutinize it. "If I could just . . ." and he reached for his belt knife.

"Oh, no you don't, Fandarel," Lessa said in alarm and retrieved her artifact. "There were other bits and pieces of the same stuff discarded in my building. Experiment on them."

"Is that all we are to have of the ancients, their bits and pieces?"

"I remind you, F'lar," Fandarel said, "their discards have already proved invaluable." The Smith then indicated the spot where Wansor's distance-viewer had been sited. "What men have once learned to do, can be relearned. It will take time and experimentation but . . ."

"We've only begun, my friends," said Nicat, whose enthusiasm had not been daunted. "And as our good Smith says, we can learn even from their discards. With your permission, Weyrleaders, I'd like to bring some experienced teams, and go about the excavations methodically. There may have been good reasons for the rank system. Each file might belong to a different craft or—"

"You don't believe, as Toric suggests, that they took everything with them?" F'lar asked.

"That's irrelevant," Nicat said, dismissing Toric's contentions. "The bed, for instance, was unneeded because they knew they could obtain wood wherever they went. The little spoon for another, because they could make more. There may be other pieces, useless to them, which might very well form the missing elements of the Records which did come down to us, in whatever mutilated fashion. Just think, my friends," Nicat held up one finger along his nose, closing an eye conspiratorially, "the sheer quantity they had to take from those buildings after the eruption. Oh, we'll find things, never fear!"

"Yes, they had to take great loads from those buildings after the eruption," Fandarel murmured, frowning as he lowered his chin to his chest in deep thought. "Where did they take their possessions? Certainly, not immediately to establish Fort Hold!"

"Yes, where did they go?" F'lar asked, puzzled.

"As far as we could tell from the fire-lizard images, they headed toward the sea," Jaxom said.

"And the sea wouldn't have been safe," Menolly said.

"The sea wouldn't," F'lar said, "but there's a lot of land between the Plateau and the sea." He stared at Jaxom a moment. "Can you get Ruth to find out from the fire-lizards where they did go?"

"Does that mean I can't excavate more thoroughly?" Nicat asked, sounding irritable.

"By all means, if you've the men to spare."

"I do," Nicat replied a bit grimly. "With three mines worked out."

"I thought you'd started to reopen the shafts Toric found in the Western Range?"

"We've been examining them, to be sure, but my Hall hasn't reached a miner's agreement with Toric yet."

"With Toric? Does he hold those lands? They're far to the southwest, well beyond Southern Hold," F'lar said, abruptly intent.

"It was an exploring party of Toric's which located the shafts," Nicat said, his eyes shifting from the Benden Weyrleader's to the Harper's and then to the Smith's.

"I told you my brother was ambitious," Sharra said softly to Jaxom.

"An exploring party?" F'lar seemed to relax again. "That doesn't make it a Holding then. At all events, mines come under your jurisdiction, Master Nicat. Benden supports your decision. I'll just have a word with Toric tomorrow."

"I think we should," Lessa said, holding her hand out to F'lar to assist her from the sands.

"I was hopeful you'd support my Hall," the Miner said with a bow of gratitude, his shrewd eyes glinting in the firelight.

"I'd say a talk was long overdue," the Harper remarked.

The dragonriders took their leave quickly, N'ton to deliver Master Nicat to Crom Hold from where they'd collect him the next morning. Robinton took Master Fandarel with him to Cove Hall. Piemur dragged Menolly off to check on Stupid, leaving Jaxom and Sharra to douse the fire and clear the beach.

"Your brother doesn't plan to hold the entire Southwest, does he?" Jaxom asked when the others had dispersed.

"Well, if not all, as much as he can," Sharra replied with a laugh. "I'm not being disloyal to him telling you this, Jaxom. You have your own Hold. You don't want Southern lands. Or do you?"

Jaxom considered that.

"You don't, do you?" Sharra sounded anxious and put her hand on his arm.

"No, I don't," he said. "No, much as I love this Cove, I don't want it. Today on the Plateau, I'd have given anything for a cool breeze from Ruatha's mountain, or a plunge in my lake. Ruth and I will take you there—it's such a beautiful place. Only a dragon can get to it easily." He picked up a flat pebble and skated it across the quiet swells that lapped the white sands of the beach. "No, I don't want a Southern Hold, Sharra. I was born in Ruatha, bred to Ruatha. Lessa obliquely reminded me of that this afternoon. She reminded me, too, of the price of my Holding and of all she's done to insure that I remain Lord of Ruatha. You do realize, don't you, that her son, F'lessan, is a Ruathan halfblood. That's more than I am."

"But he's a dragonrider!"

"Yes, and weyrbred, by Lessa's choice so that I would remain the uncontested Lord of Ruatha. I'd better start acting like one!" He rose and drew Sharra up.

"Jaxom?" and her tone was suspicious, "what are you going to do?"

He put both hands on her arms, looking her squarely in the eyes. "I've a Hold to manage, too, as your brother reminded me . . ."

"But you're needed here, with Ruth. He's the only one who can make sense out of fire-lizard images . . ."

"And with Ruth, I can handle both responsibilities. Manage my Hold and please myself. You'll see!" He drew her closer to kiss her, but suddenly she broke away from him, pointing over his shoulder, her face mirroring hurt and anger. "What's the matter? What have I done, Sharra?"

She pointed to the tree where two fire-lizards were intently watching.

"Those are Toric's. He's watching me. Us!"

"Great! Let him have no mistake about my intentions toward you!" He kissed her until he felt her taut body responding to his, till the angry set of her lips dissolved into willingness. "I'd give him more to see but I want to get back to Ruatha Hold this evening!" He rapidly drew on his riding gear and called to Ruth. "I'll be back in the morning, Sharra. Tell the others, will you?"

Do we have to leave? Ruth asked even as he bent his foreleg for Jaxom to mount.

"We'll be back in no time, Ruth!" Jaxom waved to Sharra, thinking how forlorn she looked standing there in the starlight.

Meer and Talla circled once with Ruth, whistling so cheerfully that he knew Sharra had accepted his precipitous departure.

His abrupt compulsion to return to Ruatha and set in train the formalities of his confirmation as Lord Holder was by no means entirely due to Toric's barbed comments. His own suppressed sense of responsibility had been heightened by Lessa's odd nostalgia at the mound. But it had also occurred to him, at the fireside, that a man of Lytol's vitality and experience might find the Plateau's mysteries a challenge sufficient to replace Ruatha. His return to his birthplace had the same inexorable quality of his decision to rescue the egg.

He asked Ruth to take them to Ruatha. The sharp bitter cold of *between* was instantly replaced by a damp moist cold as they entered Ruatha's skies, leaden and showering a fine light snow that must have been in progress for some time to have piled drifts in the southeast corners of the courts.

I used to like snow, Ruth said as if encouraging himself to accept the return.

Wilth trumpeted from the fire-heights in surprised welcome. Half the fire-lizards of the Hold exploded into the air about them, giving raucous greetings and spurts of chittering complaint about the snow.

"We won't stay long, my friend," Jaxom reassured Ruth, and shuddered with the damp cold even in his warm flying gear. How had he forgot the season here?

Ruth landed in the courtyard just as the Great Hall door opened. Lytol, Brand and Finder surged to the steps.

"Is anything wrong, Jaxom?" Lytol cried.

"Nothing, Lytol, nothing. Can fires be laid in my quarters? I forgot it was winter here. Ruth is going to feel the difference even through dragonhide!"

"Yes, yes," Brand said, jogging across the court toward the kitchen, yelling for drudges to bring coal fires, while Lytol and Finder hurriedly ushered Jaxom up the steps. Ruth obediently followed the steward.

"You'll take a chill changing climates like this," Lytol was saying. "Why didn't you check? What brings you back?"

"Isn't it about time I did return?" Jaxom asked, striding to the fireplace as he stripped off his flying gloves and let his hands take warmth from the blaze. Then he burst out laughing as the other men joined him there. "Yes, at this fireplace!"

"What? At this fireplace?" Lytol asked, pouring wine for his ward.

"This morning, in the hot sun of the Plateau, while

we were digging up one of the mounds the ancients left to puzzle us, Lessa told me that she had been taking ashes out of this fireplace the day my unlamented sire, Fax, escorted my lady mother Gemma to this Hold!" He raised his cup in a toast to the memory of the mother he had never known.

"Which obliquely reminded you that you are Lord of Ruatha now?" Lytol inquired, a slight lift to the corner of his mouth. His eyes, which before had seemed so expressionless to Jaxom, twinkled in the firelight.

"Yes, and showed me where a man of your talents could be better used now, Lord Lytol."

"Oh, tell me more," Lytol said, gesturing to the heavy carved chair which had been placed to get the most benefit of the fire.

"Don't let me take your chair," Jaxom said courteously, noticing that the cushions bore the recent imprint of buttocks and thighs.

"I suspect you're about to take more than that, Lord Jaxom."

"Not without due courtesy," Jaxom said, dragging a small footstool beside the chair for his own use. "And a challenge in its place." He was relieved at Lytol's placid reaction. "Am I, sir, ready to be Lord of Ruatha Hold now?"

"Are you trained, do you mean?"

"That, too, but I had in mind the circumstances which have made it wiser to leave Ruatha in your charge."

"Ay, yes."

Jaxom keenly watched Lytol to see if there was any constraint in his manner as he answered.

"The circumstances have indeed altered over the past two seasons," Lytol almost laughed, "thanks to you, in great part."

"To me? Oh, that wretched illness. So, there is now no real bar to my confirmation as Lord Holder?"

"I see none."

Jaxom heard the harper's soft intake of breath but he was watching Lytol closely.

"So," Lytol almost smiled, "may I know what has prompted you? Surely not just the realization that pressure is eased in the North? Or is it that pretty girl? Sharra, is that her name?"

Jaxom laughed. "She's a large part of my haste," lightly emphasizing the last word and then catching Finder's grin from the corner of his eye.

"A sister to Toric of the Southern Hold, isn't she?" Lytol pursued the subject, testing the suitability of the match.

"Yes, and tell me, Lytol, has there been any move to confirm Toric as a major Lord Holder?"

"No, nor any rumor that he's asked to be." Lytol scowled as he reflected on that circumstance.

"What's your opinion of Toric, Lord Lytol?"

"Why do you ask? Certainly the match is suitable, even if he hasn't rank to match yours."

"He doesn't need the rank. He has the ambition," Jaxom said with sufficient rancor to attract the undivided attention of both guardian and harper.

"Ever since D'ram became Southern Weyrleader," Finder remarked in the silence that ensued, "I've heard it said that no holdless man is turned away."

"Does he promise them the right to hold what they can?" Jaxom asked, turning so quickly on Finder that the harper blinked in surprise.

"I'm not sure . . ."

"Two of Lord Groghe's sons have gone," Lytol said, pulling at his lower lip thoughtfully, "and my understanding from him is that they will hold. Of course, they retain their birthrank of Lords. Brand, what was Dorse promised?" he asked as the steward returned.

"Dorse? Has he gone south looking for a hold?" Jaxom gave a chuckle of relief and wonder.

"I saw no reason to refuse him the opportunity," Lytol replied calmly. "I didn't imagine you would object. Brand? What was promised him?"

"I think he was told he could have as much land as he wanted. I don't believe that the term *hold* came into the discussion. But then, the offer was made through one of the Southern traders, not directly from Toric."

"Still, if a man offered you land, you'd be grateful to him, and support him against those who had denied you land, wouldn't you?" Jaxom asked.

"Yes, gratitude would be reasonably expressed in loyalty," Lytol moved restlessly, considering another aspect of the situation. "However, it was clearly stated that the best land was too far from the protection of the Weyr. I gave Dorse one of our older flamethrowers, in good repair of course, with spare nozzles and hose," Lytol added.

"I'd give anything to watch Dorse in the open in Threadfall without a dragonrider in sight," Jaxom said.

"If Toric is as shrewd as he appears to be," Lytol said, "that may be the final consideration as to who may hold."

"Sir," Jaxom rose, finishing the rest of his wine, "I'll return tonight. Our blood's not yet thick enough for a snowstorm in Ruatha Hold. And there's a task set for Ruth and myself tomorrow. Would you be free to come South again? If Brand can hold matters in our absence?"

"At this time of year, I would welcome the sun," said Lytol.

Brand murmured that he could cope.

When Jaxom and Ruth returned to Cove Hold, grateful for the balmy warmth of the starlight night, Jaxom was more certain than ever that Lytol would not find the change hard to make. Even as Ruth circled to land, Jaxom felt himself relaxing in the warm air. He'd been very tense at Ruatha—tense not to rush Lytol and still achieve his own ends, and worried by the report of Toric's clever machinations.

He slid down Ruth's shoulder to the soft sand, at just the spot where he had so recently kissed Sharra. Thoughts of her were comforting. He waited until Ruth had curled into the still warm sand and then he made for the Hall, tiptoeing in, surprised to see even the Harper's room dark. It must be later than he thought in this part of the world.

He crept into his bed, heard Piemur mutter in his sleep. Farli, curled beside her friend, opened one lid to peer at him, before going back to sound sleep. Jaxom pulled the light blanket over him, thinking of the snows in Ruatha, and went gratefully to sleep.

He woke, abruptly, thinking that someone had called his name. Piemur and Farli were motionless in the crepuscular light that briefly heralded the dawn. Jaxom lay taut, expecting a repetition of that call, and heard none. The Harper? He doubted that, for Menolly was attuned to wake at his call. He touched Ruth's sleepy mind and knew that the dragon was only just rousing.

Jaxom was stiff. Maybe that was what had awakened him for his shoulders were cramped, the long muscles in his arms and across his midriff ached from yesterday's digging. His back was uncomfortably warm from the sun on that Plateau. It was too early to be up. He tried to court sleep but the discomforts of his muscles and skin were sufficient to keep him wakeful. He rose quietly so as not to disturb Piemur or be heard by Sharra. A swim would ease his muscles and soothe his burn. He paused by Ruth and found the white dragon waking, eager to join him for Ruth felt certain that all the mud had not been washed from his hide the evening before.

The Dawn Sisters were clearly sparkling in a sun which was not yet visible over the far horizon. Could his ancestors have gone back to them for refuge after the eruption? And how?

Wading out to his waist in the quiet Cove, Jaxom dove and swam under water, mysteriously dark without the sun to lighten its depths. Then he shot himself to the surface. No, there must have been some other sanctuary between the settlement and the sea. The flight had been channeled in one direction.

He called Ruth, reminding the grumbling white dragon that the sun would be much warmer on the Plateau. He collected his flying gear and grabbed some cold meatrolls from the larder, listening for a long moment to see if he had roused anyone else. He'd rather test his theory now and surprise everyone with good news on waking. He hoped.

They were airborne just as the sun became visible on the horizon, touching the clear cloudless sky with yellow and gilding the benign face of the distant cone mountain.

Ruth took them *between* and then, at Jaxom's suggestion, circled wide and lazily above the Plateau. They'd made new mounds of their own, Jaxom noticed with amusement, from the debris which the dragons had clawed from the two ancient buildings. He lined Ruth up in the direction of the sea. That goal would have been a long day's march for terrified people. He decided against calling the fire-lizards at this point; they'd only overexcite themselves repeating memories of the eruption. He had to get them to a spot where their associative memories tapped a less frantic moment. Surely they would have something to recall of their men in whatever refuge the fleeing people had set out to reach.

Had there perhaps been stables for beasts and wherries built at some distance from the settlement? Considering the scale on which the ancients operated, such a stable would have been large enough to shelter hundreds from the burning rain of a volcano!

He asked Ruth to glide toward the sea, in the general direction of the panic-driven ancients. Once past the grassland, shrubs began to hold root in the ashen soil, giving way to larger trees and thicker vegetation. They'd be lucky if they could spot anything unusual in that thick green mass. He was just about to ask Ruth to turn back and fly another swath when he noticed a break in the jungle. They glided out over a long scar of grassland, several dragonlengths wide and several hundred long. Trees and bushes were sparse on either side, as if struggling to find soil for their roots. Ribbons of water glinted at the far end of the curious scar, like shallow interconnected pools.

Just then the sun rose above the rim of the Plateau, and turning his head to the left to escape that brilliance, Jaxom saw the three shadows lengthening across the top end of the grassy scar. Excitedly, he urged Ruth to the spot, circling until he was certain that these hills couldn't be hills and certainly were unlike the shape of the ancients' other buildings. For one thing, their placement was as unnatural as their shape. One was seven dragonlengths or more in advance of the other two, and there'd be ten or more dragonlengths between them.

He had Ruth fly past and noticed the curious conformation: a larger mass was discernible at one end, while the other tapered slightly downward, a difference visible despite grass, earth and the small bushes that covered these so-called hills.

As excited as he was, Ruth came to rest between the leading two. The hills were not as obviously unnatural on the ground but they would have appeared odd even to someone arriving on foot.

No sooner had he asked Ruth to land than firelizards erupted about them, chittering with wild excitement and unbelievable pleasure.

"What are they saying, Ruth? Let's try to keep them calm enough to make sense. Do they have any images about these hills?"

Too many. Ruth raised his head, crooning softly to the fire-lizards. They were dipping and darting about so erratically that Jaxom gave up trying to see if any were banded. *They are happy. They are glad you are come back. It has been so long.*

"When was I first here?" Jaxom asked Ruth, having learned not to confuse the fire-lizards with generations. "Can they remember?"

When you came out of the sky in long gray things? Ruth sounded bewildered even as he relayed the answer.

Jaxom leaned against Ruth, scarcely crediting the reply. "Show me!"

Brilliant and conflicting images stunned him as he saw vistas, unfocused at first, then resolving into a clear picture as Ruth sorted out the myriad impressions into one single coherent view.

The cylinders were grayish, with stubby wings that

411

were poor imitations of the graceful pinions of the dragons. The cylinders bore rings of smaller tubes at one end while the other was blunt-nosed. Suddenly an opening appeared about a third of the way from the tubed end of the first ship. Men and women walked down a ramp. A progression of images flashed across Jaxom's mind then, of people running about, embracing each other, jumping up and down. Then the images Ruth obtained from the chittering bugling fire-lizards dissolved into chaos—as if each separate fire-lizard had followed one person and each was trying to give Ruth *his* individual image rather than a group view of the landing and ensuing events.

There was no doubt in Jaxom's mind that here was where the ancients had taken refuge from the volcano's havoc, the ships that had brought them from the Dawn Sisters to Pern. And the ships were still here because for some reason they couldn't go back to the trio of stars.

The opening into the vessel had been a third of the way from the tube end? With ecstatic fire-lizards doing acrobatics about his head, Jaxom paced the grass covering the cylinder until he thought he'd reached the appropriate spot.

They say that you have found it, Ruth advised him, nudging Jaxom forward. His great eyes were spinning with yellow fire.

To support their verdict, scores of fire-lizards settled on the bush-covered place and began to tug at the vegetation.

"I should go back to the Hold and tell them," Jaxom muttered to himself.

They are asleep. Benden is asleep. We are the only ones awake in the world!

That was, Jaxom had to admit, rather likely.

I dug yesterday. I can dig today. We can dig until they wake, when they can come help us.

"You have claws. I don't. Let's get some of the tools from the Plateau."

They were accompanied in both directions by excited, happy fire-lizards. With a shovel, Jaxom marked out the approximate area he wanted them to unearth to reach the door to the vessel. Then it was only a question of supervising Ruth and the sometimes obstructive assistance of the fire-lizards. They stripped the tough grass from the earth, first, the fire-lizards depositing it in the bushes beyond the scar. Fortunately the covering was firmly packed dirt blown over the landing site in the course of thousands of Turns. Even so, rain and sun had hardened a thick covering. When his shoulders began to ache, Jaxom eased his pace. He munched on a breadroll, occasionally urging squabbling fire-lizards back to work.

Ruth's claws scrabbled on something. *It isn't rock!* Jaxom jumped to the spot, slamming his shovel through the loose dirt. The edge hit a hard, unyielding surface. Jaxom let out a wild yell that set all the fire-lizards gyrating in midair.

Brushing away the last of the covering dirt with his hands, he stared at what he had unearthed. With cautious fingers, he touched the curious surface. Not metal, not the stuff of the mounds, rather like—improbable as it seemed—clouded glass. But no glass could be that hard!

"Ruth, is Canth awake yet?"

No. Menolly and Piemur are. They wonder where we are.

Jaxom crowed in triumph. "I think we'll go tell them!"

They were waiting for him and Ruth when they arrived from *between* in Cove Hold—the Harper, Menolly and Piemur. Over their babble of questions about his disappearance to Ruatha the night before, Jaxom tried to explain what he'd found. The Harper had to silence the babble with a huge bellow that stunned every fire-lizard into *between.* Having obtained silence, the Harper took a deep breath.

"Who could think or hear in such noise? Now, Menolly, get us some food! Piemur, get drawing materials. Zair, come here, my beautiful rascal. You've to take a message to Benden. You are to bite Mnementh's nose if necessary to wake him. Yes, I know you're brave enough to fight the big one. Don't fight! Wake! High time those lazy louts at Benden were up anyway!" The Harper was in great spirits, his head high, his eyes sparkling, his gestures broad. "By Shard and Shell, Jaxom, you've started a dull day with a bright promise. I was laggard in bed because there was nothing to rise for but more disappointment!"

"They may be as empty . . ."

"You said the fire-lizards imaged the landing? People emerging? Those cylinders could be as empty as grudging forgiveness but they'd still be worth seeing. The actual ships which brought our ancestors from the Dawn Sisters to Pern!" The Harper expelled his breath slowly, his eyes brilliant with excitement.

"You're not too stimulated, are you, Master Robinton?" Jaxom asked, looking about for Sharra. "Where is Sharra?" He saw Menolly and Piemur running on their errands. Surely Sharra wasn't still asleep. He glanced among the fire-lizards for Meer and Talla.

"A dragonrider came for Sharra last evening. There's some illness at Southern and she was urgently needed. I've been selfish, I suppose, keeping you all about me when the real need is over. In fact," the Harper said, "I'm surprised to find you here and not at Ruatha still." Robinton's eyebrows arched as an invitation to explain.

"I should have been back in my Hold some time ago, Master Robinton," Jaxom admitted in a contrite tone, then he shrugged at his reluctance to leave the Cove. "Furthermore, it was snowing when I got there. Lord Lytol and I had a long talk . . ."

"There'd be no opposition to you taking Hold now," the Harper said with a laugh, "and no more hedging and hawing about lands and you being a dragon's rider." The Harper's eyes twinkled as he mimicked Lord Sangel's pinched tones. Then his face altered and he put his hand on Jaxom's shoulder. "How did Lytol react?"

"He wasn't surprised," Jaxom said, allowing his relief and wonder to color his voice. "And I've been thinking, sir, that if Nicat continues to excavate the

Plateau buildings, someone with Lytol's gift for organizing . . ."

"My own thinking exactly, Jaxom," the Harper said, giving Jaxom another clout on the shoulder in his enthusiasm. "The past is a fit occupation for two old men . . ."

"Sir," Jaxom cried in outraged tones, "you'll never be old. Nor will Lytol!"

"Kind of you to think so, young Jaxom, but I've had warning. Ah, here comes a dragon—Canth, if I don't mistake in the sun's glare!" Robinton shielded his eyes with his hand.

The glare might also account for the frown on F'nor's face as he strode up the beach toward them. Zair had given him the most confused images, which had excited Berd, Grall and every fire-lizard in Benden Weyr to the point where Lessa had told Ramoth to banish the whole lot. In proof of which, the air above the Cove was filled with fair upon fair of fire-lizards, making a tremendous clamor.

"Ruth, settle them down," Jaxom asked his dragon. "We'll not be able to see or hear for fire-lizards."

Ruth gave such a bellow he startled himself and drew an awed whirl of Canth's eyes. The ensuing silence was broken by a frightened lone chirp. And the sky emptied of fire-lizards as they rapidly found perches on the tree-ringed beach.

They obeyed me. Ruth sounded amazed, and smug.

The display of control put F'nor in a considerably better frame of mind.

"Now, tell me what you've been up to so early in the morning, Jaxom?" F'nor asked, loosening his flying belt and helmet. "It's getting so Benden can't turn around without Ruatha's assistance."

Jaxom peered intently at F'nor in surprise, but the brown rider gave him such a look that Jaxom realized F'nor was being exceptionally cryptic. Could he be referring to that damned egg? Had Brekke mentioned something to him?

"Why not?" he said in answer. "Benden and Ruatha

415

have the strongest ties, F'nor. Blood, as well as mutual interest."

F'nor's expression turned from daunting to amused. He clipped Jaxom hard enough on the shoulder to make him lose balance.

"Well said, Ruatha, well said! So, what did you discover today?"

With no little satisfaction, Jaxom recounted his morning's labor, and F'nor's eyes widened with excitement.

"The ships they landed in? Let's go!" He tightened his belt, fastened his helmet and gestured for Jaxom to speed up his dressing. "We've Thread tomorrow at Benden, but, if this is as you say . . ."

"I'm coming, too," the Harper announced.

Not even the boldest fire-lizard chirped in the silence that followed that remark.

"I'm coming, too," Master Robinton repeated in a firm reasonable tone to override the protest he saw in every face. "I've missed too much. The suspense is very bad for me!" He placed his hand dramatically on his chest. "My heart pounds harder and harder with every passing moment that I'm forced to wait until you decide to send me dribbles and drabbles of tantalizing details." He held up his hand as Menolly recovered her wits and opened her mouth to speak. "I will do no digging. I will merely watch! But, I assure you that the vexation, not to mention the loneliness and suspense while you are off making Records, will put a totally unnecessary and dangerous strain on my poor heart. What if I collapsed from the tension, with no one here?"

"Master Robinton, if Brekke knew . . ." Menolly's protest was very weak.

F'nor covered his eyes with one hand and shook his head at the Harper's base tactics. "Give the man a finger and he'll take a length." Then he looked up and shook his finger at Robinton. "If you move a muscle, pick up a pinch of dirt, I'll . . . I'll . . ."

"I'll sit on him," Menolly finished, giving her Master

such a fierce glare that he pretended to ward off her glance.

"Get my flying gear, Menolly, there's a dear child." The Harper, with a cajoling expression, gave her a gentle push toward the Hold. "And my writing case from the worktable in my study. I really will behave myself, F'nor, and I'm certain I wouldn't come to harm in such a short journey *between*. Menolly," he raised his voice to a carrying roar, "don't forget the half-sack of wine on my chair! It was bad enough yesterday being unable to see the Plateau buildings!"

As soon as Menolly returned with his requirements, the wine sack bouncing on her back, there was no more discussion. F'nor mounted the Harper and Piemur on Canth, leaving Jaxom to settle Menolly behind him on Ruth. Fleetingly he wished that Sharra were still here. He wondered if Ruth could bespeak her all the way to Southern and then restrained the impulse. Day had not yet dawned that far west. The two dragons ascended with a dense escort of fire-lizards. Ruth gave Canth the direction and, even as Jaxom worried that the Harper's action was very rash, they had gone *between* and were gliding toward the three peculiar hills.

Jaxom grinned with delight at the response to his discovery. Menolly's arms gripped him more tightly and she cried out an intricate arpeggio in her excitement. He could see the Harper gesticulating wildly, and hoped he had a good grip on F'nor's belt. Canth, never taking his eyes from the hole in the hill, veered to land as close to it as possible. They settled the Harper in the nearest spot of shade and had Jaxom ask Ruth to get the local fire-lizards to image things for himself and Zair while he admired their labors.

To the chirping conversation of fire-lizards, the others began to dig, Ruth standing to one side since Canth could move far more earth than he and there was only room for one dragon. Jaxom was keenly aware of an internal excitement that had been utterly lacking at the Plateau.

They dug perpendicularly now, for Jaxom had unearthed the top of the vehicle. Canth's enthusiasm often showered the Harper with clods of dirt as they worked down to the door area, but they'd been digging only a short time before the seam of the doorway, a fine crack in the otherwise smooth surface, came to light. F'nor had Canth shift the angle of excavation slightly to the right and very shortly the entire upper edge of the opening was uncovered.

Much encouraged, fire-lizards joined Canth and the riders, and dirt flew everywhere. When the opening was all but clear, they had also uncovered the rounded, leading edge of one of the stubby wings as well, proving, as the Harper was quick to point out, that the fire-lizards did recall accurately what their ancestors had seen. Once you could get them to remember, of course.

When the whole doorway had been cleared, the workers stood aside for the Harper to approach and examine it.

"I think we really had better contact Lessa and F'lar now. And it would be unkind in the extreme to exclude Master Fandarel. He might even be able to tell us what they constructed this ship of."

"That's enough people to know of this," F'nor said before the Harper could include any other names. "I'll go for the Master Smith myself. It'll spare time and prevent gossip. Canth will tell Ramoth." He rubbed sweat from his face and neck and the worst of the mud stains from his hands before he shrugged into his flying gear. "Don't any of you do anything while I'm gone!" he added, glaring at each one in turn and most fiercely at the Harper.

"I wouldn't know what to do," the Harper said in a reproving tone. "We shall take refreshment," he said, reaching for the wineskin, and gesturing the others to sit around him.

The diggers welcomed a respite and a chance to contemplate the marvel they were unearthing.

"If they flew in those things . . ."

"If, my dear Piemur. No doubt obtains. They did. The fire-lizards saw those vehicles land," Master Robinton said.

"I started to say that if they flew in those things,

why didn't they fly them away from the Plateau after the explosion?"

"A very good point."

"Well?"

"Perhaps Fandarel can answer, for I certainly can't," Robinton said truthfully, regarding the door with some chagrin.

"Maybe they'd need to take off from a height, the way a lazy dragon does," Menolly said, casting a sly glance at Jaxom.

"How long does it take F'nor to go *between?*" the Harper asked with a wistful sigh, squinting up at the bright sky for any sign of returning dragons.

"Takes longer to take off and land."

The Benden Weyrleaders arrived first, Canth with F'nor and Fandarel only a few seconds behind them so that all three dragons landed together. The Smith was first off Canth, rushing to the new wonder to run reverent hands over the curious surface, murmuring under his breath. F'lar and Lessa came striding through the long grasses, picking their way past dragon-strewn dirt; neither took their eyes from the softly shining doorway.

"*Aha!*" the Smith cried in sudden triumph, startling everyone. He'd been examining the rim of the doorway minutely. "Perhaps this is meant to move!" He dropped to his knees to the exposed right-hand corner. "Yes, if one excavated the entire vessel, this would probably be man-height! I think I ought to press." He put action to words and a small panel slid open to one side of the main door. It displayed a depression occupied by several colored circles.

Everyone crowded about him as his big fingers wiggled preparatorily and then hovered first over the upper rank of green circles. The bottom ones were red.

"Red has always meant danger, a convention we undoubtedly learned from the ancients," he said. "Green we will therefore try first!" His thick forefinger hesitated a moment longer and then stabbed at the green button.

At first nothing happened. Jaxom felt a clenching, like a cold hand on his guts, the prelude to intense disappointment.

"No, look, it's opening!" Piemur's keen eyes caught the first barely perceptible widening of the crack.

"It's old," the Smith said reverently. "A very old mechanism," he added as they all heard the faint protest of movement.

Slowly the door moved inward and then, astonishingly, it moved sideways, into the hull of the ship. A *whoosh* of rank air sent them reeling and gasping backward. When they looked again, the door was fully retracted, sunlight streaming onto flooring, darker than the ship's hull but, when the Smith rapped it with his knuckles, apparently made of the same peculiar material.

"Wait!" Fandarel restrained the others from entering. "Give fresh air a chance to circulate. Did anyone think to bring glows?"

"There're some at the Cove," Jaxom said, reaching for his flying gear and jamming his helmet on his head as he raced to Ruth. He never did bother to belt up and the frigid moment of *between* was a shocking cooler after the exertions of digging. He got as many glow baskets as he could carry. On his return, he realized no one seemed to have moved in his brief absence. Awe of the unknown beyond that great entrance had restrained them. Awe and perhaps, Jaxom decided, a reluctance to repeat the disappointment of the Plateau.

"Well, we will never know anything standing out here like numbwits," Robinton said, taking a glow basket from Jaxom and unshielding it as he strode forward into the ship.

It was mete, Jaxom thought, as he passed out the other baskets, that the Master Harper should have the honor of entering first. Fandarel, F'lar, F'nor and Lessa walked abreast through the opening. Jaxom grinned at Piemur and Menolly as they fell in behind.

Another great door, with circular wheel for locking thick bars ceiling and floor, lay open and inviting.

Master Fandarel was making inarticulate noises of praise and awe as he touched the walls and peered at what looked to be control levers and more colored circles. As they penetrated further, they came upon two more doors, an open one on the left and one closed on their right which would lead, Fandarel was certain, to the rear, tube-encircled end of the vehicle. How could tubes make a cumbersome, snub-winged thing like this fly? He simply had to bring Benelek here, if no one else was to see it.

They all turned to the left and entered a long narrow corridor, their boots making muffled noises on the nonmetallic floor.

"More of the substance they used for pit supports, I think," Fandarel said, kneeling and pressing his fingers against the floor. "Ha, what was in these?" he asked, fingering brackets which were empty now. "Fascinating. And no dust."

"No air or wind to carry it in here for who knows how long," F'lar remarked in a quiet tone. "As in those rooms we discovered in Benden Weyr."

They moved along a corridor of doors, some open, some closed. None locked, for Piemur and Jaxom were able to peer into the emptied cubicles. Holes in the flooring and on the inside walls proved that there had been fittings.

"All of you, come here!" came the excited voice of the Harper, who had prowled ahead.

"No, here!" F'nor called from further beyond the Harper. "Here's where they must have controlled the ship!"

"No, F'nor, this is important to us!"

And F'lar seconded the Harper's vibrant claim.

As everyone gathered about the two, their glow baskets adding to the illumination, it was clear what had arrested their attention. The walls were covered with maps. In great detail, the familiar contours of Northern Pern and the not-so-familiar Southern Continent, all of it in its immensity, had been drawn eradicably on the wall.

With a sound—half-moan, half-shout—Piemur

touched the map, tracing with his forefinger the coast which he had so arduously tramped, but which was only a small portion of the total shoreline.

"Look, Master Idarolan can sail almost to the Eastern Barrier Range . . . and it's not the same range I saw in the west. And . . ."

"Now what would this map represent?" F'nor asked, interrupting Piemur's excited comments. He was standing to one side, his glow basket lighting another chart of Pern. The outlines were the same, but the bands of different colors covered the familiar contours in puzzling configurations. The seas were depicted with varying shades of blue.

"That would indicate the depth of the water," Menolly said, running her fingers along what she knew was the Nerat Deep, here colored a deep blue. "Look, here are arrows to indicate the Great South Current. And here's the Western Stream."

"If that is so," the Harper said slowly, "then this ought to indicate the height of the land? No. For here where there should be mountains in Crom, Fort, Benden and Telgar, the color is the same as this part of the Telgar Plains. Most puzzling. Whatever could this have meant to the ancients?" He glanced from Northern to Southern spheres. "And none of that shade except this little bit here on the underside of the world. Perplexing. I shall have to study this!" He felt along the edges of the map, but it was evidently drawn on the wall itself.

"Here's one for Master Wansor's eyes," Fandarel said, apparently so engrossed in the section he was studying that he hadn't attended Robinton's words.

Piemur and Jaxom turned their glows toward the Smith.

"A star map!" the young Harper cried.

"Not quite," the Smith said.

"Is it a map of our stars?" Jaxom asked.

The Smith's big finger touched the largest circle, a brilliant orange with licking flames jagging out from its circumference.

"This is our sun. This must be the Red Star." His

finger described the orbit about the sun which had been designated for the wanderer. He now touched the third, very small, round world. "This is our Pern!" He grinned at the others, for the humble size of their world.

"What's this then?" Piemur asked, putting his finger on a dark-colored world on the other side of the sun, away from the other planets and their described lines of orbit.

"I don't know. It ought to be on this side of the sun, as the other planets are!"

"And what do these lines mean?" Jaxom asked, having traced the arrowed lines from the bottom of the chart to the Red Star and then off the edge of the chart on the far right.

"Fascinating," was all the Mastersmith would allow, rubbing his chin as he stared at the enigmatic drawings.

"I prefer this map," Lessa said, smiling with a great deal of satisfaction at the two continents.

"You do?" F'lar asked, turning from his examination of the star map. "Ah, yes, I take your point," he said as he watched her hand cover the western section. Then he laughed. "Yes, I quite agree, Lessa. Very instructive."

"How can that be?" Piemur asked with some scorn. "It's not accurate. Look," he pointed, "there's no sea volcanoes beyond the Plateau cliffs. And there's far too much shore in this section of the South. And no Great Bay. It doesn't go like that. I know. I've walked it."

"No, the map isn't accurate anymore," the Harper said before Lessa could level a criticism at Piemur. "Notice Tillek. There's a good deal more of the northern peninsula than there should be. And no mark for the volcano on the south shore." Then he added with a deep smile, "But I suspect the map was accurate, when it was drawn!"

"Of course," Lessa said in a cry of triumph. "All the Passes, each one stressing our poor world, caused upheaval and destruction . . ."

"See, this spur of land, where the Dragon Stones are now?" Menolly cried. "My great-grandsire remembers the land falling into the sea!"

"No matter that there have been minor changes," Fandarel said, dismissing these casually, "the maps are superb discoveries." He frowned again at the one with the anomalous shadings. "That shade of brown designates our first settlements in the North. See, Fort Hold, then Ruatha, Benden, Telgar," he looked at F'lar and Lessa, "and the Weyrs. They all are placed in this same coloration. Is that what it means, perhaps? Places where people could settle?"

"But they settled the Plateau first of all, and it's not that same brown," Piemur said, disgruntled.

"We must seek Master Wansor's opinion. And Master Nicat's."

"I'd like to see Benelek look over the controls by the doors and perhaps investigate the rear of the ship," F'nor said.

"My dear brown rider," the Smith said, "Benelek is very clever with mechanical things but these . . ." His broad gesture indicated that the highly advanced technology on the ship was well beyond his apprentice's skill.

"Perhaps one day, we will know enough to fathom all the ships' mysteries," F'lar said, smiling with intense pleasure as he tapped the maps. "But these . . . are current and exceedingly valuable to us, and Pern." He paused to grin at Master Robinton, who nodded his head in comprehension, and Lessa, who continued to smile, her eyes dancing with a mischief only the three seemed to share. "And, for the time being, no mention is to be made of them!" He was stern now, and held up his hand when Fandarel began to protest. "A short time only, Fandarel. I have very good reason. Wansor must certainly see these equations and drawings. And Benelek can puzzle what he may. As he talks only to inanimate objects, he's no risk to the necessary secrecy I feel we must impose on these ships. Menolly and Piemur are harperbound, and you've already proved your dis-

cretion and abilities, Jaxom." F'lar's glance, direct
and intense, caused Jaxom an inner pang because he
was certain then that the Benden Weyrleader did know
of his episode with the dratted egg. "There's going to
be quite enough to confuse Hold, Craft and Weyr on
that Plateau without adding these riddles." His eyes
went back to the broad expanse of the Southern
Continent and, as he shook his head slowly, his smile
and those of the Harper and Lessa increased. Suddenly a shocked expression crossed his face, and he
looked up. "Toric! He said he'd be here today, to
help excavate."

"Yes, and N'ton was to collect me," Fandarel
said, "but not for an hour yet or more. I was dragged
from my couch by F'nor . . ."

"And Southern is in Telgar's time area. Good!
However, I want a copy of this map. Which of you
three can we best spare today?" he asked.

"Jaxom!" the Harper said quickly. "He copies
neatly and when the rider came for Sharra last evening, Jaxom had gone to Ruatha. Besides, it is wise
to keep Ruth apart. The local fire-lizards will bear
him company here and not chatter to Toric's trio."

The matter was quickly decided and Jaxom left
with copying materials and all the glows. A screen of
branches was contrived to hide the opening from any
chance observer. Ruth was asked to entice the local
fire-lizards to him and hopefully get them to nap.
Because the morning's exertions had tired Ruth, he
was quite willing to curl up in the sun and sleep. The
others departed to Cove Hold and Jaxom began to
copy this peculiarly significant map.

As he worked, he tried to figure out why it had so
pleased the Weyrleaders and Master Robinton. To
be sure, it was a gift to know the extent of Southern
without having to walk it all.

Was that it? Of course. Toric didn't know how
large the Southern Continent was! And now the
Weyrleaders did. Jaxom regarded the Hold perinsu-
la, estimating how much Toric and his holdless men
had managed to explore. Never could Toric, even

with his Hold swollen by younger sons from every Hold and cothold in Northern Pern, explore this vast continent. Why, even if he tried to Hold as far as the Western Range in the south, to the Great Bay in the west . . . Jaxom smiled, so pleased with his deduction that he nearly smeared the line he was drawing. Should he mark in the Great Bay as they now knew it, or copy the old map faithfully? Yes, it was this one that mattered. And when Toric finally saw it . . . Jaxom chuckled, imagining with intense pleasure the chagrin which Toric would feel at first sight.

CHAPTER XXI

Next Day at the Mountain, Cove Hold, and the Southern Hatching Ground, 15.10.21

"I KNOW WHAT was originally conceded to Toric," Robinton was saying to the Benden Weyrleaders as they sat drinking klah at Cove Hold.

"To Hold what he had acquired when the Old-timers left the Southern Weyr," F'lar amended. "The purist would argue that, as the Oldtimers have not indeed all passed *between,* Toric may continue to extend his Holding."

"Or secure the loyalty of others in Holding?" Robinton remarked.

Lessa stared at him, absorbing his meaning. "Was that why he was amenable to settling so many hold-less men?" She looked indignant for a moment and then laughed. "Toric is a man we shall have to watch these next Turns. I'd no idea he'd prove so ambitious."

"Farsighted, too," Robinton said in a dry tone. "He achieves as much by gratitude as by possession."

"Gratitude has a tendency to sour," F'lar said.

"He's not fool enough to rely on that alone," Lessa said with a rueful expression then looked about her, puzzled. "Did I see Sharra at all this morning?"

"No, a rider collected her last evening. There's illness at—oh!" The Harper's eyes widened to em-

phasize his surprised dismay. "Now there's no foo
like an old one. It never occurred to me to doubt tha
message. Yes, he'd use Sharra, and his other sisters
He has several daughters as well to bind men to him
Jaxom will react to this situation, I think."

"I hope so," Lessa said with some asperity. "I
rather approve of Sharra as a match. If this is not a
simple case of his being grateful for her nursing . . ."
She clucked her tongue at the mention of gratitude

Robinton laughed. "Brekke feels, and so does
Menolly, that the attachment is sincere on both
sides. I'm delighted you agree. I've been daily hoping
he would ask me to officiate. Especially in view of
today's reflections. By the way, only it isn't exactly
by the way but to our point, Jaxom went back to
Ruatha Hold last evening. He approached Lyto
on the subject of his confirmation as Lord Holder."

"Did he?" F'lar was as pleased as his weyrmate.
"Prompted by Sharra? Or by Toric's not-too-subtle
jibing yesterday?"

"I missed far too much not being permitted to go
to the Plateau yesterday," the Harper said irritably.
"What jibing?"

The bugling of Ramoth and Mnementh outside
effectively prevented further discussion.

"N'ton's here, with Master Nicat and Wansor,"
F'lar said. He turned to Robinton and Lessa as he
rose. "Shall we just let matters proceed naturally?"

"That's usually best," Robinton said.

Lessa smiled cryptically as she strode toward the
door.

N'ton had brought three journeymen miners as
well as their Master. F'nor arrived immediately
thereafter with Wansor, Benelek and two young apprentices apparently chosen for their generous size
Without waiting for Toric to appear with D'ram
they all went *between* to the Plateau, landing as close
to Nicat's little mound as possible. Daylight provided
the answer to its function—numerals and letters
paraded as design across the far end, and rather fascinating animals, large and small and bearing no re-

semblance to anything walking Pern's surface, marched across the two long walls.

"A harper's room, for the very young learning first Teaching Songs and Ballads," the Harper said, not nearly as disappointed as the others since the building applied to his Craft.

"Well, then," Benelek added and, turning on his heel, pointed to the mound immediately on the left. "This is where the advanced students would be. If, of course," he sounded dubious, "the ancients followed a logical sequence and progressed to the right in any circular formation." He executed a curt bow to the Weyrleaders and the three Craftmasters and, gesturing to one of the apprentices, marched decisively out, picked a shovel from the pile and proceeded to cut the grass from the inner end of the chosen mound.

Lessa, waiting until Benelek was out of hearing, gave way to laughter. "And if the ancients disappoint him, will he bother with any more mysteries?"

"It's time to unearth my large mound today," F'lar said, trying to imitate Benelek's decisiveness as he gestured the others to pick up tools and join him.

Bearing in mind that the entrances tended to be on the short ends, they abandoned F'lar's original trench on the roof. Ramoth and Mnementh obligingly shifted enormous mounds of the curious gray-black soil from the center of the end. The entrance was shortly revealed as a door, large enough to admit a green dragon, sliding on rails; a smaller opening pierced one corner. "Man size," F'lar said. It opened on hinges that were not of metal, a fact which delighted and puzzled Masters Nicat and Fandarel. Just as they opened the small door, Jaxom and Ruth arrived. No sooner had they landed on the mound's top, than three more dragons burst into the air.

"D'ram," Lessa said, "and two Benden browns that went south to help."

"Sorry to take so long, Master Robinton," Jaxom said, handing the Harper a neat roll as if it were of no moment. "Good morning, Lessa. What was in Nicat's building?"

The Harper tucked the roll carefully in his belt pouch, pleased with Jaxom's dissembling. "A children's hall. Go take a look."

"Could I have a word with you, Master Robinton. Unless . . ." Jaxom waved his hands toward the mound and the little door hanging so invitingly open.

"I can wait until the air is cleared out," Robinton said, having noticed the tense look in Jaxom's eyes and his air of polite entreaty. He moved with the young man to one side of the others. "Yes?"

"Sharra is being restrained at Southern by her brother," Jaxom said in a low voice that did not reveal his agitation.

"However did you find that out?" Robinton asked, glancing up at the circling bronze that bore the Southerner.

"She told Ruth. Toric has plans for her to marry one of his new holders. He considers the Northern lordlings useless!" There was a dangerous glint in Jaxom's eyes and a sternness to his features which, for the first time since Robinton had known the lad, gave him the look of his father, Fax, a resemblance which afforded Robinton some small pleasure.

"Some of the lordlings undoubtedly are," Robinton replied, amused. "What have you in mind, Jaxom?" he added, for there was no answering response to his drollery in the grim-faced young man. Somehow, the Harper had failed to appreciate the maturing that had occurred in Ruatha's Lord Holder during the past eventful two seasons.

"I intend to get her back," Jaxom said in a quiet firm tone, and gestured to Ruth. "Toric forgot to reckon with Ruth."

"You'd fly into Southern and just carry her off?" Robinton asked, trying to keep his expression straight, though Jaxom's romantic manner made it difficult.

"Why not?" Suddenly the glint of humor was restored to Jaxom's eyes. "I doubt if Toric expects me to take direct action. I'm one of those useless Northern lordlings!"

"Ah, but not before you receive some direct action yourself, I fancy," Robinton said in a quick undertone.

Toric and his group had dismounted in the clear space between two of the mound ranks. He had left his people to sort themselves out and, stripping off his flying gear, was striding toward Lessa and those clustered about the mound door. But, after giving her a greeting, he changed directions and there was no doubt his goal was Jaxom.

"Harper!" he said, coming to a halt with a courteous nod for Robinton before he looked at Jaxom.

To Robinton's pleasure, Ruatha's Lord did not so much as straighten his shoulders or turn to face Toric.

"Holder Toric," Jaxom said over his shoulder in a cool indifferent greeting. The title, which was certainly proper as Toric had never been invited to take full rank by the other Lord Holders of Pern, brought the Southerner up short. His eyes narrowed as he looked keenly at Jaxom.

"Lord Jaxom." Toric's drawl made an insult of that title, implying that it was not fully Jaxom's as yet.

Jaxom turned slowly toward him. "Sharra tells me," he said, noting as Robinton did the surprise twitch of Toric's eye muscles, and a quick darting glance at the fire-lizards about Ruth, "that you do not favor an alliance with Ruatha."

"No, lordling. I do not!" Toric flicked a glance at the Harper, a broad smile on his face. "She can do better than a table-sized Hold in the North." The last word held contemptuous emphasis.

"What did I hear, Toric?" Lessa asked, her voice light but with a hint of steel in her eyes as she squarely ranged herself beside Jaxom.

"Holder Toric has other plans for Sharra," Jaxom said, his tone more amused than aggrieved. "She can

431

do better, it seems, than a table-sized Hold like Ruatha."

"I mean no offense to Ruatha," Toric said quickly when he caught the flicker of anger in Lessa's face, though the Weyrwoman continued to smile.

"That would be most unwise, considering my pride in my Bloodline and in the present Holder of that title," she said in the most casual tone.

"Surely, you might reconsider the matter, Toric," Robinton said, as affable as ever despite the palpable warning he conveyed that the Southerner was on very dangerous ground. "Such an alliance, so much desired by the two young people, would have considerable advantages for you, I think, aligning yourself with one of the most prestigious Holds on Pern."

"And be in favor with Benden," Lessa said, smiling so sweetly that Robinton almost chuckled at the man's predicament.

Toric stood there, absently rubbing the back of his neck, his smile slightly diminished.

"We should discuss the matter. At some length, I think." Lessa tucked her arm in Toric's and turned him about. "Master Robinton, will you join us? I think that little cot of mine would be an admirable spot in which to talk undisturbed."

"I thought we were here to dig up Pern's glorious past," Toric said, with a good-natured laugh. But he did not disengage his arm from Lessa's.

"There's surely no time like the present," Lessa continued at her sweetest, "to discuss the future. Your future."

F'lar had joined them, falling in step at Lessa's left, apparently aware through the link between Mnementh and Lessa of what had just occurred. The Harper shot a reassuring look over his shoulder to Jaxom but the young man was looking at his dragon.

"Yes, with so many ambitious holdless men pouring into Southern," F'lar said smoothly, "we've been remiss in making certain you'll have the lands you want, Toric. I don't fancy blood feuds in the South.

Unnecessary, too, when there's space enough for this generation and several more."

Toric's answer was a full-bodied laugh and although he had adjusted his stride to match Lessa's, he still gave Robinton the impression of invulnerable self-assurance.

"And since there's so much space, why should I not be ambitious for my sister?"

"You've more than one, and we're not talking of Jaxom and Sharra just now," Lessa added with a hint of irritability as she dismissed the irrelevant. "F'lar and I had intended to arrange a more formal occasion to set your Holding," she went on, gesturing to the ancient, empty structure in which they now stood, "but there's Master Nicat wanting to formalize Minecrafthall affairs, and Lord Groghe is anxious that his two sons do not hold adjacent lands, and other questions have come up recently which require answers."

"Answers?" Toric asked politely as he leaned against one wall and crossed his arms on his chest.

Robinton began to wonder just how much of that pose of indolence was assumed. Was Toric's ambition going to overpower good sense?

"One answer required is how much land any one man should Hold in the South?" F'lar said, idly digging dirt from under his thumbnail with his knife point. He had lightly emphasized the *one*.

"And? Our original agreement was that I could Hold all the lands I had acquired by the time the Oldtimers had passed on."

"Which, in truth, they haven't," Robinton said.

Toric agreed to that. "I shan't insist on waiting," he admitted with a slight inclination of his head, "since the original circumstances have altered. And, since my Hold is thoroughly disorganized by the indigent and hopeful lordlings, and holdless men and boys, I am reliably informed that others have eschewed our help and landed wherever their ships can be beached."

"All the more reason to be sure you are not deprived of one length of your just Hold," F'lar said. "I know that you have sent out exploring teams. How far have they actually penetrated?"

"With the help of D'ram's dragonriders," Toric said as Robinton noticed how keenly he watched F'lar's face to see if this unexpected assistance was known to Benden, "we have extended our knowledge of the terrain to the foot of the Western Range."

"That far?" The bronze rider appeared surprised and perhaps a trifle alarmed.

Robinton knew from that auspiciously discovered map that, while the area from the sea to the Western Range was immense, it was but a small segment of the total area of the vast Southern Continent.

"And, of course, Piemur reached the Great Desert Bay to the west," Toric was saying.

"My dear Toric, how can you possibly Hold all that?" F'lar seemed politely concerned.

"I've small cotholders with burgeoning families along most of the habitable shoreline, and at strategic points in the interior. The men you sent me these past few Turns proved most industrious." Toric's smile was more assured.

"I suspect they have pledged loyalty to you in return for your original generosity?" F'lar asked with a sigh.

"Naturally."

Lessa laughed. "I thought when we met at Benden that you were a shrewd and independent man."

"There's more land, my dear Weyrwoman, for any man who can hold it. Some small holds could turn out to be far more valuable than larger spreads, in the eyes of those who truly appreciate their worth."

"I'd say then," Lessa went on, pointedly ignoring Toric's allusion to Ruatha's size, "that you'll have more than enough to occupy you fully and to hold, from sea to Western Range to the Great Bay . . ."

Suddenly Toric straightened. Lessa had been looking at F'lar, obliquely seeking his approval for what she granted Toric, so it was only Robinton who caught the full alertness, the look of intense surprise and displeasure in the Southerner's eyes. He recovered himself quickly.

"To the Great Bay in the West, yes, that is my hope. I do have maps. In my Hold, but if I've your leave . . ."

He had taken one stride to the door when Ramoth's bugle halted him. And as Mnementh chimed in, F'lar moved swiftly to block his way.

"It's already too late, Toric."

As Jaxom watched the Benden Weyrleaders and the Harper walk toward the excavated house with Toric, he expelled with a deep breath the anger he had contained for Toric's belittling manner.

" 'Ruatha a table-sized Hold?' " Indeed! Ruatha, the second oldest and certainly one of the most prosperous Holds on Pern. If Lessa hadn't come then, he'd have shown—

Jaxom took another breath. Toric had the height and reach of him. He'd have been slaughtered by the Southerner if Lessa hadn't interfered and saved him from sheer folly. It had never occurred to Jaxom that Toric might not be honored by an alliance with Ruatha. He'd been stunned when Ruth had informed him of Sharra's contact—that she had been lured back to Southern—and told that Toric would not countenance a marriage for her in the North. Nor would Toric listen to Sharra's avowal of a true attachment to Jaxom. So he had set his queen on her two fire-lizards to keep her from sending messages to Jaxom. Toric hadn't known that Sharra could talk to Ruth, something she had done as soon as she'd awakened that morning. There was a hint of amusement in Ruth's tone for the secret exchange.

Jaxom waited until the four had entered the little dwelling before he moved to Ruth. "Fly into Southern and carry her off," the Harper had said in jest, but that was exactly what Jaxom intended.

"Ruth," he asked in his mind as he closed the distance between them, "are there any fire-lizards of Toric's about you?"

No! We are going to rescue Sharra? Where shall I tell her to meet us? We've only been to the Hatching Grounds in Southern. Shall I ask Ramoth?

"I'd prefer not to involve the Benden dragons in this. We'll go to the Hatching Ground. That egg is coming in useful to us after all," he added, appreciating the irony of the situation as he vaulted to Ruth's back. "Give her the picture, Ruth. Ask her if she can reach the place?"

She says yes.

"Let's get there then!"

Jaxom began laughing openly as Ruth took them *between*.

They came in low from the east, just as they had not quite a Turn before. Now, however, the ring of warm sand was unoccupied. Only briefly, for firelizards swooped down in cheerful greeting.

"Toric's?" Jaxom asked, wondering if he should dismount and search for Sharra.

She comes! Toric's queen is with her. Go away! You displease me, watching my friends!

Jaxom had no time to be astonished by his dragon's fierce attitude. Sharra, trailing a blanket which she was endeavoring to wrap about her thinly clad body, came running across the Ground. She pelted toward him, her expression anxious, and she almost tripped on an edge of her blanket as she looked back over her shoulder.

She says two of Toric's men are after her. Ruth half-sprang, half-glided toward Sharra, while Jaxom leaned down, holding his hands out to catch her and swing her onto Ruth's neck. Two men, swords drawn, came tearing onto the Ground. But Ruth launched himself, leaving the two men swearing helplessly at them as the Ground dropped away. The watchdragon of the Southern Weyr called out to Ruth, who replied in a greeting as he beat upward on the warm air.

"I think your brother has miscalculated, Sharra."

"Take me away from here, Jaxom. Take me to Ruatha! I've never been so furious in all my life. I

436

never want to see that brother of mine again. Of all
the devious, misguided . . ."

"We have to see your brother again, for I'm not
hiding from him. We'll have it out in the open today!"

"Jaxom!" There was real concern in Sharra's voice
now. She clutched him tightly about the waist. "He'd
kill you in a fight."

"Our affair will cause no duel, Sharra," Jaxom
said with a laugh. "Bundle yourself well in that blanket. Ruth will take us *between* as quick as he can!"

"Jaxom, I hope you know what we're doing!"

Ruth took them back to the Plateau, caroling a
greeting as he circled down.

"Oh, I'm frozen, but they took my flying gear
away," Sharra cried. Her bare legs on Ruth's neck were
blue with chill. Jaxom leaned over to rub warmth
into them. "And there's Toric. With Lessa, F'lar and
Robinton!"

"And the largest of the Benden dragons!"

"Jaxom!"

"Your brother does things his way, I do them in
mine! In mine!"

"Jaxom!" There was surprise as well as respect in
her voice and her arms tightened again about his
waist.

Ruth landed and when they had dismounted, he
walked to Jaxom's left as the two young lovers went
to meet the others. Toric no longer wore his customary smile.

"Toric, you cannot contain Sharra anywhere on
Pern where Ruth and I cannot find her!" Jaxom said
after the barest of nods to the Benden Weyrleaders
and the Harper. There was no hint of compromise in
Toric's hard expression. Nor did he expect it. "Place
and time are no barriers to Ruth. Sharra and I can
go anywhere, anywhen on Pern."

A piteously crying queen fire-lizard attempted to
land on Toric's shoulder, but the man brushed her
away.

"Further, fire-lizards obey Ruth! Don't they, my
friend?" Jaxom rested his hand on Ruth's headknob.

"Tell every fire-lizard here on the Plateau to go away!"

Ruth did so, adding as the wide meadow was suddenly empty of the little creatures, that they didn't wish to leave.

Toric's eyes narrowed slightly at that show of ability. Then the fire-lizards were back. This time he permitted his little queen to land on his shoulder, but his eyes held Jaxom's.

"How did you know Southern? I was informed that you've never been there!" He made a half-turn as if to accuse Lessa and F'lar of complicity.

"Your informant erred," Jaxom said, wondering if it had been Dorse. "Today is not the first time I've retrieved something from the Southern Weyr which belongs to the North." He laid his arm possessively about Sharra's shoulders.

Toric's composure deserted him. *"You!"* He extended his arm, pointing at Jaxom; his face was a mixture of anger, indignant outrage, disappointment, frustration and, lastly, a grudging respect. *"You* took the egg back! You and that . . . but the fire-lizards' images were black!"

"I'd be stupid not to darken a white hide if I make a night pass, wouldn't I?" Jaxom asked with understandable scorn.

"I knew it wasn't one of T'ron's riders," Toric cried, his fists clenching and unclenching. "But for you to . . . Well now," and Toric's whole attitude changed radically. He began to smile again, a trifle sourly as he looked at the Benden Weyrleaders and then the Harper. Then he started to laugh, losing anger and frustration in that laughter. "If you knew, Lordling . . ." again he pointed fiercely at Jaxom, "the plans you ruined, the . . . How many people knew it was you?" Now he did turn accusingly on the dragonriders.

"Not many," Robinton said, wondering quickly if indeed Lessa and F'lar had ever guessed.

"I knew," Sharra said, "and so did Brekke. Jaxom

worried about that egg the whole time he was fevered." Her gaze on his face was proud.

"Not that it matters now," Jaxom said. "What does matter is, do I now have your permission to marry Sharra and make her lady of Ruatha Hold?"

"I don't see how I can stop you." Toric's broad gesture of frustration took in the people and the dragons.

"Indeed you couldn't, for Jaxom's boast about Ruth's abilities is valid," F'lar said. "One must never underestimate a dragonrider, Toric." Then he grinned without softening the implicit warning. "Especially a Northern dragonrider."

"I shall bear that firmly in mind," Toric said, the intensity of his big voice indicating his chagrin. The affable grin reappeared on his face. "Especially in our present discussion. Before these impetuous youngsters interrupted us, we were discussing the extent of my Hold, were we not?"

He turned his back on Sharra and Jaxom, and gestured to the others to return to their temporary hall.

AFTERWORD

SPRING HAD COME again to Northern Pern and Ruatha Hold. Once the winter's damages had been repaired and the first crops set, there had been great business on the Hold itself, all aimed to have the old place look its best on the one spring morning when Wansor's equations said no Thread would fall anywhere but harmlessly far to the west at sea.

Ruatha's walls were scrubbed, its paving brightly sealed, and this day banners hung from every unshuttered window while flowers decked every corner of the courts and the Hall. Southern vines had been flown in the night before to garland the fire-heights. The broad meadows below the Hold proper were covered with tents and divided into fields for the runner beasts of the guests. Dragons began to arrive, greeted by the old brown watchdragon, Wilth, who would surely be hoarse from bugling welcome before the ceremonies began.

Fire-lizards were everywhere and had to be constantly called to order by dragon and friend. But the atmosphere was so relaxed, so jubilant, that pranks and antics, human or creature, were amicably tolerated.

To cater to so many guests, half Pern north and south it seemed, Fort Hold and Weyr, as well as Benden, had joined kitchen staffs with Ruatha. Toric had obligingly sent from Southern meadows dragonloads of fresh fruit, fish, wild bucks and wherries whose flesh was prized for its tender gamey taste, so distinct from Northern meats. Great roasting, baking and steaming pits had been in operation since the previous evening, the aromas commingling to set mouths watering.

There had been festivities the night before, dancing and singing until early morning, for traders had arrived well in advance, no one minding the multiple uses of this occasion. Now more people poured up the roads, flew down from the skies as the momentous hour for the ceremonious confirmation of the young Lord of Ruatha Hold drew close.

The Harper comes, Ruth told Jaxom and Sharra as the white dragon pushed open the doors of his weyr and stepped into his courtyard.

Jaxom and Sharra, in the main room of their ground-level apartment, heard his joyous bugle of welcome, just as if he hadn't said goodnight to the Harper in the early hours of that morning.

Lioth says for you to wait here. Harper and N'ton want to speak to you without other ears.

Jaxom turned to Sharra in surprise.

"Oh, it can't be anything untoward, Jaxom," she said, smiling. "Master Robinton would have told us last night. I still think that tunic is too tight across your chest."

"All the spring digging at Ship Meadow, my love," Jaxom said, inhaling so that the fabric of his brown tunic strained at the seams.

"If you split this new material, you'll have to wear it mended!" She smiled as she spoke her scold then kissed him.

Sharra's kisses were to be enjoyed whenever possible, so he held her tightly.

"Jaxom! I will not go mussed to your Confirmation."

Ramoth and Mnementh are here! Ruth rose on his haunches to bugle a sufficiently honorable greeting.

"You'd think he was the one being Confirmed as Lord Holder," Sharra said, her rich voice filled with laughter.

"It's been a joint effort," Jaxom said, grinning

broadly. He hugged her swiftly just once more, relieved that the winter's uncertainty had given way to spring.

He'd never been busier: managing the Hold and delving into the ancient mysteries of the Plateau and the Ship Meadow whenever he could spare a few hours. Lytol, as Jaxom had hoped, had found himself tremendously involved in the excavations, spending more and more time with the Harper at Cove Hold. With his Confirmation now a certainty, Jaxom had been admitted to the inner councils of the Lord Holders, as much because of his association with Toric as his own rank. Jaxom doubted that Toric would tolerate much more of the conservatism that dominated the Lord Holders' attitudes to anything. Larad of Telgar Hold, Asgenar of Lemos, Begamon and Sigomel seemed more of Toric's mind, and Jaxom found himself willing to be ranked with them rather than side with Groghe, Sangel and some of the older men. Some of the old Lord Holders simply didn't understand the needs of today—nor the call of the vast Southern lands with their infinite variety and challenge.

Today's formalities were token and excuse for a gathering of Weyr, Craft and Hold, a festival of the end of the cold months of the Turn, a happy day when no Thread fell on any part of Pern.

Lioth landed in the small kitchen courtyard, Ruth backing into his quarters to give the great bronze dragon sufficient space. The Harper slid from his shoulder, waving a thick roll, and N'ton's crack-faced grin indicated they had news of great import.

"Lessa and F'lar must hear our news, too," N'ton said, as he and the Harper joined the young Holders. "They're just coming now." He signaled Lioth to the fire-heights.

The two men removed their flying jackets, Robinton never relinquishing hold on the roll as he did so. They watched with growing impatience as first golden Ramoth and then bronze Mnementh discharged their passengers and ascended to the fire-heights to join Lioth.

"Well, Harper, Mnementh says you're bursting with news," F'lar said, handing Jaxom his flying gear as Sharra assisted Lessa.

"Indeed I am, Benden," and the Harper exaggerated each syllable, brandishing his roll in emphasis.

"So, what have you here?" Lessa asked.

"Nothing but the key to that colored map in the ship!" the Harper said, grinning at their response. "Piemur figured it out, working with Nicat, because we had the feeling it had something to do with the lay of the land. It does! The rock underneath the land, to be precise." He was unrolling the map with Lessa and F'lar holding corners. "These dark-brown patches indicate very old rock, in places that have never known earthquake or volcanic action. Never changed from this map to our present ones. The Plateau, shaded here as yellow, obviously had to be abandoned because of the eruption. See, here and here on the south and in Tillek, we have the same coloration. My dear friends, the ancients came to the North, to Fort, Ruatha, Benden, Telgar, because that land was safer from natural disasters!"

"Thread being an unnatural disaster?" Lessa asked in a droll voice.

"I prefer to cope with my disasters one at a time," F'lar said. "Being attacked from the ground and the air would be a bit much!"

"Then Nicat and Piemur have also deduced where the ancients discovered metals, black water and black stone. The deposits are clearly marked both North and South! We've already worked many of the Northern mines."

"More in the South?" F'lar asked, deeply interested. "Show me!"

Robinton pointed to half a dozen small markings. "How rich the deposits are is not yet known but I'm sure Nicat will tell us soon enough. He and Piemur make a potent team."

"How many mines are in Toric's Hold?" F'lar asked.

N'ton chuckled. "No more than he's already discovered and produced. There're far more to be worked in dragonrider country," he said, tapping the southeast. "When this Pass is over, I think I'll turn miner!"

"When this Pass is over . . ." F'lar echoed the words, his eyes catching the Harper's, suddenly aware that neither of them were likely to see that moment.

"When this Pass is over," Jaxom said eagerly, his eyes scanning the map, "people can begin to concentrate on what we've found at the Plateau, too, and in those ships. We can rediscover the South! Maybe even solve the mystery of the ships—and how we can get dragons to cross that airless void to the Dawn Sisters . . ." Jaxom's gaze went to the southeast, to beacons now hidden from his sight.

"And how to wipe out forever the threat of Thread from the Red Star itself," Sharra said in a whisper.

F'lar gave a rueful laugh, brushing from his forehead the lock of hair, now gray-streaked, that fell across his eyes. "I once thought to reach the Red Star. Maybe you young people won't find it so daunting a task once we've caught up on what men used to know."

"Don't belittle your accomplishments, F'lar," Robinton said sternly. "You've kept Pern Threadfree and united . . . in spite of itself!"

"Why, if it hadn't been for you," Lessa said, looking about her, eyes flashing angrily for F'lar's self-denigration, "none of this would have happened!" Her gesture meant Ruatha bannered for a happy day and secure in the knowledge that no Thread would mar the occasion anywhere.

"LORD JAXOM!" Lytol's bellow rang clearly from an upper window of Ruatha Hold.

"Sir?"

"Benden? Fort? The other Weyrleaders and all the

Lord Holders of Pern, North and South, have gathered!"

Jaxom waved his hand in acknowledgment of the summons. F'lar rolled up the map and handed it back to Robinton with a bow.

"I'll examine it more closely later, Robinton."

Jaxom offered his arm to his Lady Sharra and would have gestured for the Master Harper and the dragonriders to precede them.

"By no means, it's your day, Lord Jaxom of Ruatha Hold," the Harper said, and he bowed low, his arm coming up with a flourish to indicate the honor of precedence.

Laughing, Jaxom and Sharra strode out into the court, N'ton and Robinton behind them. F'lar presented his arm to Lessa but she had turned her eyes about the small kitchen courtyard and it wasn't hard for the bronze rider to sense her thoughts.

"It's your day, too, Lessa," he said, taking her hand to his lips. "A day your determination and spirit made possible!" He turned her into his arms and made her look up at him. "Ruathan Blood Holds Ruatha lands today!"

"Which proves," she said, pretending to be haughty though her body was pliant against his, "that if you try hard enough, and work long enough, you can achieve anything you desire!"

"I hope you're right," F'lar said, unerringly turning his gaze toward the Red Star. "One day dragonriders will conquer that Star!"

"BENDEN!" The Harper's roar startled their private moment of triumph.

Grinning like errant children, Lessa and F'lar crossed the kitchen courtyard and raced up the steps to the Great Hall. The dragons on the fire-heights rose to their haunches, bugling their jubilation on this happy day while fire-lizards executed dizzy patterns in the Thread-free sky!

Dragondex

THE WEYRS IN ORDER OF FOUNDING

Fort Weyr

Benden Weyr

High Reaches Weyr

Igen Weyr

Ista Weyr

Telgar Weyr

Southern Weyr

THE MAJOR HOLDS AS BOUND TO
THE WEYRS

Fort Weyr

Fort Hold (oldest hold), Lord Holder Groghe

Ruatha Hold (next oldest), Lord Holder Jaxom, Lord Warder Lytol

Southern Boll Hold, Lord Holder Sangel

Benden Weyr

Benden Hold, Lords Holder Raid and Toronas

Bitra Hold, Lords Holder Sifer and Sigomal

Lemas Hold, Lord Holder Asgenar

High Reaches Weyr

High Reaches Hold, Lord Holder Bargen

Nabol Hold, Lords Holder Fax, Meron, Deckter

Tillek Hold, Lord Holder Oterel

Igen Weyr

Keroon Hold, Lord Holder Corman

Parts of Upper Igen

Southern Telgar Hold

Ista Weyr

    Ista Hold, Lord Holder Warbret
    Igen Hold, Lord Holder Laudey
    Nerat Hold, Lords Holder Vincet and Begamon

Telgar Weyr

    Telgar Hold, Lord Holder Larad
    Crom Hold, Lord Holder Nessel

Southern Weyr

    Southern Hold, Holder Toric

THE PRINCIPAL LORDS
(AND THEIR HOLDS)

Asgenar (Lemos)

Banger (Igen Plains)

Bargen (High Reaches)

Begamon (Nerat, 2)

Corman (Keroon)

Deckter (Nabol, 3)

Fax (Nabol, 1)

Groghe (Fort)

Jaxom (Ruatha)

Larad (Telgar)

Laudey (Igen)

Lytol (Ruatha Warder)

Meron (Nabol, 2)

Nessel (Crom)

Oterel (Tillek)

Raid (Benden)

Sangel (Boll)

Sifer (Bitra, 1)

Sigomal (Bitra, 2)

Toric (Southern)

Toronas (Benden 2)

Vincet (Nerat 1)

Warbret (1st)

CRAFTMASTERS AND MASTERCRAFTSMEN

Crafter	Rank/craft	Location
Andemon	Masterfarmer	Nerat Hold
Arnor	Craftmaster, scrivenor	Harpercraft Hall, Fort Hold
Baldor	Weyrharper	Ista Weyr
Belesdan	Mastertanner	Igen Hold
Bendarek	Craftmaster, woodsmith	Lemos Hold
Benelek	Journeyman machinesmith	Smith Hall
Briaret	Masterherder	Keroon Hold
Brudegan	Journeyman harper	Harpercraft Hall, Fort Hold
Chad	Harper	Telgar Weyr
Domick	Craftmaster, composer	Harpercraft Hall, Fort Hold
Elgin	Harper	Half-Circle Sea Hold
Facenden	Craftmaster, smith	
Fandarel	Mastersmith	Smithcraft Hall, Telgar Hold
Idarolan	Masterfisher	Tillek Hold
Jerint	Craftmaster, instruments	Harpercraft Hall, Fort Hold
Ligand	Journeyman tanner	Fort Hold
Menolly	Journeyman harper	Harpercraft Hall, Fort Hold
Morshall	Craftmaster, theory	Harpercraft Hall, Fort Hold
Nicat	Masterminer	Crom Hold
Oharan	Weyrharper	Benden Weyr
Oldive	Masterhealer	Harpercraft Hall, Fort Hold

Crafter	Rank/craft	Location
Palim	Journeyman baker	Smithhall
Petiron	Harper	Half-Circle Sea Hold
Piemur	Apprentice/journeyman	Harpercraft Hall, Fort Hold
Robinton	Masterharper	Fort Hold
Sebell	Journeyman/Masterharper	Harpercraft Hall, Fort Hold
Sharra	Journeyman healer	Southern Hold
Shonegar	Craftmaster, voice	Harpercraft Hall, Fort Hold
Sograny	Masterherder	Keroon Hold
Tagetarl	Journeyman harper	Harpercraft Hall, Fort Hold
Talmor	Journeyman harper	Harpercraft Hall, Fort Hold
Terry	Craftmaster, smith	Smithcraft Hall, Telgar Hold
Timareen	Craftmaster, weaver	Telgar Hold
Wansor	Craftmaster, glassmith	Smithcraft Hall, Telgar Hold
Yanis	Craftmaster	Half-Circle Sea Hold
Zurg	Masterweaver	Southern Boll Hold

OWNERS OF FIRE-LIZARDS

Owner	*Lizard(s)*
Asgenar	brown Rial
Baner	—
Bargen	—
Brand	blue
Brekke	bronze Berd
Corman	—
Deelan	green
Famira	green
F'nor	gold Grall
Groghe	queen Merga
G'sel	bronze
Kylara	gold
Larad	green
Menolly	queen Beauty; bronzes Rocky, Diver, Poll; browns Lazybones, Mimic, Brownie; greens Auntie One, Auntie Two; blue Uncle
Meron	bronze
Mirrim	greens Reppa, Lok; brown Tolly

Nessel	—
Nicat	—
N'ton	brown Tris
Oterel	—
Piemur	queen Farlir
Robinton	bronze Zair
Sangel	—
Sebell	queen Kimi
Sharra	bronze Meer, brown Talla
Sifer	—
Toric	queen; two bronzes
Vincet	—

SOME TERMS OF INTEREST

Agenothree: a common chemical on Pern, HNO_3.

Between: an area of nothingness and sensory deprivation between here and there.

Black rock: analogous to coal.

Day Sisters: a trio of stars visible from Pern.

Dawn Sisters: an alternate name for Day Sisters.

Deadglow: a numbskull, stupid. Derived from glow.

Fellis: a flowering tree.

Fellis juice: a juice made from the fruit of the fellis tree; a soporific.

Fire-stone: phosphine-bearing mineral which dragons chew to produce flame.

Glow: a light-source which can be carried in a hand-basket.

High Reaches: mountains on the northern continent of Pern (see map).

Hold: a place where the common people live; originally they were cut into the mountains and hillsides.

Impression: the joining of minds of a dragon and his rider-to-be at the moment of the dragon's hatching.

Interval: the period of time between passes, generally 200 Turns.

Klah: a hot stimulating drink made of tree bark and tasting faintly of cinnamon.

Looks to: is Impressed by.

Long Interval: a period of time, generally twice the length of an interval, in which no Thread falls and Dragonmen decrease in number. The last Long Interval is thought to herald the end of Threads.

Month: four sevendays

Numbweed: a medicinal cream which, when smeared on wounds, kills all feeling; used as an anesthetic.

Oldtimer: a member of one of the five Weyrs which Lessa brought forward four hundred Turns in time. Used as a derogative term to refer to one who has moved to Southern Weyr.

Pass: a period of time during which the Red Star is close enough to drop Thread on Pern.

Pern: third of the star Rukbat's five planets. It has two natural satellites.

Red Star (sic): Pern's stepsister planet. It has an erratic orbit.

Rukbat: a yellow star in the Sagittarian Sector, Rukbat has five planets and two asteroid belts.

Sevenday: the equivalent of a week on Pern.

Thread: (mycorrhizoid) spores from the Red Star, which descend on Pern and burrow into it, devouring all organic material they encounter.

Turn: a Pernese year.

Watch-wher: a nocturnal reptile distantly related to dragonkind.

Weyr: a home of dragons and their riders.

weyr: a dragon's den.

Weyrsinger: the Harper for the dragonriders, usually himself a dragonrider.

Wherries: a type of fowl roughly resembling the domestic Turkey of Earth, but about the size of an Ostrich.

Withies: water plants resembling the reeds of Earth.

PERNESE OATHS

By the Egg

By the first Egg

By the Egg of Faranth

Scorch it

Shards

By the shards of my dragon's egg

Shells

Through Fall, Fog, and Fire

THE PEOPLE OF PERN

Abuna: Kitchen head of Harpercraft Hall, Fort Hold

Alemi: Third of Seaholder's six sons, at Half-Circle Sea Hold

Andemon: Masterfarmer, Nerat Hold

Arnor: Craftmaster scrivenor, at Harpercraft Hold

Balder: Harper, at Ista Weyr

B'dor: at Ista Weyr

Bedella: Oldtimer Weyrwoman, at Telgar Weyr; dragon queen Solth

Belesdan: Mastertanner, Igen Hold

Bendarek: Craftmaster Woodsmith, at Lemos Hold

Benelek: Journeyman machinesmith, Smithhall

Benis: one of Lord Holder Groghe's 17 sons, at Fort Hold

B'fol: rider, at Benden Weyr; dragon green Gereth

B'irto: rider, at Benden Weyr; dragon bronze Cabenth

B'naj: rider, at Fort Weyr; dragon queen Beth

Brand: steward at Ruatha Hold; blue fire-lizard

B'rant: rider, at Benden Weyr; dragon brown Fanth

B'refli: rider, at Benden Weyr; dragon brown Joruth

Brekke: Weyrwoman, at Southern Weyr; dragon queen Wirenth; fire-lizard bronze Berd

Briala: student at Harper Hall

Briaret: Masterherder (replaces Sograny), Keroon Hold

Brudegen: Journeyman of chorus, at Harpercraft Hall, Fort Hold

Camo: a half-wit at Harpercraft Hall, Fort Hold

Celina: queenrider, at Benden Weyr; dragon queen Lamanth

C'gan: Weyrsinger at Benden Weyr; dragon blue Tegath

Corana: sister of Fidello (holder at Plateau), Ruatha Hold

Cosira: rider, at Ista Weyr; dragon queen Caylith

Deelan: milkmother to Jaxom, at Ruatha Hold

Dorse: milkbrother to Jaxom, at Ruatha Hold

D'nek: rider, at Fort Weyr; dragon bronze Zagenth

D'nol: rider of dragon bronze Valenth, at Benden Weyr

Domick: Craftmaster composer, at Harpercraft Hall, Fort Hold

D'ram: Oldtimer Weyrleader, at Ista Weyr; dragon bronze Tiroth

Dunca: cot-holder, girl's cottage, at Harpercraft Hall, Fort Hold

D'wer: rider, at Benden Weyr; dragon blue Trebeth

Elgion: the new harper at Half-Circle Sea Hold

Fandarel: Mastersmith, Smithcraft Hall, Telgar Hold

Fanna: Oldtimer Weyrwoman, at Ista Weyr; dragon queen Miranth

Fax: Lord of Seven Holds, father of Jaxom

Felena: second to the Headwoman Manora, at Benden Weyr

Fidello: holder, at Plateau in Ruatha Hold

Finder: Harper, at Ruatha Hold

F'lar: Weyrleader at Benden Weyr; dragon bronze Mnementh

F'lessan: rider, at Benden Weyr, son of F'lar and Lessa; dragon bronze Golanth

F'lon: Weyrleader, at Benden Weyr, father of F'nor and F'lar

F'nor: wingsecond at Benden Weyr; dragon bronze Canth, fire-lizard gold Grall

F'rad: rider at Benden Weyr; dragon green Telorth

Gandidan: a child at Benden Weyr

Gemma, Lady: First Lady of Fax (Lord of the Seven Holds) and mother of Jaxom

G'dened: Weyrleader-to-be, at Ista Weyr, son of Old-timer Weyrleader D'ram, dragon bronze Baranth

G'nag: at Southern Weyr, dragon blue Nelanth

G'narish: Oldtimer Weyrleader at Igen Weyr; dragon bronze Gyamath

G'sel: rider, at Southern Weyr; bronze fire-lizard, dragon green Roth

Groghe: Lord Holder at Fort Hold; fire-lizard queen Merga

H'ages: Wingsecond at Telgar Weyr; dragon bronze Kerth

Horon: son of Lord Groghe; Fort Hold

Idarolan: Masterfisher, Tillek Hold

Jaxom: Lord Holder (underage) at Ruatha Hold; dragon white Ruth

Jerint: Craftmaster for instruments, at Harpercraft Hall, Fort Hold

Jora: Weyrwoman preceding Lessa, at Benden Weyr; dragon queen Nemorth

J'ralt: rider, at Benden Weyr; dragon queen Palanth

Kayla: drudge, at Harpercraft Hall, Fort Hold

K'der: rider, at Ista Weyr; dragon blue Warth

Kenelas: a woman of the lower caverns, at Benden Weyr

Kern: eldest son of Lord Nessel (the Lord Holder of Crom)

Kirnety: a boy, at Telgar Hold; Impresses dragon bronze Fidirth

K'nebel: Weyrlingmaster, at Fort Weyr; dragon bronze Firth

K'net: rider at Benden Weyr; dragon bronge Pianth

K'van: rider, at Benden Weyr; dragon bronze Heth

Kylara: a sister of Lord Holder Larad and a Weyrwoman at Southern Weyr who moved to High Reaches Weyr when Oldtimers were banished; dragon queen Prideth

Lessa: Weyrwoman at Benden Weyr; dragon queen Ramoth

Lidith: Queen dragon before Nemorth, rider unknown

Ligand: Journeyman tanner at Fort Hold

L'tol: rider, at Benden Weyr and, as Lytol, Warder of Ruatha Hold; dragon brown Larth (dies)

L'trel: father of Mirrim, at Southern Weyr; dragon blue Falgrenth

Lytol: Lord Warder for the underage Lord Holder Jaxom at Ruatha Hold; dragon brown Larth (dies)

Manora: headwoman at Benden Weyr

Mardra: Oldtimer Weyrwoman at Fort Weyr, banished to Southern Weyr; dragon queen Loranth

Margatta: senior Weyrwoman at Fort Weyr; dragon queen Ludeth

Mavi: Seaholder's (Yanis) Lady at Half-Circle Sea Hold

Menolly: Journeyman at Harpercraft Hold, Fort Hold, fire-lizards (10): gold Beauty, bronzes Rocky, Diver, Poll; browns Lazybones, Mimic, Brownie; greens Auntie One and Auntie Two; blue Uncle

Menolly: youngest child (daughter) of Seaholder (Yanis) of Half Circle Sea Hold

Merelan: mother of Robinton (Masterharper of Harpercraft Hold)

Merika: Oldtimer Weyrwoman, at High Reaches Weyr; exiled to Southern Weyr; dragon queen

Mirrim: greenrider, fosterling of Brekke at Benden Weyr; dragon green Path; fire-lizards: green Reppa, green Lok, brown Tolly

Moreta: ancient Weyrwoman at Benden Weyr; dragon queen Orlith

Morshall: Craftmaster for theory, at Harpercraft Hall, Fort Hold

M'rek: wingsecond, at Telgar Weyr; dragon bronze Zigith

M'tok: rider, at Benden Weyr; dragon bronze Litorth

Nadira: Weyrwoman, at Igen Weyr

Nanira: *see* Varena

Nicat: Masterminer, Crom Hold

N'ton: wingleader at Benden Weyr on dragon bronze Lioth; then Weyrleader at Fort Weyr (after T'ron), fire-lizard brown Tris

Oharan: Journeyman harper at Benden Weyr

Oldive: Masterhealer, at Harpercraft Hall, Fort Hold

Old Uncle: great grandfather of Menolly, at Half-Circle Sea Hold

Palim: Journeyman baker at Fort Hold

Petiron: the old Harper at Half-Circle Sea Hold

Piemur: Apprentice/Journeyman, at Harpercraft Hall, Fort Hold; fire-lizard queen Farli; runner-beast Stupid

Pilgra: Weyrwoman, at High Reaches Weyr; dragon queen Selgrith

P'llomar: rider at Benden Weyr; dragon green Ladrarth

Pona: granddaughter to Lord Holder Sangel, Southern Boll Hold

P'ratan: rider, at Benden Weyr; dragon green Poranth

Prilla: youngest Weyrwoman, at Fort Weyr; dragon queen Selianth

Rannelly: nurse and servant of Kylara

R'gul: Weyrleader before F'lar, at Benden Weyr; dragon bronze Hath

R'mart: Oldtimer Weyrleader, at Telgar Weyr; dragon bronze Branth

R'mel: rider, at Benden Weyr; dragon Sorenth

R'nor: rider at Benden Weyr; dragon brown Virianth

Robinton: Masterharper at Harpercraft Hall, Fort Hold; fire-lizard bronze Zair

Sanra: supervisor of children at Benden Weyr

Sebell: Journeyman/Masterharper, Robinton's second, Harpercraft Hall, Fort Hold; fire-lizard queen Kimi

Sella: Menolly's next-oldest sister, at Half-Circle Sea Hold

S'goral: rider, at Southern Weyr; dragon green Betunth

Sharra: Journeyman healer, at Southern Hold; fire-lizards bronze Meer and brown Talla

Shonagar: Craftmaster for voice, at Harpercraft Hall, Fort Hold

Silon: a child at Benden Weyr

Silvina: headwoman at Harpercraft Hall, Fort Hold

S'lan: rider, at Benden Weyr; dragon bronze Binth

S'lel: rider, at Benden Weyr; dragon bronze Tuenth

Sograny: Masterherder, Keroon Hold

Soreel: wife of the First Holder at Half-Circle Sea Hold

Tagetarl: Journeyman at Harpercraft Hall, Fort Hold

Talina: Weyrwoman at Benden Weyr, queenrider

Talmor: Journeyman teacher, at Harpercraft Hall, Fort Hold

T'bor: Weyrleader at Southern Weyr, later moves to High Reaches when the Oldtimers are exiled; dragon bronze Orth

Tegger: holder at Ruatha

Tela, Lady: one of Fax's ladies

Terry: Craftmaster smith, Smithcraft Hall, Telgar Hold

T'gran: dragonrider at Benden Weyr; dragon brown Branth

T'gellan: wingleader at Benden Weyr; dragon bronze Monarth

T'gor: rider at Benden Weyr; dragon blue Relth

T'kul: Oldtimer at High Reaches Weyr, exiled to Southern Weyr; dragon bronze Salth

T'ledon: watchdragon rider at Fort Hold; dragon blue Serith

Tordril: fosterling at Ruatha Hold, prospective Lord Holder at Igen

Torene: ancient Weyrwoman at Benden Weyr

Toric: Lord Holder of Southern Hold

T'ran: rider, at Igen Weyr; dragon bronze Redreth

T'reb: rider, at Fort Weyr; dragon green Beth

T'ron: Oldtimer Weyrleader at Fort Weyr; banished to

Southern Weyr; dragon bronze Fidranth; also called T'ton

T'sel: dragonrider at Benden Weyr; dragon green Trenth, fire-lizard bronze Rill

Vanira: see Varena

Varena (also called Vanira): rider, at Southern Weyr; dragon queen Ralenth

Viderian: fosterling (Seaholder's son) at Fort Hold

Wansor: Craftmaster glassmith, Smithcraft Hall, Telgar Hold; also called Starsmith

Yanis: Craftmaster and Seaholder at Half-Circle Sea Hold

Zurg: Masterweaver, Southern Boll Hold